MW01596494

SILENT FOOL

A Chief Mattson Mystery

Join my mailing list at richardryker.com for new releases, offers for free books, and more.

Books by R.L. Ryker

Chapter 1

"I can't believe I let you talk me into this," Brandon said. He peeked around the corner of the makeshift theater constructed for the first annual Forks Renaissance Fair. The benches were already packed for the sold-out performance. Apparently everyone in Forks, WA wanted to watch the chief of police stumble through a few lines of Hamlet in breeches and a feather-adorned floppy hat.

Emma, his sixteen-year-old daughter, appraised his outfit. "I think you look cute."

He turned his attention to his ex-wife, Tori. "What are you grinning at?"

"Nothing," Tori said, a wry smile crossing her lips as she considered Brandon's costume. "It does highlight those muscular thighs."

"Gross, Mom," Emma said.

Brandon scowled at his ridiculous costume—silver and blue striped shirt, puffy pants, and black hose. He'd been asked...no...begged by the local theater company to appear in a montage of scenes from Shakespeare. He had only agreed because the proceeds would be donated to the local arts. Somehow the theater owner had learned Brandon had been a star thespian in high school and, to a lesser degree, college.

Delilah Lewis, owner and operator of the Forks Playhouse, waved wildly from behind the stage. "Chief Mattson! It's time!"

Brandon and Delilah waited behind the curtain stage left as a group of local high school students finished up a scene from *Taming of the Shrew*.

Delilah passed Brandon a prop rapier. The sword had a dull tip and more give than the real thing.

"You got this?" Delilah asked.

"Sure."

"Come on, Chief. I've got to know your heart is in this. If we do good today, think of the attention it could bring the Forks Playhouse."

Delilah was an African American woman in her early forties with extensive theater experience in Chicago. Seeking escape from big-city life, she and her husband had relocated to Forks a few years back.

"I got it," Brandon replied.

"Nervous?"

"It's been decades since I've been on stage," he said.

She squeezed his arm. "I believe in you, Chief."

"That makes one of us."

The crowd cheered enthusiastically as the Forks High School Drama Department gave a bow before exiting stage right.

"That's your cue," she said.

Brandon strolled onto the set.

Cheers and a few catcalls greeted him. Several spectators had donned Renaissance or medieval era costumes—everything from lords and ladies to knights in chainmail. Others had come to observe the festivities in typical modern-day attire—shorts, t-shirts, and sunglasses.

Brandon forced his attention away from the standing room-only audience.

He was joined on stage by two ladies—actors from the Forks Playhouse. He pressed through the scene, gaining confidence with each remembered line.

Brandon's antagonist appeared on stage. The two women gave convincing shrieks before exiting stage right. The robust young man challenged Brandon to a duel, dramatically freeing his sword from its sheath.

His adversary was Zach, a kid from Forks High who happened to be Emma's boyfriend. Brandon had nothing against Zach, except for the fact he was dating Brandon's daughter.

They advanced, swords raised. Zach's costume was a better fit for the duel—a leather breastplate over a cotton shirt and leggings. In character, Zach hurled an insult at Brandon, earning a cheer from the crowd.

Brandon swiped the rapier at Zach. He parried the attempt and countered.

Zach went on the offensive, offering several attacks, all of which Brandon blocked. Zach was a big kid, and fast. He continued the assault. His eyes hardened.

His back to the audience, Brandon continued to retreat. He was running out of stage.

Zach's approach to the scene had become a little too aggressive for Brandon's liking.

The fight was supposed to include a sprinkling of back-and-forth dialogue, but both were too focused on the melee. Brandon tried to remember his lines...

His heel crept over the edge of the stage.

This had gone on long enough.

Brandon surged ahead with a few quick swipes, then lowered his shoulder into the young man. Zach stumbled back, catching himself at the last second. Midstage now,

Brandon jabbed his rapier at Zach, forcing him into the thin curtain that veiled the back of the set.

Fear flickered in Zach's eyes. He blinked as Brandon raised his sword for another blow.

"Brandon!" Delilah whispered loudly from her perch stage left. "I think that's enough."

He turned his head. Her wide eyes were a warning. He was taking it too far.

She was right. This wasn't a suspect he was battling.

Just then Zach thrust his rapier into Brandon's gut.

Brandon stumbled back.

The crowd gasped.

Zach lowered his sword. "Sorry."

An obnoxious cackle rose above the general murmur. Brandon tried to ignore it.

"Not your fault. Let's finish this scene."

"That's what you get for picking on a kid," a voice called out.

Brandon scanned the benches for the source.

"I've seen better fighting from a barmaid."

Brandon's eyes settled on a man standing just outside the picket fence that enclosed the outdoor theater's seating area. His balding head was somewhere between sunburned and tan with a hedge of wiry blonde hair. His shirt and pants looked to be made of sackcloth. A rope belt was tied around his waist, holding his beer gut aloft.

It was every performer's worst nightmare and one that seldom came true. Not only screwing up during a performance, but being called out for it. Brandon's gaze landed on Tori in the front row. She rolled her eyes dismissively at the man. Emma smiled at Brandon pitifully.

"Poor fellow is speechless," the mocker continued. "Dumb as a cobbler's hammer."

The audience crowed with laughter.

Brandon's hand twitched, his fingers squeezing the rapier's hilt.

It was all he could do not to hop off the stage and make a beeline for the man.

The mocker swept his arm dramatically. "Can't talk. Can't even beat a boy in simple swordplay. Maybe the pantyhose squeezed the testosterone out of his—"

Brandon stepped to the edge of the stage.

The mocker stood a little straighter, surprised by Brandon's reaction. Still, he was at least fifty feet away.

"Enough!" another man shouted. He was a few rows from the back. "We're trying to enjoy the show."

"You mind your own business, MacDuff."

"Mr. Mattson?"

Brandon turned to Zach.

"Are we going to finish the scene?"

"Sorry," Brandon said. "Let's get to it."

He glanced toward the back of the theater where the mocker had stood a moment earlier. He was gone.

A few minutes later, they'd finished. Unfortunately for Brandon, there were two more scenes involving himself and a handful of regulars from the Forks Playhouse. Brandon checked the back row at the start of each scene, but the mocker had disappeared for good, it seemed.

After a hearty round of applause, followed by the compulsory curtain call, the cast regrouped backstage.

Delilah hugged Brandon. "Thank you so much for doing this. I know it wasn't easy."

"I'm a little rusty, to say the least."

"You're welcome back anytime," Delilah said. "We're doing *Cats* in the fall."

"Thanks, but no thanks," Brandon said.

Tori and Emma appeared at his side. "My dad hates anything that isn't Rogers and Hammerstein," Emma said. "He doesn't like cats, either."

Delilah smiled. "Well, maybe another time, then."

When Delilah had left, Tori asked, "Who was that guy?"

"The mocker? I have no idea."

Emma held up a copy of the Forks Renaissance Fair's official program. She flipped through the pages, pointing to a younger-looking photo of the man.

"His name is *Drool*," she said. "He's a comic."

"He's a real hoot," Brandon said, taking the program. According to the guide, Drool was the stage name for *the West Coast's premier Renaissance and medieval fair comedian.*

"It says he's from San Francisco," Brandon said.

"I wouldn't worry about it," Tori said. "He's just doing his job."

"Yeah, well, you weren't the one on stage."

Tori nestled her arm in his. "Let's get something to eat. I think your blood sugar is low."

She was right, he was getting worked up for no good reason. He hated to admit it, but more than a year after their divorce, Tori still knew him better than anyone else. It was too bad they got along better now than when they'd lived together.

Her gray eyes smiled back at him.

Things hadn't always been that bad, had they?

He shook the thought off. Things were just fine the way they were. Shared custody of a smart, beautiful, kind daughter, despite living more than three hours apart. Everything was the way it was supposed to be.

"Dad?"

"What?"

"Can Zach come with us, too?"

Brandon sighed. "Okay. But I'm not buying his lunch."

Tori saved a table for the four of them while Brandon stood in line with Emma and Zach. On a nearby stage, a troubadour recounted the tale of Robin Hood and Maid Marion, accompanying himself on the lute.

Brandon ended up paying for Zach's hamburger and fries. Like most dads, he was a pushover for his daughter. He was already spending 30 bucks for second-rate fair food. What was ten more dollars?

It was the first day of the "Ren fair", a month-long event that was the brainchild of Mayor Sara Kim. Like most schemes the mayor concocted, the event was an attempt to increase the town's tourism revenue. As the impact of the Forks-based *Moonbeam Darklove* series faded, she explained, they would need to branch out into other pursuits.

For Brandon and his limited police force, events that attracted outsiders meant increased crime, more overtime, and the risk of a packed jail.

The fair was on a ten-acre pasture that had, in years past, featured a now-defunct dairy farm. The Robinson family farm had been part of the west county area for over a hundred years. As the dairy industry consolidated to larger, more centralized farms, the Robinson's were forced to abandon the family business. The remaining heirs to the legacy had tried their hand at pumpkin patches and corn mazes in recent years—with mixed results.

Now the family had won a five-year lease with an out-of-state entertainment group. The Renaissance fair was the first event—with concerts and other festivals planned for the future. As for their part, the fair's owners had taken an impressive first step in making the event a success. They'd constructed a permanent cluster of buildings resembling a medieval town square. Near the square, a fenced-in field hosted jousting and other tournaments. The acres surrounding the makeshift town were filled with canvas tents hosting a variety of shops hawking jewelry, costumes, handcrafted woodwork, and that ancient medieval staple—cotton candy.

Brandon had commented to Emma that there was a difference between the medieval and Renaissance periods. Her response had been, "I know that, and you know that, but I don't think anyone cares."

The trio of twenty-somethings that passed by just then made her point. Their costumes included knee-length black leather boots, black lace skirts, a leather corset with buckles across the front, and a top hat. Emma called the style "steampunk", a genre based on the Victorian period. Most of the fair's attendees, at least those in costume, stuck to the period the fair pretended to represent.

After waiting in line for 15 minutes, they had their food and headed to the table Tori had reserved.

She wasn't there.

"Where's mom?" Emma asked.

He scanned the area.

"Save our spot. I'll find her."

A moment later, Brandon felt a tap on his shoulder.

He turned, blinked, then did a double-take. Tori had changed into a velvety azure dress, almost form-fitting. Its flowing sleeves were rose and gold. She'd grown her sable hair out over the winter, and it trailed over her shoulders.

Brandon had to guide his eyes from the larger-than-life cleavage on display thanks to the costume's push-up feature.

"You like it?" she asked.

Was he blushing? For God's sake. This was Tori, his ex-wife.

"Ahh...yes."

Tori shifted, adjusting the straps. "I worried it might be a little too revealing."

When they sat down at the picnic table across from Emma and Zach, Emma stared at her mom wide-eyed.

"Wow, mom."

Tori grimaced. "Is it that bad?"

"I mean. It's a nice dress," Emma said.

"What?"

"Well, I was going to say...put those things away."

"Emma..." Brandon started.

"But I get it. When you're older you want to feel pretty."

Brandon shook his head. Sometimes even the best kids could say the meanest things.

"Leave her alone," he said.

"I'm just giving her a compliment."

"*Right*," Brandon said.

After lunch, they roamed the fair. Those vendors not busy with customers greeted any passers-by with invitations to try their wares. Brandon waited while Emma, Zach, and Tori browsed the various shops—candle makers, bowyers,

9

pewter trinket sellers, even a mock gypsy wagon offering tinctures and cure-alls. But the fair offered more than merchants. They'd stopped for a performance featuring two young women in peasant outfits performing sweet but sorrowful Celtic tunes on the fiddle and harp.

Eventually, Emma and Zach ditched Tori and Brandon, leaving the two of them alone for the first time in months.

"What are you going to do with yourself all summer?" Tori asked.

Emma lived with Brandon during the school year, with Tori taking her for the summer breaks and every other weekend. Tori had made the trip from Seattle to see Emma off to her job as a camp counselor. After camp, Emma would return home with Tori.

Without Emma around, the house would be quieter than usual. Not that she was home often, between Zach and her job at Carl's Pizza. And, Brandon realized, his time with her was running out. In the fall, Emma would be entering her final year of high school. She was already making plans for college.

"Go fishing, maybe."

"You always said fishing was boring," Tori said.

They turned the corner to another row of shops, moving out of the way as Queen Elizabeth and her entourage passed by.

He shrugged. "People change."

"Do they?"

He turned to her. The meaning behind her question held him fixed to the spot.

"I mean...yeah."

She pursed her lips together. "If you say so."

"Spoken like a prosecutor," Brandon said, hoping to lighten the mood.

Tori was a deputy prosecutor with the King County Prosecutor's Office.

"Chief Mattson!"

Brandon twisted toward the sing-song voice of Phoenix Weaver.

"Who is that?" Tori asked.

"You don't want to know." He wrapped an arm around her waist. "Let's get out of here."

"Chief Mattson! I know you hear me!"

Tori whispered, "Don't be rude, Brandon."

He clucked his tongue. "Okay. But you'll see."

As he turned, his eyes landed on a modest red and black velvet tent. There, shrouded in the shadow of lace and curtains, Phoenix sat behind a flimsy card table. A deck of tarot cards lay fanned out in front of her. A glass orb rested tenuously on the edge of the table.

Brandon approached, keeping his distance. Tori stood at his side.

"Come closer." Phoenix wore a midnight black flowy dress with a moon and stars print. The crescent moons wore eerie smiles. Her wide sleeves flapped as she motioned to him.

"I'm fine here," he said.

A year earlier, he'd had to interview Phoenix about a local vampire coven with potential links to the murder of a young woman out on Second Beach. That time, she'd made a prediction about Brandon's family that had come true. Mere coincidence, in his opinion.

"Please, won't you sit down? Maybe your lady friend would like to know what the future holds?"

"Wouldn't we all?" Tori asked, sarcastically.

11

"The cards will tell me," Phoenix said.

"Okay. Good seeing you, Phoenix," Brandon said. He tugged on Tori's hem. "We've got to get going."

"Wait!" Phoenix said, reaching out. "I sense love in your future!"

Tori froze. "Me, or him?"

"Both of you!"

"That's nice," Brandon said.

"Does he not believe in love?" Phoenix asked, eyeing Tori.

Tori looked up at Brandon. "He does. Or at least he used to."

"What's that supposed to mean?"

"Well..."

"I do believe in love, just not this nonsense." He motioned to Phoenix.

"I know," Tori stammered. "Just...forget it."

Brandon scowled at Phoenix. She tilted her head back so that her long nose pointed up at him. "I have been right before, no?"

"That was luck," he said.

Phoenix's eyes fluttered, then closed. She inhaled deeply. Hand over her bosom, she proclaimed, "Chief Brandon Mattson. I see your future and there will be true love kindled again. Don't let it go this time."

"Really?" Tori asked.

"That's enough," Brandon exclaimed. "Goodbye, Phoenix."

But there was a slight waver in his voice. Did he actually believe her?

"Suit yourself," she replied. "But don't blame me if you lose such a lovely woman..."

12

What Phoenix didn't know (or did she?) was that he'd already lost Tori. That was over a year ago. Plenty of time for both of them to get over the divorce.

As they scampered away, Tori said, "I like her."

Brandon grunted. "Of course you do."

The weather was warm for June in Forks, and the clouds had parted that morning to reveal a cobalt blue sky. The sun, the atmosphere of the fair, and having Tori at his side—all of that somehow gave him a jolt of verve he hadn't experienced in years.

He wasn't going to let Phoenix ruin that.

They strolled past Weaponsmith's Row, a section of the fair dedicated to purveyors of swords, daggers, chainmail, and other implements of war. Aside from the obvious wooden or plastic toys, most of the weapons for sale appeared dangerous enough to kill.

A town full of wannabe warriors and deadly weapons within easy reach. One more thing to worry about. But he'd been assured the fair didn't allow fairgoers to unsheathe their daggers or swords—the medieval equivalent of an open-carry prohibition.

A familiar cackle rose from the end of the row of blacksmith shops.

"Let's see what it is," Tori said.

About two dozen spectators had gathered around Drool, the performer who had heckled Brandon earlier. A tent had been erected over a temporary stage.

Tori checked the fair guide. "There's nothing scheduled."

"And that one," Drool exclaimed to the crowd. "She's a pretty one, isn't she?"

They still couldn't see who the jester was talking about. Drool continued, "I said yes, pretty, except for those teeth. I've seen less of an overbite on a chipmunk."

A few in the crowd reacted with muted laughter. Brandon never understood how others found humor in humiliating others.

"That's not funny," a young man replied. The voice was familiar.

As they neared the platform, Brandon recognized Zach's tall, sizeable frame. Then, Brandon understood who Drool was targeting with his most recent onslaught of insults—it was Emma.

Chapter 2

Brandon charged through the crowd.

The jester's eyes widened at Brandon's approach. He was holding court on a three-legged stool in the middle of a low wooden platform. The flicker of fear that crossed Drool's face faded quickly. His lips drooped into an apathetic frown.

"Look who's here, ladies and gentlemen. It's my panty-wearing friend," Drool continued. "Is this your offspring?" He swept a hand at Emma.

Emma's eyes were red with angry tears.

Brandon halted inches from the stage.

"That is my daughter, yes. And now, I'd like you to apologize."

"Hah," Drool exclaimed. His breath fumed with the stink of stale wine and cigarettes.

Making fun of Brandon was one thing. And Emma might be a strong, independent young woman. But she was still his daughter.

"Get up," Brandon said.

Drool bared his teeth in an arrogant sneer. "What are you going to do? Beat me up?"

"We are going to have a conversation."

Drool looked past Brandon at the growing crowd. "I don't talk to men in tights."

No one laughed.

"I said, stand up."

The joker's face hardened.

Drool stood, shoving the stool back. "Okay, tough guy. You want to come here and ruin my act?" The jester had at least five inches on Brandon. Despite his beer gut, he looked like he could throw a punch.

"I don't give a damn about your act," Brandon said. "You will not, under any circumstances, talk to my daughter like that."

"And what are you going to do about it?"

Brandon knew better than to respond to schoolyard taunts. He was the chief of police. Threatening another person in front of this many people, even an ass like Drool, could lose him his job.

But still...

Brandon climbed onto the platform. He was inches from Drool and had to crane his neck up at the fool. He whispered. "Take a swing, big guy, and you'll find out."

Drool blinked.

"Come on," Brandon said, quiet enough, he hoped, that none of the gawkers would hear him.

Drool's menacing grin faded. "Just get out of here, I'm trying to make a living."

"Apologize," Brandon said.

"Why are you bothering me?"

"Because I don't like people that pick on other people."

Brandon stepped back. Loud enough for the crowd to hear, he said, "Now, I'd like you to apologize to my daughter."

Drool's nostrils flared.

"Fine." He glared at Emma. "I am sorry, young lady. I should not have said what I said. You have a beautiful smile."

Emma wiped her eyes.

Zach replied, "That's right, she does!" He released Emma's hand and leaped onto the stage. He poked a finger at Drool's chest. "You're lucky the chief of police is here. Otherwise, I'd kick your—"

"Hold on," Brandon said, hedging himself between Zach and Drool.

Drool pursed his lips. "Get this kid off my stage."

"I'll take you any day," Zach exclaimed. Brandon turned the youngster on his heels and guided him away.

"You've made your point," Brandon said.

Emma smiled at Zach. "Thanks for standing up for me."

Tori rubbed his shoulder. "Thanks, Zach."

Brandon's jaw dropped. What exactly had Zach done?

"Wait a minute," Drool said. "Did that kid say you're the chief of police?" Drool plopped onto his stool. "I've got to get out of this crap hole of a town."

"If you need a ride, let me know." Brandon winked at him. "And uh, Mr. Drool, or whatever the hell your name is, public intoxication is still a crime here in Forks. Even for fools like you."

That evening, Brandon and Tori had dinner with Emma before Zach picked her up. Brandon had hoped to give Emma a ride down to Aberdeen, where she was to stay for the evening before heading off to camp. Emma had wanted Zach to drive the two-hour trip, and Tori had convinced Brandon to let it happen. But not before he had given Zach his usual spiel about boundaries, prompting Emma to exclaim, "Dad, we know. You can trust me, okay?"

He did trust her. It was Zach he was worried about. He didn't want to think about the sort of trouble two teens—one 17, the other almost 17—could get into over a hundred-plus mile stretch of highway.

17

Brandon packed Emma's sleeping bag and two suitcases into Zach's truck.

Tori and Brandon loitered on the front lawn of the home Brandon had rented for the past year. Emma hugged each of them then skipped away to Zach's truck. She opened the passenger door, then paused. "Aren't you leaving, too, Mom?"

"I will. Don't worry about me."

Emma narrowed her eyes at her parents. "You guys are acting weird."

"Nobody is acting weird," Tori said.

Emma frowned. "I'll call you guys when I get there. And Dad, don't forget to feed Caesar."

Caesar was the gray and black kitten they'd adopted nine months earlier. Brandon had only agreed to take in the abandoned pet under duress when Emma had guilted him into it.

"Love you," Brandon said, waving at her.

Zach's truck growled to life as he fired up the engine. A puff of oil smoke drifted across the lawn. They waited for Zach to pull away, just to make sure he made it down the block.

Brandon resisted the urge to have an officer follow Emma and Zach until they made it out of the county. What if they broke down in the middle of nowhere? There wasn't cellphone coverage...

"Come on," Tori said, reading his expression. "They'll be fine."

Back in the house, Brandon said, "She seems worried about us."

A smile touched Tori's lips. "I can't imagine why."

Sure, Brandon hadn't been himself since Tori's visit to Forks. He'd even felt a tinge of youthfulness each time their eyes met.

But Tori was his ex-wife. Their relationship had ended almost two years earlier. Things that were over were meant to stay that way.

Still...

"It doesn't help that you can't keep your hands off me," Brandon teased her.

"And I haven't seen you flirt like that since the first time we met."

Brandon smiled.

It had been almost two decades since they'd first met in a crowded conference room at the King County courthouse. Brandon had been a rookie patrol officer. Tori was twenty—already a college senior and intern preparing to start law school. By the time she'd finished her Juris Doctorate, they were married with a one-year-old.

"It's a long drive back to Seattle," he said. Depending on traffic, the trip could take four hours.

She nodded with a tilt of her head. "True."

"You want to get dinner?"

"Wouldn't that keep me out even longer?"

"It'll be quick," he said.

"Like fast-food quick?"

"I'm not that cheap."

* * *

Three hours later, they were on Brandon's couch, a near-empty bottle of merlot at their feet. Caesar sprawled in Brandon's recliner. Occasionally the kitten would open one eye, considering Tori curiously, but the novelty wore off, and soon he was snoozing.

Brandon poured another half glass and offered it to Tori. Dinner at the local Mexican restaurant had taken longer than they expected, thanks to the second round of drinks they'd both ordered and an expanding conversation that began with memories of Emma's childhood but soon turned to the early years of their marriage. At some point in the evening, they'd decided to pick up a bottle of wine on the way home.

"I can't drive like this," Tori said, her eyes fuzzy from her second glass of Merlot.

"I couldn't let that happen," Brandon said. "I'd have to arrest you on the spot."

"You're worse off than me," she said, taking a long drink. She handed him the glass.

"I'm just getting started," he said.

"Same old Brandon."

"What?"

"Trying to prove yourself. In everything."

He fought back the urge to defend himself. "Not everything," he said. He drained the glass and set it on the floor.

She rested a hand on his knee. "I didn't say I didn't like it."

Brandon nudged the wine bottle away with his foot.

"Now what?" she asked, searching his face. Her gaze lingered on his lips.

A dozen replies came to him but he was smart enough to know that anything he said would risk losing the moment.

"Well..."

"How about I get the bed and you get the couch," she said, patting his thigh.

"Right."

Chapter 3

Brandon blinked at the sliver of morning sun that seemed to be targeting his tired eyes. His work cell was ringing. Instinctively, he reached for the nightstand.

He wasn't in bed. He was on the couch.

Brandon rummaged around on the floor and found the phone. It was Isabel Jackson.

Jackson was his lead officer and sometimes detective. A first-generation Cuban-American, she had moved from Florida to Oregon for college and worked her way up to detective in the Portland PD before taking time off to stay home and focus on her two children. Not long after she and her husband had landed in Forks, Brandon had brought her on full time.

"What's up?" he asked.

"You sleeping in?"

He searched his memory—what day of the week was it? It was too early for that kind of math.

"It's my day off," he said, hoping he was right.

"Well, vacation's over, boss. We've got a situation out here at the Renaissance fair."

"Isn't it too soon for trouble? The fair's pub doesn't open until ten."

"It is ten o'clock," she replied.

He checked the time. How had he slept so long? Then, he recalled he'd been up past two.

Brandon sat up, gathering steam. "Jackson, get to the point."

"There's been a murder."

He pinched the bridge of his nose.

"Okay. You have my attention now."

"Remember that guy who was mocking you on stage yesterday?"

"You saw that?" he asked.

"I was patrolling the fair. Not bad, by the way," she said.

"My acting?"

"It was okay," she said. "Except the part where you let Emma's boyfriend jab you. You've got to keep your guard up—"

"Remind me again why you woke me up," Brandon said.

"The performer, Drool," she said. "His boss found him dead about a half an hour ago."

"You said there was a murder. Dead and murdered aren't the same thing," he reminded her.

"Really?" Jackson said. "I didn't know that."

"Sorry."

"Apology accepted. I'll let you see for yourself *why* this is obviously a murder."

"I'll be down," he said, hanging up.

Tori appeared in the hallway wearing one of his work shirts and a too-large pair of shorts.

"I'm too hippy for Emma's clothes," she said. "Too small for yours. Except I do like this shirt."

"You bought it for me," he said.

"I know." She plopped down onto the couch, next to him. "What's going on?"

"That clown from the fair. Apparently, he's dead."

"The one who made fun of Emma?"

"Same one."

"How did he die?"

"He was murdered. That's about all I know."

"Well it makes sense," she said, frowning. "I mean, think about how he treated Emma. Our baby isn't the only person he's hurt."

"I have to treat it just like any other case," Brandon reminded her. "Even if he was an ass."

He swept the blanket aside and ran a hand over his face. He stood, considering Tori. "I had a great time last night, by the way."

"I had a little too much vino," she said.

"Same here. If you're not feeling up to driving back yet, you can stay here as long as you want. No hurry."

She stared back at him.

"You don't have to," he said. "I mean, I know you're busy."

She smiled. "Maybe I'll stick around."

"You don't have work?"

"Remember, I took the week off. I was supposed to head down to Moclips for some alone time on the beach. But since I'm here..." She paused. "I mean, if it's going to be awkward—"

"Not at all."

Despite the invitation, Brandon wasn't sure how he felt about Tori staying. Was he lonely? Sure. And Tori had been his best friend for longer than anyone he'd known. The truth was, had things gone the way he'd wanted the night before...

Now that he was sober he realized that would have been a bad idea.

"You're sure?" she asked.

He held her hand. "I'm glad you're here. We'll do something fun tonight."

"I've heard that before."

"Is that a challenge?"

24

Tori stood and pulled him to his feet. She patted him on the rear. "Get to work, Chief Mattson."

The property hosting the Forks Renaissance Fair was about 15 minutes outside Forks proper. Thanks to an agreement between the Clallam County Sheriff's Department and the City of Forks, Brandon's department had jurisdiction over the westernmost reaches of the county. It was a cost-cutting tactic on the county's part that had been implemented just before Brandon's arrival as the chief of police a year earlier. Expanding the scope of the department wasn't a problem for Brandon—he'd earned his experience at Seattle PD—where a precinct covered more lives than the entire population of Forks.

The downside to the current arrangement was Brandon had two bosses—the mayor of Forks and the sheriff—both of whom weren't his best fans, especially Sheriff Hart.

The fair's entrance was a castle gate guarded by two tall turrets, giving the impression you were crossing a drawbridge into another time. Hanging from the turrets, a sign read *Prepare thyself for merriment.* Already patrons in medieval and Renaissance costumes were lined up at the ticket booth, oblivious to the homicide that would likely consume Brandon's attention for the next several days and weeks.

The head of security was waiting for Brandon.

"Alex Winfield," the guard said.

They shook hands. Alex was a thirty-something Black man and, unlike most security guards, had the physique of someone who could handle a hands-on confrontation if it came to that.

"Your officers asked me to meet you," Alex said. "Appreciate it."

Drool's motorhome was a red and tan behemoth parked on a patch of grass apart from the other temporary homes—everything from pop-up trailers and fifth-wheels to full-sized RVs. The closest trailer was at least 30 feet from Drool's abode.

"Are these trailers personal or provided by the company that operates the fair?"

"Everyone's responsible for their own accommodations," Alex said. "Sometimes full timers like Drool get a housing allowance."

Officers Isabel Jackson and Josiah Trent stood on either side of the motorhome's entrance. "He's waiting for you," Jackson said, pointing a thumb at the trailer.

"What's this guy's real name? It can't be Drool."

"Darren Rule," Alex said. "You know, like D. Rule."

"Ah," Brandon said.

"You need anything else from me?" Alex asked.

"No witnesses?"

"None that we know of," Alex said.

"Who found the body?"

"Mrs. Blackburn. She's the production manager."

"We'll need to talk to her for a start," Brandon said. "And how about the names of everyone in the cast?"

Alex nodded, "I can do that."

After Alex had gone, Brandon asked Jackson, "What am I walking into?"

"Mr. Darren Rule was in his early forties. Multiple stab wounds and some bruising. I took a quick peek at the body and decided to wait until you got here. A crime scene tech and Lisa are on their way down from Port Angeles."

Lisa was the county coroner.

Jackson had set her evidence kit outside the motorhome's screen door. Brandon donned a pair of gloves and snapped them tight. They would have to wait until the crime scene tech arrived to get everything collected in an organized manner.

"It's a mess in there," Josiah said.

"An altercation?"

"No, just a mess. And not much room for moving around."

Brandon climbed into the motorhome. To the right, bags of dirty laundry occupied the driver's seat. To the left, a kitchenette and cramped table and booth hugged the outer wall. He made his way down the narrow hallway, passing a bathroom and mini closet, alert for any signs of struggle. The passageway opened into a bedroom with a queen-sized bed and a single dresser.

The bed was covered in pillows and wadded up blankets. Darren Rule's body lay back on the bed, but his feet were still touching the ground. It was as if he'd passed out and fallen back while sitting on the edge of the mattress.

Brandon leaned over to get a closer look at the jester's wounds. Bruises clouded the side of his face. That meant the assault had occurred a while before death. He had at least two puncture wounds in his neck.

The murder weapon was easy enough to identify.

Sticking out of Darren's mouth was a medieval-looking dagger. It had been thrust into the back of his throat. The dagger had an 'M' on one side of the hilt and an upright, sword-wielding lion on the other.

Blood pooled around the victim's neck. At least it had been quick.

27

"How about that card?" Jackson asked.

Brandon tilted his head. That's when he noticed the playing card shoved into the victim's mouth. It appeared as though the killer had inserted the card in and then pierced it with the dagger as an afterthought.

It wasn't just any playing card, it was a tarot card.

"It's two dogs barking at the moon," Jackson said, pointing her flashlight inside Darren Rule's gaping mouth.

"You did more than take a cursory look," Brandon said. "What does it mean?"

"I'm a detective, not an astrologer."

"True."

"His mouth is cut," she said.

What Brandon had assumed was blood pooling out of Drool's mouth was actually two cuts, one on each side of his lips. The effect was to cast his lips in a gruesome grin.

"Those weren't made by this dagger," Brandon said.

"Yeah?"

"This blade is for stabbing. The edge doesn't appear sharp enough for that sort of cut."

"So we're missing a weapon," she said, scanning the room.

Brandon stepped back for a better view of the body. Darren Rule wore a black Portland Trailblazers t-shirt and shorts.

"Check that out," Brandon said, pointing to Rule's knees where they bent over the side of the bed.

"Someone beat the hell out of him," Jackson said.

His knees were bloodied, bruised, and swollen.

"Looks like they took a baseball bat to him."

"Before stabbing him?"

Brandon kneeled down for a closer look. "Those bruises are at least several hours old. We'll let the coroner decide."

Jackson cocked her head. "She's 'the coroner' now? Not *Lisa*?"

He waved a hand at her. "Drop it."

"Sorry. I just thought, you know..."

He stood.

"You know we're not together anymore. So, like I said..."

Jackson's hands shot up. "Okay. Not a peep from me."

"Is that a promise?"

He surveyed the room. The place reeked of alcohol and sweat but the body hadn't been there long enough to join the room's madrigal of diverse but entirely putrid smells. An air conditioning unit whirred from the ceiling. The room had to be ten degrees cooler than outside. Mounds of clothes, empty bottles of whiskey and cans of cheap beer were scattered across the floor.

There was surprisingly little blood splatter and all of it had remained within the confines of the bed. The crime scene techs would find more, no doubt.

Back outside, they regrouped.

"We'll wait for the coroner and techs to do their work," Brandon said. "Josiah, you know the routine. Start a crime scene log."

"Already on it," he said, handing Brandon the clipboard. He recorded his name, badge number, and the time he'd arrived.

"Good. Call for backup and, once they arrive, I want you to give Jackson a hand with interviews. You're more useful to me as part of the investigation than standing out here."

Josiah beamed. Still the greenest member of the Forks PD, he had initiative and a willingness to learn. He'd helped Brandon and Jackson with homicide cases in the past, even if he'd needed redirection from time to time.

"Will do, Chief."

Brandon turned in time to notice the head of security return. A shorter woman in her thirties with short blonde hair and cat-eye glasses trailed behind Alex, struggling to keep up with his quick stride.

"Chief Mattson," Alex said, "this is Mrs. Blackburn."

"I'm the production manager," she said, shaking his hand. "This is horrible. So horrible."

"You found him?"

"He was late," she said. "Drool's job is to greet our visitors at the gate. Doing his usual schtick. Mostly making fun of people."

"So you came here looking for him?"

"It wouldn't be the first time I had to wake him up."

"Was the door locked?" Brandon asked.

"No."

"Did you touch anything?"

"Of course not," she said. "I watch CSI."

"Nice," Brandon said. Despite the negative effects of the public's obsession with crime shows, knowing to leave a crime scene untouched was one positive development.

"Can you think of anyone who would want to do this?" Jackson asked.

She tilted her head down, studying Jackson over the rims of her glasses. "Have you ever met Drool?"

"Yes," Brandon said.

30

"Then you'll know that he's not the most likable character. In fact, he was a monster."

"A monster?"

She crossed her arms. "I don't want to speak ill of the dead."

"Just tell us the truth. We'll figure out the rest," Jackson said.

"Well, he was rude, sexist, a boor, a drunk...what else do you need to know?"

For someone who didn't want to speak ill of the dead, she was doing a great job.

"Anyone in particular who would want to murder Mr. Rule?" Brandon asked.

Mrs. Blackburn bit on her bottom lip. After a moment, she said, "To be honest, I couldn't pin it down to less than a dozen or so people, and even then I'd be guessing."

"Any idea where he was last night?"

"Probably at the pub."

"Which one?" Jackson asked.

"The one here at the fair. It's open until 10:30."

"Anywhere else he might have been?"

She scoffed. "If I were you I'd check that hotel of yours in town. The one where you keep all the prostitutes."

"We don't *keep* any prostitutes," Jackson said.

"You know what I mean."

Brandon knew exactly what she meant. The Forks Inn had a growing reputation for sex trafficking. After a couple of arrests, Brandon had hoped they'd applied enough pressure on the owner to discourage him from allowing pimps and prostitutes at the hotel. Apparently, they hadn't.

31

"With large fairs like this, we tend to get hangers-on who follow us from town to town," Mrs. Blackburn added.

"And some of them are prostitutes?" Brandon asked.

"Well they ain't here to teach Vacation Bible School," she said.

"And Mr. Rule was known to associate with these women?" Brandon asked.

"Ask anyone," she said. "He didn't even try to keep it a secret."

"Okay," Brandon said. "I'll need you to give a statement to Josiah here. We'll contact you if we have more questions."

Brandon pulled Jackson aside. "Go ahead and get started on interviews. We'll need statements from every employee living on the grounds."

"Where are you going?"

"To check on this prostitution angle," he said.

"The Forks Inn?"

"Right. Call me if the techs get here before I'm back."

Chapter 4

Brandon pulled his SUV into the only empty spot in the Forks Inn's parking lot. The shabby hotel was rarely more than half-full, even in the busy summer months. Earlier that year, Brandon had researched the establishment on one of the online reservation sites and found the average guest rating was three out of five stars.

That was being generous.

The popularity of the Renaissance fair had meant packed rooms for all three of the hotels in town, not to mention the sprinkling of Airbnb homes in the surrounding area.

But it wasn't the medieval enthusiasts and sightseers Brandon was interested in. The Forks Inn was owned and operated by Benjamin Frey, a man who'd tolerated prostitution at the hotel in the past. That meant, Brandon assumed, Benjamin was getting a cut from the pimps.

The Forks PD had shut a local pimp down a few months earlier, solving the problem. He'd already put Benjamin on notice that the police were watching his place.

If Mrs. Blackburn was right, Benjamin had returned to his old ways.

Brandon approached the hotel's abandoned front desk and smacked the bell. He took in the room. Same worn carpet, same torn leather couches. The moss lining the bottom of the windows was only lessened by the fact that summer was approaching.

"Oh, Lord."

He turned to Benjamin. The hotel owner's peppered stubble had grown to a full beard since their last meeting. He wore a bright, tropical-themed shirt that had to be straight off the 1990s rack at the local thrift store.

"Benjamin," Brandon said, nodding. "How's the family?"

"Fine. My daughter graduated. Moved in with her mom over in Tacoma."

Good for her, Brandon thought.

"You keeping clean?"

"If you mean am I staying off the dope? Sure. Attending two meetings a week."

That's not what Brandon meant. He knew Benjamin smoked but wasn't aware of any other drug use.

"Here's the deal, Ben. We've received a tip—"

Benjamin raised his hands. "I'm one hundred percent above-board, man. Promise. No prostitution. Swear to God."

"It's not a good idea to use the Lord's name in vain, Benjamin."

Brandon considered the man. He'd aged quite a bit in the year since Brandon's return to town. Years of drug use were finally catching up to him.

"One of your *guests* might know something about a homicide I'm investigating," Brandon said.

Benjamin ran his fingers through his beard. "I don't want anything to do with this, Chief. I'm getting too old. I'm just a hotel owner. The people that stay here, what they do is their business."

"What they do is called sex trafficking. Most of the time, these girls are sold on the street from the time they're kids. You have a daughter—"

"Stop."

He'd gotten Benjamin's attention. "What if it was your daughter being sold—"

"I'll tell you what I know," he said, whispering. "Just leave me alone, okay?"

"I'll leave you alone when you stop breaking the law in my town. In the meantime, I need to know who the pimp is."

Benjamin leaned in closer to Brandon. "His name is Cory. I don't know anything about him. I'm not getting a cut, I promise."

"Does Cory have a last name?"

"Hold on."

Benjamin donned a pair of reading glasses and logged into the hotel's reservation system.

"His name is Cory King."

Brandon pulled out his notebook and wrote the name down.

"Car?"

Benjamin squinted at the screen. "A '96 Dodge Caravan. Blue."

A minivan. No doubt it had tinted windows.

"License plate?"

"I don't ask," Benjamin said. "Anyway, he got here about the same time as that Renaissance fair going on outside of town. He told me he works for the fair and had a couple of lady friends that would be staying in the hotel, too."

"How many rooms?"

"Three."

"Which rooms?"

Benjamin hesitated. "If he finds out I told you... This guy, he's got sort of a scary look about him. I don't want any trouble."

"It sounds to me like you're aware of sex trafficking at your hotel and did not notify the police."

Benjamin glanced over Brandon's shoulder. A couple dressed in medieval garb was passing through the lobby.

"He's in room 213. The girls are in 215 and 217," Benjamin said. "But they've already left for the day."

"To?"

"How would I know?"

Brandon tapped on the counter. "You learn anything else, you let me know. This is your last chance, Benjamin. Got it?"

He frowned. "Got it."

Brandon tried Room 213 despite Benjamin's insistence that Cory King had gone for the day. No one answered, so he exited through the back door. He made his way through the parking lot adjacent to the hotel.

He spotted the Dodge Caravan.

Leaning on the hood was a dark-haired man in his mid-twenties. He wore a black sweatshirt and jeans. He took a hit from a cigarette and passed it to the young woman next to him.

Noticing Brandon's approach, the man snatched the cigarette from the woman and tossed it on the ground. He rubbed it out with his foot.

Not a cigarette. Marijuana.

"Cory King?"

"Yeah?" He crossed his arms. "How can I help you, officer?"

The woman next to Cory pulled a vape pen from her purse and took a puff. She appeared to be mixed race—Asian and Black. Her hair had been straightened. She wasn't wearing much makeup, but her crop-top shirt and leather miniskirt were more than revealing.

"You have an ID?"

"Me?" Cory asked.

"Both of you."

"What did we do wrong?" the girl asked.

"That's what I'm trying to figure out," Brandon answered.

"Can he ask us for our ID?" the girl asked Cory. "We didn't break any laws."

"Just do it," Cory said.

She shrugged and plucked her ID out of a silver clutch purse. Cory handed his license to Brandon.

The girl's name was Arianne Young. According to her ID, she was 22 and lived in Salem, Oregon. Cory was from Los Angeles. Brandon wrote their names and information in his notebook.

He went to his Ford Interceptor and checked their info. Neither had any outstanding warrants. When he returned, he said, "Oregon and Southern California? How'd you two meet?"

"Mutual friend," Cory said.

"And what brings you to Forks?"

"We like the Renaissance fair," Arianne said.

"Is that so?"

"That's right," Cory said. "Arianne grew up in one of these things. What was it your dad did?"

"My dad was a prick," she said. "My grandpa was from Japan and sold traditional Japanese weapons."

"Like samurai swords?" Cory asked.

She rolled her eyes. "You wouldn't understand."

"And what do you do here, Cory?" Brandon asked.

37

"I work with the Ren Fair. Do odd jobs. Repairs," Cory said.

"Will the operators vouch for that?"

Arianne's eyes slid sideways to Cory, waiting for his response.

"Sure," he said.

"Who's your contact there?"

"Duke Sterling," Cory answered. "He's the owner."

"I take it that in your association with the Renaissance fair you've met some of the performers?"

"Yeah. A few," Cory said.

"You too?" Brandon asked Arianne.

She pulled another puff from the vape pen. "I've made some friends."

"Is one of your *friends* a man named Darren Rule?"

"Never heard of him."

"He goes by the name Drool," Brandon said.

She squinted at him. "That prick? No way."

Cory seized Arianne's arm.

"What?" she asked. "That bastard tried to—"

"Enough," Cory said.

Brandon returned their IDs.

"Look," he said. "I know you're a pimp and I know Arianne here works for you. Do I like that? No, I don't."

Arianne rolled her eyes.

"And if I catch you doing what you do in my town, I'll make sure you do the time." He considered Cory. "Especially you."

"Hey, I haven't done nothing—"

"Save it," Brandon said. "What I need to know is what Drool did that upset you."

"Why does it matter?" Arianne asked.

"Because he's dead."

They both seemed surprised, despite their very different reactions. Cory appeared as though he might wet himself.

Arianne chortled. "Ha! Good."

"How did he die?" Cory asked.

"We're not releasing that information at this time."

"Probably overdosed," Arianne said. "Dumbshit."

"I take it Drool was one of your clients?"

"I handed him off to Kaitlyn," she said.

"Will you shut the hell up?" Cory demanded.

"Cory," Brandon said, "you seem worried. You want to tell me what it's about?"

"I don't like cops, that's all."

"Who is Kaitlyn?"

"Our friend," Arianne said. "She's staying here with us."

"What are you not telling me about Drool?"

"I don't know anything else, man."

"You on good terms with him?" Brandon asked.

Again, Arianne waited for what Cory would say.

"Okay. He hurt one of my girls."

"Kaitlyn?"

"He raped her," Arianne said.

"Did she contact police? Go to the hospital?"

Arianne scoffed.

It was hard enough for rape victims to submit to the grueling process of a rape investigation. Add in a distrust of the police, and it made it highly unlikely someone in Kaitlyn's position would ask for help.

"Okay," Brandon said. "And then what?"

"Then nothing," Cory said. "I told him if he did it again, he'd pay."

"*Did* you make him pay?" Brandon asked.

"No."

"You're sure."

"I told you, no."

"What's Kaitlyn's last name?"

"I don't remember," Cory said.

"So you're pretty close friends then?"

Cory didn't answer.

"Where's Kaitlyn now?"

Cory shoved his hands in his pockets. "She's at work."

"Meaning?"

"I don't keep track of her. She's just a girl I know. That's all I'm going to say about it," Cory said.

Brandon's phone buzzed. He checked the text message. It was from Jackson.

The coroner and CST are here.

He handed each of them a card. "Tell Kaitlyn to call me."

If Darren Rule had been a client of Kaitlyn's and had sexually assaulted her, she might know more about what happened to him. And if what Cory and Arianne said was true, she certainly had motive to kill him.

Chapter 5

When Brandon arrived back at the Renaissance fair, Lisa Shipley was outside Darren Rule's trailer, speaking with Jackson.

"Michael's inside checking the scene," Jackson said. "We were waiting for you before we got started."

Michael was the crime scene tech most often assigned to Forks. Two counties—Jefferson and Clallam—and a handful of municipalities had banded together to fund a shared crime scene force that would cover all the area's jurisdictions.

Lisa was the Clallam County coroner and medical examiner—and Brandon's ex-girlfriend.

"Chief Mattson," Lisa said. "Good to see you."

Lisa had resorted to calling him by his title since their breakup.

"You, too."

They stood staring at each other. Jackson cleared her throat. "I'll be inside."

"Be there in a second." He turned to Lisa. "What are your impressions?"

"He died early this morning. I'll have more info soon. Rigor mortis has set in and that's even with the air conditioning on. You spotted the stab wounds to the neck?"

"Two."

"Three, actually. And the bruising."

"His knees looked pretty bad."

"Ribs, too," she said. "Standing here, I'd guess he'd been assaulted with a blunt object at least four hours before death."

"Any defensive wounds?"

"From the dagger? Not that we can see so far," she said. "Based on what information we have now, I'd say he died from the stab wounds. The knife down the throat, that was just for show, if you ask me. I'll know more once we get him back to Port Angeles."

"The cut to his lips. That was a different knife?"

"Not sure yet, but it appears so," she said.

Brandon bobbed his head in agreement. He probably looked ridiculous. "So. How are things going?" he asked.

"What do you mean?"

The relationship had ended abruptly six months earlier. What Brandon had assumed was a misunderstanding grew into a full-blown breakup. She'd wanted more time together. He needed space, especially in light of his obsession with solving his brother's murder. The fact that they lived over an hour apart didn't help. Not to mention, Brandon was a single father—and the chief of police.

The end of their relationship, though painful at first, was an outcome he eventually accepted. The awkward thing was that they had to work together, at least whenever someone died under suspicious circumstances.

"You know," he said. "Life. Work."

"Great, actually." She peeked at her watch. "Let me know when I'm good to take Mr. Rule off your hands."

"Will do."

Michael stood in the doorway of Darren's bedroom. The white-haired, but still physically fit, sixty-something

42

crime scene investigator was the most experienced tech in the region. "That's a new one," he said.

"The card?"

"The knife down the throat *and* the card—it reveals a certain creativity, don't you think?"

"You could call it that," Brandon said.

"Anything special you need from me?" Michael asked. It was both a request and a reminder to stay out of his way while he got to work.

"Do your magic. It's too damn crowded in here for more than one person. We didn't notice any blood splatter beyond the area of the bed. We're assuming he was killed where he sat."

Michael nodded. "I'll get working on photos and the crime scene sketch."

"We'll leave you here. Jackson and I can work on prints for the rest of the motorhome. The door, those bottles."

Michael eyed Brandon doubtfully. "I prefer you let us handle the entire vehicle—just in case there's biological evidence..."

"Alright. It's your castle. Just trying to make things go faster."

"Thanks," Michael said. "I have another tech on her way."

Brandon had to appreciate the man's thoroughness and pride in his work, even if it meant he didn't fully trust Brandon and Jackson's basic crime scene processing skills.

Outside, Jackson turned to Brandon. "Tiniest crime scene I've seen."

"It's going to be a while," Brandon said.

They stepped aside as Michael's assistant arrived and checked in with the officer guarding the motorhome.

Just then, Josiah returned from his initial interviews.

"I was about to ask Jackson what you learned while I was gone," Brandon said.

"I showed a photo of the dagger to the blacksmiths," Josiah said. "Just the hilt, not the actual blade in the victim's mouth."

"Anyone recognize it?"

"Everyone agreed it was the work of a guy named Hamish MacDuff here at the fair."

"What did Mr. MacDuff have to say about that?"

"It's his," Josiah said. "At least, one he sells. Apparently, the lion symbol with the letter 'M' is a pattern he uses. I asked him if he's sold any since the fair opened and he wasn't sure. He's going to check through his receipts."

"Okay, so that one is a definite re-interview," Brandon said. "What about the tarot card?"

"I talked to the production manager. There are only two booths at the fair that offer readings. One is a lady named Madame Bonaparte. She's got a solid alibi. She and her husband were with another couple until at least two in the morning."

"Is she missing a tarot card?"

"She showed me the deck she uses. The style is different from the card in the victim's mouth."

"You're sure?"

"They were brighter. More colorful."

"Who is the other tarot card reader?"

"Phoenix Weaver."

Brandon sighed. "Of course." He'd somehow forgotten about Phoenix's offer to read his future the day before.

"What did Phoenix have to say?"

"Her shop wasn't open yet."

Phoenix tended to be a late riser. She was notorious for not opening her *Darklove Damsel* shop in town until almost noon. He would pay Phoenix a visit later.

"Anything else?"

"The couple of people I interviewed before Lisa got here all had the same story," Jackson said. "Everyone hates Drool, and no one saw him late last night."

"And when you ask who would want to kill him, the answer is always the same: Who *wouldn't* want to," Josiah added.

"It's going to take a while to make it through everyone, considering the place is packed with tourists and assorted geeks dressed up as characters from World of Warcraft," Jackson added.

"Has that head of security been any help?" Brandon asked.

"Alex? He's offered, but I wasn't sure if you wanted him involved," Jackson said.

"He seems professional enough. We can use him to get preliminary information. Don't share any of the evidence with him, though."

They could use any help they could get. The department had been down one full-time officer since his most senior officer, Will Spoelman, retired six months earlier.

Brandon sent Jackson and Josiah back to interviewing the other cast members while he waited outside the motorhome. About half an hour later, Lisa was ready to transport Darren Rule up to Port Angeles. Brandon offered to help but Lisa and Michael were able to maneuver the body out of the cramped quarters.

Once Mr. Rule was safely in the van, Lisa turned to Brandon.

"I'm out of here," she said. "By the way, his pockets were empty."

"Okay, good to know."

"Alright," he said.

"Good seeing you."

She slipped her gloves off.

"Brandon?"

"Yeah?"

"I'll get you a report as soon as I can."

"Thanks."

He was watching Lisa pull away when someone called out his name.

"Chief Mattson!"

Brandon turned at the voice of Mayor Sara Kim. The mayor was in her late thirties and had forgone her usual power business attire for a bright fuchsia, conservative version of the medieval dresses many of the women at the fair wore.

She'd recently returned from a trip to visit family in Korea and was more focused than ever on her goal of making Forks into a tourist mecca.

"Mayor."

"Don't look at me like that," she said. "I know you're working. This won't take but a second. I'd like you to meet Duke Sterling. And before you ask why I'm all done up, it's because Mr. Sterling here has chosen me as the guest of honor this week."

Duke Sterling had dark but graying short-cropped hair. His tan was a shade shy of burnt-orange. He wore dress slacks and a polo shirt that fit tight on his muscular build.

"You're the owner?" Brandon asked.

"That's me." Sterling flashed Brandon a smile. It quickly faded to a frown. "So sorry to hear about Mr. Rule."

"You might be the only person who's going to miss him," Brandon said.

"I don't understand."

"He wasn't a popular person."

"Drool got under people's skin," Sterling said. "But that was his job."

"Any idea who might want him dead?"

"Like you said—he wasn't the most beloved cast member."

Brandon motioned to the motorhome. "Mr. Rule had a nice getup, compared to most of the trailers around here."

"Paid for it himself," Sterling said. "Don't ask me where he found the money."

"Chief Mattson," Mayor Kim said, "what's important is that the people here know they are safe."

"I'm not responsible for how they feel. But keeping them safe, yes. That's my job," Brandon reminded the mayor, not for the first time.

"I'm sure the good captain knows his responsibilities," Sterling said.

"Chief," Brandon corrected him.

"Who?"

"Chief, not captain."

Sterling eyed Brandon dismissively. "If you say so."

Brandon headed back to his vehicle and submitted an electronic warrant request, outlining Mr. Rule's death and why they needed to search the motorhome. Without a warrant, the investigation would be restricted to anything they found line-of-sight. Twenty minutes after submitting the request, he received an electronic copy of the signed order. The county's participation in the electronic program, with judges on-call 24/7, saved the department from having to wait around for permission to fully investigate a scene.

He made a quick call to Jackson and asked her to meet him at the motorhome with her evidence kit.

They met up just as the techs were loading evidence into their vehicle.

"What's the news?" Brandon asked.

"We're taking the linen and clothing," Michael said. "There are more stains on those sheets than a pay-by-the-hour motel."

Jackson scrunched her face. "Eww."

"We've got prints off the walls, dresser, doors, and a few other locations."

"I obtained a warrant to poke around, so Jackson and I can get started on that. We'll bring anything else we find up to the lab."

"Sounds good."

Chapter 6

Brandon and Jackson gloved up and headed for opposite ends of the motorhome. Brandon started in the bedroom. The techs had turned off the air conditioner and now the stagnant atmosphere amplified the stench of stale alcohol and general filth he'd encountered earlier.

Michael had removed the sheets, blankets, and clothes from the bed. A round, basketball-sized bloodstain marked the spot where Darren Rule had bled out.

An acoustic guitar leaned against one corner of the room. A lute rested on a pile of dirty clothes atop the only dresser. Probably props for the jester's acts. Darren Rule didn't seem the artistic type.

The floor was slightly cleaner now that the techs had confiscated much of the laundry and empty beer cans. Hopefully at least one of the containers held DNA evidence from whoever had killed Rule. Based on what the techs had found, it appeared Darren had made a habit of inviting company into his room.

Brandon kneeled down and checked around the bed. Finding nothing of interest, he rose, eyeing the dresser.

The top three drawers were mostly bare, with a jumble of (apparently) clean undergarments and t-shirts. The bottom drawer was stuck.

He tugged on it and the front panel broke off easily. Inside was a plastic grocery bag. Untying the knot revealed several pairs of women's panties. He retrieved a pair and held them up. Too small for Darren Rule.

That ruled out cross-dressing. Brandon resealed the bag and saved it as evidence.

Brandon returned to the dresser and rifled through the pile of clothes on top, recognizing the shirt and pants Darren had worn the day before at the fair. There were socks and more undergarments. This time they were men's and were Darren's size.

Brandon was about to move on from the bedroom when he had an idea. He peeked behind the dresser. It wasn't uncommon to find evidence that ended up—purposefully or not—in the dark and dusty spaces behind everyday furniture. He tugged on the dresser. It was bracketed to the wall. One screw was loose already, so he used his Swiss Army knife to remove the other brackets. Brandon maneuvered it away from the wall, revealing a manila envelope.

He unclasped the envelope and carefully extracted several photos. Flipping through the pictures, most featured scantily-clad women. There was at least one photo of a young man. Several of the subjects appeared intoxicated or asleep. Possibly passed out. He found only one photo where a woman was alert, and in fact seemed to pose, topless and wearing only a pair of frilly black and red panties.

Darren Rule was not in any of the photos.

Brandon considered the room. At least half of the shots had been taken there.

The seemingly involuntary nature of the poses might be a motive for murder. Had the killer come searching for the photos and instead ended up killing the man who'd snapped the compromising pictures?

He made his way back up the hallway, checking the vents, bathroom, and cupboards for clues. There wasn't much else of interest. An assortment of bottom-shelf liquors occupied most of the cupboard space. A search of the garbage container answered why they hadn't found anything in the way of real sustenance—it was overflowing with fast food and takeout containers.

Jackson had finished searching the front of the motorhome.

"I pulled everything out—spare bed, hidden storage, you name it," she said.

"And?"

She held up two evidence bags. "Meth pipe and about a gram of crank."

"No surprise there," he said. "Anything else?"

Jackson revealed another bag. Inside was a tube of lipstick.

"Sweet tangerine."

"Huh?"

"It's the name of the lipstick color. I found it under the table there."

"Has it been used?" he asked.

"It's about half gone."

"Good find," he said.

"Thanks," she said. "Anything in the bedroom besides blood and beer cans?"

"A bag of panties and several pictures of individuals in compromising positions."

"What every man needs," Jackson said.

"Funny."

"The panties are his?"

"Too small," Brandon said.

"Trophies?"

"Maybe," he said. "The question is, were they given to him voluntarily?"

He explained the conversation he'd had with Cory King and Arianne, and the accusation that Darren Rule had raped another prostitute named Kaitlyn.

"One more reason for everyone to hate him," Jackson said. She considered the lipstick. "I wonder if this is a trophy too."

"Maybe one of his victims—or the killer—dropped it."

"You know what we haven't found?"

"What's that?" he asked.

"His cellphone," she said.

"And Lisa said his pockets were empty. We'll need to figure out which carrier."

"Already know," she said. "Hold on."

She returned from the front of the motorhome with a stack of papers. "Cellphone bill, banking information, you name it."

"Good find. Work on a warrant for the cell records. If we're in luck, it's still active. And we'll have to identify who all these people are." He passed her the envelope.

Jackson flipped through the pictures.

"Interesting taste in photography," she said.

"So far we've got sex and drugs as potential motives."

"I'm sure money is involved in this somehow," she said, referring to the three most common reasons for murder: sex, drugs, and money. "It's going to be nearly impossible to identify the photos."

"That's why I'm handing them off to you," he said, smiling.

"Gee, thanks. I'll get copies of these after I print them. We'll need to ask around. If we can figure out who some of these people are—"

"Maybe not the *full* photo," Brandon said.

She held up the picture of the woman wearing just panties. "This is why I won't let my husband take pictures of me..."

Brandon raised an eyebrow. "Too much information, Jackson."

She pursed her lips. "Not everyone is an old prude, Chief."

"Old? I'm barely forty."

"Fine, then you're just a prude."

"If that means I don't enjoy snapping pictures that might end up on the internet—or in some pervert's trailer—fine, call me a prude."

It was nearly seven in the evening by the time he left the station. They'd recorded the new evidence, written their reports, and started a summary of the case on the whiteboard in Brandon's office. Josiah and Jackson had interviewed almost two dozen of the fair's regular entertainers. It was generally accepted that Darren Rule was hated by everyone, spent most nights drunk or high, and had frequented prostitutes in every town they visited. He'd been married and divorced at least three times. His parents had passed away before he joined the fair. There was a rumor he'd had a child some years back.

Thanks to the new electronic warrant system, Jackson was able to get a judge to sign off on accessing Darren Rule's cellphone records. Getting a response from the carrier was another story. Sometimes it took several days, even weeks, to get the information back. Something else they hadn't found was a personal computer. If the killer had taken the phone and the computer, then there was a chance he was hoping to obtain something off the devices—or prevent others from doing so. There weren't any other signs of burglary. The television and a handful of other valuables were untouched.

They would have to wait for the coroner's report, but the cause of death appeared to be the stab wounds to the neck and the final jab down his throat. The addition of the tarot card suggested a message—maybe revenge of some sort. They'd have to research the meaning behind that particular card.

The fact that the dagger had come from one of the fair's blacksmiths provided some direction. Brandon would follow up on Josiah's interview with the weaponsmith in the morning. The photos could indicate a blackmail scheme. Then again, they could be trophies—like the women's undergarments. Then there were the narcotics Jackson had found. The murder might have been the result of a deal gone wrong. To check that angle, Brandon had his officers scour the west county area's suspected dealers to see what they knew.

So far, every dealer they'd interviewed denied having ever met or sold to Darren Rule.

The first day of the investigation had turned up more questions than answers, and he was okay with that. As long as you were asking the right questions, you'd eventually separate the truth from the lies. And in his experience, usually more than one person familiar with a murder victim had reason to lie.

* * *

It wasn't until Brandon climbed into his truck that he realized he'd forgotten to call Tori. He'd thought about texting her to let her know how things were going, but the investigation or some other interruption had pulled his attention away before he had a chance to connect.

He started the truck, reveling in the familiar thrill—and exhaustion—that came with a new case. Probably not the best time for Tori to visit.

Considering he hadn't spoken to her since morning, hadn't even checked in, it was possible she'd headed home—or to the beach where she'd planned on spending her days off.

He considered their interaction the night before. What had happened between them? Nothing physical—yet. Had the last day been a turning point in their relationship? Did it mean they were back together? The implications of *that* flooded him. His mind turned to the reasons they'd split in the first place. Could they overcome their differences this time? What would that mean for his career? For Tori's? What would Emma say?

He tried to shake the growing sense of dread that threatened to ruin his evening. *One day at a time,* he told himself.

Brandon smiled as he rounded the corner to his street. Tori's car still hugged the curb in front of his house.

She hadn't left, after all.

He opened the front door and was greeted by a sharp whiff of citrus-scented cleaner. Neat vacuum lines crossed the living room carpet. The pillows on the couch and love seat were neatly tucked into their corners.

"I'm in here," Tori said from the kitchen.

"You didn't have to do all that," he said over the swoosh of the dishwasher.

"I was bored." Tori was at the table, her laptop open. "But I got plenty of work done. I fed the cat, too."

She'd changed into jeans and a form-fitting t-shirt.

"I thought you were on vacation," he said.

"You know how it is," she said.

Tori adjusted the red bandana that held her hair back. There was a glow about her, one he hadn't noticed—at least in recent years. Had he taken her natural beauty for granted? No, he'd appreciated every moment of it. But it had been too long since he'd had the chance to just *look* at Tori.

He was staring at her.

She smiled at him.

"Well?" she said.

"You, ah. Do you want to go out tonight? I don't have much to eat here."

After grabbing some takeout, they headed for the ocean.

Bonfires dotted Rialto Beach as the sun set over the Pacific.

It was still June. The evenings would be chilly, and he wished he'd stopped by the Quinault Quick Stop for firewood. At least they'd brought a blanket and had each other to keep warm. They ambled along the shore, crossing the smooth, ebony rocks that made Rialto unique to the area.

A few seagulls hopped lazily across the stones in search of a stray crab or forgotten clam as an evening snack.

When Brandon and Tori had traversed far enough from the clusters of campfires, they left the water for the sandy, log-strewn area just past the high tide mark.

After a few minutes spent lumbering through the sand, they found a lonely log.

Darkness and a smoky haze descended over the beach as the day surrendered to twilight.

Brandon draped the blanket over them and they leaned against each other, their shared warmth a bulwark against the relentless breeze. Brandon sucked in the cool air, heavy with the salty scent of kelp and shoreline sea life.

Tori shivered. He found her hand and wrapped his fingers through hers.

They talked about work, about the case Brandon was working, then more about Emma and her future, what college she might attend. Tori told Brandon she was considering a job out-of-state once Emma graduated.

"Why move now?" Brandon asked.

Their heads were leaning against each other, their eyes fixed on the night-darkened whitecaps just offshore.

"You mean at *my age*?" she asked.

"*Our* age," he said. "I'm barely forty. You're still in your thirties. And you're active enough to do whatever you want. I mean, Colorado, that's pretty far."

"Are you saying you'd miss me?"

A hundred feet away, a woman screamed near one of the campsites. Brandon turned his ear to listen. A moment later, there was raucous laughter and the woman's voice joined in the response. The group's conversation fell to a murmur again.

"Always expecting the worst," Tori said, squeezing his thigh.

"Not always."

"Hmm."

"What?" Brandon asked.

"Don't ruin the moment," she said. "I'm enjoying this. Us."

The wind wrapped around them, creeping up and under the blanket where it dangled at their feet. After a minute, he said, "I don't think the worst of us if that's what you meant."

She lifted her head, smiling at him. "I know."

"I wanted...want..."

She waited for him to finish.

"What is it you want, Brandon Mattson?"

Right there, in that moment, what he wanted was Tori.

Not just Tori, but everything they'd had, everything they'd been.

Her eyes searched his.

"I miss you," he said.

Her gaze fell to his lips. "I miss us."

He wrapped his arm around her waist. She leaned into him and they kissed, slow and passionate. A gust swept off the ocean, passed over them, their embrace impenetrable in the suddenly warm blanket.

They hesitated long enough to watch each other smile. Brandon kissed her neck and made his way up to her lips again.

Tori's phone dinged in her back pocket.

"Do you need to get that?"

"No," she said, pecking him on the lips.

"You sure?"

"It's probably work. It can wait."

She slid her hand up his thigh, halting just shy enough to tease him.

"Let's go home," she said.

On the way back to Brandon's house, their hands remained clasped, neither wanting to let go, to risk releasing the growing tension within and between them.

Neither said a word.

It was a race to the front door and the house's warmth enveloped them. It was suddenly too hot. Oppressively hot. They tossed their shoes and coats off, leaving them by the door like a couple of messy kids.

Later, Brandon would recall that it was new and different and the same but better, all at once. It was like the first time, but nothing like the first time. A falling into the security of the familiar as if you were experiencing it anew. And somehow, it was like the past two years hadn't happened at all.

Chapter 7

Brandon was awake by seven. He lay in bed, listening to the empty house.

Then, he heard the shower door slide open as Tori turned the water on.

He made coffee and considered scrambling some eggs, then found none in the fridge.

While Tori changed in the bedroom Brandon showered and got dressed for work. He found her at the kitchen table, sipping on a cup of coffee.

He smiled at her.

"What?" she said.

They were both, he imagined, wondering the same thing. The night before had happened, there was no getting around it. Where did they go now? Would they resort to the cordial distance they'd developed after the divorce? Or pretend like they were still together, playing house for a few more days until one of them acknowledged what was happening.

He leaned back against the counter, hands behind him. "Well."

Tori stood. He waited to see what she would do.

"About..." he started.

At the same time, "Brandon..."

"You go," he said, pushing himself off the counter.

"No, you."

"I was just going to say..."

She drifted closer to him. Tori slipped her hands into his. Her gray eyes glistened in the morning sun splashing through the kitchen window.

"Yes?" she asked.

"Let's get breakfast."

On the way to the Forks Diner, Tori said, "You'll be working on the homicide for a while."

"It looks like it," he said. "What are you up to today?"

"I've run out of things to clean in your house," she said.

"Are you thinking about heading back?"

"I don't want to overstay my welcome, Brandon..."

"No. Not at all," he said. "You want to tag along with me today?"

"During a murder investigation?

"You can at least come down to the station and meet everyone."

He wasn't sure why, but it seemed important to show her more of his new life. After all these years, he still wanted to please Tori. He could show her he'd made a good decision moving to Forks and abandoning his career as a detective.

During breakfast, an uneasy closeness hovered tenuously between them. They were still feeling out what they were, how to act. They'd swayed from one extreme—a friendly aloofness—to passionate intimacy in record time. Those opposites were easy compared to the unmapped wilderness they had to navigate now.

They were leaving the diner when Brandon spotted Cory King and Arianne Young stepping out of Cory's minivan.

A third woman exited the vehicle.

"Hold on a second," Brandon said to Tori.

Arianne noticed Brandon's approach. "Great," she groaned.

"Quiet," Cory warned her.

Brandon considered the third person.

Hoping to grab Brandon's attention, Cory said, "Hello, Chief. I hope you're having a fine morning with your lady." He jutted his chin in Tori's direction. To Brandon's surprise, Tori appeared at his side.

"Who's your friend?" Brandon asked, considering the young woman.

"Kaitlyn, say hello to the officer," Cory said.

Kaitlyn had blonde hair with dark roots and baby blue highlights. She wore an oversized flannel shirt that loosely covered jean shorts that looked a size too small. Her nose and eyebrow each had a single loop piercing.

She yanked her shirt lower over her shorts. "Hi."

Kaitlyn couldn't have been older than 18.

"Did you get the business card I left?" Brandon had asked Cory to tell Kaitlyn he needed to speak with her.

"I was going to call."

"Okay," Brandon said to Cory and Arianne. "Why don't you two go inside and find a place to sit while I talk to Kaitlyn for a moment."

"I'm not hungry," Cory said.

Brandon peered down his nose at the recalcitrant pimp. "Then take a walk," he said. "Now."

Cory opened his mouth to respond, then thought better of it. "Come on, Arianne."

They made their way across the parking lot and sucked on their vape pens as they hovered outside the diner's door.

"You have an ID?"

Kaitlyn unclasped her crossbody purse and pulled out a state ID.

"You don't drive?"

"Never took the test," she said.

That left her even more vulnerable to men like Cory. Without transportation, she'd have to depend on others to get where she was going—or escape from dangerous situations.

The ID indicated she'd turned 18 three months earlier. Her name was Kaitlyn Gallagher.

"How long has he been trafficking you?" Tori asked.

Brandon eyed Tori. This wasn't what he needed right now. Sure, Tori had years of experience. But as a prosecutor, not a cop.

Kaitlyn narrowed her eyes at Tori. It was the face of an angry teenager about to unload on her mother.

"No one's *trafficking* me," she said. "I chose to be here."

"Oh, sweetie, we know that's not true," Tori said.

"Ok. One thing at a time," Brandon said. "I've received some info that you were involved with Darren Rule—the performer they called Drool."

Her eyes wandered to where Cory and Arianne stood by the diner's entrance.

"I need the truth," Brandon said. "Not what Cory or Arianne told you to say."

She turned her attention back to Brandon. "He was a customer."

"Meaning he paid you for sex?"

"Meaning he was supposed to but raped me instead."

"When was this?"

"I don't know, less than a week ago."

"Did you contact law enforcement?"

"Why?"

"To report what he'd done to you."

"Cops don't believe people like me," she said.

"I don't know what you've experienced before, Kaitlyn. But I will listen to you. First, I need to know if you know anything about what happened to Drool."

"He was killed."

"How did you find out?"

"Cory told me. He said everyone is talking about it."

"When was the last time you had contact with Mr. Rule?"

"A few days before he died." She crossed her arms. "You think I killed him because of what he did to me?"

"Did you?" Brandon asked. Out of the corner of his eye, he noticed Tori staring at him. Like it or not, the question had to be asked.

He would have to continue the interview down at the station, away from distractions. And her potential involvement with Darren Rule warranted an official statement.

"That douchebag isn't worth murder," she said. "There's no way I'm going to prison for him."

Rule hadn't just been stabbed. He'd been beaten before his murder.

"What about Cory?" Brandon asked. "Maybe he roughed Drool up a bit?"

She shrugged. "Ask him yourself. I don't know what he does with his free time."

Brandon thought back to the evidence they'd found in the trailer.

"Did you ever spend time in Drool's trailer?"

"A few times. Until the time he raped me."

"I'm sorry that happened," Brandon said. "I'd like to refer you to the sexual assault center—"

"I don't need that," she interrupted.

Tori said, "I know you don't think you do, but they have counselors—"

"I know the number, okay?"

"Okay. But if you need to *remember* the number at any point, let us know," Brandon said.

"Yeah. Are we done? Cory is going to be pissed at me for talking to you."

"I'll take care of Cory," Brandon said. "I only have a couple more questions. Did Drool ever say anything about anyone wanting to kill him?"

"No," she said.

"Did he ask about or talk about collecting women's undergarments?"

She snorted. "Why, was he a crossdresser or something?"

"He didn't ask you for yours?"

"Hell no. I can't afford to go giving away my panties to every perv that wants a trophy..."

"Okay. Here's the deal. I'll need an official statement from you."

"Right now? I'm supposed to eat breakfast with those guys." She pointed to Cory and Arianne.

"It won't take long. I'll spot you for the breakfast," he said.

Brandon motioned for Cory and Arianne. They crossed the parking lot.

"Can we go now?" Cory asked.

"I'm taking Kaitlyn for a quick statement," Brandon said. "In the meantime, I need to know if any of you own a knife."

"Not me," Kaitlyn said.

"You're sure?"

She opened her purse. Inside were several business cards, a bank card, lipstick, and perfume. There were a handful of condoms, too.

The lipstick reminded him of the tube they'd found in the motorhome.

"Do either of you use sweet tangerine lipstick?"

"What the hell?" Cory asked.

"No," the girls said.

Noticing Brandon's eye on her purse, Arianne opened it. The contents were no different from Kaitlyn's, except she had a container of pepper spray. Arianne picked out a neon blue condom package and dangled it in front of Brandon. "You want one for you and your lady?"

If she was trying to embarrass Brandon, it wouldn't work. He'd been a cop for too long to be embarrassed about sex or anything related to it. As for Tori, he glanced sideways at her in time to notice the heat rising in her neck.

"Funny," Brandon said. "Where's your lipstick?"

She cast him a wry smile and squeezed it out of her hip pocket. "Succulent cherry."

"You have my card," he said to Cory. "Anything you learn, you let me know."

"When are you going to have Kaitlyn back?"

"When we're done talking," Brandon said. "You don't need her for anything, do you? Seeing as how you are all just friends?"

Cory's eyes shot Kaitlyn a warning. What was he trying to tell her? "Right," he said, turning his attention back to Brandon.

66

"We're going to need fingerprints," Brandon said. "From all three of you."

"I told you we didn't have anything to do with Drool's death," Cory said.

"Good to know. Then you won't mind us printing you."

"What about her?" Arianne said, pointing to Kaitlyn.

"We'll get hers too."

"I got stuff to do," Cory said. "I don't have time for this shit."

"Make time," Brandon said. "In fact, we'll be happy to give you a ride."

Brandon drove Tori and Kaitlyn to the station. He had an officer meet Cory and Arianne in the lobby. Cory had insisted on driving himself. So far, he'd been cooperative—barely.

After printing Kaitlyn, he ran a check on her. There was a missing person report from two years earlier, when she was a minor. He found a photo of a much younger and happier version of Kaitlyn on the state patrol's missing person website. They would have to notify the program she was no longer missing.

Her record check came back clean.

Brandon took Kaitlyn's statement in the station's interview room. After having her go over her knowledge of Darren Rule and the statement she'd made in the parking lot, he turned to her background.

"Looks like your dad reported you missing a while back."

She scoffed. "As if."

"You don't get along with him?"

"I'm pretty sure he only reported me missing to make himself look good to his latest girlfriend," she said.

"The report said you're from Mercer Island."

The island, nestled on the east side of Lake Washington, was a short drive from Seattle and home to several multimillion-dollar properties.

"Are you asking how a rich kid like me could end up a prostitute?" she asked.

"No, but that is a good question."

She considered her hand and began picking at the porcelain white fingernail polish.

"Let's see. Mom left, dad chasing any woman who was willing to put out after a couple glasses of wine..."

Her voice trembled with anger.

"And?" Brandon asked.

"You want more? I was supposed to be the intelligent one. I do have a sister. Anyway, the brainy nerdy kid gets bored at school and a friend offers her some Oxy."

It wasn't the first time he'd heard a story like hers. For girls, the addiction could lead to selling themselves for more pills. Their self-regard in the tank, it wasn't much of a step to street prostitution.

"I want you to know," he said. "We have places that can give you treatment."

"For the Oxy?" she asked. "Haven't touched it in a couple of months."

"Good. But you don't have to sell yourself. There are other options."

"Not for this much money," she said. "And now I'm no good for anything else."

"That's not true."

Her eyes slid to the door. "Can I go now?"

68

He sighed. "Okay, Kaitlyn. But if you need anything, you call me, got it?"

She stared at him for a moment before replying, "If you say so."

He had one of his officers give Kaitlyn a ride back to the diner. As promised, he spotted her money for breakfast—20 dollars was more than enough to cover a meal at Forks' greasy spoon diner.

The chances of Kaitlyn reaching out for help were slim to none. She'd been hurled into the world of prostitution when she was 16, a world that was nearly impossible to escape without support.

Her father had made a missing person report. He must care about her, despite what Kaitlyn believed.

Brandon's thoughts turned to Emma. Had he done enough to protect his own daughter against addiction? He'd heard stories of people experiencing an injury only to fall into the trap of opiate addiction through legally prescribed medications.

There was too much about life you couldn't control. Especially when it came to those you cared about.

Chapter 8

It wasn't ideal having Tori wait in his office, but he wanted to get the interview out of the way.

When Brandon stepped back in, Tori was behind his desk, typing on her cellphone.

She shoved it into her back pocket when she noticed him enter.

He turned at the sound of Jackson's voice. She was in the bullpen area, just outside his office.

"Chief?"

"Yeah?"

"You got a second?"

"Sure," he said.

Brandon grimaced at Tori. "Be right back."

The room they called the bullpen consisted of a conference table, chairs, and a few desks, one of which belonged to Jackson. A kitchenette occupied one corner. Jackson sat on the edge of her desk, arms crossed.

"What is she doing here?" she asked.

"I was interviewing her. I also found out there's a missing person report—"

"I wasn't talking about the girl."

"You mean Tori?"

"Is it *bring your ex to work day,* because if that's the case..."

"Don't get started. Yes, she's my ex. She's also a prosecuting attorney for King County. It's not like I'm bringing a stranger in here."

Jackson unfolded her arms. "I'm just saying. I hope this doesn't interfere with the investigation."

"You know me better than that," he said, "I'm just introducing her to everyone."

"Does this mean you two are back together?"

He'd had enough of her interrogation. He respected Jackson, but this wasn't the first time she'd crossed a boundary, especially considering she reported to him.

"One, none of your business. Two, just because you're friends with Lisa doesn't mean you have to hate anyone else I'm seeing."

Jackson and Brandon's ex, Lisa, had grown close over the last year. He was well aware of Jackson's disapproval of their breakup.

The only other officer in the room, Josiah, said, "I'd be happy to meet her. I think it's great when divorced couples get along. It helps with co-parenting—"

Jackson sighed. "Josiah, don't be a brown noser."

Tori appeared in the doorway.

Brandon extended an arm. "This is Tori. Tori, Isabel Jackson and Josiah Trent."

Josiah rose from his desk to shake her hand. "It's a pleasure to meet you, Miss..."

"Still Mrs. Mattson," Tori said, smiling. "Or, I suppose, Ms. Mattson. But call me Tori."

Jackson's lips curved in a weak smile.

Tori's eyes shifted from Jackson to Brandon. "Well, I'd better let you all get back to work."

"Nice meeting you," Jackson said, unenthusiastically.

"You know," Tori said, "I heard you mention the missing person report on Kaitlyn. I could check with my contacts in King County."

"Or we could do that," Jackson said.

Tori pressed her lips together. "Sorry. I didn't mean to step on anyone's toes. I know you're busy."

"We can handle the case," Jackson replied.

Now she was just being petty. Brandon held Jackson's gaze. She looked away, shaking her head.

"Tori's contacts can give us more info than a quick background check. She's not stepping on our investigation. Just doing us a favor."

Jackson stared at Brandon for a long time before saying, "Okay, Chief."

She swiveled her chair around and turned her back on Brandon before sitting at her desk.

Tori raised an eyebrow.

"We'd better get going," Brandon said.

"Nice meeting you all," Tori said.

Josiah grasped her hand again. "You, too."

Out in the parking lot, Brandon said, "You can take my truck. I'll drive a department vehicle home. And, about Jackson...she'll get over it."

"Over what?" Tori asked.

He paused, unsure how much to tell her.

"Remember the person I was dating? The coroner?"

"Yes."

"Jackson and Lisa are pretty close."

"It's not an excuse for being snotty. Is that the only reason she hates me?"

"What do you mean?"

"She seems jealous for your attention."

"Wait a minute," he said. "Like I said, she's a happily married woman."

Actually, he had no idea whether her marriage was happy. But she was married, and Brandon had never sensed anything but professionalism from Jackson.

"It doesn't have to be romantic for someone to crave being around you," she said.

"I hadn't thought of that," he said. His hands circled her waist. "Is it romantic when I *crave* being around you?"

She gazed up at him. "Only you can answer that."

Not knowing what to say, he kissed her instead.

"I'll see you tonight. If you're still here."

"Trying to get rid of me?" she asked.

He kissed her again, more deeply this time, hoping that was answer enough.

She smiled, slipping a hand into his pocket.

He scanned the parking lot. What was she thinking?

Tori plucked his keys free.

"I'll need these if you want me to take the truck."

He exhaled. "Right."

When Brandon returned to the bullpen, Jackson and Josiah were at the conference table. They grew silent as he opened the door.

Brandon poured himself a cup of black coffee. The charred drink bit at his tongue.

"How old is this?"

"Night shift," Josiah said.

Brandon tossed the coffee and made a new pot.

"What's the plan for the homicide case?" Josiah asked.

"Good question. Let's review what we know so far."

Mostly, he wanted to get Jackson focused back on the task at hand. She was his most experienced officer, and he needed her investigative skills.

To Brandon's relief, she joined the conversation. "The one thing we know for sure is pretty much everyone is happy he's dead," she said.

"Have you heard anything back from Lisa's office about the official cause of death?"

"Not yet," Jackson said. "She promised something by today."

"We have the murder weapon," Brandon said. "That's a start. The dagger and the tarot card in the mouth make this a pretty unique case."

"So, we'll have better luck making the connection between what's unusual about this case instead of focusing on motive?" Josiah asked.

"Possibly," Brandon said. "But motive will help us narrow the suspects. Not everyone who hates a person has motive to kill them. Motive requires a reason to take someone's life. Few people have such extreme feelings, even about their worst enemy."

"The dagger connects the victim to the swordsmith, Hamish. The card, to someone who reads fortunes. There are only two at the fair and one has an alibi."

"I'll work on Phoenix today," Brandon said. "And I want to take a look at this Hamish myself. Wasn't he supposed to get you information on his inventory?"

"He's checking if anything's been stolen, or if he'd sold a dagger matching the one that was used to kill Mr. Rule."

Josiah asked, "What did you learn from the prostitute girl?"

"Her name is Kaitlyn," Brandon said.

"Sorry. Kaitlyn."

"She's a runaway from over in King County. Got into drugs. Now's she's a victim of sex trafficking."

"Does she need treatment?" Jackson asked.

"She said she's sober now."

"But she keeps selling herself."

"She made a comment about not being good for anything else," Brandon said.

Jackson shook her head. "If men weren't willing to pay for sex, we wouldn't have this problem."

"Not all men," Josiah said defensively.

She looked sideways at him. "I wasn't talking about you, goodie-two-shoes."

He narrowed his eyes at her, leaning forward. "I'm proud I was homeschooled, in a good Christian home."

Jackson waved a hand at him. "You're a good man, Josiah. This isn't about you."

Josiah leaned back, still scowling.

"Kaitlyn and Arianne both denied using the lipstick color we found in the motorhome," Brandon said, trying to rope his two officers back into the conversation.

"Women rarely use just one hue," Jackson said.

"Okay. It's a piece of evidence we'll have to keep considering."

"What about the bruises on Darren Rule?" Josiah asked. "We need to ask around about that too."

"Good points," Brandon said. "Let's get down to the Renaissance fair and start asking questions."

The police station receptionist stuck her head in the room.

"There's a man here to see you, Chief Mattson."

The station's usual admin staff, Sue, was on vacation for the next two weeks. Lucy was Sue's niece. Both were members of the nearby Hoh tribe. Brandon was concerned about managing his department without Sue's knowledge and no-nonsense handling of the public, but Lucy had done a great job filling in.

"He says he's head of security for that geeky circus outside of town," Lucy said.

Lucy shared her aunt's gift for candor.

"It's a Renaissance fair," he said.

"Technically, the performers are dressed more medieval than Renaissance," Josiah said.

"You had it right the first time, Lucy," Jackson said. "Geeky circus."

Brandon met the fair's head of security in the lobby.

"Chief, I brought the list of employee names you asked for," Alex said.

"You didn't have to bring this down here," Brandon said, impressed by Alex's initiative.

"No trouble." He handed a manilla envelope to Brandon. Inside was a list of all the employees with their names, ages, and home addresses.

"These performers," Brandon asked, "how often do they return home?"

"Some of them have post office boxes, that's it. Their trailer is their home. Others only work the summer months."

"Thanks for this," Brandon said. "I'll let you know if we need anything else."

He turned to leave.

"Chief," Alex said.

"Yeah?"

"Any news on who might have done this?"

"We're working on it," Brandon said.

"Just so you know, I've been thinking about the whole tarot card thing..."

"Who told you about that?"

"Your officer. What was her name...Jackson?"

Brandon glanced at the door leading to the bullpen. He'd have a talk with Jackson about sharing evidence with those outside the team.

"It's not her fault," Alex said. "She was showing the picture of the card around. I noticed a speck of blood on the card and, well, it's a safe assumption it had to be part of the crime scene. Otherwise, she wouldn't be asking."

"So, what about the card?"

"It's the moon card."

"Okay," Brandon said, recalling the creepy moon face staring down at two baying dogs.

"Don't you think it has some sort of meaning?" Alex asked.

"We checked online. It has something to do with hidden enemies, deception, that sort of thing. Makes sense to me."

"But which direction was the card facing?"

Brandon thought back to the scene. "What do you mean?"

"Was it upside down? From your point of view...looking at him."

"I'll have to check the photos. But I think it was upside down, meaning the bottom of the card faced away from us."

"That's what they call reversed," Alex said.

"You seem to know a lot about tarot cards," Brandon said.

Alex held up his phone, revealing a tarot reading website. "When it's reversed like that, it can be related to silence."

"And?"

"The killer is sending a message. Something about Drool keeping silent. Maybe he knew something. A secret..."

"And someone was making sure he didn't reveal it?"

"Right."

77

"It's an interesting theory," Brandon said. "I'll keep it in mind."

Alex nodded. "Let me know what else I can do to help, Chief."

Brandon tapped on the envelope. "Thanks again. We'll be in touch."

"What did Alex want?" Jackson asked.

Brandon tossed the list of employee names onto the table.

"More people to interview," Josiah said.

"That's a good thing," Jackson said.

"What's not a good thing is you discussing evidence with a security guard," Brandon said.

Jackson stared back at him until it dawned on her what he was talking about.

"I showed him the picture of the tarot card and the knife, just like I did with others who might identify them. He noticed the blood and figured it out himself."

"Figured what out?"

"That it had been in the victim's mouth."

"He told you that?"

"Wait," Jackson said. "Are you thinking Alex had something to do with the murder and he's dropping hints?"

It wasn't unusual for a killer to offer the police help. Jackson knew that as well as Brandon did.

"Do you want me to keep an eye on him?" Josiah asked, sitting up straight in his chair.

"No," Brandon said. "I want us to be careful."

"Are you saying we're not careful?" Jackson asked. It was more of an invitation to an argument than an actual question.

Brandon looked to Josiah. "Start on the list. Mark off everyone we've already talked to and get working on the rest. If you need help locating any of them, it's fine to ask Alex."

"Got it," he said. "What are you going to do?"

"Jackson and I are going to revisit Hamish about the dagger and then, if we have to, drag Phoenix out of bed to get a statement from her about the tarot card."

Chapter 9

Brandon started the Interceptor SUV with Jackson in the passenger seat. The radio crooned an old John Prine folk tune. Jackson reached over and turned the volume to zero.

"How can you listen to that?"

"What?"

"Banjos and fiddles. What is this, the 1800s?"

"It's a mandolin. And, sorry, I don't have any Cuban music for you."

She glared at him. "Just because my family is Cuban does not mean that's the only music I like."

"Okay, what do you want to listen to?"

"Just, forget it."

He turned to Jackson. "Are you okay?"

"What?" she asked.

"You seem...irritable."

"So what, are you going to ask me if I'm menstruating? Because..."

"No," he said, shaking his head. That was the last thing he needed to know. And he'd never been dumb enough to ask a woman such a stupid question, even before being sunk in years of sensitivity training over in King County. "Just making sure we're okay."

"I just don't get it," she said.

He wasn't sure what she meant, so he waited.

"You know?" she continued.

"You're going to have to be a little more specific."

"Okay, you want specific, but don't get all up in my ass about getting into your personal life."

She wanted to talk about *that.*

"You and Lisa had something special," Jackson said.

"That doesn't mean it was meant to be," he said.

Why were they talking about this now? He should have kept his mouth shut.

"So you rebound to your ex-wife?"

"You could say Lisa was a rebound from my divorce."

"No, that would have been Misty."

He tapped his fingers on the steering wheel, avoiding her gaze. "That didn't last long enough to count."

His first month back in Forks, Brandon had almost rekindled his romance with his high-school sweetheart, Misty Brooks. Soon after, Misty had relocated to Aberdeen, saving both of them from what was bound to be a repeat of the train wreck that had ended their relationship decades earlier.

She grunted. "Whatever."

"Tori is easy to get along with. You ought to try it."

"I'm sure she's a real peach," Jackson said.

Brandon shifted the car into drive.

"She's going to be part of my life. Not that it has anything to do with my job," he said.

"Okay, I get it. Mind my own business," Jackson said.

Yes, please.

Josiah pulled up next to them and rolled down his passenger window. He leaned over. "You guys coming?"

"We'll be there," Brandon said.

Josiah nodded and drove off.

"I just don't want you to get hurt," she said.

"I can take care of myself." He edged up to the street and flipped the blinker on.

"Does Tori talk much about her home life?" Jackson asked.

He wasn't sure what she was getting at.

"You mean work?"

"I mean dating. If she's seeing anyone."

"She hasn't mentioned anything, no." He studied Jackson. "Why are you asking me this?"

She was staring out the passenger window.

"You're right. It's none of my business."

Brandon turned onto the street. He didn't like the way the conversation was going. He trusted Jackson. They'd be friends if he wasn't her boss. But because he was the chief, that meant keeping the boundary between work and home, hard as that was in a town the size of Forks.

"Alex has got this theory about the tarot card we found in Darren Rule's mouth," Brandon said, signaling an end to the conversation about his personal life. He explained Alex's theory about the direction of the card and how that might mean the killer was sending a message about keeping quiet.

"It's an interesting theory," Jackson said. "But a little convoluted. Still, he's got the making of a good cop."

"Who said he wants to be a cop?" Brandon asked.

"He's a security guard."

She had a point.

"Did he tell you he was interested in police work?" Brandon asked.

"No, but by the way he's going out of his way to help, it sure seems like it."

"That," Brandon said, "or he's covering his tracks."

She turned in her seat, watching him. "Do you trust anyone?"

"Do you?"

She smiled. "Touché."

A minute later, she said, "Jazz."

"What?"

"You asked me what kind of music I like. Jazz. Classical too. Almost anything. As long as it doesn't have banjos."

"Good to know."

They arrived at the Renaissance fair just after 11:00. Most of those roaming the grounds at that hour were performers out for a morning stroll before the masses arrived. Many of the shops were just opening. As they passed through the open-air food court, the candied aroma of barbeque ribs drifted over the plaza.

Brandon and Jackson approached *MacDuff's Iron Blade*, one of several merchants selling melee weapons, armor, and ranged weapons like recurve bows and crossbows. MacDuff's shop was a wide, multi-pole tent with a wooden facade for the storefront.

The man raising the store's canvas porch had the build of someone who'd spent hours leaning over an anvil banging chunks of metal into deadly weapons.

Hamish MacDuff turned at their approach. He had dark blonde hair and a wild beard split into five or six parts with rubber bands. He wore a kilt as if to add legitimacy to his last name. He appeared to be in his mid-forties.

"Officers. How can I help you?"

Brandon smiled at the accent. He really was Scottish.

"We had a few questions about one of your daggers," Brandon said.

"Let's go in back," he said, pointing over his shoulder with his thumb.

Behind the counter, the display table and wall were covered with sabers, two-handed swords, short swords, and daggers of all shapes and sizes. Some were dull, dark steel. Others had a mirror-like polish.

Hamish led them to a back area nearly twice as expansive as the front.

There were boxes, a bed and dresser, assorted trunks, and a television. The space was enveloped in a canvas tent of white and indigo stripes.

"You sleep here?" Jackson asked.

"Me and the lady."

"Where's your workshop?" Brandon asked.

"Further back," he said.

Just then, a woman entered, drying her amber hair with a towel. Her attire was gypsy-like, with a black cotton corset over a bone white, shoulderless blouse. She had a red and black Tartan sash wrapped around her waist.

The soothing fragrance of lavender followed her into the tent. She started when she noticed they had company.

"More questions about the Drool situation," Hamish said. "Officers, this is my wife, Daisy."

There was something familiar about Daisy. Maybe he'd seen her at the fair in one of the performances. She had a wide mouth and lips some women paid for, but she wasn't smiling now.

Daisy grimaced at Hamish. "Did you check the paperwork like you told them you would?"

Hamish lowered his head before glancing at Brandon. "I'm working on it. The problem is, you see, I keep everything on paper."

"But the knife in the photo you were shown was one of yours?" Brandon asked.

"It's got my family crest on it," he said, pointing to a tapestry on the wall behind Brandon. The crest matched

84

the sword-wielding lion on the dagger found in Darren Rule's mouth.

"That doesn't mean we sold it to the killer," Daisy said, moving to Hamish's side. "It could have been stolen."

"Okay. So what can you tell me about the inventory? Are you missing a dagger?"

"I don't think there are any missing."

"Then we need to know who you sold daggers to since arriving here."

"I don't keep track of that," he said.

"What about the receipts?" Jackson asked.

Hamish approached a pile of boxes in the far corner and lifted the top one. He set it on a table next to Brandon.

"Look for yourself."

Inside were carbon copies of handwritten receipts. The only information on the papers were basic descriptions like 'sword' or 'dagger' and the sale amount.

"Can you tell by the sale price?"

"Not really," he said. "Sometimes a customer negotiates lower."

"How many daggers have you sold here in Forks?" Brandon asked.

Hamish thought about it for a second.

"Maybe ten. Twelve."

"And you have no idea who you sold them to?" Jackson asked.

"Like I said..."

"Wouldn't you have noticed a missing dagger?" Jackson asked.

"Well..." Hamish started.

"Hamish is a good man. Strong and hardworking," Daisy said. "But he's not organized."

Brandon considered Daisy. "Have we met before?"

"I don't think so," she said.

Jackson whispered to Brandon, "The photos."

"Huh?"

"In the motorhome."

Then, it hit him. Daisy was the topless blonde in the stack of pictures he'd found behind Darren Rule's dresser. Her hair was darker now, but it was definitely her.

They'd have to ask her about the photo at some point.

"What are you whispering about?" Hamish asked.

"What's your job with the fair?" Brandon asked Daisy.

"If you mean, why don't I help out with Hamish's bookkeeping, I do what I can," she said. "But I have work of my own."

"What is that?" Jackson asked.

"I'm a performer."

"She's more than a performer," Hamish said, leaning down and kissing her on the forehead. "She's part of the *Royal Equestrians Horse Troupe.*"

"Like doing tricks on horses?" Brandon asked. He'd seen that sort of thing on television. Performers hanging off a horse with one leg or doing flips as the beast rushed around the arena.

"A little more complicated than tricks," she said.

"So remind us again where you two were the night Darren Rule was murdered," Brandon said.

"We were here in the tent," she said. "All night."

"Starting when?" Jackson asked.

Hamish's eyes swept to Daisy before he answered. "I don't know, maybe after eight. We watched a movie."

"Which one?" Jackson asked.

86

"Gladiator," Hamish said. "We have the DVD."

"I fell asleep," Daisy added.

"But then I woke you up. Remember?" Hamish said with a silly grin.

She slapped him on the chest. "They don't need to know about that."

Jackson and Brandon stared at each other. He tried not to roll his eyes.

"How long had the two of you known Darren Rule?" Brandon asked.

Daisy's gaze dropped. Almost imperceptibly, she drifted away from Hamish.

Hamish spoke first. "He didn'tae deserve her," he said, his accent suddenly thicker.

Had Daisy been another of Darren Rule's sexual assault victims?

"Quiet," she said. "I can't change the past and neither can you."

"I take it you and Darren were together at some point?" Jackson asked Daisy.

Her eyes revealed a memory pricked by a long-ago pain.

"We were married," she said.

That shed light on the photograph. Considering she appeared older now, it might have been taken during the marriage.

"When did it end?" Brandon asked.

"Long ago. Maybe ten years."

"We've been together for six years," Hamish said. "And then he had to show up again."

"What did you mean by show up again? Had he been gone?"

"He was traveling with another troupe until this year. I have no idea why Mr. Sterling hired the git. Everyone hates him. He's not even funny."

"And since he's been back," Brandon asked Daisy, "what's your relationship been like with him."

Hamish flinched, then took a half-step toward Brandon. "What's that supposed to mean?"

"It means what you think it means," Brandon said. "We have to consider everything."

"There is no relationship," she said.

Jackson looked to Brandon. They couldn't leave without addressing the topless photo.

"Daisy," Jackson said, "We have a few personal questions we'd like to ask. Maybe you'd like to speak to us somewhere else?"

Daisy wrapped her arm in Hamish's. "I don't have anything to hide."

I wouldn't be so sure about that, Brandon thought.

"I don't know what this is about," Hamish said. "Daisy hasn't done anything wrong."

"You're sure?" Brandon asked Daisy.

Daisy began fastening the black corset over her blouse. After the third hook, she paused. She eyed Brandon calmly. "I have no secrets from Hamish."

They were about to find out if that was true.

"We found some photographs in Darren's bedroom."

Her fingers caught on the top fastener. "So?"

She knew.

"One of the photos is of you. Topless."

"That is not true," Hamish said. "Impossible."

Brandon and Jackson stared at Daisy, waiting for a response.

"You should leave now," Hamish said to Brandon.

"We're not done yet," he replied.

Hamish stepped closer to Brandon, his frame towering over him. "And so what if there's a picture of my wife? It must be from a long time ago. When she didn't know any better."

Brandon looked past Hamish to Daisy. "How old is the photo?"

Before she could answer, Hamish gripped Brandon's shoulder. "Get out!"

Brandon shifted to the side, swinging free of Hamish's grasp. By the time he separated himself, Jackson had her hand on her pistol.

"Stop!" Daisy said. "Hamish, get back here now."

He cast Brandon a menacing glare before returning to her side.

"Where I come from," Hamish said in a thick accent, "Cops don't need guns."

"They come in pretty handy around here," Brandon said. "And the next time you lay a finger on me, you'll be spending time in a cell."

Hamish huffed. "Put the guns away and let's see who's the real man."

"Silence yourself," Daisy said. She frowned at Jackson. "It was during our marriage. He wanted to take pictures of me. I was okay with it. It was stupid, I know."

"We're all guilty of doing dumb shit for men at one point in our lives," Jackson said.

Brandon's head swiveled to her, but she didn't look back at him.

"But was he using the picture against you?" Jackson asked. "For blackmail?"

"No," she said. "I didn't even remember it until now."

"Have you had any contact with him since the fair arrived in Forks?" Jackson asked.

"No."

Her cheeks were crimson with embarrassment, her eyes red and wet. They'd asked enough questions for the time being.

"Okay," Brandon said. "If you recall anything, you need to let us know."

"We will," Daisy said, sliding her hand into Hamish's.

They left the tent, Hamish's gaze boring into the back of Brandon's neck.

"He doesn't like you," Jackson said as they strolled away from the weapon maker's shop.

"No man likes the idea of another man having a topless photo of his wife. Much less implying she might have hooked up with her ex."

"You think he's playing dumb about the dagger?" Jackson asked.

"That, or he's just plain dumb."

"Maybe Daisy has brains enough for both of them," Jackson said.

"I'm not buying that she had no contact with Darren Rule after their divorce. They're in the same fair."

"Not by choice, according to her."

"Maybe not," Brandon said, "but there's something both of them are hiding."

"Agreed," Jackson said. "What's next?"

Brandon motioned toward the crowded row of tents that trailed away perpendicular to the armor and weapon section of the fair. "A visit to my favorite fortune teller."

Chapter 10

Phoenix Weaver's merchant tent was sealed, the table she'd used for her tarot cards and other fortune telling wares gone.

Brandon checked the time. It was past eleven.

"She was nowhere to be found yesterday, either," Jackson said. "You want to try later?"

Brandon held a hand up, listening. A rustle came from within the tent.

He stepped closer. "Phoenix, we know you're in there."

There was a clanging of metal.

The tent flap opened. Phoenix emerged wearing the same moon and stars dress she had worn two days earlier.

"You made me spill my Chex," she said, holding out a half-empty bowl.

"It's nearly lunchtime," Brandon said.

She eyed him critically. "Do I tell you when to eat?"

"We have some questions about your tarot cards," Jackson said.

She set her bowl down on the grass and approached Jackson. "You would like to know your future?" She grasped Jackson's hand and turned it palm up.

"Phoenix...."

"What do you see?" Jackson asked.

"Really?" Brandon asked.

"Good things," Phoenix said. "True love."

"Now I know you're lying," Jackson said, sarcastically. She yanked her hand back.

"Why?"

"I've been married ten years."

"Ouch," Brandon said.

"It was a joke," Jackson said.

Brandon asked Phoenix, "What do you know about the performer who died?"

Phoenix squinted at Brandon, considering the question. "What does any of us know about another soul?"

"A lot, depending on the person," Brandon said.

She tightened the black sash around her waist.

"I've seen him around."

"Ever talk to him?" Jackson asked.

"Once or twice. Seemed kind of pervy."

"How so?" Jackson asked.

"The sort of man who might be into kinky stuff." She winked at Jackson. "You know the type."

Jackson stared back at her.

"I could do a couples reading for you and your husband," Phoenix said. "My customers will tell you it has done wonders in the bedroom. Not that I would know anything about that personally."

"Ah, no thanks," Jackson said.

On a hunch, Brandon asked Phoenix, "Did Darren Rule come on to you?"

"Eww," she said. "I'm not so desperate to be with a man like that."

That wasn't what he'd asked her.

"So, the answer is no?"

"Of course," she said, flipping her long blonde curls over one shoulder.

"We'll need to see your cards," Jackson said.

"Why?"

"Just get the cards," Brandon said.

She huffed before disappearing into the tent. A minute later she emerged with a hand-sized mahogany box.

"What's that smell?" Brandon asked.

"Sandalwood incense," she said. "It's a cleansing. A protection..."

"From?"

She eyed him. "Well, I didn't need it before you arrived."

Phoenix opened the lid, showing the cards to Brandon. He reached for the deck but suddenly she clutched it to her bosom.

"I don't like your energy," Phoenix said. She held out the box for Jackson.

Jackson lifted the cards out. Brandon pulled out his phone and scrolled to the picture of the card in Darren Rule's mouth.

"Find the moon one," he said to Phoenix.

"Why?"

Jackson handed the box back. "It's of interest to us."

Phoenix lifted the cards and seemed to find the moon card immediately.

She held it flat in her palm. The drawing of two dogs baying at a dour-faced moon didn't match the one they'd found with Darren Rule. Phoenix's deck was stylistically more medieval than the other.

Brandon held up the photo of the tarot card in the victim's mouth.

"You know anyone who uses a deck like this?"

She squinted at the screen. "That's a newer set. Probably less than a few years old."

She carefully placed the cards back in the box and closed the lid. "My deck is antique, used by my mother and my grandmother. Have you asked the other so-called seer that travels with the fair?"

"Her deck is similar to yours," Jackson said. "Not an exact match but—"

Phoenix pressed her lips together. "*My* deck was handcrafted, officer. Nothing about my gifts or tools has been manufactured. There are only two in existence. And they are both mine. I even checked on eBay. Not one for sale."

Phoenix peered over Brandon's shoulder. "I have a customer."

Jackson looked to Brandon. They'd reached the end of the interview.

They stepped aside. The customer was Arianne Young.

"You hear anything, Phoenix, you let us know," Brandon said.

Phoenix tucked the box under her arm. She considered Arianne. A scowl crossed her face. "I don't do readings for free."

"I have money," Arianne said.

"Okay, but I can't promise your future will be any better than the present."

Brandon and Jackson left them.

"What was that about?" Jackson asked.

"No idea, but she obviously doesn't like Arianne. Could be because she knows how Arianne earns her money."

Jackson pressed her lips in disgust. "Victim shaming. *Eso es una mierda.*"

"Agreed," Brandon said. He wasn't sure exactly what she'd said, but the tone conveyed her meaning.

Brandon and Jackson turned at the sound of Duke Sterling's voice.

"I don't have time for this, Alex."

Alex Winfield, head of security, had a hand on Sterling's arm.

"This won't take long, I'm sure," Alex said.

"What's going on?" Brandon asked.

Alex stepped aside, motioning to Sterling.

"Here he is, sir."

Sterling wore a gold-embroidered scarlet tunic with matching pants. His hand rested on the hilt of a short sword tucked into a sheath at his side. Brandon stared back, confused.

Jackson cleared her throat. "This is my fault."

"I was in the middle of our daily knighting ceremony," Sterling said.

"Knighting?" Brandon asked.

"For a nominal fee, our guests have the privilege of being knighted by the Lord Mayor." His nose rose in the air. "That's me."

"I mentioned in passing that we needed to speak to Mr. Sterling at some point," Jackson said.

Brandon asked Alex, "And you decided that should be now?"

"Sorry, sir," Alex said. "I figured it must be important to your investigation."

Alex's penchant for wanting to help was beginning to grate on Brandon. It was one thing to do what he was asked, but at this point, he was inserting himself into the case.

"Is there somewhere we can talk?" Brandon asked Sterling. "Privately."

Sterling led Brandon and Jackson to a mobile trailer situated behind the fair's main stage. He'd somehow squeezed a desk, two chairs, and a leather love seat into the tight quarters. Photographs of Sterling with important-looking people were tacked to the wall behind his desk. Brandon recognized the governor of California and at least two former presidents.

He asked them to have a seat and they did.

"Have you given any more thought to who might want to kill Darren Rule?" Brandon asked.

Sterling opened a drawer in his desk and grabbed himself a plastic water bottle. He twisted the lid off and swallowed a long drink.

"Not really."

"You're not concerned there might be a killer in your fair?" Jackson asked.

Sterling spread his hands out. "Like I said, nobody liked Darren. I'm sure most of the cast was glad to see him go."

"Does that include you?" Brandon asked.

"I'm not in the cast."

That wasn't the point of the question.

"Mr. Sterling, were you glad to see Drool go?" Brandon asked.

He motioned to Brandon with the water bottle. "I get where this is going. The answer is no. Hell no. I'm not stupid enough to kill a clown like Rule just because he insults me. I have a good life. Too much to lose."

"You married?" Jackson asked. "Have kids?"

"I've had a few," he said. "Wives, I mean. Kids and I don't get along."

"How long have you been in the entertainment business?" Brandon asked.

Sterling leaned back in his chair. His face loosened. "Twenty years. Cut my teeth managing a handful of acts. Now, all this is mine." He sat up. "Not just this. I operate three Renaissance fairs, eight carnivals, and six award-winning festivals, including the renowned *Macaroni and Cheese Festival* in Orange County."

"Nice," Brandon said.

"You wouldn't know about the relationship between Daisy MacDuff and Mr. Rule?" Jackson asked.

Sterling sighed. "To be honest, I don't have time to track the soap-opera of relationships that fester in an environment like this. It's close working quarters. People live, eat, drink together. Someone's bound to get killed, eventually."

"Your concern for your employees is touching," Jackson said.

"I'm not their parent. And technically, I don't even have to be here. I'm the owner. That's why I have an operations manager and a head of security."

"How long has Alex Winfield worked for you?" Brandon asked.

"Too long."

"You're not happy with him?"

"He's over the top. Thinks he's a cop," Sterling said. He finished the last of the water and made a show of squashing the plastic container before tossing it in a garbage can, ignoring the recycling receptacle a few feet away. "I hired Mr. Winfield in California a couple months back. Some sob story about wanted to work closer to his family. I'm not sure we'll keep him."

"Why?"

"Because I don't like him. And I'm the boss," Sterling said.

"Alright," Brandon said. "Do you plan on staying in town?"

"Unfortunately, yes. This is our first fair in the state. If we're able to expand our market share, we'll have competing fairs begging to join us by next season."

"You and the mayor must get along," Brandon said. Mayor Kim shared Sterling's cutthroat approach to business, especially when it came to tourism.

Sterling flashed a smile. "Sara Kim is a lovely lady. She has that killer instinct."

"Right," Brandon said. Two peas in a pod.

"He's a piece of work," Jackson said on their way back to the car.

"People like that, you wonder if they're successful because of their general disregard for other people, or if the disregard came after their success."

She shrugged. "Who has time to worry about all the prideful gits in the world?"

"We've got plenty of suspects to check up on," Brandon said. "Hamish and Daisy. Sterling, although he's not technically a suspect, yet."

"Phoenix?"

"We already know her," Brandon said. "But do a check just to make sure."

"And the pimp and his two girls?"

"We already have the info on them. No hits on their records. I'm looking into Kaitlyn Gallagher's past. One more thing," Brandon said. "Do a background check on our stellar security guard."

"You're that worried about him?"

"Making sure we cover all our bases," he said.

"Got it. I'll head back to the station and get working on researching our suspects."

"I'll find Josiah and help with the list of employees," Brandon said. "In the meantime, remind your buddy Alex to stay in his own lane. He's stepping on our investigation. If we need to interview a witness, we can get ahold of them without his help."

Chapter 11

Brandon, Jackson, and Josiah regrouped at the station that afternoon.

"Any breaks?" Jackson asked, leaning back in her chair. Josiah was at his desk, Brandon at the bullpen conference table.

"Yeah. Everyone hates Darren Rule," Josiah said.

"Same," Brandon said.

"I asked around about his cellphone since you mentioned it was missing from the crime scene," Josiah said. "A few people remember him bragging about having the newest iPhone."

"That doesn't narrow our search by much," Jackson said.

"Any news back from the carrier?" Brandon asked.

"Not yet. I'll keep bothering them, but you know how it is."

"Wait, there's something else," Josiah said. "Apparently the cellphone cover had a picture of a naked woman on it. A painting, according to the production manager."

"A painting?" Jackson asked.

"Maybe he was a fan of fine art," Brandon said.

"I'm sure."

"That's good information, Josiah. Sounds like it won't be hard to miss if it turns up." Brandon turned to Jackson. "What did you find out about Alex Winfield?"

"He's clean. I even checked with his former employer. He's just a guy hoping to become an officer in our state, closer to his daughter."

"Fine. But he's not an officer. Not yet."

"I checked everyone else, too. Daisy is clean. Hamish has an arrest for second-degree assault but the charges were dropped."

"What about Sterling?"

"He's got lawsuits, all civil stuff," she said.

"What sort of lawsuits?" Brandon asked.

"Breach of contract. Property rights disagreements. Some cases filed for him, some against him."

"And Phoenix?"

"Clean as the virgin snow," she said. "And speaking of virgin, or whatever the opposite of that is, I'm about finished with Darren Rule's background."

"Don't tell me. Everyone hates him," Brandon said.

She flipped through her notebook. "He's from San Francisco originally. We knew about his reputation. Assault. Sexual assault reduced to assault. Domestic violence."

"A real winner," Brandon said.

"Here's the kicker. He's got a son."

"How old?"

"Ten."

"Well I guess we can rule the son out," Brandon said. "What about the mother?"

"She's in Texas. Lisa's office already notified her. She wasn't surprised or overly sad to hear about Rule's death. But that's understandable, considering who he was."

"Still, he was the father of her child," Brandon said.

"Father meaning sperm donor?" Jackson said.

"Okay," Brandon said. "I get it."

"And she has an alibi," Jackson said. "I checked on it, just to be safe."

"Good work, Jackson. You too, Josiah. We're making headway, even if it doesn't seem like it."

"How?" Josiah asked.

"By eliminating alternatives."

"Deduction," Josiah said. "Like Sherlock Holmes."

"But we're not geniuses."

"Speak for yourself," Jackson said, smiling.

"Okay. Except for Jackson."

"Any progress on the photographs?" Brandon asked.

"I haven't had much time. The few individuals I've asked don't have a clue. I don't believe the people in the pictures are from the fair—except Daisy. It's going to be near impossible to locate them."

"I'm sure you'll figure it out. You are a genius, after all."

"Don't be a *cabrón.*"

"Watch it, Jackson."

"I know. You're the chief."

Jackson settled her feet on the chair across from her. "Any other news?"

"Tori is doing some digging on Kaitlyn. She's going to update me tonight."

Jackson huffed.

"Anyway," Brandon said. "We'll meet here tomorrow and talk about next steps."

He stood and Jackson swung her feet off the chair.

Josiah hopped up and grabbed his coat.

"Where are you off to in a hurry?" Brandon asked.

He hesitated. "I have a date."

It wasn't often Josiah got out. His father had died years back from multiple sclerosis, prompting Josiah to move back in with his mother to care for her.

"Wow," Jackson said. "Don't stay out too late."

102

"Don't listen to her," Brandon said. "Have fun."

When Josiah had gone, Jackson said, "Say hi to the wife."

He rolled his eyes. "Now who's being a *cabrón*?"

When he arrived home, Tori was on the couch reading a book. Caesar was asleep at her feet.

Tori sat up and the cat scrambled away. Brandon kicked off his boots and took Caesar's place.

"Any news?" Tori asked.

"Let's see. Phoenix Weaver's tarot cards didn't match the one found with the victim. One merchant, Hamish MacDuff, acknowledged the dagger used on Darren Rule was his but doesn't keep records on what he sells. And the owner of the Renaissance fair is arrogant and generally not helpful."

"In other words, you had a great day," she said.

"Exactly. What did you learn about Kaitlyn Gallagher?"

"Kaitlyn was a runaway, but you already knew that," Tori said.

"She hinted her father wasn't there for her—but is that enough to cause her to turn to prostitution?"

"Could be. There are so many factors involved. Including being at the wrong place at the wrong time," she said.

"Kaitlyn did mention her addiction issues. She claims she's sober now."

Tori reached for a notebook on the floor next to the couch. She flipped a couple of pages, then began reading her notes. "Her father was a real estate broker, then made a killing on the market. Apparently, the mom disappeared a while back."

"And he's been enjoying the bachelor life ever since," Brandon said, recalling what Kaitlyn had said about her father.

"He's no father of the year, but nothing criminal or negligent," she said.

"What else?" Brandon asked.

"There isn't much here. I'm sorry."

Brandon nodded. "Thanks for checking."

"Wait a minute," she said, glancing at her notes. "I have the father's number. But it sounds like at some point he gave up on her."

She handed him the notebook and he removed the page with the number. "I'll give him a call."

"I can have King County notify him we've found her. She is over eighteen, though."

"Right," he said. "Still, I'd like to talk to him."

She considered him. "Don't go getting mixed up in this."

"It's my job," he replied.

"I mean the relationship between the dad and his daughter. I know how you are."

"And how is that?"

"You want things to work. People to do the right thing."

"So?" he asked.

"Families are complicated. You're a cop, not a social worker."

Kaitlyn's father had nothing to do with the investigation, but that didn't mean Brandon should abandon Kaitlyn to her current situation. There was still hope for her—if only she would accept it.

"Who's playing therapist now?" he asked.

She smiled. "True."

He rose and held out his hands. She held them and stood too.

"Let's go out tonight."

"Where to?" he asked.

"I was thinking..." she paused. "You might not like this idea."

"Whatever you want, I'm game."

"Promise?"

He narrowed his eyes at her. "What are you thinking?"

"The Forks Renaissance Fair."

"That's hardly romantic."

"It is," she said. "And tonight is the Midsummer celebration. There's going to be Celtic music, dancing, beer."

"Well, if there's going to be beer..."

Still, it would be awkward spending an evening out at the same location where someone had been murdered. A crime he hadn't solved yet.

"I'll rent one of those dresses again."

He recalled the dress she'd donned the day Emma left.

"Sold," he said, smiling.

He reminded himself that Darren Rule's motorhome, not the entire fair, was the crime scene. And the motorhome was up in the evidence garage in Port Angeles.

"I'll go get ready," she said.

He stood there, watching her form, wondering where the evening would lead them. He knew where he wanted it to take them. Whether that was a good idea or not, that was something entirely different.

Tori was still in the bathroom when he'd finished changing into his civilian clothes. He picked up the paper with the number for Kaitlyn's father on it.

Hopefully, her father hadn't changed numbers in the last two years.

He dialed the number. Brandon thought about what he'd say. *Good news, Mr. Gallagher. We've found your daughter.* He'd let Kaitlyn explain the rest. His stomach lurched at the thought of Emma in the same situation. Lost for years, only to come home broken and bitter at having been forced into a life of prostitution. A life she was refusing to leave now that she had a chance.

Brandon would love Emma no matter what choices she made. That's what fathers did.

The call went to voicemail.

"Mr. Gallagher. This is police chief Brandon Mattson from Forks. I'd like to speak with you about your daughter Kaitlyn." He left his number and added, "It's urgent. And you'll be happy to learn we've found her. Alive."

Brandon disconnected, then waited a minute. People screened their calls. When the father learned what Brandon had called about, he'd call back right away.

After a few minutes, he slipped the phone into his pocket. He was sure to contact Brandon soon.

Chapter 12

The Forks Renaissance Fair was packed—the evening audience noticeably older if not more mature. The families with small children had headed home before sundown, leaving the nighttime festivities to the mostly over-21 crowd.

Despite Tori's badgering, Brandon had refused to don the outfit he'd worn for the theater performance. Waiting for her to rent the dress, he found a commoner's outfit, loose-fitting and plain. He'd die if one of his officers recognized him decked out like a cos-play, Dungeons and Dragons convention escapee.

You're doing this for Tori, he reminded himself. *Grin and bear it, and soon you'll be back at home, alone with her.*

They found an open spot in the beer garden next to what was called the Wild Rover Stage (sponsored by Pistol Annie's, a firearm dealer in town). Tori got her fill of Celtic jigs and reels and Brandon was able to relax with a couple of pints. He hadn't eaten since lunch, so the alcohol was making itself known.

They ordered dinner from a place offering "steak on a stick"—basically overpriced shish kabobs—and ordered a few with a side of vegetables. They watched a couple more shows...a magician with a pet ferret as his assistant, and then a fire-eating comic who, though funnier than Drool, was just about as raunchy.

After a few hours, the sun had set and Brandon was ready to head home and spend the rest of the evening with Tori. He was about to say as much when she veered toward the arena that had hosted a jousting tournament earlier that day.

Inside the fenced-off pitch, three men in plate armor were engaged in a melee. Portable generator-fueled spotlights cast a white glow over the dirt and sand field.

The trio of armored men circled each other, weapons ready to strike. Each knight had a colored band on his bicep—yellow, blue, or red. A bulky knight wearing the red band swung a double-headed axe at the yellow opponent. He ducked easily, then shoved a foot into his rival, sending him stumbling onto the dirt. Now the yellow knight stalked the broadsword-yielding blue fighter. Blue parried the thrust, but again, yellow kicked blue onto his backside. By then, the colossal red soldier had climbed to his feet and took another swing at yellow.

This went on for several minutes, a choreographed match as realistic, Brandon guessed, as the Hulk Hogan and Andre the Giant duels of the 1980s.

When it was all done, yellow had bested his foes, raising his hand in victory under a wave of cheers.

"Totally fake," Brandon said.

"Still...don't you think it would be fun?"

Just then, the field of battle emptied and a medieval emcee rushed into the stadium, microphone in hand.

"Ladies and gentlemen, our next event will be the amateur battle to end all battles."

The crowd cheered. The field was an oval with risers on the two farthest sides. Brandon and Tori watched from a standing-room-only, longer portion of the pitch. Directly across from them was a tall platform where several elegantly dressed men and women surveyed the combatants. Brandon hadn't noticed them until now. Resting in the most regal of chairs was Duke Sterling.

Mayor Kim perched at his side in a throne just a little shorter than his.

Beneath her wide smile, Brandon guessed Mayor Kim was probably fuming about the height difference.

"You ready to go?" Brandon asked.

"I want to see what happens."

The emcee continued. "Are there any men brave enough among you to step forward?" His eyes swept over the crowd of onlookers, men measuring the risk of playing the fool against the potential reward of saying, what? That you could kick someone's ass if it were eight centuries ago?

"I am *woman* enough," a lady shouted from the stands, "to take all you men."

"I'm sure you are, fair lady, in more ways than one."

The crowd shrieked with laughter.

Brandon hated sophomoric humor. Noticing his reaction, Tori tapped him on the arm. "Oh, Brandon. Lighten up."

"And to be fair," the announcer said, "the ladies' tournament will commence once the men are done pummeling each other."

Still, no men stepped forward. The emcee approached the wooden fence where Brandon and Tori stood.

"You, sir. Here is a man truly stout of heart."

Brandon tried to look away.

"What's your name?" He stuffed the microphone in Brandon's face.

"Brandon," he said, wanting to be anywhere but there.

"Aren't you the fellow who almost lost a sword fight to a young lad on stage a few days back?"

"No."

The emcee took a dramatic step back, pointing a finger at Brandon lazily. "Come now, show us you still have something left in those old bones of yours."

Who was he calling old?

"Do it," Tori said, squeezing his biceps.

The crowd egged him on, forming a chorus. "Brandon, Brandon..."

This wasn't going to turn out well. The chief of police getting beat by some pimple-faced kid who'd been practicing swordplay since he was five.

"What's my weapon?" Brandon asked.

"Take your pick," the emcee said, motioning to a pile of swords, axes, staffs, and other weapons stacked in the center of the field. All wooden.

It couldn't be that bad.

"For me?" Tori asked.

He couldn't hide his smile. "Fine."

The crowd cheered.

She kissed him on the lips and he slipped through the fence.

Emboldened by Brandon's decision, other men crossed onto the field. Brandon sized up the six opponents.

He recognized Hamish MacDuff among the contestants. Hamish was a potential suspect in a criminal case. Brandon's eyes flashed to Tori.

"We need one more," the emcee announced. "Who is man enough?"

Across the field, a familiar frame entered the arena.

It was Josiah.

Hamish, a suspect, and now Josiah, one of his officers.

Brandon sidled over to the fence, armor and helmet on. "I shouldn't do this," he said.

"You'll be fine," Tori said, tying a swath of blue cloth around his arm.

"What's this."

"It means I'm the lady for whose honor you battle," she said. "Now get out there and kick some ass."

The emcee went through a list of rules for the competition. Something about no thrusting of weapons. If the judge determined you'd lost a limb, you were no longer allowed to use that limb, and so on. Each fighter donned headgear and simple body armor. It was like suiting up before a football game back in high school. That was where the comparison to anything he'd ever done before ended.

Once the rules were explained, each contestant was required to sign a waiver form—releasing the fair from any liability for loss of life or limb.

Brandon's only experience with swordplay was the playacting choreography lessons he'd had in high school and college. Pretending to be knocked upside the head onstage didn't compare to a real-life whack with a battle axe—even if it was wooden.

Lucky for him, he wasn't the first to do battle. He watched from the sidelines as two evenly matched thirty-somethings duked it out mid-arena. Both were aggressive, making for an interesting fight. One held a pike—a weapon long enough to block some blows and deadly enough to strike from a distance. His opponent wielded a short sword and shield. After several back-and-forth blows, the pikeman landed a strike to the swordman's leg. The judge, a man dressed in a red and white striped outfit and holding a long staff, instructed the sword wielder he could no longer use the leg. A moment after dropping to his

111

knees he was struck in the head and chest and the match was over.

Brandon was up next. He picked through the weapons and selected a shield and medium-sized sword.

He met his foe near the middle of the pitch. The ground was covered in a thin layer of gravelly sand. Not as firm as packed dirt, but hardly enough to soften a fall.

He considered the young man—he was probably in his late twenties. Jerking back and forth, hopping up and down, he swirled a samurai sword in front of him. The judge instructed them to bow to each other.

They did, and immediately the samurai kid charged. Brandon twisted aside, letting the kid's blow land on his shield. As Brandon turned, he charged again, this time with a loud, "Arrgh!"

Brandon swept the blow aside again. The samurai wore leather armor, enhancing his agility even more so compared to Brandon's bulky plate armor.

Twice more the kid attacked. On the fifth attempt, Brandon stepped to his right, a maneuver the kid didn't expect. Brandon swept his sword across the kid's abdomen. For good measure, he thwacked the kid's back as he passed by.

This, he thought, *is kind of fun.*

Brandon was declared the winner, having struck a fatal blow. He shook hands with the kid and returned to Tori.

She gave him a congratulatory kiss—he could get to like this. They watched as Hamish disposed of his opponent—a burly fellow almost his size—in less than 20 seconds.

Josiah was up next. After a long, drawn-out, mostly defensive melee, Josiah was victorious. The suddenly confident officer sauntered over to a young lady near the stands. She wrapped her arms around him and kissed him on the cheek.

Brandon smiled. So that's what this was about. Josiah wasn't the sort of person to go looking for a fight. But if he was trying to impress a lady...

Good for him.

The next match would feature Brandon versus his youngest officer.

Hopefully, Josiah didn't take it personally when he lost to his boss in front of his lady friend.

"Don't be too hard on him," Tori warned him as he made his way to the center of the stadium. Brandon donned the helmet and selected the same sword and shield.

They approached each other. Josiah flexed his grip around his sword's hilt. "Chief."

"You sure about this?" Brandon asked.

"You're not scared, are you?"

He'd never heard the young officer trash talk before. Brandon didn't know he had it in him.

"We'll see about that," Brandon replied.

Josiah's armor was chainmail. Otherwise, his sword and shield were about the same size as Brandon's.

On the signal, the two circled each other. Brandon figured, after watching Josiah's mostly-defensive last match, that the officer wouldn't strike first.

He'd figured wrong.

Josiah hurled himself at Brandon, smacking his shield against Brandon's with a loud clack. Josiah cast an overhand swing followed by a side attack, repeating the pattern before taking a swipe at Brandon's legs.

Brandon pulled back. Under the shadow of Josiah's helmet, his dark eyes betrayed cold determination.

He *really* wanted to best Brandon.

Brandon leaned left, then right, narrowly avoiding Josiah's attacks. He was getting closer with each swing.

Brandon was losing ground. It was time to go on the offensive.

He shoved hard against Josiah. The officer careened, caught himself, then hunted Brandon, poking and prodding, testing Brandon's defenses. Brandon attempted an overhead chop but Josiah parried the attempt. Brandon swung from the side, unsuccessfully attacking Josiah's left and then right.

Josiah lunged and Brandon's heel caught in the uneven sand. He faltered and Josiah landed a glancing blow to Brandon's shoulder.

The judge ordered Brandon to hold his left arm behind his back.

Brandon tossed the shield aside as he and Josiah cut a ring into the dirt, circling each other, just out of reach.

Suddenly, Josiah charged. Brandon twisted away and tumbled onto his backside, kicking up sand and dust.

Josiah stalked him, sword poised to strike.

"Don't go easy on me, now," Brandon said, scooting back.

"I wasn't planning on it," Josiah replied. His sword swept over Brandon's head as he ducked, rolled to one side, and leaped to his feet. Josiah swung again, but this time, he'd left an opening. Brandon dropped to his knee and whirled his sword into Josiah's exposed ribs.

A rush of air fled Josiah's lungs.

"Halt!" the judge said. "We have a winner!"

Josiah was half-bent, nursing his side.

Brandon slipped off his helmet. Josiah kept his on, but it did little to hide the disappointment in his eyes.

They shook hands. "Good job, kid. You okay?"

He straightened with a grimace. "Yeah."

"I was lucky," Brandon said.

"True."

Brandon smiled. He liked this newer, tougher version of Josiah.

"Who's the girl?" Brandon asked, pointing his chin at the young lady who'd been at Josiah's side earlier.

"Her name is Alena," he answered. "This is only our second date."

Brandon patted him on the shoulder. "I'm sure she's real proud of you."

"Except I lost."

"But you showed you were willing to fight. That matters."

Josiah nodded with a tilt of his head. "I suppose."

"Well, get over there," Brandon said. "Don't make her wait all night."

Brandon had barely caught his breath by the time Hamish eliminated his pike-wielding opponent.

Brandon grabbed his trusty sword and shield for the final match and made his way onto the pitch.

Hamish swiveled his sword with a flourish, pressing his lips into a smug grin. Besides brute strength and, Brandon assumed, more experience with these weapons, Hamish had another advantage over Brandon—rage at what he perceived was a slight against Daisy because of the questions they'd asked her about the topless photo.

Hamish only wore a kilt, long leather boots, a helmet, and a loose-fitting peasant's shirt—no body armor. Apparently, he wasn't worried about an opponent lasting long enough to cause him any real damage.

Brandon shouldn't be there. Sure he was off-duty, but Hamish was connected to Darren Rule's murder—loosely, but still connected. It would be in his better judgment to forfeit the match, as little as he liked the idea of appearing like a coward in front of the whole town—and Tori.

He was about to suggest a forfeit when the judge shouted, "Begin!" Hamish swept his long broadaxe at Brandon's midsection. Brandon's arms had been down at his sides, so he was forced to suck in his gut to avoid the blow.

He hoisted his shield and sword, now stalking Hamish.

Brandon offered an overhand swing. Hamish held the axe between his hands, blocking the attempt. Brandon attacked from the side, but the brawny Scot was nimble for his size and was unharmed.

Brandon lowered his shoulder and rammed his shield into Hamish, taking a page out of Josiah's book. It didn't have the desired effect.

He ricocheted off the giant like a rubber ball flung against a concrete wall.

"You remember what I said last time we talked?" Hamish asked.

"What?"

"You're not so brave without your guns."

Hamish targeted Brandon's shield. The axe landed with a shudder, the blow stinging his forearm. Hamish persisted, swinging the axe again and again like an old-time lumberjack felling a tree.

Brandon's shield arm tingled. It was going numb.

He raised the shield like an umbrella to ward off an overhead stroke. His arm gave way as the shield cracked in two. Pain shot up to his shoulder as he worked to free his hand from the straps.

116

With a swift side swing, Hamish aimed for Brandon's defenseless ribs. He parried the axe at the last second, but the strike sent his sword soaring across the arena.

The five spikes of Hamish's dark blonde beard wagged over the top of his unbuttoned shirt as he sneered at his weaponless opponent. "I told you, Daisy is no whore."

Brandon stumbled back. "I never said she was—"

He leaped back as the axe swooshed inches from his neck.

"You said she slept with Drool," Hamish said.

"They *were* married..."

Not a smart thing to say, considering he was unarmed.

With a guttural Braveheart growl, Hamish lunged at Brandon with a chopping motion—his target Brandon's skull. Brandon veered to the left and let Hamish pass him by, then gave the Scot a swift kick in the ass.

The stadium roared with approval.

Brandon dashed for his sword. Gripping it with his one good hand, he turned to the Scot.

Hamish shouted at him, 15 feet away. "That wasn't funny."

Stalking Brandon with the axe in a baseball bat grip, he planted his feet and swung high. Brandon ducked. The axe bounced off the tip of his helmet. He kept his eyes on Hamish's ribs. The axe swing had left him exposed. Brandon aimed high, but he'd lost his balance.

He landed a solid stroke on Hamish's thigh.

"That's a hit," the judge declared. "On your knees."

"Not a hit," Hamish said. He jabbed the butt of the axe into Brandon's gut.

Brandon stumbled back, the world spinning for a moment as he fought for air. He gathered his wits enough to keep his distance, holding his sword out defensively.

117

The crowd jeered at the cheap shot.

"I thought the rule was no jabbing," Brandon said.

"That is the rule," the judge said. "On your knees, Hamish."

Hamish glowered at the judge. He fell to one knee.

"Come and get me," he insisted, motioning to Brandon. "You coward policeman."

Brandon stood tall, sucking in oxygen.

It was time to get this over with.

Brandon approached the Scot, wary of his next move.

It didn't take long to find out.

As soon as Brandon stepped within range, Hamish attacked, but not with a swing or a thrust.

Hamish stretched the broad axe an arm's length in front of him. Brandon raised his sword horizontally to block what he thought would be a chopping motion. Instead, Hamish used the axe head as a hook, yanking Brandon toward him. Hamish lowered his head. With a mighty tug, he hammered his helmet into Brandon's groin.

The pain was worse than anything he'd experienced. A thousand spots filled his vision.

He didn't have time for pain.

Brandon yanked the sword free with his right hand then shoved his knee into Hamish's face, causing the Scot to fold back onto his haunches. Without a second's hesitation, Brandon held the sword to Hamish's throat.

"We have a winner!" the judge declared.

The crowd roared. Brandon stumbled a safe distance from the Scot, bent over, and vomited.

Tori was at his side a moment later.

"Let's get you out of here," she said. "Before that brute kills you."

He turned his head to her. "Kills me? I'm the one who won."

"You look half dead. He just looks...mad. Here he comes."

Brandon stood the best he could, still bent like an octogenarian.

Hamish was unarmed, but that didn't mean the fight was over.

"I am not happy," Hamish said. "But you won." He held out a hand. Brandon hesitated a moment before taking it. To his surprise, the Scot's grip wasn't overpowering. "Congratulations." He stared down at Brandon's groin. "We're even now. For what you said to Daisy."

"I didn't...never mind."

* * *

It took a while for him to walk off the pain, and after a brief ceremony where Sterling awarded Brandon a six-inch plastic trophy with the dubious title *Provisional Knight of the Realm*, Tori agreed it was time to head home. He'd turned down Sterling's offer to become a full-time knight, despite the half-off discount he'd receive for winning the contest.

They were exhausted by the time they reached home. In the evening's excitement, they'd both forgotten to return their costumes. Brandon fell into bed as soon as they arrived. A few minutes later, Tori returned from the kitchen with an ice pack.

"I figured you'd need this," she said, glancing at his groin. "For, you know..."

"I had something else in mind," he said, sitting up on the edge of the bed.

She cocked her head at him. "Are you sure?"

He rose and embraced her, whispering in her ear, "I'm as sure as I've ever been about anything."

His only worry in the world at that moment was how he was going to make his way through the seemingly endless number of buttons on her medieval dress fast enough.

Chapter 13

Brandon awoke with a start. His room was drenched in shapeless shadows and the fragrant scent of Tori's perfume. She lay in bed next to him, her breath brushing against his arm.

He glanced at the clock. It was just after one in the morning.

Brandon thought he'd heard something, but now he wondered if it was only a memory from a fading dream. The sound had come from the living room. It couldn't be Emma. She wasn't due home for a couple of weeks.

He slipped out of bed and Tori rolled over to take up the space he'd abandoned. Lifting his pistol from the closet, he advanced down the hallway, listening.

He peered into the bathroom, where the cat opened one eye with a questioning *meow.*

Brandon continued to the living room, pistol ready but pointed down.

"Who's there?" he asked.

Outside, a car engine revved, then drove away. He crept through the kitchen, checking the door, then the living room. Convinced no one had entered the house, he slid the front curtains aside.

He searched his memory for what exactly he'd heard in the half-lucid seconds before he awoke. Metal. The screen door.

He checked the peephole and, seeing nothing, opened the door.

There, taped to his front door, was a tarot card.

"What is it?" Tori asked.

He started at the sound of her voice.

"Sorry," she said.

"It's nothing to worry about."

She peeked around his shoulder.

"Isn't that like the card they found with Drool?"

"It's similar, but not quite the same."

Still, it looked familiar.

"The style is closer to the ones Phoenix Weaver showed us." He wouldn't be sure until he compared the card with her deck.

"You think she did this?"

"I don't know why she would," he said. "We've seen her cards. She'll be the first person we talk to tomorrow."

"If Drool's killer did this...it means they know where you live."

"Everyone knows where I live," he said. "This is Forks."

Brandon grabbed an evidence kit from the Interceptor and donned gloves before placing the card into an evidence bag. On first inspection, it didn't appear the card or even the tape had any fingerprints. Whoever had placed it there had probably been wearing gloves. Still, he'd send it to the techs for a better look.

He closed the door and held the card up to the light. The picture was of a tall, white stone tower atop a rocky outcrop. A bolt of lightning descended from some unseen power—a cloud or maybe a supernatural force. Where the bolt struck, fire rose from the top of the tower. Flames roared out of the tower's windows. Two figures were shown plummeting to their deaths on the rocky shore below.

"It represents an unexpected turn for the worse," Tori said.

"How'd you know that?"

"I looked it up," she said, holding up her phone. She read more. "You assume you're safe, but soon life will teach you otherwise. What you have believed to be true has been nothing more than a lie."

She lowered the phone. "Do you think it's the killer?" she asked, her eyes worried. "Warning you to back off?"

"Back off from what? We don't have a main suspect yet."

Brandon recalled Alex's theory about the tarot card having special meaning.

"It could be someone trying to advance the idea that the tarot card was symbolic, meant to send a message."

"It makes sense," she said.

"Maybe, or maybe someone is trying to point us to the cards as a distraction."

"Who?"

"That's the question," he said, "for tomorrow."

He stored the card in his evidence case and went to Tori, holding her hands. "Are you okay?"

"You mean am I scared?" she asked.

"It's okay if you don't want to stay here."

Tori rolled her eyes. "I was married to a homicide detective for how many years?"

"Good point."

She turned away. "Let's go to bed."

Brandon checked the locks again and joined her.

Tori drifted to sleep, leaving Brandon to his thoughts.

Who would be bold enough to leave what was obviously a threatening tarot card on the chief of police's front door? He thought back to Alex and his intensity around the tarot cards. What was his motive in advancing the importance of the cards?

123

Was the killer sending a message, or was it a distraction? Or was it a copycat seeking attention?

Mind reeling and ears primed for any hint of disturbance around the house, he slept little over the next few hours.

* * *

Brandon was showered and ready to go by seven. The steamy water over his back had been a relief. It hadn't taken more than a few seconds awake for his body to remember the pain Hamish had inflicted on him the night before.

He had a long day ahead of him. They had plenty of leads to follow, but so far no particular path was more promising than the others. Now, there was the added twist that the killer, or someone pretending to be the killer, was targeting his home. He'd have to get the tarot card into evidence and figure out what connection, if any, it had to the one found with Darren Rule.

At first glance, the card didn't appear to match the style and size of the card at the crime scene. It seemed familiar, though, and the only other tarot card he'd seen in recent years was the set Phoenix had shown him.

Tori found him in the kitchen, downing the last spoonful of his cereal.

"Big plans for today?" she asked, joining him at the table.

"There's this whole card thing, on top of what we were already working on. How about you?"

He hoped, more than he ought to, that she wasn't planning on leaving yet.

124

"I'm supposed to be on vacation but I think I'll do some work. I have a few briefs to prepare. I might head out to visit dad," she said.

Brandon's father had always been a fan of Tori, even if it had taken his mother a while to warm up to her.

"How's he been?" she asked.

"Back to his usual ornery self," Brandon said. "He's fully recovered from his knee surgery."

Brandon visited his father about once a week. They'd even gone fishing a couple of times that spring. Their relationship had experienced a bit of a renaissance after Brandon had solved Eli's murder. Eli, Brandon's brother, had been a Forks police officer before Brandon took over as chief. He'd been killed in the line of duty just outside town. Eli's murder and Brandon's desire to catch his brother's killers was one reason he'd returned to Forks.

"You want to do lunch?" he asked.

"Where at?"

"I'll call," he said.

On his way out the door, she pecked him on the lips. "Bye."

It was the familiar kiss of a long-married couple. He stared at her. What were they doing but playing house? How long could they keep it up?

"What?" she asked, searching his eyes.

"Nothing," he said. "I'll see you at lunch."

He had already processed the tarot card and arranged for transport up to Port Angeles by the time Jackson and Josiah arrived. They were mid-conversation as they entered the bullpen.

They both looked up at Brandon.

"Hey, Chief," Josiah said.

"I heard you got your butt handed to you last night," Jackson said.

Brandon eyed Josiah before asking Jackson. "Who told you that?"

"Not what I said," Josiah insisted.

"You just told me the chief was lucky he could still walk."

Brandon's brow furrowed in confusion. "Josiah must be talking about someone else."

Jackson waved a hand at him. "I'm just giving him a hard time. He did tell me you beat that oaf MacDuff. Sort of like David and Goliath."

"He's not that much bigger than me," Brandon said.

Jackson scoffed. "Okay."

"Are you two ready to work? I have news."

Jackson opened the fridge and set her lunch inside.

Brandon tossed his notebook on the table and grabbed a chair. Josiah and Jackson joined him.

"Someone left a tarot card on my door." He pushed a photo printout he'd made across the table.

"Damn," Jackson said. "Were you home?"

He nodded. "Middle of the night. I heard something, but they drove off before I could spot them."

"Were there any prints?"

"I don't think so. I'll wait for the lab to do their magic, just in case."

"What does it mean?" Jackson asked.

"Something about believing lies, the truth coming out. An unexpected event. Nothing good."

"That card is a match with Phoenix's deck," she said.

"I thought the same thing. She'll be our first stop today."

126

"That reminds me," Josiah said. "I got a call from Alex after you left last night. Apparently, he was interviewing a witness—"

"You were going to tell him to stay in his lane," Brandon said to Jackson.

"What's the harm?" Jackson asked. "We're short-staffed as it is."

"I don't need that damn security guard interfering with my investigation."

"It might be useful info," Jackson said.

"It might be, but every time you interview a potential witness, you risk contaminating their memory. Meaning a defense attorney could have a field day getting our testimony tossed out of court."

"Sorry, Chief," Josiah said.

"It's not you, it's Alex."

"I can bring him in for an interview," Jackson said, "if you're that worried about it."

Brandon thought about it, then said, "You've got enough on your plate. This merits a conversation between Alex and me."

Josiah asked, "Do you want to hear what I learned from him?"

"Right," Brandon said, motioning for him to continue.

"One of the merchants told Alex they were passing by Darren Rule's trailer and heard him arguing with someone just after midnight the night he was killed."

"Was it a man or a woman?" Brandon asked.

"A man. With a Scottish accent."

"MacDuff," Jackson said.

"Right," Josiah said. "Wasn't he convicted of assault?"

"Charged," Brandon said. "Never prosecuted."

"And it was his dagger found in the victim's throat," Josiah said.

"A dagger he made," Brandon said. "We're not sure who it belonged to."

And Hamish claimed he had no idea who had bought—or stolen—the dagger.

"We'll need an official statement from the person who witnessed the argument," Brandon said.

"Will do," Josiah said.

"So MacDuff is our first stop this morning, I take it? Then Phoenix?" Jackson asked.

"Agreed," Brandon said. "But first, any progress on the pictures we found in the trailer?"

"Josiah and I can keep working on passing them around—compromising positions out of view, of course."

"No bites yet?"

"Nope. Besides Daisy, there's not a person in those photos that matches anyone who works at the fair. We've taken Daisy's out of circulation."

"Interesting that none of the cast claimed to recognize her that first day we were passing them around."

"They were probably afraid to," Josiah said. "Considering the way Hamish reacted to you and Jackson—that's probably how he treats everyone."

"Good point," Brandon said. "And that makes me wonder what else people aren't telling us. Josiah, you finish up any interviews of cast members. Take the pictures with you."

Jackson dragged a stack of paper off her desk and tossed it on the table. She'd copied and enlarged each photo with any exposed or otherwise embarrassing body parts covered.

"Try not to get too excited," she said to Josiah.

"It's not like I haven't seen a naked person before."

His cheeks bloomed red while Jackson and Brandon stared back at him.

"Okay, well..." Brandon said. "Let's get to work."

Before they left, Brandon checked his phone. Kaitlyn's father should have listened to Brandon's voicemail by now. There were no new messages and no missed calls.

He called the father again and left another message, reminding him he had important information about his daughter. "This is good news," he added. "Call me as soon as you get this."

Chapter 14

MacDuff's shop was open for business by the time Brandon and Jackson arrived. They waited until he finished speaking with a young couple who were eyeing a wicked-looking broadsword that was probably well out of their price range. Hamish, noticing the officers' looming presence, seemed distracted. The customers left without purchasing anything.

"You here to arrest me for the beating I gave you last night?" Hamish asked.

Jackson looked to Brandon. "I thought you won."

"Barely," Hamish said.

"We're here about the Darren Rule homicide," Brandon said.

"I still don't know who I sold the dagger to," he said. "Or who stole it."

"How hard did you look?" Jackson asked.

The blacksmith's thick, veined neck twitched. "Very hard," he said, his words thick with a Scottish accent.

"That's not what we're here about," Brandon said.

"What, then?"

"In private," Brandon said, motioning to the shop.

Hamish narrowed his eyes at Brandon. His head swiveled, causing the banded splits in his beard to wiggle. Brandon stood his ground and, a moment later, the weaponsmith relented. "Fine."

Hamish closed the front of his shop by removing two sticks that held up a long piece of plywood. He led them to the back tent where they'd spoken earlier.

"I'm losing money standing here," he said.

130

"You lied to us," Brandon said.

Hamish crossed his arms but remained quiet. The man's biceps bulged.

"You told us you were in your tent with Daisy the night Darren Rule was killed."

"So?"

"We have a witness that heard you arguing with him."

"Who said that?"

"So it's true?"

Hamish slumped into a folding chair. The chair disappeared under his sizable frame. Hamish lowered his face into his hands. After a moment, he looked up at Brandon. "Yes, I argued with him. Nothing else. I swear."

"What time?"

"I don't know. Around midnight."

That jived with the witness' statement.

"What did you argue about?" Brandon asked.

He sighed. "We were here in the shop. It was late."

"We?"

"Daisy and me."

"Okay, then what?"

"Darren showed up and wanted to brag about coming into some money."

"Money? How much?"

"Hell if I know," Hamish said. "I figured he was talking out his arse. It wouldn't be the first time."

"He didn't mention how he'd gotten the money?" Jackson asked.

"No. But he was wasted. Drunk, high on God knows what."

"Okay, so what caused the argument?" Jackson asked.

"Besides him being an ass? He started making advances on Daisy."

"Did he harm her?"

He squinted at her. "You think I would let him do that?"

"Then what happened?" Brandon asked.

"I took him outside. We said a few things. To be honest, I told him if he returned or ever talked to Daisy like that again I'd knock his head off."

"You didn't touch him?"

"No," Hamish said. "But I'll tell you what. Someone had already beat the hell out of him. His face was all messed up and he was walking sort-of crooked, you know?"

His description matched the bruises they'd found on Rule's body.

"He didn't mention who'd done it?" Brandon asked.

"No. And whoever did it probably had a good reason." Hamish considered the two officers. "You don't believe me, do you?"

"You've got a history of assault—"

"That was never proven."

"Let me finish," Brandon said. "There's the assault charge. Someone heard you arguing with a homicide victim just before his death. He came on to your wife, who happens to be his ex. And he was killed using a knife from your shop."

"Are you arresting me?"

"Not yet. But I need you to stick around until we figure this out."

"Where am I going to go?" He motioned to his shop. "This is my life. And Daisy is all I have."

"We're going to collect your fingerprints," Brandon said. "Daisy too."

"Daisy has nothing to do with this," he said.

"Then she has nothing to worry about."

On the way to Phoenix's store, Jackson asked, "What do you think?"

"Hard to tell. Maybe his prints are in the motorhome, maybe not."

"Worse, what if Daisy's are in there?"

"Meaning she was having a fling with her ex-husband?" Brandon asked.

"It's been known to happen," Jackson said, studying him with a skeptical gaze.

Brandon shook his head, refusing to meet her eyes. "Sometimes I have no idea why I keep you around."

Phoenix was alone at the card table in front of her tent when they arrived. The orb and a few trinkets were on the table, an oversized map of a palm with the various lines for life, death, and even number of children was on a tripod behind her. Noticing their approach, she looked up from her phone.

"Now what?"

Brandon made a show of scanning the area for customers. There were none. "You're not too busy to talk are you?"

"You're quite the comedian, officer."

He had a photocopy of the tarot card he'd found on his front door. He dropped it on the table. "Last time we were here, you said there were only two sets of your particular deck. Tell me that doesn't match yours."

"Where did you get this?" she asked.

"I found it. On my front door."

Phoenix clutched her dress. "Impossible."

133

"You want to show us your cards again?" Jackson asked.

Last time, she'd let them inspect the one deck while claiming she owned a matching set. The only two ever made, according to Phoenix.

"You're saying I lied about the uniqueness of my cards."

"Or someone stole one of your decks," he said.

"Then again," Jackson said. "Maybe you taped the card to his door."

She scowled at Jackson. "As if I have time to harass police officers. On the contrary, *I'm* the one being harassed."

"Just check your cards," Brandon said.

She sighed but rose and entered the tent. They waited while she rummaged through her belongings. Suddenly, there was a clamor and a thud.

"You need help?" Brandon asked.

"I'm fine," she shouted from inside the tent. "Just hold your horses."

A minute later, she ducked through the tent flaps. She held out a wooden card box matching the one she had shown them previously.

"This one," she said, pointing to the deck already on the table, "is always with me." She held out the second box. "And these I keep hidden."

"Tell me if the card with the tower is missing."

Worry creased Phoenix's brow.

"I certainly hope that's not the card you were given. It could mean..."

She opened the box.

It was empty.

"My cards...this is impossible."

She closed the lid and then reopened the box as if the cards might reappear. Her free hand moved to her neck.

"Have you left it unattended at all?" Jackson asked.

"No. I mean, well, when I go on breaks. But I close the tent."

Anyone slight enough could slip under the canvas material.

"You're sure it's missing?"

She cast him a sullen glare. "Yes, I'm sure. I never take it out of the box. Those cards belonged to my grandmother. They were imbued with two generations' insight."

Tears welled in her eyes. "Who could have done this?"

"I was going to ask you the same thing," Brandon said.

Her shoulders dropped. "I don't know."

"We'll need to get you printed," Brandon said, making the request of a third suspect that day.

"You believe I put the card on your house?"

"I would like to rule that out," Brandon said.

"Fine," she said. "But in the meantime, maybe you can do your job and find out who stole my family heirloom."

Finding the thief would lead them to whoever had been bold enough to send Brandon the late-night warning—possibly the same person who had killed Darren Rule. That, of course, assumed Phoenix was not the culprit behind the warning.

Brandon headed back to his office, leaving Jackson to take care of the prints for Hamish, Daisy, and Phoenix along with a report on what they'd learned that morning.

He used the rest of the morning to catch up on paperwork and some of the political responsibilities that went along with being chief of police. That included finding a replacement for his most experienced officer, Will Spoelman. Will had been with the force almost as long as Brandon had been alive. He'd retired, against Brandon's protests, six months earlier.

Brandon had been dragging his feet selecting Will's replacement. There'd been plenty of applications, but none that met his standards. Plenty of officers from larger jurisdictions were willing to give Forks a shot. But, as far as he could tell, most of them were scouting for a place to retire. There was nothing wrong with that, but the few applicants he'd interviewed seemed more interested in an on-the-job retirement.

By the time he'd caught up on emails and a handful of new applications—none that overly impressed him—it was almost noon.

A grumbling in his stomach reminded him he'd promised to meet Tori for lunch. He didn't have much time. He wanted to check in on how Josiah was doing with the final interviews, too.

He texted Tori, telling her to meet him at the fair.

Before he left the office, he tried the number he had for Kaitlyn's father again. He'd left two messages already. This time, when it went to voicemail, he hung up.

Chapter 15

Brandon led Tori through the staff entrance to the fair. "It's not the Metropolitan Grill," he said, referencing Tori's favorite Seattle restaurant.

"And you're sneaking me in for free," she said. "You really are penny pinching."

"Official police business," he said, grinning back at her.

They found a picnic table under a shady oak tree. They'd both ordered gyros from a food truck offering Greek fare along the fair's restaurant row. Like everything else at the Forks Renaissance Fair, the gyros were overpriced, but the servings were generous, as was the amount of tart but creamy Tzatziki sauce the restaurant slathered over the beef and lamb meal. They shared a side of overly salty fries between them. Brandon didn't like soda and, while a beer sounded good, it was barely past noon—and he was on the clock.

"Have you heard from Emma?" Tori asked.

"She's texted me a few times," Brandon said. "Checking in."

"It's nice she communicates with one of us," Tori said.

"You guys are close. Just in a different way."

Tori and Emma had been inseparable most of her young life. Then, somewhere around 15, their relationship had grown contentious. It wasn't until Emma had moved to Forks to live with Brandon during the school year that her relationship with Tori improved.

"So you say," she said.

"How's dad?" Brandon asked.

137

"Good," she said. "Talked about you, mostly. How you solved Eli's case."

"Did he mention how he almost got himself killed by sticking his nose in the middle of it?"

She considered Brandon. "He's proud of you. I hope you know that."

Brandon swallowed hard. His relationship with his father had been a sore spot for most of his life. Things were going well now and, at this point, his main goal was to avoid knocking their tenuous relationship off balance.

"I do," he said.

"He did say you haven't been out for a couple of weeks," she said.

"I am busy running a department. Raising our daughter..."

"Okay. No need to get defensive."

He looked away. "I'm not being defensive."

When he looked back at her she was focused on her cellphone.

"I know," she said, absently.

Brandon finished his gyro and crumbled the foil wrapper, tossing it into his basket.

She glanced up from her phone.

"Work?" he asked.

"Yeah. A case."

"Want to talk about it?" he asked.

She set the phone on her lap. "No."

"Alright then," he said. "I'd better get back to work."

"Hey," she said. "I'm sorry. I'm just distracted."

"You sure you don't want to talk about it?"

Her lips were set in a line of worry, her eyes gazing off into whatever it was that was bothering her.

"I'm sure."

She grabbed his basket and tossed both in the garbage.

"You want to take a walk?" she asked. "Tell me about the case."

He shrugged. "Sure."

Brandon wasn't sure why he was annoyed with her. It wasn't like he needed—or even wanted—her undivided attention. But something seemed off and he couldn't figure out what it was.

They perused the various shops and stages, most of which they'd already visited, briefly slowing to wonder at a demonstration on the art of making linen from flax. He updated her on where they were with the case and his annoyance with Alex. After passing a marionette performance of *Twelfth Night*, Tori and Brandon ended up behind set—where the performers' trailers and motorhomes were parked.

"Which one was his?" Tori asked.

"It was over there," he said, pointing to the spot where the motorhome had been. "It's in an evidence garage now."

"You said it was a big one," she said. "How much can a comic like Drool make?"

"Not much, I imagine."

"Some of those cost upwards of a hundred grand," she said.

"You been pricing motor homes?" Brandon asked.

"Actually, yes. Nothing extravagant. I was thinking about taking a cross-country trip with Emma after she graduates. You want to come along?"

"Ah, maybe," he answered.

He was considering the other motorhomes and trailers but could sense her staring at him, judging his answer.

"So you found some drugs, panties, lipstick, and some compromising photos of unknown individuals?" she asked, making an obvious effort to change the topic.

"That about sums it up," he said.

"Sounds like a mixed bag. Feels like blackmail, though."

He nodded. "Until we figure out who is in the pictures, we're stuck with that line."

"You sure you checked everywhere?" she asked. "Inside the motorhome, I mean."

"We have crime scene techs. And you know, I do have some experience as a detective."

She rested a hand on his arm. "I know. I was just thinking out loud."

"We searched all the usual secret compartments."

"Underneath?"

"The motorhome? Sure," he said, not recalling whether the techs had searched there or not.

"What about the engine?" she asked. "I watched a crime show once where someone stashed documents inside the air filter compartment."

He cast her a wry smile. "Tori, dear. You are an awesome prosecuting attorney. The best I ever met. And you're smart—"

"Smartest you ever met?"

"Yes. But look, trust me to do my job. Just like I used to trust you to do yours..."

"Used to?"

"You know what I mean. When we worked together."

She pecked him on the cheek. "Ok. I'll leave you to it. But seriously, I've got a feeling there's more to this."

They headed back to the fair's concourse. Brandon was about to say goodbye when he spotted Kaitlyn

140

Gallagher. She was standing near the entrance to the food court, balancing herself on high heels and wearing a short leather skirt and low-cut blouse. Nothing about the outfit indicated she was there to enjoy a Renaissance fair.

A man in his late thirties approached her. A moment later he reached for his wallet and showed her its contents. She pointed to the exit.

They strolled off together.

"What's wrong?" Tori asked.

"That's Kaitlyn."

"Where?"

"With that man."

Brandon hustled after the pair, catching up with them just as they neared the exit.

He latched onto the man's shoulder.

"Hey," the man responded. "What the..."

His eyes caught on Brandon's badge. The color drained from his face.

"I ah..."

"ID," Brandon said, holding out a hand.

The man fumbled through his wallet, searching for his driver's license. He handed it over. His name was Dan Coker. Brandon pointed at the wallet. "You plan on using those condoms anytime soon?"

Dan's cheeks went pink. "No."

"So you picked up the young lady here for, what? A walk around the neighborhood."

"Um."

"It says here you're from Port Angeles," Brandon said. "You in the habit of picking up hookers there, too?"

Kaitlyn shifted her weight. "We're friends," she said.

"How long have you known each other?" Brandon asked.

Kaitlyn's eyes darted to the parking lot.

Brandon poked a finger in the man's chest. "I asked you a question."

"Ow!" Dan threw his hands up and stumbled back dramatically as if Brandon had gut-punched him.

A throng of spectators had gathered to watch the confrontation.

Alex Winfield and Duke Sterling approached.

"Is there something I can assist with?" Alex asked.

"Yeah, Alex. There is. It seems you've got a prostitution racket thriving right here in your fair."

"That's a serious accusation," Sterling said.

"The only kind I make," Brandon replied.

Sterling turned to the gawkers. "Move along folks. Nothing to worry about here. Just a family disagreement."

"If we had a prostitution problem," Alex said. "I would know about it."

"Well, you didn't. And it appears to be an ongoing issue."

"You're saying I'm not doing my job," Alex said, squaring his shoulders against Brandon.

"I'm saying maybe if you spent more time managing your own security staff instead of sticking your nose in my murder case..."

"I was only trying to help," Alex said.

"Well, don't."

"What I do know," Sterling said, smoothing his voice out, "is that it doesn't help anyone to have the police roughing up our customers."

"Even when your customers are soliciting prostitution?"

Sterling tilted his head back with a dismissive eye roll. "Fine. Take him away." He stiffened his back. "If there's one thing I won't tolerate it is crimes against a young woman's honor." His eyes passed dismissively over Kaitlyn.

Brandon's jaw clenched.

"What do you want me to do with these two?" Alex asked.

"I've got it under control," Brandon said.

"It didn't look like that when I arrived just now," Alex said.

Brandon stared down Alex. Dan broke the tension. "Hey, man. I promise I won't do it again. I was just..."

"You were just *what?*"

"I don't know." Dan's voice wavered. He was on the verge of a breakdown.

Brandon radioed Josiah. He was still at the fair and arrived in less than a minute.

"Boss?"

"Run a check on our friend Daniel here. If he's clear, send him on his way." He turned to Dan. "Stay the hell out of here, and stay the hell out of Forks, is that clear?" Brandon's eyes landed on the man's ring finger. "And hope your wife doesn't find out."

Daniel's right hand covered his left as if to ward off the thought of his wife learning what he'd done—or at least attempted to do.

"Josiah," Brandon said. "You can take Alex here with you."

Josiah left with Dan and Alex. Sterling turned his attention to reassuring the few stragglers there was nothing to worry about.

"Can I go now?" Kaitlyn asked.

"Where's your pimp?"

"I don't know what you're talking about."

Brandon sighed. "Kaitlyn, I want you to know there's help for you, okay?"

She crossed her arms and cast her eyes anywhere but on Brandon.

"I don't need your help," she said.

"What about your family?"

"They don't give a damn about me."

"You don't know that. Your father reported you as missing."

She let out a dark laugh. "So he'd look good to his friends."

"I left him a message to let him know you're okay."

She narrowed her eyes. "That was none of your business."

"It is my business," he said.

"And did he call back?"

"I'm still waiting."

"Exactly," she said.

"Kaitlyn..."

She twisted on her heels to leave. Brandon grabbed her arm. "Wait."

Kaitlyn turned on him, yanking her arm away. "Am I under arrest?"

"Not yet," he said, his voice hardening.

"I can leave?"

As much as he wanted to keep her off the streets, she was right. He had no reason to hold her.

"Yes."

It wasn't until she was gone that he noticed Tori at his side.

"That went well," she said.

"I don't want to talk about it."

"I told you to stay out of her family's business."

144

"She has a missing person report—"

"And she's an adult now," Tori said.

"Prostitution is illegal," he said. "Even at this damn Renaissance fair."

"I know. But you can't save everyone."

"I can try," he said.

Kaitlyn had expected her father wouldn't call Brandon back. So far, she was right. Three tries and still no response. Could it be he didn't care what happened to his eighteen-year-old daughter? If Emma had gone missing, Brandon wouldn't stop searching until he found her. And when he did, it wouldn't matter what had become of her or what she'd been through. He'd welcome her with open arms and never let her go again.

Back at the office, he left one final message for Kaitlyn's dad. "Call me back or I'll send out an officer to ensure we get a response from you."

It wasn't an idle threat. Brandon still had a few contacts at the King County sheriff's office. In his years as a Seattle PD detective, he'd done the county more than a few favors and, if need be, he was willing to call one in for Kaitlyn's sake.

Chapter 16

Jackson and Josiah were back at the station by four that afternoon.

They'd just gathered at the bullpen table to discuss the case when someone buzzed at the sallyport.

"I'll get it," Jackson said.

She returned a minute later.

"Look who's here," she said, moving aside.

"Hey, Chief." Lisa had donned her burgundy skater dress—the one with the lace sleeves. He remembered she'd called it a skater dress when she wore it on their first date together.

"Hey," he said.

Lisa held a folder under her right arm. "I emailed the results but figured I'd deliver them in person."

"That's a long drive," he said. Port Angeles was over an hour away.

"She was coming down anyway," Jackson said. "Girls' night out."

"In Forks?"

"Don't knock your hometown," Jackson said. "There's plenty to do after dark."

"If you say so."

They assembled around the table. Lisa slid the folder to Brandon.

"You want me to give a report?" she asked.

"Go for it."

He found his eyes avoiding hers. There was something about being with someone, getting used to the idea of gazing into their eyes and it always meant something, or at least it did most of the time. Then, after a breakup, you were supposed to stare into those same eyes as if they belonged to a total stranger.

His thoughts turned to Tori. Maybe the slow deterioration of their relationship had made the transition less bumpy. But how was it possible—that a person you'd been passionate with for so many years and raised a child with, that you were supposed to be in their presence with no feeling at all?

But what was going on between Brandon and Tori now? What did he feel when he looked into her eyes?

"What?" Lisa asked.

"Huh?"

"You shook your head. Is something wrong?"

"Ah...no. I'm fine."

He selected a marker and began outlining the case on the whiteboard.

"Victim Darren Rule stabbed in the throat, how many times?"

"Three," Lisa said. "The same dagger they stuck in his mouth."

Brandon swallowed hard at the image of the dagger protruding from the victim's mouth.

"The sideways cuts to his lips and the tarot card suggest some sort of message or meaning behind the murder."

Lisa sipped the coffee she'd brought with her. "Different knife," she said.

Brandon nodded. He and Jackson had figured the same when they first noticed the cut.

"You're looking for two knives," she said. "The one used to cut his lips left a jagged wound. A serrated knife."

They hadn't found any other weapons at the scene, meaning the killer had kept the weapon or tossed it.

"Alex figures the tarot card was a warning to keep silent," Josiah said. "Or maybe the victim didn't stay quiet and he was being punished."

"Who's Alex?" Lisa asked.

"Head of security for the fair."

"Brandon's not a fan," Jackson said.

"I just don't like security guards stepping all over my investigation."

"Except the tarot card left on your door sort of makes his point," Jackson said.

"What tarot card?" Lisa asked.

"Sorry," Brandon said. "I figured the lab would update you. I was asleep a couple of nights ago and heard something. I found a card taped to the front door. Tori looked it up and figured it was some sort of warning about believing lies."

"Tori?" Lisa asked.

"She's my ex."

"I know who she is," Lisa said.

Brandon turned to Jackson. She bit her bottom lip. At least Jackson hadn't told Lisa that Tori was staying with him. Not that it should matter.

"You think the card was a threat?" Lisa asked.

"I'm not sure. Copycat, threat, it means something. I'm still waiting for prints."

"Okay. But next time, let me know when you learn something this important."

"Got it," he said, irritated at the implication he hadn't done his job. "I'll send you the police report."

They were staring at each other when Jackson attempted to break the tension. "Okay, what else do we know?"

Lisa sucked in a deep breath, then continued. "Bruises on his torso. Two cracked ribs."

"Baseball bat?" Jackson asked.

"Most likely," Lisa said.

"What about toxicology?" Brandon asked.

"Nothing too unusual. Positive for amphetamines and THC. His blood alcohol was .15—high but not enough to contribute to his death. But if you're asking if he was poisoned? No. And believe it or not, despite his lifestyle, he was in generally good health."

"Some people have all the luck," Jackson said. "I gain 10 pounds and my cholesterol goes through the roof."

Brandon scribbled the list of evidence on the board. "Lipstick at the scene. Meth and drug paraphernalia. Pictures of God-knows-who in compromising positions."

"He frequented prostitutes," Josiah said. "One claims he raped her."

"A revenge killing?" Lisa asked.

"Or blackmail," Jackson added. "Considering the photos."

Brandon added the names of the potential suspects to the board.

"Any news on DNA from the crime scene?" Brandon asked.

"Pubic hairs, body hair, semen. You name it."

"Any hits?"

She tilted her head at him. "How long have you been doing this?"

He tried to judge if her sarcasm was meant to be joking or biting. He decided to pretend it was in the spirit of the former. He grinned. "I know. It takes time."

"Lots of time," she said. "You have any other leads?"

"The dagger was forged by a fair regular, Hamish MacDuff," Brandon said. "And he has a history of assault."

"And he argued with Darren Rule just after midnight," Josiah said. "He could have committed the murder then."

"Probably not," Lisa said. "I'm limiting the time of death to about two or three in the morning."

"Then it wasn't Hamish," Josiah said.

"Unless he returned," Brandon said.

Still, the new information about the time of death deflated his hopes of pinning the murder on MacDuff.

"Hamish claims Darren was already banged up before their confrontation," Jackson said.

"So we're potentially after two perpetrators," Lisa said. "One who beat him and, later, another who killed him."

Brandon stepped back from the board. "There are too many people with motive. Everyone on here, from Kaitlyn and Arianne to Hamish and just about everyone who knew him."

"Did you check who uses those particular tarot cards?" Lisa asked.

"No match for the one with Darren Rule," Brandon said. "The one on my door matches a set stolen from Phoenix Weaver."

"You sure it was stolen?"

"I can only go on what she says at this point. She's a suspect, but unless we have more to go on, it's unlikely she's the perpetrator."

"That's about all I have." Lisa motioned to the report.

"As far as the motorhome," Jackson said, "the knife and card were clean. The techs did find prints on the walls and dresser. No hits, yet."

"Anyone who might be in the database was smart enough to wipe the area," Lisa said.

"At least smarter than your average killer," Jackson said.

"What's next?" Josiah asked.

"We keep asking questions," Brandon said. "Eventually we'll discover the nexus between motive, means, and opportunity. I'm not ruling anyone out. Now that we have confirmation about the serrated knife cuts, tomorrow we'll ask Hamish if he's aware of a knife like the one Lisa described."

"Will do," Josiah said.

Brandon slid the folder off the table and stood.

"Thanks for this. And, uh, you all have fun tonight," he said unenthusiastically.

"You sure you don't want to come along?" Jackson asked.

Brandon eyed her. "I'm busy."

"Oh yeah, the ex—"

"Jackson..."

She threw her hands up. "Ok, Chief."

"Good seeing you again," he said to Lisa.

"You too, Brandon."

Her eyes held his for a moment. Was that sadness? Resolve?

It didn't matter. Their relationship was over, for better or worse. They'd stayed on good speaking terms. He didn't want to rock the boat. More importantly, he didn't want to douse the feelings that he and Tori had rekindled over the past week.

151

Before leaving the office, Brandon texted Tori to ask if she wanted him to bring something home for dinner.

He waited a few minutes for a reply. None came.

She was probably busy working.

He poked around the office for a while longer, then decided to head to the store to pick up some groceries. Maybe they could throw something together for dinner. Just like the old days.

The house was dark when Brandon arrived home. The porch light was off. He scanned the street. Tori's car was gone.

He had a feeling she wasn't just out for a drive.

Brandon opened the door and flipped the lights on. He set the groceries on the kitchen counter next to a folded piece of notebook paper.

He already knew what it would say: I'm sorry, Brandon. The last few days were a mistake. They never should have happened. What were we thinking...?

He retrieved the rest of the groceries from the truck and loaded them in the fridge.

He opened a beer and leaned against the counter, staring at the unopened note.

Screw it.

He unfolded the paper. His hands trembled.

Brandon, I'm sorry.

Yep, just what he'd figured.

He read on.

I need to go to Seattle for a work issue. I'll be back soon as I can. Love, Tori.

He reread the note, searching for some hidden meaning behind the words. She was coming back? When? Why hadn't she just texted him?

152

Brandon microwaved a can of soup and a homemade quesadilla. After eating, he plopped himself down in front of the television, a bag of tortilla chips resting between his legs.

He was a bachelor again, at least for a couple of days.

He stuffed a handful of chips in his mouth and swallowed a long drink of beer to fill up the sudden emptiness he felt at Tori's absence.

Chapter 17

Saturday morning, Emma called from camp. He'd planned on sleeping in, but he wouldn't miss the opportunity to speak with his daughter, even if it was seven in the morning. She'd only been gone five days but he already hated the silence of the house, made doubly worse now that Tori had gone.

"How's camp?"

"It's alright," she said. "The girls in my cabin aren't too extra."

"Extra?"

"It means drama. Like dramatic. Emo."

"Oh," he said. "You like being a counselor then?"

Emma had flirted with the idea of majoring in psychology, but for the last several months had been set on criminal justice. She wanted to be a cop, like her dad. Brandon wasn't thrilled about his daughter becoming a law enforcement officer.

"I'm not a real counselor," she said. "They have those here too. I'm not sure I could sit around all day listening to other people's problems."

"You and me both," he said.

"Anything exciting at work?" she asked.

Brandon wasn't keen on sharing his work with Emma. Especially when it came to homicides. But he knew that in a small town like Forks, she was bound to hear the rumors.

"What have you heard?" he asked.

"Well, that jester guy got killed. I know that."

"That's about all I'm focusing on right now."

"You haven't solved it yet?"

"No, sweetie, not yet."

"I know," she said. "It isn't like on television."

"Have you heard from mom?"

He was curious if Tori had shared the incident with the tarot card on the front door of their home. He hoped she hadn't. Emma would be a bundle of nerves. Based on what Brandon knew of his daughter, she'd be more worried more about her old man than her own safety.

"She texted me yesterday. I heard you kicked ass in some tournament. I wish I was there to see it."

He didn't like the way the term *kicked ass* rolled off his daughter's tongue so easily. She *was* almost 17. But still...

"It was a close fight. I'm still sore. Did Mom tell you anything else?"

"No, why?"

It sounded like Tori hadn't mentioned the tarot card incident.

"Just asking."

"Mom's not there with you is she?"

"No," he said, telling the truth, technically. "Why?"

"It's just...you two were acting weird before I left."

"Weird how?"

"Like you were about to get back together."

Brandon would have to tread carefully. If he outright denied anything between Tori and himself, and it turned out they did rekindle their relationship, or Emma somehow learned the truth, she'd feel betrayed.

"Would that bother you if we did?" he asked.

Brandon suffered through the interminable silence that followed.

"Emma?"

155

"What?"

"I just...it was hard enough the first time around," she said.

"The divorce."

"Yeah. I don't want to go through that again."

"Me either," he said.

"Besides," she said, "I don't think mom is in a place to be dating you."

"What's that supposed to mean?"

More silence, and then, "I better get going. I have to get my cabin to breakfast."

"Okay, but Emma—"

"Love you," she said.

"I love you too."

When the call ended, Brandon stared at his phone. *Not in a place to be dating me?*

Either Emma was grasping at straws, doing her best to prevent her parents from reuniting, or she knew something Brandon didn't.

He selected Tori's number from his contact list and was about to hit dial.

No. This was probably Emma freaking out about her parents. He didn't disagree with her. The emotional risks to everyone involved were high.

He would not force Emma to endure another parental breakup. If he and Tori were going to get back together, it had to be for good. Truth be told, he wasn't sure what they were—on a weekend fling or tenuously reunited. It was too early to say.

In the meantime, Tori wasn't there and he had a murder case to solve.

Brandon checked his phone again, just to make sure he hadn't missed a call from Kaitlyn's father.

He hadn't.

He spent the early morning catching up with a couple of on-call officers. It was Jackson's day off so it would be Brandon and Josiah working the case. With no relevant fingerprint matches and a collection of clues that raised more questions than answers, the investigation had stalled. Lipstick, photographs, a tarot card, and a dagger. Like most difficult cases, it was like staring at a thousand puzzle pieces without knowing what the picture was that you were trying to assemble.

They had the report about the serrated knife used on the victim's lips, but that wasn't exactly new information. Still, they would ask Hamish MacDuff what he knew about the missing knife.

In the meantime, they were waiting for any DNA matches, but even that was a shot in the dark. By all accounts, Darren Rule liked parties and prostitutes. DNA could only confirm the individual had been in the room, not prove them guilty of murder.

He recalled Tori's suggestion that he check the motorhome's engine compartment. It was worth a try, but the motorhome was up in Port Angeles, over an hour's drive away. If he had time, it might be worth the trip.

Jackson had left him a note. She'd heard back from Rule's bank. He had made multiple cash deposits over the past several months, between one and five-thousand at a time. The last had been dropped the day before he was murdered.

The deposits reinforced the theory that blackmail was a potential motive in his murder.

They were missing the piece of the puzzle that would link the motive to the person or persons who had reason to kill him.

Based on the number of deposits, he'd probably targeted multiple individuals.

Brandon spent a few minutes reviewing the crime scene evidence. He studied the photo of the bag of panties they'd found in Rule's motorhome. The actual undergarments were out for DNA testing. Before sending them up to the lab, they'd taken individual shots of each pair. The variety of sizes and designs was astonishing.

Without meaning to, he thought back to a pair of Tori's panties he'd found mixed with his laundry that morning. The design—tiger print—wasn't the sort of thing she wore while they were married. He wondered if a woman's choice in undergarments somehow reflected their personality. What did it say about Tori? Did she perceive herself as wilder, more outgoing sexually since their divorce?

He caught himself.

Why am I even thinking about this? And what the hell does it matter what panties she wears?

He turned back to the photo. One pair caught his eye. They were midnight blue with a pattern of golden stars and ashen crescent moons. He'd seen a similar pattern before. Not on undergarments. On a dress.

"You ready to go?" Brandon asked Josiah.

"To interview Hamish about the knife?"

"Later," Brandon said. "First we'll pay a visit to the fortune teller. Phoenix Weaver."

They found Phoenix at the curb in front of her Forks shop, loading her car with supplies. Brandon parked behind her. She ignored them, retrieving another box from her store.

"Phoenix," Brandon said. "We need to ask you a few questions."

She shoved the last container into her Subaru and closed the hatch.

"I'm busy," she said, turning to him. "Very busy."

"Isn't it a little early for you to be opening shop?"

"I'm not sleeping well nowadays." She flung a mass of her blonde curls over one shoulder. "Due to the crime in this town. I'm considering moving elsewhere, if at least for my own mental health."

"Good to know," Brandon said. "In the meantime, let's go inside and talk."

She glowered at him as if that would make him leave her alone. A tuft of her curly bangs drooped over her eyes. "Fine."

Phoenix locked her car and followed them into the shop, positioning herself behind the counter. The store was a potpourri of faux occult and vampire-themed items. Phoenix prided herself on not being as "touristy" as the other merchants in Forks. Onyx curtains draped the walls, a few stained-glass lamps providing the only light. The coal-black candles and incense sticks weren't lit, but the place gave the impression you'd stumbled into a séance.

"What is this about?" she demanded.

"How well did you know Darren Rule?"

"I don't know," she said, running her fingers over the long string of beads around her neck. "Not at all, really."

"You'd met him?" Josiah asked.

"Maybe. I don't know. There are lots of performers at the fair. You can't expect me to remember everyone I meet."

The last time they'd interviewed Phoenix, she'd said she'd met him at least a couple of times. She'd even described him as "pervy".

"You ever visit his RV?" Josiah asked. On the way to Phoenix's shop, Brandon had briefed Josiah on his find—the moon and stars patterned undergarment.

She tilted her chin back. "Of course not."

"Not even once?" Brandon asked.

"Not once."

Brandon held out the photo of the star and moon panties.

"Are these yours?"

Her fingers clutched the bead necklace draped over her bosom.

"No," she said, her voice wavering.

"I don't believe you," Brandon said.

"Of course you don't. Police officers don't believe anyone."

He considered her dress. Not the moon and star one he'd seen her wear before, this one was indigo and covered with melancholy suns, moons, and astrological symbols.

He still held the photo out. "Why was your underwear in Darren Rule's room?"

"Those are not mine."

He slid the phone into his back pocket.

Phoenix cast him a self-assured grin. "I suppose you want a peek at my underwear drawer, too?"

"Not yet," he said.

"Ugh. You are impossible," she said.

160

"We will need a DNA sample," Brandon said. "To compare against any fluids or other biological material we've found at the scene, and on the undergarments."

She glared at him. "That is disgusting."

"So you're okay giving a sample?" Brandon asked.

She tilted her head back. "I have nothing to hide."

Yes, you do, Brandon thought. He wasn't sure what it was, but she wasn't even coming close to telling the truth.

"Any sign of the tarot card deck you lost?"

"Of course not. It's gone. Forever. And despite what you think about me, I did not put a tarot card on your front door. I wouldn't waste a card on *you*."

"Take her to the station for the swab," Brandon said to Josiah.

Phoenix locked her shop and Josiah led her to the police vehicle.

Josiah turned and cast Brandon a *please don't leave me alone with her* look.

"Don't worry, it will be over soon enough," Brandon said to him.

"I'm standing right here," Phoenix said.

"We'll be chatting more soon. In the meantime, if you decide you want to tell me the truth, you know my number," Brandon said.

As she ducked into the backseat of Josiah's squad car, Phoenix said, "I see horrible things in your future, Chief Mattson."

He ignored her.

Her voice straining now, she added, "Your love life is cursed. *Cursed!*"

Like I need you to tell me that, Brandon thought.

Josiah closed the door, silencing her condemnation.

161

"What do you want me to do after I'm done with her?" Josiah asked.

"Make the rounds again," Brandon said to Josiah. "Ask around about any rumors about blackmail. Especially if Darren Rule had spilled the beans about knowing anyone's secrets, that sort of thing. And don't forget to ask Hamish about the serrated knife."

"Sounds good," Josiah said.

"I'll be heading up to Port Angeles," Brandon said.

"What for?"

"I want to take another look at Rule's motorhome."

It was a long shot, but he needed new evidence or the case would remain stuck.

Chapter 18

An hour and a half later, Brandon was in a makeshift auto storage unit—essentially a garage with nothing in it but the motorhome. He'd checked in with the evidence technician and was given free rein with the vehicle.

His first step was to do one more sweep of the motorhome, covering the ground he had during the initial investigation. He doubled back on the areas Jackson had checked, too. Not because he didn't trust her. It was impossible to catch every clue, even with experienced officers and crime scene techs.

The vehicle was as trashed as the first time he'd seen it. The stench left behind by Rule's life and death, however, was worse. During the initial hours after Rule's death, the air conditioning had been on. No such luck now in the stuffy, room temperature garage.

He popped the hood and examined the engine compartment. The engine was fairly clean, which made sense. It was a newer model motorhome. Remembering Tori's comment about the air filter compartment, he snapped it open only to find...an air filter.

"Good idea, Tori," he said to himself. "But no luck."

After a quick check for any nooks and crannies under the motorhome, he locked the vehicle.

He was at the garage door when he thought of something.

Opening the motorhome's passenger door, he popped the glove box. Inside were the registration and an owner's manual. He poked and prodded underneath, hunting for the latch. Finding it, he removed the box's door and set it on the floor.

All newer vehicles, he knew, had in-cabin air filters.

He pressed his hand under the dash and grasped for the filter. It was missing. Sticking his head under the dash, he found his prize: a red folder. It had been shoved into the filter compartment. He yanked it free and a shower of papers scattered across the passenger side floor.

"Thank you, Tori," he said.

He gathered the documents and fell into the motorhome's passenger seat. Most were court documents, others were financial reports. Thumbing through his trove, he found several different individuals named in the papers.

There was now no doubt Darren Rule had engaged in blackmail. The question was which one of Rule's targets was scared enough to kill him?

He met up with Josiah outside the fair's turreted entrance. It had been a warm afternoon and sun-weary fairgoers were headed to their cars, some toting tired toddlers, or leading straggling groups of older children— kids and adults ready for a nap.

"How did it go with Phoenix?" Brandon asked.

"I got the DNA swab," he said. "But she insisted on reading my palm..."

"Tell me you didn't let her."

"There was nothing I could do. She grabbed my hand and then her eyes sort of rolled back in her head."

"Been there, done that," Brandon said.

His first month back in Forks, Phoenix had accosted Brandon with an omen of impending family problems. Soon after, Tori arrived in town to drop off Emma for the summer. Exactly the opposite of what they'd agreed to in their parenting plan. He was still convinced that, despite the accuracy of Phoenix's prediction, it was mere coincidence. Besides, having Emma live with him in Forks had been a blessing—not a curse.

"What was her dire warning this time?" Brandon asked.

"That I wouldn't get married until I was at least 30. Maybe longer."

"That's not so bad," Brandon said, patting Josiah on the shoulder.

"But I want to be married."

"Marriage is wonderful," Brandon said. "And a lot of work. Enjoy the single life while you can."

It was evident Josiah wasn't convinced.

"Alright, how did it go with the interviews?"

"Nothing new," he said. "I asked Hamish about the serrated knife. He only makes straight-edged weapons. Apparently, anything else is too complicated. Did you find anything new in the motorhome?"

"Lots of court papers and other documents. This is looking more like blackmail every day."

"You need help with the documents?" Josiah asked.

"I will, but in the meantime head back to the station to finish your reports."

As for Brandon, there was someone else he wanted to speak with.

The security office was housed in a temporary shelter of wooden poles and a weatherworn canvas. A faded laminated sign that read *Security/Lost Children* was stuck to the front of the tent with a diaper pin.

Brandon slowed as he heard raised voices from within the tent.

"Dammit," Sterling said, "I expect better than this. Either do your job or I'll find someone who will."

"I am doing my job," Alex answered. "Pets are not allowed in the fair. It's your policy."

"If the mayor of this Podunk town wants to bring her Pomeranian into the fair, let her. Do you have any idea how much money she's saving us?"

"No, sir. I wouldn't have any idea how much money you're making."

"Watch it."

"I don't like double standards," Alex said. "Either the rule applies to everyone or it doesn't apply to anyone."

"Don't talk to me about rules. You can't even prevent a murderer from knocking off one of my cast members..."

Brandon stepped into the entrance. He cleared his throat.

They both turned to him.

"Gentlemen," Brandon said.

"Chief Mattson," Sterling said. "I was just speaking to Alex here about the investigation."

"Were you?"

"Yes. Have you found Mr. Rule's murderer yet?"

"Not yet."

"To be honest," Sterling said, "both the mayor and I are concerned about how this is going to impact ticket sales."

It sounded like the sort of thing Mayor Kim would be worried about.

"We're doing our best," Brandon said. "And thanks to Alex, we're getting closer to solving this case every day."

Alex's eyes widened with confusion.

Sterling's head swiveled from Alex to Brandon. "Really?"

"But I did have a question for you, Mr. Sterling. What was Darren Rule's monthly salary from the fair?"

"I'd have to check with payroll. I don't know each cast member's income."

"You do sign the checks?"

"The payments are electronic," he replied.

"Any idea how Darren would have the means to deposit several thousand dollars in cash each month?"

Sterling waved a hand at Brandon. "No idea. I don't pay in cash if that's what you're asking."

"Could he have been blackmailing someone?"

"Could he? Why not? The scoundrel was guilty of just about any other crime."

"Then why keep him around?" Brandon asked. "A man with his background would be a liability to your business."

He shrugged. "People thought he was funny."

"Did you?" Brandon asked.

Sterling's jaw twitched. "No, I didn't."

He straightened his back, checking his watch. "I have a meeting, so I'll leave you to whatever it is you law enforcement types like to discuss." He pointed a finger at Alex. "And yes, the mayor's dog is allowed on grounds."

When Sterling had left, Alex said, "Yeah, and he probably wants me to pick up its crap, too."

Brandon chuckled.

"I'm surprised at the vote of confidence," Alex said. He retreated to a folding chair behind a cheap wooden table at the back of the tent.

"What do you mean?" Brandon asked, settling into the only other chair.

"It wasn't that long ago you were telling me to stick my nose somewhere else."

"About that..."

"I get it, I'm security, not police. I'll stay in my lane," Alex said.

"I hear you," Brandon said. "But I do want to apologize. You've been helpful, but being a detective most of my career—"

"I'm the guy who keeps trying to solve the case, which makes you wonder if I'm the perp."

"That possibility crossed my mind."

"You know that stereotype about security guards being wannabe cops?"

"Yeah, I know that one," Brandon said.

More often than not it was true.

"I have law enforcement experience. I took this position because I need to pay the bills. I'm waiting for the right job," Alex said. "Something close to my kid."

"What did you do before you worked for this outfit?"

"You want the long or short version?"

Brandon leaned back in the chair. "I have a few minutes."

"I went to Cal on a scholarship, majored in psych and criminal justice."

Those were good choices for a future officer.

"What was your scholarship for?" Brandon considered Alex's stocky frame. He had the build of a running back.

"Gymnastics," Alex said. "And tennis."

"Really?"

Alex grinned. "I'm just kidding, man. I don't play tennis. But yeah, gymnastics. I won the all-around title in vault and bars three years out of four."

Brandon didn't know what that was, but it sounded impressive.

"I considered football," he said, pointing to his head, "but I'm interested in keeping this brain of mine healthy for as long as I can."

"Good point."

"Out of college, I joined the Army. Reenlisted once. Ended up with MP. After discharge, I worked as a patrol officer down in Daly City."

"That's outside San Francisco," Brandon said.

"Right. I was there for about two years. But my daughter's mom moved up here to Port Angeles to be closer to her family."

"How old?"

"She's three."

"Fun age."

"I love her more than anything. I haven't told Sterling, but once this fair heads to the next town at the end of summer, I'm out."

"What will you do?"

"Keep looking for work. If I can't get hired on anywhere, I'll keep with security." He shook his head. "It's damn depressing."

"I can't promise you anything," Brandon said, "But Forks PD has an opening."

"I saw that," Alex said. "But after, you know..."

"After I chewed you out?" Brandon said.

"Yeah."

"If you're interested, it's an option."

"I'll take a look," Alex said.

The files Brandon discovered in Darren Rule's motorhome belonged to at least seven distinct parties. Five were court cases. Three cases were civil including divorce, custody, and domestic violence situations. Two were criminal. The remaining two documents were financial records.

Back at the station, he split the cases with Josiah, and by the end of the afternoon, they had contact information for most of the litigants. Brandon was at the bullpen table, Josiah at his desk.

"You think he was blackmailing all these folks?" Josiah asked. "That seems like a lot of work."

"I'm sure he had plenty of time on his hands, considering his only job was to be on stage a few hours a day," Brandon replied.

"If we assume each one of these has a motive for murder, then we'll need to establish alibis," Josiah said. His tone was more of a question than an answer. Brandon had been working on the young officer's confidence.

"Exactly right," Brandon said. He glanced at the clock. It was getting late, but there was plenty of work left to do. "You got plans for tonight?"

"I can cancel if I need to."

"A date?" Brandon asked.

"Dinner at home with my mom. But my girlfriend is coming over. I'm supposed to cook."

"Well, get going," Brandon said. "I wouldn't want to keep the two most important ladies in your life waiting."

Josiah swiveled his chair, facing his desk. "Ha, ha."

"I'm just giving you crap," Brandon said. "You know, when someone teases you, Josiah, you can flip it back at them. Sort of like you did during our match at the Renaissance fair."

Josiah turned back to him. "That was different."

"How?"

"I was pumped. Sort of mad."

"You don't have to be mad to speak your mind."

"So you're saying I should disagree more often?"
Brandon winked at him. "As long as it's not with me."
"I figured you'd say that."

Chapter 19

Brandon spent the next hour writing up what they'd found in the documents, including any available contact information and next steps. Because he had the time, he drafted a list of potential blackmail-worthy dirt within each document. Mostly criminal charges and accusations of abuse. The financial documents were trickier. Without context, it was impossible to discern incriminating info from a spreadsheet.

Brandon pulled into the Forks Diner parking lot just after seven. He'd skipped lunch and was famished. It wasn't until he parked his truck that he realized he hadn't spoken with Tori for over 24 hours.

She'd left the day before, but he figured she'd at least text or call him. He ran through their last conversations. Had he said something to upset her? Scare her off?

No, everything had been going great. At least that's what he'd assumed.

Unlocking his phone, he scrolled through his messages. After a minute of deliberating, he sent a text: *I hope everything is okay.* He added, but then deleted *Miss you.*

He'd reached the diner's door when raised voices caught his attention. Passing by on the other side of the street were Cory, Kaitlyn, and Arianne.

Cory turned on Kaitlyn, finger in her face.

Arianne shoved his hand away.

Brandon crossed the street. They cast him a chorus of dark looks.

"What's going on?" Brandon asked.

"There isn't anything going on," Cory said.

"That's not what I saw," Brandon said.

"We were having a disagreement," Arianne offered. She was trying to appear calm, but her almond skin burned pink in her cheeks.

"What I witnessed was you," Brandon pointed at Cory, "acting aggressively toward this young lady."

Kaitlyn's *please leave* look made it clear she didn't appreciate his intervention.

"I didn't touch her," Cory insisted.

The small-time pimp had gotten under Brandon's skin from their first meeting. If he had anything to arrest him on, he would have and then sent him packing with a one-way bus ticket back to Los Angeles.

"Beat it," Brandon said to Cory.

"Okay," Cory said. "Let's go girls."

"Not the ladies," Brandon said.

Cory tucked his hands under his armpits. He pointed his chin at Arianne and Kaitlyn. "These are my girls."

"These *girls* don't belong to you or anyone else," Brandon said. "Unless you're admitting to promoting prostitution."

"Not what I said, man."

Brandon made a motion, dismissing Cory. The pimp scowled before turning away.

"We don't have anywhere to stay without him," Arianne said.

"I can talk to county social services. There's a program for girls coming out of human trafficking. It's called Scarlet Road—"

"Look," Arianne said. "We know all about that stuff. We're not interested."

Brandon studied Kaitlyn. She hadn't said a word.

"What about you?"

Kaitlyn shrugged.

"She knows too. Okay. I'm going to get back to work."

Cory had strayed half a block down the street and was now loitering under a stop sign.

"Tell you what," Brandon said. "I'll buy dinner for both of you and we can talk about options."

"Hell, no," Arianne said. "You know what people would think if they saw me hanging out with a cop?"

"What's that?"

"They'd think I was a narc. That I was setting them up."

She had a point. In fact, Brandon would love it if every creep in town believed these two girls were off-limits.

"I gotta go," Arianne said, scuttering away.

She paused, glancing at Kaitlyn.

"I'll take free food," Kaitlyn said.

Arianne tugged her arm. "Come on."

She yanked her arm free. "No."

"*Now*," Arianne insisted.

"Arianne, Cory is waiting for you," Brandon said.

"Screw you," Arianne said.

"I just want something to eat," Kaitlyn said. She glared defiantly at Cory. "Without him."

"He's gonna be pissed."

"I don't care."

Arianne's nostrils flared. "This is not cool."

She stomped away—the best she could in her heels—to where Cory was waiting.

Cory shook his head dismissively.

"Come on," Brandon said. Kaitlyn followed him across the street to the diner.

174

Tammy, the diner's long-time waitress greeted him. "Hey, Brandon." Her gaze held on Kaitlyn.

Kaitlyn wrapped her windbreaker closer over her tight-fitting skirt and top.

"Who's your friend?"

"Kaitlyn, this is Tammy. We go way back."

"Brandon used to have a crush on my little sister," Tammy said.

"Other way around."

Kaitlyn ignored the conversation, her eyes scanning the restaurant like a squirrel about to cross a four-lane highway. Brandon wondered if any of her customers were at the diner.

"This way," Tammy said, grabbing two menus.

After a few awkward minutes where they both scanned their menus in silence, Tammy returned with coffee.

She held out her order pad.

"What will you have, dear?" she asked Kaitlyn.

"Whatever he's having."

"The number one," he said. "Eggs sunny side up."

"Breakfast?" Kaitlyn asked.

"I like breakfast for dinner," Brandon said. He lowered his voice, "And the burgers here aren't the greatest."

Tammy crossed her arms. "Really?"

"Can I get my eggs scrambled?" Kaitlyn asked.

"Sure thing, hun."

Once Tammy left, Kaitlyn asked, "Did my dad ever call you back?"

The question was like a punch to his gut. It was more of an accusation than a question.

"Not yet," he said. "But I'll keep trying."

175

"He won't call back," she said, pouring three packets of sugar into her coffee.

She was probably right. He'd tried four, five times. Brandon stifled his emotions—it wouldn't do any good to reveal what he really thought about her father.

"Why did you leave home?" he asked.

"There was no reason to stay. My dad had other interests."

"His girlfriends?"

She cupped her hands around the mug. "Yes. Not that he didn't have time for my sister."

"Is she still at home?"

"She's at Boise State."

"Ah," Brandon said.

"Sorority, all that crap."

"You ever talk to her?"

Kaitlyn scoffed. "Yeah, right."

"Have you tried?"

"Haven't you learned yet? My family doesn't want anything to do with me."

Brandon sipped his coffee. He was stalling, unsure what to say to her statement.

"You said earlier you went into treatment," he said. "What happened?"

"Nothing happened. I got clean. Mostly. I mean, I don't do Oxy or whatever."

"But—"

"Not the happily ever after story everyone expects, right? Going to treatment is one thing. But then what? You break one rule at a clean and sober house and you're kicked to the curb."

"Is that what happened?"

"No."

He waited for her to continue.

"I met a guy. He was in recovery too. So I moved in with him. He relapsed, got sent back to jail. I had nowhere to go. That's when I met Cory and Arianne. They had just come up from California."

"And because you'd been in the business before..."

"It was like, you know, the only way I know to make money where I'm not looking for a new place to crash every night. And at least I know I'm wanted."

Tammy arrived with their food. "Here you go. Anything else, darling?"

"We're good," Brandon said.

Tammy considered Kaitlyn. She bent down. "Are you okay, hun?"

"I'm fine," Kaitlyn said, an edge to her voice.

Tammy straightened, raising an eyebrow at Brandon. "Ok. Well, let me know if you need anything."

Kaitlyn picked up her fork and poked her scrambled eggs. "Why does everyone have to be so condescending?"

"People want to help."

"Like you," she said. "I can tell you think you can rescue me or be some kind of hero or something." She paused, took a bite. "No offense. But we aren't like that. People like Arianne and me."

"Aren't like what?"

"Waiting for someone to rescue us. Sometimes, life sucks. And it's going to stay that way."

"But it doesn't have to," Brandon said. "That's the point."

His words seemed to sink in the space between them. She continued eating as if he hadn't spoken.

After a while, he said, "What's next after the fair leaves Forks?"

"I don't ask. That's up to Cory." Her face lit up. "I hope it's somewhere sunny during the winter. Like Arizona. I always wanted to see the Grand Canyon."

Brandon smiled. "That sounds like fun."

"Have you been there?" she asked.

"A few times. When I was a kid, my aunt and uncle lived in Flagstaff, so we used to visit all the tourist sites."

"Like Montezuma's Castle and the Painted Desert?"

"Right," he said. "You know a lot about the area."

"I used to love geography," she said. "I won first place in the statewide geography bowl when I was in seventh grade."

Her eyes sparkled for a moment, but the glimmer faded. She sipped her coffee. "I know, stupid, right?"

"Not at all," he said. "That's actually pretty impressive."

"I wish I had my stuff. You know, my academic awards, my journals. My dad probably tossed them."

"Why not ask for them back?" Brandon asked.

She sighed. "Why are you stuck on me talking to my dad?"

"I'm a father," he said. "I can't imagine not talking to my daughter, not knowing where she is."

"That's the difference between you and him." She sighed. "It doesn't matter. Life goes on. I mean, you're a cop. Bad things happen all the time, right?"

The depth of her cynicism at age 18 was bewildering.

Tammy brought the bill and Brandon handed her his card.

"I'd better get going," Kaitlyn said. "Cory's already going to be pissed. Arianne too."

"Promise me something," Brandon said.

178

She peered up at him with her dark, heavy eyes. "I don't make promises. They're too easy to break."

"At least consider it. There is housing, school, whatever you need available. You're a smart girl, Kaitlyn. And people care about you."

"Like who?"

"I do, for one. And I bet there are others too. If you would just let them help."

She slid out of her seat. "Thanks for dinner."

Brandon collapsed into his recliner. He rubbed a fist over his chest, suddenly vise-tight at the thought of how Kaitlyn would spend her night, the next night, and the weeks and years after that.

He checked himself, already aware he was losing objectivity. There was nothing wrong with wanting to help someone involved in a case. But getting emotionally wrapped up, caring too much, that could sink you.

Brandon glanced at his phone where he'd left it on the bookshelf near the front door. He wished Tori were there. He needed to unload what he was thinking and feeling on someone who would understand.

For all her youth, Kaitlyn was right. Bad stuff happened to good people all the time.

But it didn't have to be that way.

If only her father would step up, offer some sort of reconciliation. That might be the one thing she needed to move her life in the right direction.

What Kaitlyn's father needed was a man-to-man talk. Brandon had threatened to send someone out to his house if he didn't respond. Tomorrow, he would make good on the threat.

Chapter 20

It was Brandon's day off. He'd planned on going into the office but his plans to confront Kaitlyn's father meant he was heading inland to the Seattle area. He checked in with Jackson first. She'd received his email and summary about the potential blackmail documents he'd found in Darren Rule's motorhome. She and Josiah would attempt to contact those involved and get a statement regarding their relationship with Rule and where they were the night of his murder.

He'd be back by evening but was available by phone for most of the four-hour trip to the Puget Sound.

He reached Seattle by noon. His plan was to head home by early afternoon—before hitting the worst of Seattle's infamous traffic. Even on the weekend Interstate 5 could deadlock through the city. If he finished his business soon enough, he might even take the ferry from Seattle over to Bremerton and take the northern route to Forks across the top of the Olympic Peninsula.

Brandon exited I-5 and veered onto Interstate 90. This was the western edge of the longest interstate in the United States—a highway connecting two oceans, from Seattle to Boston.

The highway delved into a long tunnel that cut through the steep hills that formed the city's east side. A minute later the passage opened onto the I-90 floating bridge over Lake Washington and a spectacular view of the Cascade Mountains.

After taking the offramp to Mercer Island, he stopped at a grocery store parking lot to check his map.

On the eastern shore of Lake Washington, Mercer Island was synonymous with wealth, or snobbery, depending on which side of the lake you lived. Dotted with multimillion-dollar homes, private beaches, and stunning views, the island had been home to a number of famous people, from Microsoft co-founder Paul Allen to Steve Miller and even Barack Obama's mother, who had graduated from the local high school. It wasn't as swanky as Medina, a few miles to the north—and home to Bill Gates' sprawling mansion—but it was close.

Brandon double-checked the address he had for Kaitlyn's home. The island's main roads were one that circled the island and another that cut through the middle, north to south. He followed the outside road to a waterfront property on the south end of the island.

Brandon pulled up to the house and parked along the road, blocking the iron gate that guarded the driveway. He bypassed the call button and pushed through a walk-in gate that wasn't locked.

The house reminded Brandon of the hybrid modern and stucco-styled homes that sometimes sprang up in posh West Coast neighborhoods. It was alabaster white and had a garage at street level, topped by two additional stories with at least one balcony and two chimneys. A stone-lined path to the left led up to an unseen entrance.

Crossing the driveway, he slowed to admire the silver Porsche 718 Spyder with its top down.

It was probably considered a crime to own a normal car in a neighborhood like this. Next to the Porsche sat a gleaming white Audi A6.

The double front doors were mahogany with frosted glass inlaid with an ornate wrought-iron grapevine design.

He pressed the doorbell camera button and a long, winding melody played from within the house. A Jack Russell skidded into the entrance hallway, fighting to keep its balance on the hardwood floors. It yipped at Brandon while he waited. Eventually, the dog quieted, still eyeing Brandon.

When no one answered, he tried the bell once more and the dog started yapping again.

A woman appeared in the hallway. She wore tight, but not too tight, cutoff jeans and a black t-shirt.

She opened the door and, closer now, Brandon could see she was in her late thirties. She had the sort of tan you couldn't get naturally in Seattle and short, chestnut brown hair.

"Hi," she said, her voice as perky as the rest of her.

"I'm looking for Gary Gallagher."

"Is there something wrong?" she asked.

"I need to speak with him about his daughter."

"Is Ashley okay?"

"It's about Kaitlyn," Brandon said.

Confusion glazed her eyes. "Gary only has one daughter."

She still had her hand on the door, deciding whether to let him in.

"Are you Gary's wife?" Brandon asked.

She bit her lip as if she had to think about the question. "My name is Liz. Gary and I are together. I live here."

He nodded as if that was important information. "I'd like to speak to Gary."

Brandon's gaze stumbled onto the middle-aged man traipsing down the hallway in a bathrobe and white, fluffy slippers.

Liz stepped back to let Gary take over.

"What's the problem?"

"Brandon Mattson, chief of police of Forks."

"Yes. You called me."

"I'd like to chat with you about Kaitlyn."

"Who is Kaitlyn?" Liz asked, still lurking in the hall.

"I'll explain later," Gary said.

"I hope so." Liz stomped off to some unseen location within the palatial home.

"Come in," Gary said, stepping aside. He led Brandon to a dining room at the back of the house where there was a wide vista of Lake Washington. Yachts floated by lazily while speedboats ripped through the lake's mild waves. Further north, cars crawled over the I-90 bridge on their way to Seattle.

Gary settled into a chair at the head of an expansive polished maple dining room table. A matching buffet and sideboard adorned opposite sides of the room.

"You didn't return my calls," Brandon said, taking the chair directly to the right of Gary.

Gary's gaze wandered out to Lake Washington. "I didn't see the point."

Despite his smile lines, there was a sadness behind Gary's eyes. Brandon recognized the resemblance to Kaitlyn.

"The point is your daughter was missing and we've found her."

Gary rested his hand palm down on the table. "Look, don't get me wrong. I'm grateful she's alive."

"Kaitlyn doesn't know that. She believes you don't care about her."

Gary's lips pursed in what Brandon assumed was a superficial attempt to show concern. "I'm sorry she feels that way."

"And what are you going to do about it?"

He spread his hands out. "What can I do?"

"To start, you can talk to her."

"Officer, or chief—whatever you are—I've known Kaitlyn her entire life. I've tried to make things work, trust me."

"She needs to know her father cares. Kaitlyn needs you."

Gary's head swiveled side to side. "No, I don't think she does."

"Why?"

He leaned back, his jaw suddenly hard. "What Kaitlyn needs is a good kick in the ass. If there's anything I did wrong, it was being too easy on her."

Brandon's teeth clenched. Maybe it was a good thing Kaitlyn wasn't around this asshole. "Is pretending she doesn't exist what you call being too easy?"

"What's that supposed to mean?"

"You didn't even tell your girlfriend you have a second daughter."

"That's none of your business."

Brandon leaned forward. "Do you know what Kaitlyn has to do to stay warm at night? To feed herself?"

"I don't need to know," he said, shaking his head.

"She's a prostitute, Gary. Your little girl sells herself every night. And you don't have the balls to have one simple conversation with her." He slapped his hand on the table. The smack echoed through the room.

184

"I'm sorry, but she's made her own bed. Now she has to sleep in it."

Brandon stood, forcing the chair back so it almost tipped over.

Gary slid back, fear in his eyes.

"Get up," Brandon said.

Cautiously, Gary rose. "You don't have jurisdiction here," he said, voice quivering.

Gary assumed Brandon was going to arrest him. But being a deadbeat parent wasn't against the law, especially when the child was 18.

"Your daughter has requested some of her belongings," Brandon said.

"I won't let you go digging through my property," Gary insisted.

Liz appeared at the dining room entrance. She'd changed into dress slacks and a button-up top. "Let him get what he came for, Gary."

"Why?"

"Do it, so he leaves. And then I'll have my turn with you," she said, her voice like steel.

Gary blinked at Liz. He turned to Brandon. "Her room is upstairs, first room on the right."

"The room you keep locked?" Liz asked.

"I didn't think it was important," Gary said.

"To tell me you had another daughter?"

Gary didn't answer. He opened the middle drawer of the sideboard and pulled out a single key. He handed it to Liz.

"This way," Liz said.

He followed her up the stairs where she opened the door to Kaitlyn's room. She stood in the doorway for a

185

moment, taking in the room for the first time. "Gary, you damn fool."

She turned to Brandon. "He told me this room was for storage. I guess I should have wondered why it was locked."

"How long have you been with Gary?" Brandon asked.

"A couple of months," she said. "He's not a bad guy, really."

Could have fooled me, Brandon thought.

"I'll get you a box," she said. "And I'm sorry. I really had no idea. He told me he has one daughter off at college. That's it. I was supposed to meet her next week. I can't believe he's not helping...what was her name?"

"Kaitlyn," Brandon said. "She's eighteen."

"It's a good thing you're still here," she said sarcastically. "I might have strangled him by now."

Brandon stepped into the room. The air was heavy with the honeyed scent of vanilla candles and lavender. The walls were fuchsia pink and porcelain white. Posters of horses adorned one wall, cutouts of characters from video games the other. The bed was made, its pink floral comforter matching the curtains. The top of Kaitlyn's white dresser was neatly organized with an earring tree, jewelry box, candle, and what looked like an art class painting of a Japanese anime character.

He was still standing there, trying to imagine Kaitlyn living in this space, when Liz returned with a large Rubbermaid container. "Is this big enough?"

"Sure," Brandon said.

"Let me know if you need anything," she said, before leaving.

Brandon stared at the empty container.

What had he gotten himself into? The truth was, Kaitlyn hadn't asked him to get any of her things. But she'd mentioned she wished she had some of her belongings. A reminder of her life before her current situation might nudge her in the right direction.

Hanging from the headboard were ribbons and medals. One read *Geography Bowl State Champion.* The other two were for a science fair, first and second place. A picture frame on the shelf next to her bed showed a much happier Kaitlyn wearing the medal before her science fair board.

He slid the medals off the bed and placed them in the box.

Brandon surveyed the room, unsure what to take or leave. He opened the nightstand and found a *Teen Study Bible* and some bulletins from a nearby church. Inside the Bible, an inscription read *From Mom to Kaitlyn. Never forget you are loved by God and me.*

He didn't spot any of the journals she'd mentioned but he did find a stack of music papers with words and chords. He eyed the acoustic guitar in the corner. He'd take that, too.

He jostled the pillows and found what he was looking for. Three journals. He considered opening them, then reminded himself he wasn't processing a crime scene. Whatever was in them belonged to Kaitlyn and was none of his business.

The journals and Bible went into the box, along with a few pictures from the wall—ones with Kaitlyn and her friends. There was an assortment of stuffed animals and he picked a couple, not knowing which ones might hold any sentimental value for her.

A few minutes later, the box was full. Flinging the guitar strap over his shoulder, he hauled the instrument and the box down the stairs where Gary was waiting by the entrance.

Gary opened the door. "I wish I could say I was glad you stopped by..."

"You have my number. Any time you want to act like a father," Brandon said, "let me know."

Gary's eyes veered sideways in an expression of disinterest. "Good day, officer."

"Chief," Brandon said.

"Where was it you're chief of?"

"Forks."

"I've heard of it. Isn't that the place with the vampires?"

"Funny," Brandon said. "By the way, have you had any contact with Kaitlyn's mother?"

He huffed. "No, and no thanks. She left me years ago. Never even told me where she went."

"I can't imagine why a woman would leave a nice guy like you, Gary."

Brandon nodded at Liz as she entered the hallway.

"You two have a nice day."

Brandon loaded the box in the SUV and made his way back to I-90.

A stiff wind swept over the long and low floating bridge, the lake's choppy waves fingering at the guardrails. He was stuck on Gary's indifference to his daughter's circumstances. It was easy to blame Gary, or even her mom, for how Kaitlyn had ended up, despite having so much going for her. A nice home, good schools, smarts, and talent.

But life was complicated. It wasn't just one thing that sent people off the rails. What if she'd never been exposed to drugs? Sometimes it seemed the difference between a slightly dysfunctional life and a tragic one was simply a matter of wrong place, wrong time.

And if setting your life careening off-course was complicated, picking up the pieces and trying to make something of it after that was even harder. Based on experience, Brandon knew there was little chance Kaitlyn would accept help. But a little hope was better than none.

It was just past two in the afternoon when he made it back across the lake and into Seattle, settling on the southern route home. He wasn't in the mood for the long lines that would await him at the ferry terminal. If he spent more time in the area he'd be stuck in traffic for an hour before facing anything resembling an open road.

His heart was heavy in his chest as if Kaitlyn's losses—and those of all the other Kaitlyns he'd dealt with as a cop—weighed on him now.

He had a sudden urge to talk to Tori.

He'd promised himself he'd leave her alone, give her space. But here he was, just minutes from her home.

Maybe he'd surprise her.

Except Tori didn't like surprises.

He'd call her on the way.

Brandon headed north on I-5, taking the exit to the University District. Since their divorce, Tori had been renting a house north of the University of Washington. Why she wanted to live in Seattle, he had no idea. Not only was the cost of living one of the highest in the nation, but crime rates also continued to rise.

Driving through Seattle was like a tour of cases for him. He'd worked investigations in every neighborhood, from his time as a beat cop, to petty crimes, to the major crimes unit. He knew of murders that had occurred in some of these homes that, had the new owners known of the crimes, they never would have stepped foot in them.

Brandon had tried Tori's cell but she didn't answer.

He thought back to how she'd acted strangely after two nights of them making love. Had he scared her off?

He turned onto Tori's street, recalling Emma's comment about Tori not being in a good place to be in a relationship with Brandon. What did that mean?

He slowed to a stop in front of her home. Tori's car wasn't in the driveway.

She was probably at work.

It was getting late and now he was guaranteed to hit traffic.

Before heading for the highway, he pulled into the Cutter's Point Coffee Shop. Emma had mentioned it as one of her favorites while staying with Tori.

Brandon considered the drive-through but figured it would be better to stretch his legs before the long trek back to Forks. He'd just stepped down from the Interceptor when he noticed Tori's car two parking spaces over. From the parking lot, he scanned the café. There, near the window sat Tori. The man across from her wore a pea coat, a white dress shirt, and a black tie. Brandon looked away. Jealousy was a knee-jerk reaction.

It was probably a friend. Or a work acquaintance.

Or something more.

Again, his mind went back to the way she'd been acting. He thought back to the text messages she'd received throughout the day and late into the evening while staying with him. He'd assumed they were work. Could they have been from the man she was with now?

190

The thing was, on any given day over the last year, he had no interest in Tori's dating life. But it was different now. She and Brandon had gotten back together.

Or had they?

He was back to wondering if this was just a friend.

He texted Emma: *What did you mean when you said mom wasn't ready for a relationship?*

A minute later, she responded: *Not what I said but why?*

Just wondering, he replied.

He waited, and in the meantime, the man across from Tori laughed at something she said and rested his hand on hers. He leaned forward as if to kiss her.

Brandon backed the SUV away from the café. He glanced at Tori one more time and, it seemed, she'd caught sight of his car.

It didn't matter. He'd seen enough.

Brandon waited at a stoplight a block away. Emma finally replied: *Because she has a boyfriend and you and mom were acting like you were interested in each other again.* Then, another text: *You aren't, right?*

Brandon responded: *Right.*

The light turned green and he headed back to Forks.

Chapter 21

He'd gotten stuck in traffic in Seattle, and then Tacoma, and finally, Olympia, before he struck the open road on Highway 101. He had plenty of time to cycle through a whole gamut of emotions, thoughts, and plans. The thing was, he had been doing fine until Tori had come back into his life. Sure, things with Lisa hadn't worked out, but that was to be expected with their busy schedules and the distance between them. Not much different from the situation with Tori. But he and Tori had been together for years, had raised a family together. If she was only interested in a weeklong fling, she should have told him.

A half an hour into his trek back home, Tori had tried to call him. She'd messaged him too. That meant, he assumed, that she had noticed the Forks Police Department SUV in front of the café.

He'd call her back later. For now, he didn't have the stomach for excuses, and he was just fine stewing in silence all the way back to Forks.

Around six in the evening, he got a call from Jackson. He was outside of Aberdeen, still an hour and a half from town.

"You still working?" he asked.

"Someone has to around here," she replied. "How did it go with Kaitlyn's dad?"

"About as well as you'd expect."

"So he's not winning father of the year. Go figure."

"I got some of her belongings," Brandon said.

Jackson paused. "Did she ask you to do that?"

"Yes," Brandon said. "Sort of."

"Sort of?"

"She said she wished she had some of her things, so I'm bringing them back to her. Okay?"

"Alright, no need to jump all over my ass."

She was right.

"Sorry," he said. "It's been a long day. You have any updates on the Rule case?"

"You're gonna flip," she said.

"What?"

Jackson sometimes liked to draw out the drama in a conversation, a trait that sometimes irked Brandon.

"We found Phoenix Weaver's prints in Darren Rule's room."

"What the hell was she doing in his motorhome?"

"Good question. You remember that tube of lipstick?"

"I remember."

"Her prints were on that too."

The knife and tarot card in Rule's mouth had no prints. The only thing they had to go on were whose prints were in the room. Even then, it didn't mean much. Rule's penchant for women and parties meant they were likely to find a slew of prints.

"Phoenix claimed she didn't know Rule, which means she had no reason to be in his motorhome," Brandon said. "What else did you learn?"

"Josiah and I worked through the documents you found under the glove compartment. Everyone we got ahold of claimed an alibi, and most of them were from out of state."

"So if he was blackmailing people, it was before the fair arrived in Forks. Anything on Phoenix?"

193

"No, but there was one file on a local kid."

"I saw that," Brandon said. "An order for probation on a second-degree burglary charge."

"What did Darren Rule care about some kid's juvenile record?"

"That's what we need to find out."

"By the way," Jackson said, "I heard back about the tarot card on your front door. No prints."

"That's what I figured," he said.

"Okay, so we got the kid and the possible blackmail and Phoenix doing God knows what in Darren Rule's trailer. You want me to bring them in?"

"Tomorrow," he said. "You've been at it all day."

"My husband thanks you," she said dryly. "By the way, I haven't seen the ex around for a while. You two still a thing?"

"No."

"By the way you said that I'm assuming I'd better not ask any more questions."

"Your assumption would be correct, detective."

"Well, I'm sorry, if that makes things any better," she said, her voice softer now.

"It doesn't. But I appreciate it anyway. Goodnight, Jackson."

Brandon was back in Forks by eight. He loathed the idea of returning home to an empty house, so he headed to the fair to see if a hike around the area near the murder scene might generate any ideas. He'd left Caesar plenty of food and water, knowing he'd be out until late, so he had no reason to head home.

He made his way through the front entrance. By now, the ticket sellers knew him by name, and they let him through without questions. It was a Saturday evening and the fair's pub and beer garden were packed, but the general mood was one of joviality. He'd had assurances before the fair's arrival that alcohol sales would end at ten, at least for fair visitors. He wasn't concerned about the alcohol consumption of the crew members, as long as they stayed on the property and didn't engage in behavior requiring police intervention.

He strolled through the fairgrounds, pausing for a moment to watch another melee like the one he'd participated in a few days earlier. His groin tensed at the thought of Hamish's last blow.

He was about to leave when Alex appeared at his side.

"Reliving your glorious moment?" he asked.

"You saw that, huh?"

"That was pretty badass. Beating Hamish isn't easy to do."

"I take it you've tried your hand in the arena?" Brandon asked.

Alex scoffed. "Me? Hell no. I'm a lover, not a fighter. Besides, it wouldn't be professional, being the head of security and all..."

Brandon eyed Alex.

Alex noticed Brandon's attention. "I didn't mean it like that. You're the chief...you do what you like..."

"No, you're right," Brandon said. "I was about to step out of the contest when Hamish charged me."

"Sounds like Hamish," Alex said. He considered Brandon for a moment. "What brings you here tonight, Chief?"

"Bored. Searching for clues. Hoping something comes to mind."

Not to mention, I just saw my ex with another man, and I know it shouldn't bother me...but it sure as hell does.

"Any ideas where Darren Rule might have stashed documents, personal belongings...anything like that?"

Alex thought about it, then said, "Follow me."

He led Brandon back to the area where cast members parked their trailers, RVs, and, in some cases, tents and cars. He considered the open spot where Rule's motorhome had been parked before being hauled off as evidence.

"I should have thought of this earlier," Alex said.

Alex stopped before a small wooden shed.

"What's in here?" Brandon asked.

"It's prop storage. A bunch of stuff like torches, fake swords...all the crap performers use."

"What does it have to do with Rule?" Brandon had asked about documents or incriminating evidence, not stage props.

"Some cast members use it for general storage."

"Who has the key?"

"The cast members know the combination. As far as stealing from each other, they have a sort of honor code."

"Does that code include *thou shalt not murder*?" Brandon asked.

Alex chuckled.

Brandon hadn't meant it as a joke.

Alex's eyes narrowed. "Crap."

"What?"

"Someone's pried the lock off."

The metal loop where the lock should be hung limp from one screw.

Brandon opened the door with his foot.

"You're sure Darren Rule stored personal belongings in here?"

"It's possible," Alex said.

Bandon clicked his flashlight on and scanned the wooden structure. It was no larger than a backyard shed. Inside were theater props, a barrel of assorted weapons like pikes and long swords, and stacks of boxes with cast members' names on them.

"Is anything missing?"

Alex stroked his chin, surveying the shed. "Couldn't tell you."

"Who would know to search here, assuming it has something to do with our victim?"

"Cast members, mostly."

"So whoever it is, their prints were already all over this thing," Brandon said.

"Dozens of prints—everyone has access to the shed."

Brandon ducked as he exited the shed. Alex closed the door, doing his best to prop it shut.

"I'll have to write a report on this," Alex said.

As far as Brandon could tell, there wasn't much to see. It was doubtful Darren Rule would be foolish enough to store valuable blackmail documents in a location anyone could access.

But if his victims believed he might do so, they would check the shed.

A loud thwack rattled the wooden door just as Alex turned to face him. Brandon flinched as the object swished inches from his nose.

"What the hell?" Alex said.

He followed Alex's gaze to the shed. An arrow penetrated the door and a thin, rectangular object pierced through by the arrow's tip.

"Get down," Brandon shouted.

The next arrow swept over his head, slamming into the shed with a thud.

Brandon drew his pistol.

"Stay down," he said.

Brandon scanned the darkened lot. Twenty feet away stood a long travel trailer, to its left was a forest, to its right, several cars were parked along the path leading back to the fair. He visualized the angle of the shot—it had come from the travel trailer. He circled around to the right, sprinting for the cover of the cars, Alex on his heels.

"Alert your security staff."

"Roger."

Brandon called for backup. They were to apprehend anyone with a ranged weapon.

"It's a crossbow," Alex interrupted him.

"How do you know?"

"Those are crossbow bolts. Shorter and heavier than the arrows used with bows."

Brandon conveyed the information.

Three weak floodlights atop temporary poles added scant light to the shadowy lot.

He instructed Alex to stay put until he cleared the area. Brandon checked the trailer, then the nearby vehicles, searching underneath and behind any potential hiding place.

The shooter was gone.

Two of the department's swing shift officers met him near the arena. "Ask around. Any sign of a man or woman with a crossbow, I need to know about it."

After retrieving his evidence kit, he met up with Alex near the trailer.

"I figure this is where the shooter stood," he said. He searched for footprints, but the area had recently been covered with a fresh coat of gravel.

They headed back to the shed. "We'll get prints off those, what did you call them?"

"Bolts."

"Right."

He stopped short, considering the two bolts.

Hanging off the first was a tarot card.

"Damn," Alex said.

"Maybe you were right," Brandon said.

"About the cards? I figured you wouldn't believe me."

"To be honest, I thought maybe you wanted the cards to be important."

"Why would I want that?"

"I don't know. People do things for strange reasons."

"You mean like, I was the killer, trying to throw you off the scent?"

"Nothing that extreme."

"Well, now you know. I ain't about to get my ass shot just to prove a point to anyone. Not even you."

"I hear you," Brandon said.

He slipped on a pair of gloves and carefully freed the bolts and tarot card. The card dangled from the bolt. The shooter must have attached it before firing.

"Amazing it stayed on," Brandon said. "You want to interpret this one for me?"

The card showed a man, face down, with several long swords protruding from his back. In the background, an inky sky hung over distant mountains.

"I used Wikipedia last time."

"It's from the same set as the one they left on my front door."

199

"Of your house?"

He'd forgotten for a second that Alex wasn't part of his team, meaning he wasn't aware of all the facts of the case.

"Right."

"That's not cool," Alex said.

"Agreed. Phoenix Weaver, one of the locals taking part in the fair, said she had a deck stolen that matches this one and the one at my house."

"So you were the target, then."

"Either someone is trying hard to get me to point the blame at Phoenix or the killer just happens to own a similar deck and is trying to send a message."

"We need to figure out what this card means," Alex said. "Are you going to ask Phoenix?"

"She's not the type to wield a crossbow, but I'm not ruling her out. Not yet."

They made the rounds through the fair. Phoenix's shop was closed, as it had been earlier when Brandon passed by.

"How many shops sell crossbows?"

"There's only one bowyer here," Alex said. "Follow me."

They spoke with the bowyer and it turned out he only had two functioning crossbows. The others they sold were wood and rubber band toys that were only good for launching marshmallows.

"I should say I *had* two," the bowyer said. He was a thin, balding man in his late forties dressed up like Robin Hood.

"What do you mean?" Brandon asked.

"One went missing a couple days after we arrived. I was in the middle of offloading our inventory when I realized it had disappeared."

"Why didn't you report this?" Alex asked.

The bowyer glanced at Brandon before turning to Alex. "No offense, but in the past, security hasn't been too keen on protecting our assets. Unless Mr. Sterling owned the shop, no one seemed to care much."

Alex frowned. "That was before I started. I need to know when this sort of thing happens. If it happened to you, it could have to others."

First, Hamish's knife, now a crossbow. The murderer was an accomplished thief as well.

"Understood," the bowyer said. "But it's a little late now. That crossbow is worth at least three hundred dollars."

"I'll take a report when I'm done with the chief here."

"Did you suspect anyone in particular?" Brandon asked.

"Of course not," the bowyer said, scratching the back of his neck. "Because if I did, they'd be hearing from me, even if it meant sticking an arrow in their backside."

"Leave catching the thief to my team," Alex said. "And the police."

The bowyer nodded doubtfully. "If you say so."

Brandon searched online for an explanation of the tarot card's meaning. The card was called the "ten of swords." It made sense—ten swords protruded from the man's body. According to a couple of websites he checked, the card represented hopelessness, betrayal, loss, and painful endings. He didn't bother to determine whether the card had been "reversed" or not, which supposedly changed its meaning. Anyone attaching a tarot card to a crossbow bolt and firing at someone most likely wasn't interested in which direction it landed.

What was clear was that the card, like the one on his front door, was meant as a threat. The first card had been of two men jumping from a burning tower, and the meaning had to do with believing lies and assuming you're safe. This time the warning was of a painful ending and betrayal.

One thing was clear—someone was trying to get him off the scent, and that usually meant he was getting close to the truth. So close, someone was willing to murder to prevent him from finding it.

He'd hoped to kill a few hours after his return from Seattle. Instead, he'd almost gotten himself killed. At least his mind was off Tori—for the time being.

Chapter 22

Brandon woke up with a hangover headache—even though he hadn't touched a drop of alcohol the night before. He did his best to stomach a bowl of cereal and a cup of coffee, then fed Caesar and headed to the station.

It was just past seven when he pulled into the parking lot. It gave him a chance to check in with the overnight shift—a couple of on-call officers, one of whom had applied for the open position but Brandon wasn't so sure about. He was still too green and Brandon was looking for seasoned officers. Losing Will—his longest-tenured officer—to retirement had dropped the average years of experience in the department to well below ten.

He was on his third cup of coffee when Jackson checked in.

"Ready for the big day?" she asked.

"Don't I look it?"

"You look like someone ran over your dog."

"Maybe they did," he replied.

Jackson pointed the empty carafe at Brandon. "You know, it's common courtesy to make fresh coffee when you drink the last."

"My apologies," Brandon said.

She shook her head and made a new pot.

"You are in a foul mood," she said, her back to him.

"Well, Jackson. Life happens," he said.

She replaced the carafe and turned the machine on. Leaning on the counter, she asked, "You want to talk about it?"

"I'm your superior officer," he said.

"So that means you don't get to have feelings?"

"I don't need a damn therapist if that's what you mean."

She stared at him for a long time and he wondered what she was thinking.

"In case you're wondering," she said. "What I'm thinking is that ex of yours did a number on you. I mean, sure, I bet the Kaitlyn situation is getting you down. That happens to all of us, or at least those of us that care. But you look like a man who's had his heart broken."

He liked Jackson better when she was joking around. Work wasn't a place to talk about your feelings. Especially when you were the chief.

"Tori and I were together again, in a sense, if you know what I mean."

"I think I know what *in a sense* means," she said.

"And when I was over in Seattle, I figured I'd drop by her place—"

Jackson's jaw dropped. "Wait, you didn't catch her in the act, did you?"

"God, no," Brandon said waving his hands in front of his face as if to erase the image. "But I saw her out with another man."

"Out where?"

"At a café."

"And?"

"He was about to kiss her, so I left."

Now that he'd said it out loud, he realized how ridiculous it sounded.

"So you're sure this is what you saw?"

"And Emma told me Tori is seeing someone."

Jackson twisted her lips. "I'm sorry, Chief."

Brandon thought about it for a minute, then said, "The thing is, why the hell start a relationship again when you aren't ready to stick with it?"

"Most of the time it's the woman asking that question," she said.

"I don't know about that..."

"No disrespect, but usually it's the man that wants what he wants and, when he gets bored, wants to move on."

"That's not fair," Brandon said.

She lifted her hands. "Just telling it how I see it."

"I guess it doesn't matter," he said. "No one promised anyone anything. At least not this time around."

"That doesn't stop it from hurting," she said.

Something about the pity in her voice pricked him. He realized he was slouching in the chair.

He sat up, crinkled his empty paper cup, and tossed it in the garbage.

"Okay. The session is over. We have work to do."

Jackson smiled. "Glad you're in a better mood. What's the news for today?"

"You want some news? Alex and I were attacked last night."

He described the crossbow attack and the tarot card attached to the bolt.

"Did you find them?"

"Nope. We did discover a crossbow had been stolen a couple of weeks back."

"What was the tarot card?"

"The Ten of Swords. Apparently, it means betrayal and painful endings."

For the first time, he wondered if the card was predicting the fate of his relationship with Tori.

That was impossible. How could the shooter know about what he'd seen in Seattle? He was letting the occult nature of the cards get to him.

"I don't like this," Jackson said. "First your house, now someone takes a shot at you."

"It's a message, but I'm not sure what the message is. It would be idiotic to believe posting tarot cards on my door or taking shots at me is going to distract us from the investigation."

"The alternative is someone is trying to mislead you."

"That's my guess."

"It's a good thing Emma is at camp," Jackson said. "She'd be having a fit if she knew someone had shot at you."

"Right. And we'll keep it our little secret until she gets home. By then, we'd better have this solved, or she'll be staying with her mom in Seattle." He motioned to her desk. "Any news on the documents?"

She grabbed a file from the pile on her desk and slid it across the table to him. "Here's the one on the local kid and his court documents. Like I said, no idea why Darren Rule was interested in a juvenile case."

Brandon scanned the file. The kid's name was David Velasquez. "Did you get ahold of his probation officer?"

She nodded. "David has had his share of trouble, but nothing big. Some truancy issues. Otherwise, he's got a supportive family and pretty much keeps to himself."

"But no connection to our victim?"

"Not that we know of. And remember, Rule had only been in town for a few weeks at most before his death."

"Sounds like he knew how to make connections, and fast," Brandon said. "Let's head to the kid's house first, then we'll tackle Phoenix."

Jackson rode shotgun and played navigator as they headed to David Velasquez's home. It was a couple of miles outside of town along a backcountry road that led to the foothills.

The two-lane road narrowed but was still paved as they left the pastured flatlands and climbed a gradual incline into a forested area.

"Here," she said.

Brandon slowed to a stop in front of the New Testament Church of God.

"It's a church," he said.

"This is the address his corrections officer gave me."

The building was painted in typical church hues—baby blue with stone blue trim. Half the churches in town utilized the same blue and gray tone. Still others adopted a similar accent pattern, but in mint green. He figured it must be a denominational thing.

Behind the church, and in the same blue hues, was what appeared to be an apartment building. He pulled into the parking lot and noticed a sign on the larger building. New Testament Church of God Seminary.

"There's a Bible college out here?" Brandon asked.

"Seminary."

"What's the difference?"

"Seminary is like graduate school for pastors."

He stared back at her, surprised.

"My dad is a pastor," she said.

"I didn't know that."

She pointed a thumb at herself. "Pastor's brat tried and true."

"That explains a lot."

"You're almost as funny as Darren Rule," she said.

He smiled. "All we have is the court documents on this kid, right?"

"Yep."

"His prints weren't in the trailer?"

"We checked. His prints are on file. None were found at the crime scene."

"Got it."

The main entrance was locked but they found the church office on the opposite side of the building.

A woman in her thirties with dusky hair wrapped in an overstuffed bun sat typing at a computer.

"Can I help you?" Her voice strained above the clamor of the copy machine behind her spitting out copies of the church bulletin. The nameplate on her desk indicated she was Beatrice Postma.

"Hi, Beatrice. We are looking for David Velasquez. We were told this is his address," Brandon said.

"Is David in trouble again?"

"We just want a few words with him," Brandon said.

She considered Brandon, sizing him up. She must know something of David's history, and she certainly didn't believe the police were in her office for a friendly visit.

"I'll get Eddie."

The woman disappeared through a door at the rear of the reception area.

Why was David Velazquez living at a church? Was he a seminary student?

"Eddie's his father," Jackson said.

Beatrice returned with Eddie.

Eddie was about 40. To Brandon, he appeared to be Mexican American. He wore a navy-blue cotton tie and a white dress shirt. His armpits and brow were wet with sweat. His raven hair was slicked to one side like an old-school Baptist preacher.

"We can talk in my office."

Eddie Velasquez's office was dimly lit. A worn carpet and dark built-in bookshelves meant the church had probably been constructed in the 80s. Eddie took a seat behind a cherrywood paneled desk. Next to his computer screen were a Bible and a stack of books with titles like *Spurgeon's Sermons* and *The Problem of Pain* by C. S. Lewis.

"How can I help you?"

"We'd like a word with David Velasquez. We were told he lives here."

"David and I stay in an apartment out back."

"Where the seminary is?"

"Used to be. We're on hold right now. Low enrollment." Then, as if remembering something, his demeanor brightened. "But we'll be hosting online classes starting in the fall."

Brandon took the chair directly in front of the pastor's desk. "I'll get to the point, Mr. Velasquez. We'd like to speak to David about the death of a man named Darren Rule."

He blinked at them, then closed the Bible on his desk. "David's not here."

"When do you expect him back?"

"I can't keep track of David," Eddie said. "You know how kids are nowadays."

"Do you know of any connection between Mr. Rule and your son?" Jackson asked. "He's also known by the name Drool."

"None whatsoever."

"Any idea why this Mr. Rule would have copies of David's court paperwork?"

He tilted his head at Brandon. "Why would he have that?"

"That's what we're trying to figure out."

"So Drool never approached you or David asking for money?" Jackson asked.

"No."

Jackson pressed him. "No threat of blackmail whatsoever?"

"I would have contacted the police," Eddie said.

They asked him a handful of other questions, but it seemed Eddie knew little of his son's daily activities or contacts in the community.

"He's 18 now," Eddie said, as if to defend his lack of information. He leaned forward in his chair. "You said you found the burglary documents. Was there anything else?"

"Like?"

"I'm just wondering. I've heard blackmailers sometimes try to make things up—lies about people."

Jackson said, "If there is anything we should look for, Mr. Velasquez, we need to know."

He leaned back. "No. I just...you never know what your kids are getting into until it's too late."

They waited for him to elaborate. Instead, he stared at the stack of books on his desk, suddenly in some other place.

Brandon stood. "Call either one of us when he gets back." They both passed him a card.

"Is David in trouble? I mean, do you really believe he's involved in this?"

"Right now, we're just asking questions," Brandon said.

They followed him out through a different hallway, one that led to the church foyer. Two open doors gave them a glimpse into the empty sanctuary.

"How's business?" Brandon asked, smiling.

"We get a handful. Sixty or so on a good Sunday."

Brandon wondered if Eddie was exaggerating. The church had the dank atmosphere of a seldom-used building.

"I never knew this place was out here," he said.

"The school opened in '82. Enrollment was in the hundreds at one point. They trained a lot of good pastors here. God used this old building, in its time. I was a student here back in the day."

"What happened to the school?"

Eddie pinched the bridge of his nose. "My wife and I were called to New Testament about seventeen years ago. I'd been offered a position down in San Jose at a much larger church. But I knew I was meant to be here at the seminary."

By Eddie's tone, Brandon could tell the story didn't have a happy ending. He suddenly wondered where Eddie's wife was in all of this.

"She left you?" Jackson asked.

Eddie's head jerked back. "Did you know Susan?"

Brandon pointed a thumb at Jackson. "Don't mind her. She does that to me all the time."

Eddie eyed Jackson before continuing. "David was still in diapers when she told me she'd had enough—of the ministry, of me, of everything. She filed for divorce and there was nothing I could do to convince her to come home."

"And you're still here," Brandon said.

"I'm called here."

Brandon wondered if Eddie was still waiting for his ex to change her mind.

"Has David ever owned a set of tarot cards?" Jackson asked.

Brandon was surprised by the question, but it was a good one, considering the crime scene.

Eddie made a motion as if to ward off an evil spirit. "We don't allow the occult in our home."

"I figured," Jackson said. Then, turning the conversation, she asked, "Is David your only child?"

"Yes, ma'am. It hasn't been easy raising him alone." His shoulders sank. "I know I've let him down. Otherwise, why would he get in trouble as much as he does?"

"You do your best," Brandon said, "and hope for the best. There is such a thing as free will... you can't control everything. Especially at his age."

Eddie nodded thoughtfully. "I just pray he makes it through this."

Brandon wondered what Eddie meant by *this*. Did he mean his probation for burglary, or something worse?

"You're welcome any Sunday," Eddie said, motioning to the sanctuary.

"Thanks," Brandon said. "My daughter and I attend First Baptist in town."

"Pastor Mark is a good man." He turned to Jackson. "You're welcome too."

Jackson grimaced. "It's been a while. And my husband—"

"No pressure. The invitation is open."

"Give us a call when David comes home," Brandon said. "We can come back out."

Back in the SUV, Jackson said, "Damn. What a sad story."

"Yeah," Brandon said. "And I hope for Eddie's sake his son isn't involved in this murder."

"Wife leaves you alone with a kid. You do your best and he still ends up in the system. Man, life sucks sometimes."

"It's not all bad," Brandon said. "Sounds like you need to head to church this Sunday."

She rolled her eyes. "Very funny."

Chapter 23

They headed for Phoenix Weaver's tent at the Renaissance fair. Not only had one of Phoenix's missing cards been attached to a crossbow bolt and shot at Brandon's head, they now had evidence she'd been in Darren Rule's motorhome.

Phoenix was busy reading an older woman's palm when they arrived. They loitered several feet away. She pretended not to notice them, but Brandon could sense the seer's uneasiness.

When the customer had gone, they approached Phoenix's tent.

"I already gave fingerprints and DNA," Phoenix said. "What else do you want from me? A kidney, perhaps?"

"It's nice of you to offer," Brandon said, "but your fingerprints are exactly why we're here."

"What about them?"

"We found your prints in Darren Rule's bedroom," Jackson said.

Phoenix's eyes widened. "That's impossible."

"Not if you were in his motorhome," Brandon said. "Even though you claimed you weren't."

"I *said* I didn't know him well."

"So you admit you were in his room?" Jackson asked.

"No. Yes." She sighed and appeared as if she would swoon. "I don't understand why you are asking me all of this."

"Close up the shop," Brandon said.

"Why?"

"We're taking a trip to the station."

Her hands balled into fists. After a short but intense buildup, she exclaimed. "Ugh!"

Brandon and Jackson sat across from Phoenix in the station's interview room. They began recording, notifying her of her rights.

"Yes, I understand," she said. "Can we get this over with?"

"What's the hurry?" Jackson asked.

"I have customers," Phoenix said.

"Who need their future explained to them, right?" Jackson replied.

"You can doubt all you want. And besides, I am a small-business owner. Unlike some people, I don't get to live off the government's dime."

Jackson scooted her chair closer. Brandon tapped his hand on the table. "We're going to get started."

He eyed Jackson, warning her to cool her jets.

"Last time we talked," Brandon said, "you denied that the panties we found in Darren Rule's room were yours. Do you remember that?"

"Of course," she said.

"The thing is, Phoenix, I don't believe you."

She squinted at him. "Do you believe anyone? How about that lady you were with? Do you trust her?" She pointed a finger at him. "You obviously have relationship issues, Chief—"

"I am not here to discuss my personal life."

"Hmm."

"We found your fingerprints in Drool's room, the scene of a murder. We also found a pair of panties that, when they come back, I'm sure will match your DNA. We have your lipstick at the scene too."

215

"My what?"

"Lipstick. With your prints on it."

Her hand involuntarily moved to her side, where she might normally wear her purse.

"You were probably wondering where it went," Jackson said.

Phoenix didn't have an answer for that.

"And now we've found a tarot card—"

"That was not my tarot card. I told you, someone stole my deck."

"The fact is a tarot card placed on my front door and another attached to a crossbow bolt aimed at my head *do* match your cards."

She waved a hand dismissively. "I know nothing about that."

"Have you ever fired a crossbow, Phoenix?"

"Of course not. I am not one to use weapons. My purpose in this world is to bring insight and healing."

"But you admit the panties, lipstick, and prints from the motorhome are yours?" Jackson asked.

"Yes...No. Stop doing that."

"Why are your prints in Darren Rule's room?" Brandon asked.

"I don't know," she said, burying her head in her hands.

"You don't know or you're afraid? The best thing you can do is tell the truth."

"I am," she said. When she lifted her eyes, they were wet.

"We have your DNA. Anything that happened in that room will come to light."

"Do you carry a knife?" Jackson asked.

"No."

216

"What did Drool have on you?" Brandon asked on a hunch.

She straightened. "Have on me?"

"A secret you didn't want anyone else to know?"

She huffed. "Like what color my panties are?"

"This is serious," Brandon said. "If I find out you're lying to us, I will suggest the prosecuting attorney come down hard on you. Do you understand?"

"I have nothing to hide, Chief Mattson."

She'd gathered herself and presented a cool front, but Brandon wasn't buying it.

"Let's go," he said, standing.

Worry crossed her face.

"Am I going to jail?"

"Not yet."

They dropped Phoenix off at the fair. She left without another word. Brandon had remained silent, too. He was irked at her unwillingness to cooperate. She'd been in Rule's room. The question was why. The longer she held the truth back, the more she was getting herself wrapped up in the homicide investigation. Brandon didn't believe she'd murdered the jester. But then again, he'd been wrong before.

Back at the station, they talked through the case.

"We've got the murder weapon, motive, and a truckload of suspects," Jackson said.

They'd spread out the photos, reports, and documents on the station's conference room table.

"By motive do you mean blackmail?"

"Right," she said.

"That's one," Brandon said. "But there could be others."

"Like?"

"Revenge," he said.

"For blackmail."

"There's more than one reason people seek revenge."

"Like the girl, Kaitlyn Gallagher," Jackson said. Her lips hovered over her cup, watching for Brandon's response.

"What about her?"

"Darren Rule raped her. That's reason enough for vengeance," Jackson said.

"Kaitlyn's not the murdering type."

"You once told me there's no such thing as the *murdering type.*"

"I meant it. I'm not talking types, I'm talking about a real person. An individual."

"Okay, so you don't think she could have murdered him, even though he sexually assaulted her?"

"I'm not ruling it out, if that's what you're asking," Brandon said.

Jackson crossed her arms, considering Brandon. "You sure you don't have a blind spot here, Chief?"

"Yes, I'm sure," he insisted.

Jackson cast him a doubtful look. "Okay, what about Cory King, her pimp?"

"Revenge for what happened to Kaitlyn, considering he sees the girls as his property."

Jackson flipped through her notes from the interviews. "What about Hamish and Daisy? Something is going on there we don't know about yet."

"I don't trust them, either. But the time of death is well after Hamish's argument with Rule."

"It doesn't mean he didn't come back later."

"None of this explains the tarot card," Jackson said. "What's the connection there?"

"Alex believed it has something to do with a warning," Brandon said.

She raised an eyebrow at him. "Since when did you start listening to the security guard?"

"I might have changed my mind about him," Brandon said.

"You're saying I was right about Alex?"

"*Anyway*," he said, "the only tarot card connection is Phoenix. And we know she's lying."

"But did she kill Drool?"

"I hope not," Brandon said, pulling a chair out and resting a foot on it. "What would Forks do without its one and only fortune teller?"

Jackson arranged the files into a neat stack. "I guess we're stuck waiting for the DNA. We can keep looking into these documents."

"And keep asking questions. Someone's bound to remember something. Our killer could be any of these folks—or someone we haven't met yet." He stood. "I've got to get caught up on chief of police stuff. Applications, emails, community complaints."

"Sounds fun," she said. "I'm supposed to be covering the west side today. Let me know if anything comes up."

"Will do."

"And watch your back, Chief. Please."

"I will."

He spent the rest of the afternoon avoiding texts and phone calls from Tori. He caught up on his emails, rejected a couple of new applications for the open officer position, and responded to five complaints. Three were about his officers not taking the noise ordinance seriously—he suspected these were from the same person using multiple email addresses. Another was about the illegality of marijuana shops under the United States Constitution (not his problem), and the final was a form letter no doubt sent to hundreds of chiefs across the state, urging him to defund "the police state" and fund social programs instead. Brandon shook his head at the last one. His budget barely covered payroll, and his department had nothing close to the "military-style weapons" mentioned in the letter.

He was all for the community programs the individual demanded. Some counties even raised taxes to support alternative sentencing drug courts and the sorts of programs that helped get women like Arianne and Kaitlyn off the streets. In his humble opinion, which he was sure no one wanted to hear, both protective and social services should be funded.

He was about to check out for the day when Emma called.

"Hi, dad."

"Hey, sweetie. How's it going?"

"Oh, it's okay. I'm kind of ready to come home."

"Did something happen?"

"No, I'm just done with middle schoolers. They're so...immature."

Brandon chuckled. It was only a few years ago she was a middle schooler herself.

"Well, we miss you," Brandon said. He wasn't sure why he had said *we*.

"Did you remember to feed Caesar?"

"Did I ever forget to feed you?" he asked.

"That's different."

"It is. But yes, your cat is still alive."

"Is everything okay?" she asked. "You sound stressed."

"Just a lot going on at work, that's all."

"Did something bad happen?"

He'd already decided not to tell her about the crossbow attack. Emma wouldn't sleep knowing he was in danger. She would be upset with him later when she found out. In the meantime, he wanted her to enjoy her time at camp.

"Nothing out the ordinary," he said.

"Are you and mom talking a lot?" she asked.

"Not right now," he said, his tone too revealing.

"Why not?"

"She's busy with work."

She paused. "Hmm."

"What?"

"Mom said she's been trying to call you. She said *you* were the one that was too busy."

"Well, that is true. I am working a case right now."

"What's the deal with you and mom?"

"Nothing is the deal," Brandon said.

"Okay, if you say so. But you should call her."

He didn't like Emma getting in the middle of his relationship with Tori. She was supposed to be the child, not the parent.

"Don't worry about us. We'll figure it out. Besides, things have been going well for the last two years."

"I know. That's why I don't want you to mess that up. Promise me you won't."

"Okay," Brandon said, "I promise."

"I got to go. I have a cabin full of emo girls to get to dinner."

"Love you," Brandon said.

"Love you too."

Chapter 24

On the way home, Brandon passed by the Forks Inn and then made the circuit through town searching for Kaitlyn. He hadn't seen her since his return from Mercer Island. He had a box full of her childhood belongings and had hoped to give her some initiative to consider a turn from her current path. Unfortunately, Brandon had nothing good to report about her dad or his willingness to help. All that meant was she'd have to turn her life around without his help.

Brandon didn't find her and, after a quick survey of the fair, he headed for home.

He made himself rice and beans and had planned on adding chicken but it seemed too much work for one person. He'd recalled conversations he'd had with empty-nesters and how they complained about cooking for two. With just himself, it was damn hard not to descend into picking up fast food every night. It was too easy to pack on the pounds past 40.

He'd just done the dishes and settled into his chair with a copy of a novel Emma had bought him for his birthday, but that he'd had little time to read.

His phone buzzed.

It was Tori.

Despite his silence since leaving Seattle, he'd worked over the conversation he planned to have with her a dozen times in his head.

He wasn't in the mood to talk, but it would be better to get it over with.

"This is Brandon."

"Hey."

"Hey," he replied.

"I've been trying to get ahold of you."

"I've been busy," he said.

"How's the investigation going?"

"It's going," he said, already tired of the conversation.

"I saw your car the other day," she said. "At the café."

He swallowed the swelling sense of betrayal roiling his stomach.

"I wanted to talk to you about what happened," she said.

"I wasn't spying on you if that's what you're thinking. In fact, I was there to get a cup of coffee before heading back to Forks."

"Okay."

"I was in Seattle on work, and figured, hey, I'll stop by Tori's and say hi. But you weren't home. Little did I know you were out with your boyfriend."

"Brandon..."

"There I was, thinking, well, we made love, spent time together. It sure seems like we're back together again, whatever that means. But you disappear one day and I figure, okay, she needs some space. Shows what a damn poor excuse for a detective I am. At least when it comes to family."

"I'm not with him, Brandon."

"It sure seemed like you were. And you know what the worst part of this is, Tori? I had to find out from our daughter. What would Emma have thought of you if she knew you were in my bed while in the meantime your boyfriend has no idea—"

"Stop," she said.

224

"I was done."

In fact, as far as he was concerned, the conversation was over. He'd said his piece.

"You're not letting me explain," she said.

"Okay. Go for it."

This should be interesting, he thought.

"Yes, I was dating him," she said.

"Until when?"

"Until I came to Forks and realized I'm still in love with you," she said.

That wasn't fair. It was a punch in the gut to lead him on like this.

"And when you kissed him?"

"In the café?" she said. "I never...wait, you mean when Anthony *tried* to kiss me?"

"I saw what I saw," he said, recalling that he'd turned away before they'd kissed. It was possible she'd spurned him.

"Wait," she said, "did you tell Emma about us?"

"She already knew about you and *Anthony*."

"I mean you and me, that I'd stayed at your house," she said.

"Of course not," he said. "It would only confuse her."

It was a good thing Emma didn't know they were back together because obviously, they weren't.

"I'd better get going," he said, picking up his book. "I've got some things to work on."

"Okay, but please let me say this."

He was quiet for a moment, then said, "I'm listening."

"Anthony and I had been dating less than a month. I figured I was over you, over us..."

He didn't want to hear this. It was a hell of a lot easier knowing he and Tori were finished. He didn't have the capacity to deal with a back-and-forth relationship. And he wasn't prepared to go through the emotions of another breakup with Tori.

Being apart, the way they'd been the last two years, was the safest choice.

She continued, "But I'm not. And it's not just because we made love. I believe we have a chance..."

"You've got to get your life straight," he said, feeling a bit hypocritical. He'd not had the best experience dating since their divorce either. But at least his relationship with Lisa was over before he'd hooked up with Tori.

"That's what I'm trying to do," she said.

When he didn't respond, she said, "I'll let you go."

"Talk to you later," he said.

He waited for her to say goodbye. Instead, she said, "You were never this jealous when we were married."

"I trusted you," he said. "Back then."

"I hope you can trust me again."

"I'll see you around, Tori."

He tossed the phone onto the floor and opened his book to the page he'd been reading. After reading the same two sentences five times over, he flipped the television on. When that didn't work to keep his mind off Tori, he considered going for a drive or a walk. He did neither and instead went to bed, not feeling any better than before he'd talked to her. He wished, and didn't wish, that she'd really been with the boyfriend. That she'd stayed with this Anthony fellow and never spent the night at Brandon's house.

The possibility of a relationship, while knowing it most likely wouldn't work, was a hundred times worse than knowing you didn't have a chance at all. What was that song back in the day? Something about *owner of a lonely heart...much better than the owner of a broken heart.*

He agreed one-hundred percent.

Before heading to the station the next morning, Brandon checked around town for any sign of Kaitlyn. Instead, he found Arianne heading up Forks Ave near the diner. He pulled over and met her on the sidewalk. It was a cool morning and she'd wrapped herself in an oversized winter coat that almost reached the hem of her skirt.

Now that he stood next to her, the cloying aroma of her sickly-sweet perfume was overpowering. Brandon had always figured the difference between perfume and too much perfume was the difference between a lump of sugar and a tablespoon of saccharine.

Brandon couldn't imagine how any woman with a sense of smell could not notice the scent on her husband or boyfriend after being with Arianne. He wondered if tagging the men with her fragrance was a sort of subconscious revenge on Arianne's part.

Or maybe she just liked cheap perfume.

"You here to buy me breakfast?" she asked, winking at him.

"I offered yesterday."

"Ask me today," she said.

"I already ate."

She scowled at him. "I would have said no anyway. I don't eat with pigs."

Brandon ignored the jab. "I'm looking for Kaitlyn."

She crossed her arms, giving him the once over. "Seems like you're sort of obsessed with her."

"I have some of her belongings," he said.

That got her attention. "What kind of stuff?"

"Not your business, Arianne."

"Just don't hurt her, okay? We have to look out for each other. I don't care if you're a cop or whatever, you're still a man."

"If you cared about her, you'd let her get help."

Arianne considered her fingernails. "She lives her own life."

"You think you can protect her out here?"

"I've done it so far. No one's hurt her yet."

"Except when Darren Rule raped her," Brandon said.

Her dull eyes met his. She looked away.

"How long have you been on the street?" Brandon asked.

"Seven years," she said.

Since she was 15.

"What about you?" Brandon asked. "Why not be an example and show her the way?"

She slipped her hands into her coat pockets. "You don't know a thing about me."

"Tell me, then."

She glared at him. "I already had a counselor. Since I was a kid."

"Did it help?"

"Help me forget I was sold by my mother? That she let her meth-head tweaker boyfriends do whatever they wanted to me?"

"I'm sorry," Brandon said.

"Sorry for what?"

"That you had to go through that."

She scoffed, wiping a tear. "Screw you. Now you made me mess up my makeup."

Arianne considered Brandon. "I don't need your help. Neither does Kaitlyn. Just...leave her alone, okay? I know what's best for her."

Brandon set his jaw. "I can't do that."

When he looked up at her, she was staring across the street.

Brandon turned. Pastor Eddie Velasquez had just entered the pawnshop across the way.

"You know him?" Brandon asked.

She adjusted her purse strap, grasping it tight against her side.

"He's a pastor or something like that. Another type that assumes they can save everyone."

"You don't believe God cares about you, no matter what your circumstances?" Brandon asked.

She thought about it.

"I guess. Doesn't mean life turns all unicorns and fairy dust, does it?"

"Nope," he said. "But it's a start."

Chapter 25

There was an email from the crime lab waiting for him when he arrived at the office. They hadn't found any prints on the tarot card or crossbow bolt used in the attack two nights earlier. It was what he expected, but still a disappointment. They'd obtained prints from all the prime suspects in the case, and not one hit except for Phoenix, and she wasn't talking. No prints on the murder weapon or any item directly connected to the crime. They were stuck, half a dozen trails to follow and none more promising than the others.

Later that afternoon, Brandon was about to leave for a meeting with the mayor when he received a call from Jackson.

"You'll never guess who I just found," she said.

"Who?"

"David Velasquez."

"On a violation?"

"No, I was doing my beat, passing the skate park. I recognized one of the kids from somewhere, but I couldn't figure it out. Then it hit me. He's in one of the photos from Rule's motorhome."

"Which one?"

"It was a picture of him taking a bong hit."

`Brandon recalled that one. The kid had his shirt off, a bong in one hand, a lighter in the other. He'd appeared to be half-baked in the picture—a photo taken in Rule's bedroom.

"Bring him in," Brandon said.

"He's asking his dad to be there," Jackson said.

"That's fine. This time."

David wasn't a minor, so it wasn't a requirement to have a parent there. In fact, in many jurisdictions, it wouldn't be required even if he was under 18. But maybe his father's presence would help David understand the need to cooperate with the investigation.

Eddie and David occupied one side of the table, Brandon and Jackson on the other. David was almost a foot taller than his father, had long black hair that was curled and messy. He wore shorts, a t-shirt, and Vans—the same shoes skaters wore when Brandon was a kid.

After informing him of his rights and starting the recording, Brandon asked, "Do you own a baseball bat?"

David looked to his father. Eddie said, "Go ahead. You have nothing to hide."

"No," he said. "I don't play baseball."

"How well did you know Darren Rule?"

"I don't know who that is," he said.

"His stage name was Drool."

David blinked. "I don't know him."

"You've been in his motorhome," Jackson said.

"No."

Brandon opened his folder and set the photograph of David onto the table. David picked it up and studied it.

"That's you, correct?"

He shrugged.

"I'll need you to say yes or no for the recording," Brandon said.

"I guess it's me."

"And where was it taken?"

"I look pretty stoned," he said. "I probably can't remember."

Eddie touched his son's arm. "Don't be smart, David. Answer the question."

David twisted his shoulder away from Eddie. "I said I don't know, okay?"

"Okay," Jackson said. "When was it taken?"

"Must be a long time ago. I don't use anymore."

"He's on probation," his dad said.

"How long?" Brandon asked David.

"A year."

"Except Darren Rule only arrived in town a few weeks before his murder," Brandon said. "Meaning you violated your probation and there's photographic evidence right here."

Eddie sat up in his chair. "David came down here to help."

"And we appreciate that," Brandon said. He turned to David. "All we're asking for is the truth. We're not here to bust you for smoking pot a month ago."

It was a wonder he hadn't gotten busted yet, considering the mandatory drug tests required while on probation. Then again, a quick web search might lead an addict to dozens of sketchy websites offering workarounds for drug testing, from supplements and pills to using someone else's urine.

"Okay," David said. "I smoked pot with him in his trailer. But I didn't have anything to do with killing him."

"Do you know how he was killed?"

"The rumor is his eyes were stabbed out because he was a perv."

Brandon and Jackson glanced at each other. Either David had no idea how Darren Rule was murdered or he was playing dumb.

"What makes you say he was a perv?" Jackson asked.

"Just his reputation around town."

He'd developed a local reputation that quickly? That seemed unlikely to Brandon.

"Did he ever touch you or try to do anything that made you uncomfortable?"

His head jerked back. "No."

But David's eyes betrayed a darker memory.

"Your shirt is off in this photo. Why?"

He twisted his chair away from the picture. "I don't remember."

"Darren Rule had a history of taking advantage of people. And photographing them. If he did that to you, we need to know."

"Why? He's dead."

"Because there could be others he took advantage of," Brandon said.

And we need to know your motive for murder, he thought.

"It was hot in his RV, okay? That's why my shirt was off. I don't want to talk about this."

"Okay," Brandon said. "We're going to give you some information for victims if you change your mind, okay?"

Eddie's head sunk into his hands. "I can't believe this." He swiveled his head to his son. "I'm sorry, David."

"Dad, stop. Nothing happened, okay?"

David gripped the edge of the table. "You asked me about a baseball bat."

"Right," Brandon said.

"You asked me that because Drool got the shit beat out of him."

"David," his father said, reacting to his language.

"How'd you know that?" Brandon asked.

"Cory King told me."

233

"And he knew, how?"

"Because he's the one that did it. He told me Drool had raped one of his girls and he was going to make him pay."

"How do you know Cory?" Jackson asked.

"We partied a couple of times."

"With Drool?"

"No. He hangs out at the park sometimes with the girls."

"You're sure about this?" Brandon asked.

"Yes," David said, sounding surer than he had the entire interview.

"Thanks, David, and if you remember anything else, let us know."

When they'd written up the statement and passed the victim resources to Eddie and David, they met back in the bullpen.

"There's no way he would know Kaitlyn was sexually assaulted unless Darren Rule or Cory King told him," Jackson said.

"And the bruises on Drool aren't common knowledge."

"You think Cory King is our man?"

"Rule was already beaten and bruised hours before he was killed, according to the autopsy," Brandon said.

"And Hamish's description of him that night," Jackson added.

"But it doesn't mean he didn't come back later to finish the job. At the very least he had motive and now, proof of willingness to harm the victim."

Twenty minutes later, they were knocking on Cory King's hotel room door. When he didn't answer, they tried the girls' rooms and then scoured the town. Benjamin insisted Cory and the girls hadn't checked out.

Their last stop was the fair. Brandon called on Alex and his limited crew to search the area. Jackson and Brandon split up, making the rounds again.

After an hour of fruitless searching, Brandon drove by the Forks Inn again.

He spotted Kaitlyn and Arianne working the street in front of the hotel. He pulled into the parking lot. Arianne grabbed Kaitlyn's arm.

They both headed back to the hotel.

"Arianne," Brandon said, stepping from the Interceptor.

"What do you want? We're just hitching a ride to the fair."

"I need to speak with Kaitlyn. Alone."

She huffed, thought about refusing to leave, then returned to the street. They wouldn't have much luck "finding a ride" with a cop car ten feet away.

Kaitlyn stared up at him, arms crossed.

"I paid your dad a visit," Brandon said.

Surprise widened her eyes. She quickly returned to her mask of indifference.

"So?"

"I can see why you don't get along with him," Brandon said.

A smile touched her lips. "Was his girlfriend there?"

"Liz?"

She snorted. "That's a new one."

Brandon decided not to mention that her father hadn't told Liz he had a second daughter.

"Why did you go there?" she asked.

"He wouldn't return my calls."

She nodded in admiration. "You're stubborn."

"Yep."

"Did he say anything about my sister?"

"No, but I did get some of your belongings." He opened the back of the SUV, revealing the box.

"My guitar!" she said, lifting it out. She strummed the strings. "Did you get my tuner?"

He scrounged in the box and held it up. "You mentioned your journals, too."

"You found them?"

"I'm a detective," he said. "And no, I did not read them."

She searched his eyes for a moment and then, it seemed, decided he was telling the truth.

"You didn't have to do any of this."

"I wanted you to remember your life before..."

"I became a prostitute?"

Her eyes drifted to Arianne, who was watching them from the curb. A logging truck swept by, sweeping dust over the three of them.

For a moment, a youthful innocence had returned to Kaitlyn's face. Brandon imagined it was a hint of what little hope she'd had before leaving home.

The hardness returned, her jaw set against him.

She pressed the guitar into his hands.

"I don't want it."

"The guitar?"

"None of it," she said. When he didn't take the guitar, she shoved it back in the box. She paused, turning one of the stuffed animals so that it faced her. It was a white teddy bear. He'd brought it because its fur was tattered and worn as if it had been held more often than the others.

"Funny," Kaitlyn said, her voice tinged with sarcasm.

"What?"

"My mom gave that to me after she left. It was the last thing she sent. I guess it didn't take her long to feel guilty about leaving."

"If you don't have a place to store these, I can keep them," Brandon said.

"I said I don't want them," she said. "Take them back to him. Or toss them."

"I don't believe that's what you really want," Brandon said.

"How the hell would you know what I want?"

Arianne appeared at her side. "Is he harassing you, Kaitlyn?"

Brandon eyed the young woman. "Stay out of this, Arianne. Before I find a reason to lock you up for the next week."

"You see," Arianne said to Kaitlyn. "This is how pigs are. They act all nice as long as you do what they want. When that doesn't work, they threaten you."

Brandon sucked in a deep breath in an attempt to calm himself.

What had he expected? For a few trinkets from home—an unhappy home at that—to convince Kaitlyn to accept the help she so obviously needed?

"Where is Cory?" Brandon asked Arianne.

She pretended to pluck a bit of lint from her skirt. "How would I know?"

He closed the back of the SUV. "I'm keeping this at the station for safekeeping. In the meantime, I have a homicide investigation to run."

237

"What's that got to do with us?" Arianne asked.

"All three of you are suspects in the murder of Darren Rule."

Arianne cast him an indifferent glare, but the blood drained from Kaitlyn's face.

"Why?" she asked.

"While it's unfortunate what Darren Rule did to you," Brandon said, "it gives you motive for murder. Cory too, because of your relationship."

"You mean because he's her pimp?" Arianne sneered.

"I thought you said he wasn't a pimp."

She pulled her vape pen out of her purse and it fell to the ground, spilling her keychain and pepper spray out.

"You have pepper spray too?" he asked Kaitlyn.

"Lost it," she said.

"You're not her father," Arianne said.

"Does Cory have a baseball bat?" he asked.

Arianne blinked her artificial eyelashes at him. "No."

I'll take that as a yes, he thought.

"How about a crossbow?"

Kaitlyn stared back at him, confused.

"Those are expensive," Arianne said. "And hard to use. Unless you know how."

Brandon recalled his first conversation with Arianne when she mentioned growing up around Renaissance fairs.

"Your family owned a shop at one of these fairs," he said.

"So?" Arianne asked.

"Your grandfather sold weapons."

"No."

"Didn't he make that thing...what did you call it? A Yumi?" Kaitlyn asked.

Arianne's eyes blazed at her. "Shut up, Kaitlyn."

238

"What's a Yumi?" Brandon asked.

"It's an ancient Japanese bow," Arianne said.

"So he was a bowyer."

"He didn't make crossbows if that's what you mean," she said.

What it meant was that Arianne probably knew how to use one.

"You're sure you don't own a crossbow?"

"Yes, I'm sure."

"And you haven't operated one recently?"

"No," she said. "Can we go now?"

Brandon scanned the parking lot one more time. "Tell Cory I'm looking for him. The quicker he talks to me, tells me the truth, the better it will be for him. That goes for you, too."

Arianne looked away without answering.

Kaitlyn turned her back on him.

"When you want your stuff," Brandon said. "Let me know."

Brandon pulled onto Forks Ave, doing his best not to squeal his tires as he exited the parking lot. Arianne, he decided, was the most dangerous person in Kaitlyn's life. Cory King was a pimp, and because of that, a scumbag who belonged in jail. But Arianne had something Cory didn't—influence over Kaitlyn. With one phone call, Brandon could have a safe place for Kaitlyn to stay, treatment if she needed it, counseling, and even help with college if that's what she wanted. Arianne, with her own abuse history and jaded view of the world, might believe she was doing Kaitlyn a favor.

She wasn't. Instead, she was guaranteeing Kaitlyn would be on the street for at least another decade—if it didn't kill her first.

And what about the crossbow incident? Was Arianne behind the attempt on Brandon's life? That her grandfather was a bowyer didn't prove she was behind the attack. But it did raise a red flag. She'd expressed her frustration when Kaitlyn mentioned her grandfather's occupation. Why the defensiveness—especially when the attack wasn't common knowledge?

Chapter 26

On his way back to the station, Brandon checked in with Jackson. She hadn't had any luck locating Cory King.

"I did bump into Alex," she said. "He's been trying to get ahold of you."

"No one's called me."

"Your office phone," she said. "I'm at the fair now. I'll let him explain."

Brandon turned his SUV around and headed to the Renaissance fair.

He met Jackson and Alex outside the security tent.

"What's up?" Brandon asked.

Alex held up a hand. "First, just so you know, I wasn't investigating. I was having a conversation."

Brandon chuckled. "I get it. Tell me what you learned."

"I was at the pub last night," he started.

"The one here, at the fair?"

"Right. It's sort of a hangout for the performers and other staff. I ended up chatting with Hamish MacDuff. He's the blacksmith guy. Long beard..."

"We know him," Brandon said.

"A couple of pints and a few shots into the evening, he starts talking about his woman, Daisy."

"What about her?"

"Just how she's not as affectionate as she used to be. The usual."

Brandon wasn't sure where this was headed besides Hamish and Daisy needing marital therapy.

241

"Then he says he's hooked up with this prostitute."

"Oh, boy," Brandon said.

Alex caught himself. "I don't mean hooked up like that, I mean, you know, friendly acquaintances."

"So he's befriended a prostitute to *talk*?" Brandon asked.

"Right. I know."

"Where's this going, Alex? Because if you're telling me we have prostitutes in Forks, I already know that."

"He's getting there," Jackson said.

Alex continued. "Hamish said the girl kept returning to his shop. Being all nice and talkative."

"What's this girl's name?"

God, he hoped it wasn't Kaitlyn.

"Arianna, Aria, something like that."

"Arianne," Brandon said.

"Right. So one time she read his palm, claimed his love life was headed for a cliff. Next thing he knew, she offered to do a tarot card reading."

"Wait, so you're telling me Arianne Young reads tarot cards?"

"Exactly," Jackson said. "And that means—"

"She must own a deck of cards," Brandon said.

"Or stole one," Jackson said.

"And I was thinking," Alex said. "Considering the tarot card in Darren Rule's mouth..."

"And the ones used on your front door and the crossbow attack," Jackson said.

Brandon updated them on what he'd learned about Arianne's grandfather and her likely experience with a weapon like a crossbow.

"I bet she's our girl," Jackson said. "You want me to pick her up?"

"I just spoke to her half an hour ago at the Forks Inn. In fact, she was headed here." He looked to Alex. "Could you and your staff ID Arianne when she shows up?"

"Definitely. She's got a season pass."

"Keep an eye out for her. Call my cell if you spot her." He listed off his cell number.

"And good work, Alex. I appreciate this."

Jackson requested an APB for Arianne. She spoke with Josiah and he agreed to cover the town, including the restaurants and bus station.

If Arianne owned a deck of tarot cards, Brandon wanted a look at them. If they matched the card in Drool's mouth—or the ones used in the threats against Brandon—all the better.

"While we're searching for Arianne, let's have a word with Mr. MacDuff about his relationship with her," Brandon said.

It was a slow day at the fair, and Daisy and Hamish were chatting behind the weapon seller's counter.

Hamish's eyes landed on the two police officers. Daisy's followed.

"Now what?" Hamish asked.

"How are you feeling?" Brandon asked.

"Why?"

"I heard you had quite the time last night."

Daisy's eyes flew to Hamish. "What is he talking about?"

"Oh, nothing too bad," Jackson said. "Just a drink or two, or seven, at the pub."

Hamish stood, his hands too close to a display of daggers behind the counter. "Is it against the law for a man to drink?"

"No. But it is a crime to withhold evidence."

Daisy stood next to him now.

"I don't understand," Hamish said.

"We want to talk about your friend, Arianne Young," Jackson said.

Hamish chewed on his lip, his eyes wandering as if he had to think about the answer.

"Is that the little doxy that comes around here all the time?" Daisy asked.

"That's her," Jackson said.

Daisy crossed her arms. "Don't tell me you've been out with the hookers, Hamish. Because if you ever want to touch me again—"

"I haven't been with no hooker," he said, his Scottish accent thick.

"What did she tell you when she read your tarot cards?" Brandon asked.

Hamish glared at Brandon. "Who told you that?"

"You let her read your cards?" Daisy asked.

Hamish passed a hand over his beard. "It was just for fun. It didn't mean anything."

"And what did you pay her for it?" Daisy asked. "Our hard-earned money?"

"I didn't give her a dime," he said.

"She offered her services for free?" Brandon asked.

Hamish stared back at Brandon. The blacksmith's eyes betrayed a secret. Something so significant he'd held it back, despite the murder investigation.

"I can and will arrest you for obstruction of justice," Brandon said, reaching for his handcuffs. He kept his eyes on Hamish's hands and the weapons within his reach.

"Why don't you both step out here?" Brandon said, motioning Hamish away from his wares.

244

Daisy followed Hamish out of the tent.

"Okay," Hamish said, holding out two meaty hands. "I gave her a present."

Daisy sized him up. "A present. Is that what you call it?" She paused, understanding. "Wait a minute. Is that where the knife went?"

"No..."

"What knife?" Brandon asked.

"It's nothing," Hamish pleaded. "Daisy—"

"You think I'm going to jail because you can't keep your dobber in your pants?"

"I didn'tae touch her," he insisted.

Daisy turned to Jackson. "I sure know how to pick my men. First Darren, now..." she made a sweeping motion at Hamish, "This."

Jackson cast her a knowing frown.

"You asked us to check the inventory," Daisy said. "We found one knife missing. A dagger like the one you described was used to kill Darren."

"And?" Brandon asked.

"We couldn't figure out what had happened to it. At least that's what I thought." She looked askance at Hamish.

"What really happened?" Jackson asked.

"Sitting here now, after this conversation, I imagine he gave it to her as a gift."

"Why do you think that?"

"Because he'd let her handle it more than once. I told him, she's more likely to steal it than buy it."

"Did you give Arianne the dagger?" Brandon asked.

Hamish's voice cracked. "It's not a crime. I didn't know what would happen."

245

"Do you believe Arianne killed Darren Rule?" Brandon asked.

His head swiveled doubtfully. "I don't know."

"She never mentioned wanting to hurt him?" Jackson asked.

"Never."

"You'll need to come down to the station and make an official statement," Brandon said. He pointed his chin at Jackson. "The officer here will take you down."

On the way out of the fair, Jackson asked, "Where are you going?"

"To find Arianne."

She nodded. "Good luck. Don't do anything exciting without me."

He grinned. "I'm not making any promises."

Chapter 27

He was back at the Forks Inn 15 minutes later. So far, the APB hadn't turned up any sign of Arianne or Kaitlyn. The idea that Arianne could harm Kaitlyn had already crossed his mind. If, as he suspected, she had killed Darren Rule, there was nothing to prevent her from doing the same to Kaitlyn. And she was likely the same person who had aimed a crossbow bolt at Brandon's head.

He found Benjamin and asked him to open Arianne's room. After some initial resistance—valid because Brandon did not have a search warrant—Benjamin grabbed the housekeeping cart and told Brandon to follow him to Arianne's room.

He knocked on the door.

"I know the rules about the rights of our guests," he said. "I took a webinar on this exact topic."

"Good to know," Brandon said.

"So, while I want to help, I do need you to know I'm not technically allowing you into the room. And you might see that she's there, or not. But either way, you don't have a right to search the room."

Noticing Brandon's cold stare, he added, "In my opinion."

Benjamin knocked again. "Housekeeping."

Whatever it took for him to get in the room, Brandon was fine with that.

When no one answered, Benjamin opened the door. Brandon moved to follow him but Benjamin held up a hand. "This has to be real. I'm not getting sued for doing you a favor."

He grabbed a roll of toilet paper and two towels and cautiously entered.

"There's no one in here," he said.

Brandon jostled around the cart and surveyed the room. There was a backpack on the bed, dirty clothes were strewn across the floor.

"Just for the record," Benjamin said. "I didn't say you could come in here."

"Give it a rest, Benjamin," Brandon said. "And thanks for your help."

"My pleasure," he said, sarcastically. "Now what are you going to do?"

"I'm sure the other room needs cleaning too. You'd better check," Brandon said.

"What room?"

"The one belonging to Kaitlyn Gallagher."

Benjamin bit his bottom lip. "I don't like this."

"Don't think I can't get a warrant," Brandon warned him.

"Damn you."

"Be nice," Brandon said. "I'm doing you a favor."

"How exactly is that?"

"I'm saving you from dealing with a warrant and a whole department of police cars. How would that look to your customers?"

"Screw you," Benjamin said, sliding the key out of his pocket.

He knocked and, hearing no response, entered Kaitlyn's room. This time Brandon stayed in the hallway. Despite his frustration with the hotel owner, he had a point. His goal was to find Arianne. Any other evidence he found without a warrant wouldn't be usable in court.

"She's not here," Benjamin said, holding out his arms.

"Great. Thanks, Benjamin."

Benjamin closed the door and returned to Arianne's room. "I might as well clean it while I'm here. Are we done now?"

"I'll check Cory King's room," Brandon said.

"Don't ask me—"

"I'm not," Brandon said. He continued down the hallway to room 213 and knocked.

"What?" Cory King asked through the door.

Brandon stepped to one side, so King couldn't spot who was there.

"Housekeeping," Brandon said.

Down the hall, Benjamin poked his head out of Arianne's room. He frowned disapprovingly.

Brandon held a finger over his lips.

Cory opened the door. "Do you understand what do not disturb means?"

Brandon shoved his foot in the door. Cory's eyes widened as he stumbled back.

Brandon stepped into the room.

"What?"

"Where's Arianne?" Brandon asked.

"I don't know, man."

"You want to talk here or at the station?" Brandon asked.

Cory tugged on his sleeves, collecting himself.

"Here, but I don't know what you want."

"Good," Brandon said, accepting Cory's invitation.

"When's the last time you saw Kaitlyn and Arianne?"

"I don't know. Last night."

The queen-sized bed was a mess of blankets, pillows, and dirty clothes. A round cafe table near the window was

249

covered with empty beer cans. The television, on mute, was playing a mixed martial arts cage fight.

There was a side table next to the bed. Leaning against the table was a baseball bat.

Cory followed Brandon's gaze.

"Tell me again what you were doing the day Drool was murdered?"

"I was here in my room."

"You have anyone that can verify that?"

Cory's eyes wandered the room as if searching for a better answer than the truth.

"No."

"That's a nice baseball bat you got over there," he said, pointing his chin in that direction.

"Thanks."

"Mind if I take a look at it?"

"Can I say no?"

Brandon stared back at him.

"Okay, fine," Cory said.

Brandon moved over to the nightstand and kneeled next to the bat. It was wooden and had seen better days. He'd probably picked it up at a thrift store or stolen it from some kid's front yard, Brandon figured.

Touching just the tip of the handle, he twisted the bat around. There was a red smear on the head of the bat.

"You tried to wipe his blood off," Brandon said, standing. "But the thing is, Cory, this is wood. It's porous. The blood won't come out. Ever."

Cory looked as though he might faint. "I didn't kill him, I swear."

"But you did strike him with the bat?"

Cory held his hands out. "I don't want to go to jail. I've got anxiety issues. It's not a good place for me."

"Face the wall, and hands behind your back."

Cory obeyed. As Brandon was checking the young man's pockets, he said, "You know who else probably has anxiety problems, Cory?"

"Who?"

"The girls you pimp out. The young women you forced into sex trafficking."

"I don't force anyone to do anything," he said.

Cory's pockets were empty. He sat him down on the bed and called for backup. The bat was evidence and Cory would need to be booked into jail on assault charges.

"You mind if I look around?" Brandon asked.

"Yes."

"I'm trying to help you."

"Yeah, I can tell."

"Prove to me you didn't kill Drool."

"Check the room. I don't care," he said. "I don't got no knives or tarot cards or what the hell ever you're looking for."

Brandon stared down at him. "Who told you about the cards and the knife?"

"Arianne told me."

"Told you what?"

"That the dude's body had a knife down his throat and a tarot card in his mouth."

"How did she know that?"

"Damn, I don't know, okay? Probably some cop she was screwing told her."

"Not funny," Brandon said.

Cory frowned.

"Does Arianne own a set of tarot cards?" Brandon asked.

"She's always messing with that voodoo shit," Cory said. "I was raised by a God-fearing mom. I know better than to touch that black magic crap."

"Does your God-fearing mom know what you do for a living?"

"Yeah," he said. "I'm in the entertainment industry. I manage some acts."

Brandon's neck bulged. Cory's eyes widened and he looked away.

However long Cory King spent in jail, it wouldn't be long enough. The truth was, he'd spend little if any time locked up and would return to his "entertainment" job once released. Brandon had no real proof Cory had engaged in sex trafficking.

A search of the room didn't reveal anything more than Cory's personal items, marijuana paraphernalia, and a full fifth of whipped cream flavored vodka.

"You drink this crap?"

"It's good, man. Like candy."

"Where are Arianne and Kaitlyn?"

"I wasn't lying. I don't know."

"Where are they supposed to be?"

"They said they were going to the fair to hang out."

"Hang out, or work?"

"Naw, just playing around. They work at night."

"Let's go," Brandon said, hauling him off the bed.

"Can you save that bottle for me? Maybe store it in my belongings?"

"Nope."

Brandon was leading Cory down the hallway when they passed Arianne's room. Benjamin hadn't moved the cart, so he had to squeeze by. Brandon froze.

"What?" Cory asked.

"Shh."

The room was silent—too silent.

"Ben?" Brandon called out. When he didn't answer, he yanked Cory into the room with him.

There, face down on the floor, lay the hotel owner.

Chapter 28

"Is he dead?" Cory asked.

Brandon knelt down next to Benjamin. He turned him over and his eyes flickered.

"Wha..."

"What happened?" Brandon asked.

Benjamin pressed himself up on one elbow. "I was gonna change the sheets. I heard something behind me, then...they must have bonked me on the head."

"Who?"

"I don't know."

"Where did they come from?"

"I think...the bathroom."

"I thought you checked when I was standing out here."

He sat up, rubbing the back of his head. "I did, kind of."

Meaning he didn't.

"Any description at all?" Brandon asked.

"It was a blur...white. They were wearing a white hoodie. I saw in the mirror."

"You're sure it wasn't Arianne?"

He thought about it for a second. "I don't think so."

"Are you able to stand?" Brandon asked.

He stood, legs wobbly. "I'm fine."

"Still, you should get seen by a doctor, now."

"Alright."

"Let's go," he said to Cory.

Brandon exited through the hotel's side door, hoping to spot the attacker.

He contacted dispatch to warn his officers to be on the lookout for the suspect.

"What were they doing in her room?" Cory asked.

"Good question. Have any ideas?"

"No."

"You don't believe Arianne was blackmailing anyone?"

"If she was, I would know," he said confidently.

Brandon wasn't so sure about that.

"Hey!" Cory shouted. "What the hell!"

Brandon followed his eyes.

"That's my car."

Someone was inside Cory's minivan. Whether they were the attacker would be impossible to tell through the tinted windows. Brandon unclicked one of the handcuffs and attached Cory to a no-parking sign.

He updated dispatch, then ordered Cory, "Stay here."

"Like I have a choice. Hey! Make sure they don't steal my van!"

Brandon rushed to the van, but his target bolted from the opposite side, where the sliding door was already open.

"Stop! Forks Police Department."

The suspect crossed through the field adjacent to the hotel. He was headed for the forest.

Brandon raced over the clumps of dirt and tall grass. The suspect disappeared behind a shield of alders and underbrush.

A shot rang out.

Brandon's reflexes drew him to his haunches. The hooded figure peeked from behind a tree, pointed a handgun at Brandon, and fired again.

Brandon warned dispatch—shots fired. He unholstered his pistol.

The shrill call of sirens reverberated across the field.

The figure vanished into the trees.

Bent low, he pursued. To the right, the forest ended at the main highway. To the left, it stretched for miles in the direction of the foothills. He maintained his pursuit to the left, assuming that was the way the attacker would head.

After working his way through brush and thickets for 15 minutes, Brandon halted at a stream. No sign of the hooded figure. He checked in with his officers—they were scouring the area for any suspicious vehicles.

Brandon headed back to the hotel.

Jackson and two other officers met him at the edge of the forest. He waved them over. He directed the other two officers to hit the streets and ask around for any sign of a person meeting the attacker's description. If they had any hits from local businesses, ask for video footage.

"First," he said, "One of you bring me back an evidence bag and some gloves."

When they'd gone, Jackson said, "I've got Cory King in my SUV."

"Thanks." Brandon motioned for her to follow him. Finding the spot where the shooter had stood, he knelt down, moving the tall grass aside.

"Just so you know, I did request air support," Jackson said.

"And it was denied," Brandon said.

It wasn't the first time they'd requested, and been denied, a helicopter to help with a pursuit. The sheriff didn't like Brandon and, it seemed, that dislike extended to everyone within his department.

"Yep," she said. "Any idea who it was?"

"I didn't get a good look."

"You think it was Arianne?"

"I had a feeling it was a man. But it's impossible to know."

"You figured it was Arianne who shot the crossbow at you," Jackson reminded him.

"Why attack someone in her own hotel room?"

"Maybe she knew you were coming after her."

His eyes caught on what he was searching for. Two small brass shell casings.

"Looks like a .22," Jackson said.

The officer returned with the evidence bag and gloves. Handing them off, he returned to his vehicle.

Brandon slipped on the gloves and dropped the casings into the bag. A search of the area didn't reveal any other clues.

"You okay?" Jackson asked.

"I am. Again."

"So whoever it is that has it out for you has graduated from crossbows to firearms."

"Apparently," he said. "But in this case, I don't think I was being targeted. If I hadn't caught them in the act..."

"Cory told me all about what happened—in dramatic fashion. Josiah's inside getting a report from Benjamin."

"Good work," Brandon said. The rush was wearing off now and he was flooded by the inevitable adrenaline crash that followed a life-threatening event.

"You should take the rest of the day off," Jackson said.

He shook his head. "You know better than that. Whatever paperwork I had to do, it's doubled thanks to this." He motioned toward the wooded area where he'd lost the attacker. "Let's assume it wasn't Arianne who fled the room. What if it was someone searching her belongings?"

"Considering they targeted Arianne's room *and* Cory's van, that's a safe assumption," she said. "If they knew Cory's connection to the girls, they might assume what they were searching for might be in his car. But if Arianne killed Darren Rule—and that's still an *if*—why is someone searching her room?"

"It's becoming clear there's more to this case than Darren Rule's homicide," he said.

"What's the connection between the murder, the blackmail, and what happened here?" Jackson asked.

"Maybe someone believes Arianne has information that once belonged to Rule."

"Documents—or photos—we haven't found yet," Jackson said. "I'll work through the documents we do have and recheck everyone's alibis."

"Sounds good. I'll see you back at the station."

A check of Arianne's room didn't reveal anything out of the ordinary. Brandon was hoping for, but didn't find, any sign of tarot cards or a crossbow.

Brandon booked Cory into the jail for the baseball bat assault on Darren Rule and added the prostitution charges based on statements Cory had made. More than once, Cory had claimed some level of ownership of the girls, and had even given his reason for attacking Rule as "what a pimp does."

When Brandon interviewed Cory again down at the station, the pimp had again confessed to bludgeoning Rule to protect Kaitlyn.

"And earlier, you said that was because that's what pimps do, is that right?" Brandon asked him. The digital recorder was running this time, and Cory said, "No, I did it because she's my friend. I don't know anything about pimps."

Cory had grown a few brain cells on the way to the station. Now—at least for the prostitution charge—it would be Brandon's word against his.

"That's kind of you," Brandon replied. "You must really care about the girls."

Cory nodded enthusiastically. "I do. I'm like a brother to them."

Brandon shifted in his seat. He flipped the page in his notebook, signaling a topic change. "You must have been really mad at Rule for hurting Kaitlyn."

"Yeah."

"I'd be mad too. And how much money did you lose when he didn't pay you?"

"We had a deal," Cory said, eyes glazed over as he was lost in the memory of the event. "Fifty dollars if he sent business my way."

"So Darren Rule normally paid you 50 dollars for sex with Kaitlyn."

"Right."

"And how much did you charge other customers for Kaitlyn or Arianne?"

Cory rubbed his chin, still in his own head. "I mean, it depends. Sometimes 75, 100..."

Cory's eyes shot to Brandon. He'd suddenly remembered where he was.

"I didn't mean that!"

"You didn't mean to just tell me you sold the girls for sex?"

"That's entrapment, man."

"No, it's not," Brandon said. "Not even close."

He hadn't found the one piece of information he really wanted—where he could find Arianne and Kaitlyn. The key pieces of evidence linking Arianne to Darren Rule's murder were the knife and tarot card found in his mouth. As far as motive, revenge for what had happened to Kaitlyn was enough. Despite Brandon's misgivings about Arianne, she was protective of Kaitlyn—as long as Kaitlyn did what she wanted.

Cory King might be involved, but all the evidence indicated that the beating he gave Darren Rule occurred on or before the day of the murder—at least hours before he was killed. Hamish and Daisy stated they'd seen Rule bruised and beaten around midnight. Lisa had estimated the time of death at two or three in the morning.

Brandon had already called for an APB on Arianne. Now he added Kaitlyn. They might still be in town, somewhere in the wilderness around Forks (unlikely, if they were alone), or somewhere hitching a ride on Highway 101.

He met up with Jackson and Alex at the fair. There'd been no sign of the girls since the night before. Brandon updated Jackson on Cory's arrest and the baseball bat he'd found.

"You don't think Cory was involved in the murder?" Jackson asked.

"He'd already exacted his vengeance. Everything points to Arianne."

"And her friend," Jackson added.

"We don't have any evidence Kaitlyn was there," Brandon said.

"Except she was. That's where he raped her, right?"

"True, but that was earlier."

"I'm just saying, she's a suspect, Chief. Both of them could have done it."

Brandon didn't think that was the case. His gut told him Kaitlyn wasn't a killer.

He hoped to God he was right.

They agreed to keep searching the area. State Patrol would cover Highway 101 north and south of Forks, on the lookout for hitchhikers or vehicles with two women matching their description.

By evening, there was still no word of the girls' whereabouts. Brandon had filled his gas tank and made the rounds through town, out to the beaches, and all the way up to Lake Crescent and back again before heading south down to Lake Quinault. He'd covered hundreds of miles before returning to the Forks Inn, where there hadn't been any sign of the girls since morning.

He'd skipped lunch, settling for two quad shot lattes over a five-hour period, and now his intestines were exacting their revenge. He stopped by the store and, after hemming and hawing about what to eat, settled on a frozen pizza.

Stomach be damned—he didn't feel like cooking.

As he rounded the corner to his street he involuntarily pumped the brakes. There, in front of his house, was Tori's car.

Chapter 29

What was Tori doing in Forks?

Maybe she'd come to gather the clothes she'd forgotten. He considered going for a drive, hoping she would be gone by the time he returned. But he'd been driving all day and he was tired.

Brandon parked behind Tori's car.

He wasn't ready for this. Not after a day like he'd had. His stomach grumbled.

"Tell me about it," he said.

Brandon closed his eyes, took a deep breath, and pulled on the door handle. He'd tell her he didn't want to argue. He understood her situation with the ex and, no matter what, she and Brandon were Emma's parents. They would find a way to get along.

The front door was locked, and he was about to slip his key in when Tori opened the door.

"Sorry," she said. "I let myself in."

He'd given her a key when she'd decided to stay in Forks after Emma left for camp.

Brandon cast her a blank look.

"You look tired," she said, stepping aside to let him in. "Bad day?"

He grunted. "Something like that."

"Is that dinner?" She plucked the frozen pizza from the grocery bag.

"I wasn't expecting company."

Her eyes searched his face.

"I'll put this in the oven," she said. "We can talk later."

After taking a long shower—he needed a long shower but, truth be told, he was stalling—and changing, he joined Tori in the kitchen.

She had made a salad to go with the pizza.

Brandon took a seat at the table. "What brings you over to Forks?"

He thought, but didn't say, *is your boyfriend busy tonight?*

"What?" she asked.

"Nothing."

She bit her lip. "Brandon, I wanted to talk in person. Our phone call kind of went sideways..."

"Look, Tori—I'm not interested in—"

She held out a hand. "After dinner, okay?"

He knew better than to waste his time pressing the issue. She had driven more than four hours to get there. He'd let her say her piece and then she could head back to Seattle.

There was a grocery bag on the counter. Tori reached in and retrieved a bottle of Merlot. She scrounged around his utensil drawer and found a corkscrew. After pouring herself a glass, she asked, "You want some?"

"Nah," he said.

She opened the fridge and pulled out a beer. She popped the top and parked it on the table in front of him.

"You know I don't like drinking alone," she said.

Brandon smiled. "That makes one of us." He downed half the bottle in two drinks, then decided he'd better pace himself. Who knew what Tori planned to drop on him?

They made small talk about Emma, Brandon's dad, anything but their relationship.

After dinner and a couple of drinks each, they moved to the living room with Tori relaxing on the love seat, Brandon an island to himself in his recliner.

"How's it going with the case?" she asked. He'd expected her to dive right into the situation with Anthony, her boyfriend or ex-boyfriend...whatever he was.

He brought her up to date on the evidence against Arianne, and Cory King's arrest.

"No idea where she is?"

"With Kaitlyn," Brandon said.

"Did you ever hear from Kaitlyn's father?" Tori asked, curling her legs up on the love seat.

He nodded. "That's what I was doing over in Seattle the other day."

"Oh," she said.

The room swirled in silence for a moment, waiting for one of them to lead the conversation one way or another.

"He was just about like Kaitlyn described her," Brandon said.

"That's too bad."

Brandon's gaze dropped. "I don't get it."

"Not everyone is as a good a father as you are."

The idea of Kaitlyn stuck on the streets weighed on him. Too many girls in her position ended up dead or strung out.

It wasn't right.

What had he expected her to do, hop on the next bus to treatment and a warm home, undo years of feeling unloved, all because he'd gone to her house and retrieved a few journals?

"You okay?" Tori asked.

He stood. "I'm fine."

In the kitchen, he opened the fridge. He was out of beer.

"Can you bring me a glass too?" Tori said from the living room.

He poured each of them a half glass. "I bought two bottles," she said. "Just in case."

Apparently, she wasn't planning on driving home that evening.

When he returned, he handed her the glass. She scooted to one side of the loveseat, patting the cushion next to her.

"Sit here," she said. "I don't bite."

He sank into the seat and balanced his glass on the floor. He wasn't really in the mood for wine. Tori set hers down too. She rested her hand on his knee.

"You're really taking this hard."

He didn't answer her.

"Look at me, Brandon." She slid her finger under his chin. "I keep saying this because it's true. You can't save everyone."

"I know that."

"Then why are you blaming yourself?"

He never said he was blaming himself.

But she was right.

Sorrow from some unseen place swelled within his chest. Sadness for Kaitlyn and all the kids like her. Cynical and bitter like Arianne or on the way there. Somehow resigned to being used, to having their only worth wrapped up in the few minutes of physical pleasure they offered strangers. Men who couldn't care if they lived or died once they got what they'd paid for. Men who ignored that these girls were someone's daughter. That they too, had dreams, desires, hopes.

He remembered Emma dressing up as a princess, her love of fairy tales, and the happily ever after stories she imagined with her princess dolls. Maybe the same stories, the same dreams Kaitlyn had once had, too.

She wiped a tear off his cheek, and he tried to look away.

"I'm sorry," she said.

Tori leaned her head on his shoulder and they stayed there for a long time. Brandon blinked his eyes dry, his arm around Tori.

Brandon could have fallen asleep with Tori in his arms. But with time, his mind circled back to why she'd come to Forks.

He moved his arm and Tori sat up. She yawned, leaning back so that her legs rested on his.

"You want to talk about us now?" she asked.

"Isn't that why you're here?"

"Yes. And to see you. I sensed something was going on."

He wouldn't challenge her intuition.

"What I said on the phone was true," she said. "I agreed to meet with Anthony to make a clean break. I'd already spoken to him once, ending our relationship before it even started. But he wasn't giving up."

A pang of jealousy rippled through Brandon. "He wasn't taking no for an answer?"

She patted his knee. "Don't worry. He got the message."

"Good," Brandon said.

She smiled. "Do you believe me now?"

He thought about it for a minute.

"Yes, but that doesn't make everything back to normal."

"What's normal?" she asked.

"True."

"What happened between you and me, I can't explain it," Tori said.

He wondered what she meant by *happened*. Did that mean she considered it over, a mistake not to be repeated?

"So now what?" he asked.

She squeezed his hand. "What do you want?"

"Me?"

He wasn't ready to answer that question.

"I need to know where we're going with this," she said.

"Things were going fine. Until you left."

"Were they?" she asked. "Because at some point, after a few more days or weeks of having fun in the sack like it's 20 years ago, we would have been at this point, regardless. We can't go on pretending."

"I wasn't pretending," he said.

She sighed. "You know what I mean."

Brandon stared at her hand in his, their fingers interlocked. Did he want to be with her? Sure. Did it scare the hell out of him, the idea of breaking up with her again, of crashing to the earth like they had two years earlier?

Yes. And the question he couldn't answer was whether it was worth the risk. They had a friendship, a balance between them, that had kept everything going smoothly for the past year. Why upset that?

Tori searched his eyes and, finding something, she smiled.

"What?" he asked.

"I love you," she said.

He paused.

"I love you too."

They leaned into each other and kissed a deep, true, unabashed kiss.

Brandon buried his head in Tori's shoulder, breathing in the scent of her. The comfort of a dozen years of security rushed back to him, and he wondered why he'd ever let it go.

He lifted his head.

It wasn't that simple. Living in the past was impossible. But they had today.

"Do you mind if I stay here tonight?" she asked. "We don't have to—you know."

He pressed his lips in mock worry. "I *was* concerned you might be thinking about taking advantage of me."

They laughed. She leaned his forehead against hers and they kissed again.

"I'm exhausted," Tori said.

"Me too."

"We should probably turn in early."

"Great idea."

They made the short trek down the hallway, his hands around her hips, lips caressing her neck.

Out of habit, he closed and locked the door before they fell into each other.

Chapter 30

By the time he awoke the next morning, the empty spot next to him on the bed had gone cold.

Brandon sat up on the edge of the bed. The shower was on. Then, he heard her voice, the familiar alto—a tad out of tune but beautiful, nonetheless.

Brandon made breakfast—eggs sunny side up and toast.

"Thanks," Tori said, taking a seat at the kitchen table.

He drew in the sweet, berry scent of her conditioner, suddenly wishing he'd joined her in the shower.

But the relationship couldn't only be physical. Once again, they were ignoring the inevitable questions—what were they to each other, where did they go from here?

"I'm heading to Seattle today," she said.

"Oh."

"I'll be back tonight," she said. She rested her hand on his. "I promise."

He smiled weakly.

"Tori..."

"What's wrong?"

He glanced at the microwave clock. He would be late and he had more than a day's work to tackle. A shooter on the loose and Arianne, his main murder suspect, nowhere to be found. Not to mention, Kaitlyn.

"Nothing," he said. "I'll see you tonight."

She slid the egg over her toast. Her eyes smiled at him. "Good."

Jackson was waiting in his office when he arrived.

"Don't tell me I'm late," he said, "because I'm not."

She shook a finger at him. "My dad used to say if you're not ten minutes early—"

"Then you're late. My dad said the same thing. Sounds like a whole generation that needs to learn how to tell time." He motioned to her. "Come out here. I need coffee."

In the bullpen, he poured himself a cup and offered her one and she accepted.

"Any news?" he asked.

"About the shooter?" she asked. "No, but I did get a call about 20 minutes ago. Not related to the case—not directly at least."

"Okay."

"So this guy says he was fishing the Calawah River, just east of where..." she picked up her notepad, "the south fork joins the main river. He was under a bridge. I don't know, is that a fishing thing?"

"Sure," Brandon said. "But what happened?"

"He heard a car approach and then stop above him."

"It's Sitkum-Solduc road."

Brandon had fished there himself with his dad and Eli.

"He sees a splash in the water and the car drives off."

"What was it?"

"A cellphone."

"Did he get a look at the vehicle?"

"No."

"Is he going to bring the phone in?"

"That's the thing," she said. "He's in Montana."

"What?"

"This was the day after Darren Rule was murdered," she said.

"He's sure of the date?"

270

"It was the day before he left for home from his camping trip. He's sure."

"Why didn't he call then?"

"He didn't think anything of it. Apparently, he's done something similar in a fit of rage when his girlfriend broke up with him. Figured it was none of his business."

"Could he describe the phone?"

"The cover was of a naked woman."

Mrs. Blackburn, the fair's manager, had given a matching description of Darren Rule's cellphone.

"And he left it there?"

"When he noticed the woman on the cover, he had no interest in carrying around a phone with what he called a *pornographic cover*. People might think it was his."

"Good point. What changed his mind?"

"He heard about the murder from some local friends, figured maybe it was connected."

"Okay, we need to get out there."

Darren Rule's phone had been conspicuously missing from the crime scene. It had been a week and they hadn't heard back from the cellphone carrier yet. Technically, they had ten days to respond to requests. They often took longer. It was typical for the giant telecommunications companies to take their time responding to police inquiries—even those involving homicide.

The cellphone was right where the fisherman had said it would be. About ten feet from the bridge. It was nearer to the edge of the river. Whoever had dumped the phone hadn't thought to toss it in deeper water—or they had been in a hurry.

The current was slow and the morning sun reflecting off the river's smooth surface made Brandon wish he was

271

there for fishing, not to solve a murder. He slipped on a pair of gloves, made his way over moss-covered rocks, and plucked the phone out of a half-foot of water.

The screen was cracked, the battery removed. The cover, Brandon was surprised to learn, was a copy of the *Venus of Urbino* painting by the Renaissance artist Titian. He recognized the piece from an art history class he'd taken in college. Technically, yes, it was a naked woman reclining on a couch—but also a famous work of art.

He made his way back up the embankment to where Jackson waited with an evidence bag.

Jackson considered the phone cover. "Back when women with curves were considered sexy."

Brandon was about to respond that he liked curves just fine, but thought better of it. "I'll get this checked for prints."

"There might be some identifier on the phone, too. A serial number. Check with the carrier."

"What are you up to?" she asked.

They had driven separate cars to the river. Brandon already had the rest of his morning planned. "I'll start making the rounds on our main suspects. Maybe one of them will be wearing a white hoodie."

"Good luck with that."

It was a longshot, but he would question each suspect regarding their whereabouts during the shooting at the hotel, and whether any of them owned a twenty-two-caliber firearm. Sometimes the simplest questions caused a suspect to crack. A confession would be a hell of a lot easier than waiting for DNA results, repeating interviews, and getting shot at with crossbows and handguns.

"I'll start with David and Eddie Velasquez," he said.

The church was further outside of town, but he was already halfway there.

"Have fun with our local church hoodlum."

"Is that what they called you when you were a kid?" Brandon asked, recalling Jackson's father had been a pastor.

"Me? Heck no. I was the good one. It was my older brother who was the prodigal. Whenever we played cops and robbers, he wanted to be the robber."

Brandon arrived at the New Testament Church of God a little after 9:30. He wasn't sure of the church's hours but since Eddie and his son David lived on the property, he was likely to find one of them. The parking lot was empty except for a newer mini-SUV. He parked on the side of the lot next to the building that looked like an apartment complex but had once been the seminary's dorm. Towering Douglas firs populated the hillside around the lot, and a blanket of undisturbed nettles and pine cones over the pavement told him the seminary hadn't seen company in months.

He considered the church and seminary. It had the look of a once-bustling community, abandoned like a mining town after a boom. David and Eddie, its only remaining residents, pining for the good old days. In Eddie's case, possibly waiting for his wayward wife's return.

He hiked across the parking lot to the church office. Beatrice was behind her desk.

"Hello, Chief Mattson," she said. "How are you today?"

He was impressed she'd remembered his name.

"I'm hoping to talk to Eddie or David."

"Pastor Eddie hasn't been in all day," she said. "His car was gone when I arrived this morning."

"And David?"

"We don't see little David much nowadays." Her eyes searched the room as if trying to latch onto a now-forgotten memory. "It's sad, you know, what happened to that family."

"You mean David's mother leaving?"

"And with Eddie raising him all alone..." She shook her head. "I've known David since he was in diapers. Changed a few of them myself. It must be hard on the pastor. The boy is the spitting image of his mother."

"Any idea when Eddie might be back?"

"Sorry, no." Tapping her pen on her chin, she asked, "Is this about that murder case down in Forks?"

"Why do you ask?"

"That man came here one day, and God forgive me but he was the creepiest, meanest thing on two legs I've ever met."

"Who?"

"The clown, comic, whatever he was called. Tool or fool or something like that."

"Drool?"

She pointed her pen at him. "Yes! Acted like he owned the place. Demanded to talk to Pastor Eddie. Called me sweetheart one minute, then...I won't say what he called me when I didn't leap out of my chair and do what he asked that instant."

Why had Darren Rule been at the church? They knew about David's legal documents and the photograph of him smoking weed. But Eddie had denied any attempts by Rule to blackmail him.

"When was this?"

"Maybe..." she pressed her lips together. "I'm guessing two weeks ago?"

About three of four days before Darren Rule's death.

"Did he talk to Pastor Eddie?"

"Eventually, sure. And I don't know what it was they discussed, but listen to me, Pastor Eddie was upset when he left. I can only imagine what the fool said to him."

Brandon tilted his head. "He didn't tell you?"

"No, and I figured it's none of my business."

"When you see Pastor Eddie, let him know I'm looking for him," Brandon said.

"Will do, but I'm out of here in an hour." She lowered her voice conspiratorially. "It's not in the church budget to pay full-time staff. I do what I can on my own time, but you know, with my husband's illness and all..."

"I'm sure Eddie appreciates everything you do."

She perked up. "One hundred percent. He's a good man."

"I'm sure he is," Brandon said. "You have a good day, Beatrice."

He paused at the door. "One more question. Do you know anyone who wears a white hoodie?"

Her eyebrows wrinkled in confusion.

"No. Why?"

"Just wondering. Bye, now."

It seemed Darren Rule had attempted to blackmail the pastor and his son. But the court documents were public and, the way Beatrice had talked during his earlier visit, everyone knew about David's crimes and transgressions. What was there that was worth blackmailing Eddie or David?

He spent the rest of the day checking in with the main suspects in the case, asking about their whereabouts during the time of the shooting at the Forks Inn. Hamish had been at his shop during the time the attack occurred and Daisy had been performing with the Royal Equestrians Horse Troupe. Phoenix claimed she was reading fortunes in her tent and Cory had been with Brandon. That left Eddie and David Velasquez, Arianne, and—he hated to admit it—Kaitlyn.

Brandon couldn't imagine Kaitlyn shooting anyone, but he knew better than to make those sorts of assumptions.

After leaving the fair, he made the rounds through town and even checked the jail rosters for most of the coast and peninsula area for any sign of Kaitlyn or Arianne. For all he knew, they could be back in Seattle, Portland, or even California.

He had Kaitlyn's journals and other personal effects. Brandon still held out hope she'd come around. Hopefully, before she got herself hurt again, or got wrapped up in a crime where she was the perpetrator rather than the victim.

He didn't find David at the skate park and another pass by the church revealed an empty parking lot.

Before he left for home that evening, he checked in on their progress at the crime lab. They were close on the DNA—maybe a day or two away. The fingerprint evidence had been a dud so far—except for Phoenix's prints in the motorhome. He hoped they'd have better luck with Rule's cellphone.

Whoever was trying to prevent Brandon from revealing the truth about Rule's murder was being careful.

To Brandon, that meant a person willing to scheme, wait, and execute a plan—someone with patience.

The case presented more moving parts than most. Solid evidence implicating more than one suspect. Arianne possessing the murder weapon was the strongest link. Not to mention her history with tarot cards. Both of those facts, and her previous contacts with Rule, tied her to his death. But others, like David and Eddie Velasquez, had motive too—and Eddie had hidden the fact that he'd had direct contact with the victim. Hamish wasn't the least bit upset by Darren Rule's murder, and might even have been relieved by the performer's death. And it wasn't out of the realm of possibility that Hamish could have lied about giving Arianne the dagger used to kill Drool.

And then there were the documents. They'd found a handful of incriminating court filings, spreadsheets, and pictures. Any of those individuals, and maybe a dozen more they hadn't discovered yet, could be responsible for the killing.

But the killer wasn't the only one with patience. Brandon only hoped his perseverance would pay off—before someone else got hurt.

Chapter 31

Brandon arrived home around six and smiled as he noticed Tori's car parked in front of his house.

He found her in the kitchen at her laptop. She was wearing a charcoal black skirt, high heels, and a white blouse. Her sable hair hung in loose curls about her neck, her lipstick cherry red.

"Did you have court today?" he asked.

"I went into the office in the morning and had a couple of arraignments after lunch."

"You didn't have to drive all the way back here..."

She crossed her arms. "Getting tired of me already?"

"Ah, no."

"Besides, I decided to stay all done up so we could go out tonight."

He sighed.

"Are you too tired?" she asked.

"I've been driving all day, talking all day..."

Her smile dropped. "It's okay. I can pick up something—"

"No," he said. "Let's do it."

"You're sure?" She stood, wrapping her arms around him. "I'll drive."

"Is that supposed to convince me to go out with you?" He smirked.

She slapped him on the butt. "You know I'm a good driver."

"How about Giuseppe's up in Port Angeles?" Brandon asked.

Giuseppe's was the restaurant they'd gone to the night Tori had met his parents for the first time. It became their favorite stop-off on trips up to Vancouver Island, too.

Her eyebrows rose. "You sure?"

"Sure as I've ever been."

* * *

Brandon had made reservations but Giuseppe's was fairly empty even for a weeknight. They ordered a pizza, breadsticks, and Cabernet Sauvignon.

Tori had finished half her glass before the breadsticks arrived. She was obviously stressed, and whether it was about work, or something else, he wasn't sure.

He'd already decided to stick to one glass himself. During their marriage, they'd taken turns on outings—wine tasting in Oregon meant Tori could drink her fill while Brandon held back in order to be the designated driver. On the other hand, if they were lucky enough to do a brewery or distillery tour, it was Brandon's turn to let loose. Not that they'd had too many excursions with, at best, one babysitter able to cover their infrequent date nights. Brandon's parents had lived in Forks, hours away, and Tori's had moved to Arizona when Emma was seven.

While they waited, he asked Tori about her current caseload. He realized how often they'd discussed his work recently, while he'd heard little about the cases she was prosecuting. He inquired about her upcoming trials or, in most cases, plea bargains. Tori could get lost in the legal details of a case, citing case law and local court rules from memory as easily as she could recite the pledge of allegiance.

It was a side of the law cops rarely witnessed. A detective had to prep a case, take all the right steps and protections to make sure the evidence was clean and usable in court. Beyond that, and testifying, the courtroom wrangling of prosecutors and defense counsel often seemed little more than barriers to real justice.

But he knew court procedures were key to the justice process—and if he ever forgot, Tori was sure to remind him.

By the time their pizza had arrived, Brandon was half-stuffed on the soft, garlic butter breadsticks and the two dipping sauces that came with them—thick, creamy Alfredo and marinara. He did his best to put away a couple of slices of the pepperoni and mushroom pizza before they both decided they would need a to-go box.

When they'd finished eating, Brandon ordered a coffee. He set it in front of him, considering Tori.

"What?" she asked, smiling back at him.

"It's been nice. You and me."

"It has," she said, not looking up from her glass.

"But I wonder. Where is this going? Where are *we* going?"

Her eyes rose to meet his. "I think...I don't know, Brandon."

"How much longer can we keep doing this?"

"You mean enjoying each other's company?"

Just that morning she'd been asking the same question. Now she seemed reluctant to answer.

"Making love, playing house," he said a little too loudly as the waiter approached.

"Will there be anything else?" he asked.

"No, we're fine," Brandon said.

When the waiter had left, Tori said, "I like things the way they are."

Did she mean the way things were before two weeks ago—or after?

"In less than a year, Emma is going to graduate," Brandon said. "She'll be off to college. Even now, technically, she's old enough to drive herself to Seattle for her days with you. That means you and I don't have reason to see each other."

She rose a critical eyebrow. "Really?"

"I didn't mean it like that," he said.

"Maybe I'm wondering the same thing," she said, her tongue loosened by the wine. "Can I trust you to be there if we get back together?"

"What's that supposed to mean?"

And what did she mean by trust? She was the one that had a boyfriend—last week.

"Are you willing to put our relationship above your career?" She placed her hands on the table, carefully considering her next words. "Brandon, you've always been a great father. Always been there for Emma, no matter what."

"But not there for you," he said.

The truthfulness of the words stung him as soon as they left his mouth.

It wasn't the first time she'd criticized Brandon about his dedication to their relationship. It was the first time she'd done so in the context of his relationship with Emma.

She stared back at him and he suddenly had an urge to defend himself. Who was Tori to talk about career versus family? If she wanted to compare who brought work home more often, that wasn't an argument he would lose.

The difference was that Tori's consisted of files and piles of court documents. As a homicide detective, Brandon's daily baggage was less tangible—yet more damaging.

"I don't want to argue," she said.

"Me, either."

He rested his hand on hers.

"Can't we take this one step at a time?" Tori asked.

It wasn't what he wanted to hear. But he'd learned long ago that other people didn't always follow neat, well-planned paths in life. Neither did he, for that matter. But it sure as hell would make life a lot easier if they did.

Maybe it was the fact that she was heading home in two days. Her vacation was over, and they were as unsure about each other as the day Emma left for camp.

"I get it," he said, "we can't just pretend like we're still married."

She brushed her thumb over his. "We can, in some ways."

"Maybe. Don't get me wrong. It's been great. But I'm not the kind of guy to hop into bed with anyone..."

"I'm not just anyone."

He shrugged. "True."

Brandon's work phone buzzed. The vibration startled him out of his reverie—and his plans for the rest of the evening.

"This is Mattson."

"Chief, this is Officer Dennison."

Dennison was a reserve officer covering swing shift.

"What's up?"

"We got a situation I thought you might want to know about."

"Go ahead."

"Someone called in a shooting a few miles out on La Push Road. The homeowners found a dying woman on their front porch."

"Who?"

"No ID yet. Officer Carlsen said she recognized her as one of the prostitutes with that guy Cory King."

"Which one?" Brandon asked, his heart racing now. He wasn't sure he wanted to hear the answer.

"I'm not sure, sir. The medics transported her to the hospital. I'm there now."

"What's her condition?"

"The doctor said she passed away on the way in. She'd lost a lot of blood."

"Okay. I'm not in town. I'll be there in a little over an hour."

"Carlsen is at the house where they found her. The owner is a man named John Guthrie. Carlsen has secured the scene. I called in Jackson to help too."

"Got it."

He ended the call.

"What's wrong?"

"One of the girls was shot."

"You mean Kaitlyn?"

"I don't know," he said, the frustration seeping from his voice. "Let's go."

Chapter 32

He sped down Highway 101, barely slowing at Lake Crescent and the twisting lakeside gauntlet that passed for a road. After passing a logging truck and two tractor-trailers, he was on a clear path to town.

Tori was silent most of the way, leaving Brandon to his own thoughts and questions he didn't have the answer to. Who was the victim? Who would want to kill her? Was it the same shooter who'd targeted Brandon at the hotel?

And what was she doing way out on La Push Road—on someone's doorstep?

Dennison was waiting for Brandon at the Forks Community Hospital Emergency Department. Dennison started his report but Brandon interrupted, asking to speak to the doctor who'd handled the patient.

Dr. Wilcox recognized Brandon from the First Baptist Church where the thirty-something attended with his family.

"Chief," he said, shaking Brandon's hand.

"Where's the girl?"

"She's already passed," Dr. Wilcox said, looking to Dennison. "I thought you knew."

"I need to view the body." Then, he added, "This is part of a larger homicide investigation, and it appears she may be a victim of the same killer."

The doctor nodded.

"I'll be out here," Tori said, motioning to the cluster of chairs in the waiting area.

"Dennison," Brandon said, "give Tori a lift home, then go check on the crime scene. My place is on the way. Ask

Jackson if she needs any help." He turned Tori. "I'll be home late. It's going to be a long night."

Dr. Wilcox led Brandon through the hospital's sterile hallways. Under the blinding light, Brandon blinked through the heartbeat-rhythm speckles that blurred his vision.

God, please don't let it be Kaitlyn.

He had a ridiculous thought. What would he do with her belongings? The journals, the guitar, the teddy bear.

What a stupid question, he thought. A girl had just lost her life, her dreams, her hopes. Gone, forever.

The doctor opened the door to the morgue.

Lisa Shipley glanced up at him, matter-of-fact, before returning her focus to the body.

"This is a first," she said. "Getting a chance to examine a corpse before you arrive."

Brandon stepped forward, eyes drawn to the dead woman's face.

He blinked, his mind needing a second to make sure it really was her.

There, on the table, was the blood-stained body of Arianne Young.

He suppressed a rising tide of relief fueled by grief.

Lisa was studying the gunshot wound. She held still, then considered Brandon. "You okay?"

Brandon swallowed. "Yeah. Fine."

"You knew her?" she asked.

"No."

Her eyes studied his face knowingly. Something was wrong, she understood that much.

"Cardiac arrest due to a single gunshot wound," Dr. Wilcox said in a clinical tone. "She never made it here alive." He shook his head. "So young."

The doctor seemed to take their silence to mean they wanted professional privacy. "I'd better get back to the floor," he said.

"Thanks, doc."

Brandon considered the heart tattoo just above Arianne's sternum with the name Sam in cursive. He wondered who Sam was. A boyfriend? A child? Her left breast had been punctured by the bullet. Blood stained her chest and abdomen.

On her arms, calves, and ankles, tattoos covered her smooth, almond-colored skin. The tattoos pictured flowers, butterflies, the usual. He studied her face. Even in death, her lips held a smart-aleck pose. Not a smile or frown. Something in between. It was an *I know something you don't know* look.

Did Arianne know too much?

"Any other wounds?" Brandon asked.

"One entrance wound. No exit."

"A twenty-two-caliber," Brandon said.

"We'll see. I don't want to guess."

"It is," he said.

She stared back at him, confused.

"Someone shot at me yesterday," he said. "With a twenty-two-caliber pistol."

The small-caliber bullet made up for its size by butchering a victim's insides as it bounced around the body.

"Why didn't you tell me?" Lisa asked.

Calling Lisa hadn't come to mind. Did she mean because it might be connected to the ongoing homicide investigation?

Because he couldn't think of anything else to say, he said, "Sorry."

"I do care about you, you know," she said. "Just because we're not together doesn't mean..."

"I get it," he said. "You're right. I should have called."

"You'll want to check the shirt. It's in the bag there." She motioned to the wall. "Gloves over there."

After donning the gloves, he retrieved a bra, cami, and a powder blue San Diego Chargers sweatshirt out of a plastic hospital bag. He studied the sweatshirt, checking for telltale signs from the gunshot blast. A charred tear marred the fabric where the bullet had penetrated. Powder residue surrounded the hole.

"Had to be close range," Brandon said.

"And at a downward angle by the look of the wound. I can't be sure yet."

"So the killer might have been much taller—or there was some sort of struggle."

Brandon turned the sweatshirt over. Dust and a few strands and seeds of oat grass coated the back. That might tell him something about where she'd been killed.

"We'll get any DNA from under her fingernails, check for sexual assault, the usual."

He placed the clothing back in the bag. "I take it crime scene techs are on their way."

"They should be when they wrap up at the house where the shooting occurred."

It reminded Brandon that he needed to get out to the scene.

Lisa wrapped Arianne's left hand in a paper bag. She passed a bag to Brandon and he did the same with her right. The bag would preserve any DNA evidence on her hands and under her fingernails.

"I'll get you a report by tomorrow. Noon or maybe sooner," she said.

"Thanks, Lisa."

He tossed his gloves in the garbage.

"Any idea who to notify?" she asked.

"I know she's from Salem. That's it. I'll send over the address I have."

He was about to leave but she was still reading him.

"Brandon," she said, "I'm not getting all in your business, okay? But you don't look good."

He considered lying, making something up about the investigation or stress at work. Instead, he said, "You know. It's just hard sometimes. When you watch these kids throw their lives away. She's barely older than Emma."

Lisa's hands fell to her sides. "I'm sorry, Brandon. I could sense you were close to her..."

"It's not her. Another girl—Kaitlyn. She's still missing. I even went to see her father and tried to convince him to reconnect with her."

"What happened?"

"Nothing. That's the problem."

"I bet just knowing someone cares makes a difference to her."

"That's not what she said."

She tilted her head, twisting her lips into a wry smile. "And since when do adolescents say what they really mean?"

He smiled, grateful for the encouragement. "Right."

"I'm here if you need a friend to talk to," she said, spreading the sheet over Arianne's lifeless form.

"I know," he said.

Chapter 33

Brandon contacted an officer to give him a ride to the station to pick up his SUV, then headed out to the Guthrie place.

The property was a few miles outside of town, on La Push Road, the main route between Forks and the Quileute reservation. Thick forest hedged the shoulder, with an occasional dark driveway leading to hidden homes or, in some cases, access to the two winding rivers that framed the highway—the Sol Duc to the north and the Bogachiel to the south.

Brandon found the entrance to the property, a narrow dirt lane that led north of the road. After about 500 feet it opened into a clearing, where to the left a 1970s rambler sat on a rise above the lane. Straight ahead, the path continued deeper into the forest.

Jackson was parked in front of the Guthrie house.

She stepped out of her SUV.

"What did you learn?" Brandon asked.

"I took a statement from the owners. I figured the sooner the better."

"That's fine," he said.

"Weird as hell," she said. "Apparently, the family here was watching television. All of a sudden they hear a crash. The husband goes to check and there's a rock on his front room floor."

"The techs get that?"

"Yeah, come and gone. They tried to print the rock. Nothing. But maybe they'll have more luck in the lab.

Anyway, Mr. Guthrie gets his Smith and Wesson and comes out to confront whoever just tossed a rock through his window. That's when he stumbled over our young lady."

"Did she say anything?"

Jackson pursed her lips. "She was out before she was dropped here."

"So the murder occurred somewhere else," Brandon said.

"They didn't hear any gunshots."

It wouldn't be the first time someone hadn't heard a gunshot, especially a smaller caliber weapon like a .22.

"They didn't see anything?"

"After grabbing his gun and almost tripping over the body on his way out the door? Not much. They did notice a car's brake lights up the path here."

"So it was headed to the main road."

"Right. But no description."

The reason the shooter had hurled a rock through the window was obvious.

"They wanted to get the homeowner's attention—and get Arianne help."

"Yeah, like they'd regretted what they'd done," she said.

"Or it was an accident."

Brandon studied the dirt lane. The area in front of the home and across the way had been mowed recently. None of the tall oat grass he'd found on Arianne's sweatshirt. The road continued back into the forest.

He pointed his chin in that direction. "You check up there yet?"

"We can do it now," she said.

She moved to get back in her SUV. He waved to her. "Let's walk. I don't want to miss anything."

Flashlights out, they followed the dirt lane down into a grove of alders and maples. It helped that the moon was three-quarters full. And there was minimal cloud cover, unusual for June.

Not far from the house, oat grass hedged the road on both sides.

"Keep your eyes on the edge."

A faint set of tire tracks marked the dust, but grass had grown over the path in most places.

The road ended suddenly at a wall of evergreens. Off to the left, a John Deere rested in an area of the forest that had been clear cut.

"Looks like someone is preparing to build out here."

"You know who owns this?" he asked. "I mean, do the Guthries?"

"They said this is all their property."

"And they didn't notice a car driving past their house at night?"

"The first they noticed was the rock through the window."

That was surprising. Most people out there got up and checked if anyone came within a country block of their home. Strangers weren't the norm and were certainly not to be trusted. In this case, they were right.

"Probably watching television. I imagine the volume was up."

"So you're saying they're older."

"How much do you want to bet they were watching *Wheel of Fortune*?" she asked.

"Too late for that. It comes on at seven."

She shook her head. "Man, you are getting old."

"Funny." He set the evidence kit down. "Okay, let's spread out. See what we can find. And avoid the tire tracks if you can. Maybe we can get an impression."

Unfortunately, gravel had been added at some point, probably in preparation for the heavy equipment that would be needed to level the clearing.

Brandon swept his light over the circular area. Finding nothing interesting, he crossed to the tall grass at the edge of the road.

A spotted owl hooted from the nearby forest. The quick cadence of the bird's call reminded him of the bold yapping of a miniature dog. His flashlight halted over a swath of grass that had been pressed down as if someone had recently traveled through. He kneeled, avoiding the flattened area. Three splotches of blood stained the trampled grass.

He stood and, circling the spot, stepped further away from the road to check for more evidence. Something rustled near his boot. Instinctively, he jerked away. Shining his light, he watched a garter snake slither away. He kept his light on the reptile's glimmering scales as it sunk into the deeper undergrowth.

He held his light on the spot where the snake had disappeared.

Brandon approached, light fixed on a glint that had caught his attention.

A makeup mirror. Next to the mirror was a tube of lipstick, a woman's wallet, and...he stepped closer. A purse.

Jackson's voice startled him. "I struck the jackpot, Chief."

He turned his head. "Oh yeah?"

Jackson had followed him over, probably curious about what he had discovered. She was at the edge of the road.

"I found a shell casing," she said.

He grinned to himself. "Always trying to one-up me. Don't walk in any further."

Her voice turned wary. "What did you find?"

"Not much. Just a treasure trove of evidence."

"Shut up."

"Toss the casing in a bag and we'll check what we've got over here," he said.

Brandon retrieved the evidence kit and a pair of gloves. He snapped photos of the blood-stained grass, then moved to the purse and its contents as he'd discovered them. Jackson worked on collecting the blood—it was the only biological evidence they'd found—while Brandon secured the purse and its contents.

As they were heading back to the road, Jackson froze.

"What is it?" Brandon asked.

Jackson lifted her foot. "I stepped on something."

She bent down and searched with her flashlight. A moment later she retrieved a key chain. Attached to it was a pepper spray container.

Jackson held it out in front of her flashlight. "It's not in the safety position."

"Arianne used it?"

"Looks like it to me," she said, holding it to her nose. "Has that smell, too. What's in the purse?"

"We'll take it back to the vehicle for a look."

Ten minutes later, they had popped the Interceptor's hatch and laid out the evidence. Inside the purse, Brandon found a roll of condoms, a vape pen, a pair of leather gloves, and a lighter. Reaching deeper in the purse, his

294

hand grasped something hard and cool. He retrieved a long, thin knife.

"How much you want to bet that's serrated?" Jackson said.

Brandon opened the knife. The serrated edge glinted under the SUV's weak light.

It was the blade that had formed Darren Rule's ghastly, ragged death smile.

"Wait a minute," Jackson said. She reached for the purse. "There's something in the side pocket."

She unzipped the pouch and discovered a deck of tarot cards.

The design matched the one pinned to Brandon's home, and in the crossbow attack.

"Phoenix's missing deck," Jackson said.

"Anything else in there?"

He was hoping they'd find a deck matching the card stuffed into Drool's mouth.

"Nope."

"You know what's missing?" Jackson asked.

"The cellphone, just like with Rule," Brandon said. "Whoever killed her probably tossed it, too."

"And I doubt this time some random fisherman is going to find it for us."

They would have to follow up on the phone. Someone—maybe Cory King—might know her number and they could figure out the carrier.

Jackson pointed to the gloves. "I'll bet that's how she avoided getting prints on the cards."

"Arianne said she'd grown up around Renaissance fairs. Remember—her grandfather was a bowyer."

"So she'd know all about crossbows."

"We've got a connection to the attacks on you," she said, holding up the deck of cards. "And the knife connects her to Darren Rule's murder."

He had no doubt Drool's DNA would be on the serrated edge. The probable murder weapon, the tarot cards, and her connection to the murder weapon would have been enough to charge her, had she survived.

"Assuming no one planted these on her."

"You believe that?" she asked.

"It's possible," he said. "What I'm still not sure about is the motive—why would Arianne want to kill Drool?"

"Wasn't she close with Kaitlyn?"

"Close? I don't know. Protective, in a sort of controlling way, yes."

"Rule did rape Kaitlyn. Maybe it was revenge."

He'd thought about that, and it made as much sense as anything else.

"Chief, there's a high probability Kaitlyn is involved in this."

"You mean she killed the person who you just said protected her from Rule, or at least got him back...."

"Maybe they were both involved in the murder and Arianne got cold feet."

Brandon didn't imagine Arianne as the type to get cold feet about anything.

"It doesn't fit."

"Doesn't fit the facts, or doesn't fit what you want to be true?"

Brandon resecured the contents of the purse back into the evidence bag.

"We'll need this checked right away. Prints, DNA..."

"Go ahead, ignore my question," she said.

He eyed her. "I heard what you said, loud and clear. Do we need to locate Kaitlyn? I want that more than anyone. But for her own protection, not because I believe she killed Arianne."

"Then who?"

"That's what we need to find out."

Brandon did his best to get an impression of the tire tracks they'd found. The area didn't produce anything like a clear shoe imprint. And the front of the house where Arianne had been dropped off had been trampled over by the EMTs and the initial police response.

They prepared to head back to the station.

"That casing was a good find," he said to Jackson. "The pepper spray too."

He shouldn't have snapped at her. Had their roles been reversed, he'd probably have the same concerns about giving Kaitlyn a pass.

"The question is," she said, "why toss the purse aside?"

"Killers don't always think things through," he said.

"Or maybe the pepper spray was what he or she was really trying to hide."

"Meaning," he said, "somewhere out there is a killer with pepper spray burns on their face."

* * *

Back at the station, he helped Jackson inventory the evidence they'd found at the crime scene.

"Were you on tonight—before patrol called you in?" he asked Jackson.

"I was at home. It was supposed to be a date night with my husband."

"Must have been quick," he said, "if you were home by eight."

"It was a stay-at-home date. The kids are at his mom's. Just the two of us..."

"Tell him I'm sorry."

"I'm sure that will make him feel better," she said, bitterly. "Anyway, he's probably already asleep."

"I'll take the evidence up to Port Angeles," he said.

"I can do it. It's no big deal."

"Get out of here. I'll do the detailed report, too."

"You sure?"

He waved a hand at her. "Go. Tomorrow's a busy day."

"It's my day off."

"*Was* your day off..."

She clicked her tongue. "If I have to come in with a hangover, it's your fault."

It was 2 a.m. by the time he'd delivered the evidence to the lab up in Port Angeles. After waking the night tech and completing the chain of evidence paperwork, he headed home.

He'd sent Lisa the last address he had for Arianne and a copy of her identification. Brandon did a search for the location and it appeared to be a duplex. It was likely that Arianne, like Kaitlyn, had little contact with her family.

Jackson's statement about Kaitlyn had wormed its way into his brain in the hours since they'd left the crime scene. What if she had killed Arianne? And it wasn't out of the realm of possibility that she'd been involved in Darren Rule's death, too. He imagined the case in court.

The evidence against Arianne was compelling—the cards, both knives, her hatred for the drunken rapist.

The defense's strategy would be to cast doubt on those connections. Wasn't Arianne a victim herself? Wouldn't the real killer want to get the police on the wrong scent—by planting the knife and tarot cards on Arianne?

That didn't change the fact that Hamish had admitted to giving Arianne the knife used to murder Darren Rule.

Unless Hamish was lying, too. What if he'd killed Rule with the dagger and then claimed to have given it to Arianne? Brandon had never had the chance to ask her about Hamish's statement.

And then there was Phoenix. Her cards were found on Brandon's door and on the crossbow bolt. Was she really stupid enough to use her own cards in the attack? And her cards didn't match the one with Rule.

This case was far from over.

In the morning, they would have to reinterview everyone, get alibis, and reconsider motives.

Chapter 34

It seemed he'd just shut his eyes when his alarm buzzed him awake. He'd set it for six, hoping to get to the station before everyone else and strategize for the day's work.

He spent the morning updating the case summary on the whiteboard in his office. When he heard Jackson and Josiah arrive, he lugged the board out to the bullpen, setting it atop a filing cabinet.

"You feeling okay?" he asked Jackson, recalling her comment about a hangover the night before.

After a moment of confusion, she answered, "Oh, that? I dozed off soon as I got home. Like I figured, Peter was asleep."

Josiah and Jackson migrated to the table.

Jackson updated Josiah on the evening's events while Brandon finished making notes on the whiteboard.

"Today we reinterview each suspect," he said. "We need to know where they were last night between say, 7:30 and 8:30."

"You hear back about time of death?" Jackson asked.

"Not yet. This is based on the time of the call and that EMS was able to revive her briefly. The attack couldn't have been long before the killer tossed the rock through the Guthrie's window."

"Especially since it seems they were trying to get her help."

"Right."

"Who's our main suspect?"

Jackson looked from Josiah to Brandon. She waited for Brandon to respond.

"Jackson feels strongly that Kaitlyn may be involved," he said.

"She was closest to the victim, and we're not sure of Kaitlyn's involvement in the original murder."

"And we have to consider all suspects equally based on the evidence." He pointed to the board.

"Hamish had plenty of reason to kill Darren Rule."

"Wait," Josiah said, "I thought Arianne killed him."

"Possibly," Brandon said. "Even probably, but listen. Hamish had motive, argued with Rule, even made the knife that killed him. Yes, he claimed he gave the knife to Arianne. The question is, what motive might he have for killing her?"

"Revenge for using the knife to kill Rule. For dragging him into this," Josiah said.

Brandon wrote *revenge* under Hamish's name. He was doubtful about the connection, but they weren't ready to rule out any suspects.

"Same for his wife, Daisy."

"Right," Brandon said. "considering her reaction when she found out Hamish had a thing for Arianne."

"What about Phoenix?" Josiah asked. "Her cards matched the one on your door and in the crossbow attack."

"Phoenix claimed her cards were stolen the moment we asked her about them," Jackson said.

"Meaning Arianne hoped to pin Drool's murder on Phoenix," Brandon said.

"Phoenix didn't help herself by lying about being in Rule's room," Jackson said.

"What if Phoenix was behind the tarot cards all along?" Josiah asked.

"Why would she use her own cards? She would only incriminate herself," Jackson said.

"That's what I mean," Josiah countered. "She was trying to make it appear Arianne was setting her up, but all along Phoenix really was the killer."

"That's a bit complicated," Brandon said. "And it doesn't consider the knife angle. Especially the dagger."

"Still," Josiah said. "Why lie about being in Darren Rule's motorhome, then?"

"That's a question we'll have to ask her—again."

Brandon shifted to the next suspect, Cory. "Mr. King was in custody at the time of the murder, and when I was shot at."

"That doesn't rule him out from involvement in Rule's murder," Jackson said.

"True, and we'll need to interview him, too."

"Does he know Arianne is dead?" Josiah asked.

"I'll let him know today."

"What about David Velasquez?" Josiah asked.

"Definitely still in the running," Brandon said. "And his father."

"A pastor murdering a prostitute," Jackson said. "Doubtful, but okay."

"We know Rule visited Eddie Velasquez. Most likely something to do with blackmail. And I haven't been able to get ahold of either of them for the last two days."

"Blackmail for what?" Jackson asked. "Everyone knows his kid was in trouble."

"Not sure. Maybe there's more to the story."

"And there's still no sign of Kaitlyn?" Josiah asked.

"I assumed she was with Arianne," Brandon said.

If that were true, she might be dead too. Or, if Jackson was right, on the run after killing Arianne.

"Did you try calling her dad?" Josiah asked.

"Good idea," Brandon said. He popped the cap back on the marker. He looked to Jackson. "Any news about the phone we found in the river?"

"I have a call into a supervisor. I'm supposed to hear back today—if it is Rule's phone, we'll need the techies to work on hacking in. Still waiting for the prints."

"Both of you keep asking questions at the fair. Focus on Hamish and Daisy, then Phoenix. Press them hard. One of them might be the killer. Any sign of a crack in their alibis, let me know. I'm going to take a trip up to Pastor Eddie's church, talk to Cory, and work on locating Kaitlyn.

The church parking lot was empty again, and when he checked the office, the lights were off. He'd brought his casebook along and, finding Eddie's cell number, gave him a call. It went to voicemail.

Brandon was beginning to suspect Eddie was avoiding him. He wondered if Beatrice had mentioned to Eddie that she'd let Brandon know about the visit from Darren Rule.

On a hunch, Brandon crossed to the main entrance to the church and tried the doors.

They opened. He checked the sanctuary and, finding it abandoned, headed back to Eddie's office. It, too, was empty.

Brandon considered the shelves of Bibles, sermon books, and commentaries. He wondered if Eddie had read all those books.

He was about to leave when he had an idea.

He parked himself on the edge of the desk and used Eddie's office phone to call the pastor's cell.

Eddie answered. "Beatrice?"

"Eddie, why won't you answer my calls?"

"Who is this?"

"Chief Mattson from the Forks Police Department."

"Oh, hi, Chief."

"I've been trying to get ahold of you."

"Is something wrong? Is David alright?"

"I was hoping you could tell me," Brandon said.

"David is supposed to be at home. He's probably sleeping."

"You mind coming down to the station, Pastor? I have a few follow-up questions from our talk the other day."

"I'm out of town at a convention," Eddie said. "I plan on returning this evening."

"Okay," Brandon said. If Pastor Eddie was at a convention, that would be his alibi, but what about David?

"You said David's been at home. Does that include last night?"

"I'm sure he was," Eddie said.

"I'll need to talk to him."

"What's this about, Chief? You still haven't told me."

"Arianne Young was murdered last night."

There was a long pause. "I'm sorry to hear that. But I don't know who that is."

"She was a victim of sex trafficking. There could be a link to Darren Rule's murder."

"What does this have to do with David?"

"That's what I want to find out," Brandon said, intentionally vague.

"Okay, but I'm sure it doesn't have anything to do with him, just like the other murder."

"Speaking of Darren Rule," Brandon said, "I heard he paid you a visit."

Another pause, then, "Who told you that?"

"Beatrice."

"I didn't want to say anything."

"Why not?" Brandon stood, twisting the phone around so he could take in the rest of the room. On the far wall hung a diploma and a framed ordination certificate. On one of the bookshelves rested a "World's Best Dad" mug. Next to it, a photo of Eddie and a woman—likely his ex-wife—posing for a family photo with a newborn.

"He wanted money," Eddie said.

"For?"

"Something about David's court files. And the pictures you showed David. He was embarrassed by what people would think."

"How much did he ask for?" Brandon asked.

"Ten thousand dollars."

Ten thousand? For a picture and some public court documents?

"He must have known you didn't have that sort of money."

"I don't know what he thought. Maybe he figured I'd take it from the church."

"Did you?"

"Of course not," he answered.

"Alright, call me as soon as you're back in town. I'll need an official statement. And I still need to talk to David. The longer you both delay this, the worse it will be for him."

Brandon hung up the phone and made his way out to the car.

He hesitated in the parking lot, turning his head.

There was music coming from one of the apartments. He followed the deep thump of bass notes to the far end of the building. Suddenly, the thumping faded, leaving the air void except for the distant call of a small songbird.

Brandon held still, listening. It was impossible to tell from which of the units the sound had come.

He knocked on the doors of the last two apartments on the bottom and top floors, alert for any sound of movement. Whoever it was had hunkered down and would not make a peep until he left. He'd bet a thousand bucks it was David—and that he'd spotted Brandon in the parking lot.

Back in his car, he watched the curtains in his rearview mirror.

A few minutes later, he left empty-handed.

Brandon headed back to the station to interview Cory King. The pimp might have an idea about who killed Arianne or at least where they might find Kaitlyn. He'd denied any knowledge of the girls' whereabouts, but that was before Arianne's murder.

Before talking to Cory, Brandon stopped by his office and made a call he'd been putting off.

He dialed the number to Kaitlyn's father.

"Hello?"

It was Liz. Apparently, learning Gary was a deadbeat dad hadn't been reason enough to dump the real estate mogul.

"This is Chief Mattson from Forks PD."

"Oh, hi. I remember you."

A slight slur in her voice made Brandon wonder if she'd been hitting the Pinot a little early.

"I was hoping to speak to Gary."

"I hope you're not going to tell me Gary has *another* child I don't know about," she twittered.

"No," he said. "Is Gary there or not?"

"Hold your horses. I'll get him."

A minute later, Gary got on the line.

"Hello."

"This is Chief Mattson."

"What?" Gary held the phone away. "You told me it was a client."

Liz snickered. "Just talk to him."

"I filed a complaint about you," Gary said.

"I'm sorry to hear about that," Brandon lied. "Have you heard from Kaitlyn?"

"No. Not even a thank you after I allowed you to bring her some of her belongings."

"Why would she thank you?" Brandon asked. "It was my idea."

"The point is, I sent her those things as a peace offering."

"You didn't *send* her anything. In fact, you made it clear you wanted nothing to do with her," Brandon said.

"It doesn't matter. She's chosen her path in life. You're wasting your time with her."

"If you hear from Kaitlyn at all, you need to contact me."

"Why? What has she done now?"

"She's missing. I'm concerned she may have been harmed. Or worse," Brandon said.

After a moment, Gary said, "Fine. Although I still say you're wasting your time."

Brandon slammed the phone down.

"Piece of—"

His cellphone buzzed. It was Tori.

"What's up?" he asked.

"Just checking in."

"I'm in the middle of this case. Sorry we didn't get to finish talking last night."

"You don't sound good," she said.

He realized his hands were shaking, his breath shallow after the call with Kaitlyn's father.

"There are a thousand moving parts to this case. And we need to locate Kaitlyn."

"Is there anything I can do?" she asked.

He could use her help.

"You mind checking around for any sign of Kaitlyn? Hospitals, homeless shelters, anyone who will talk to you."

He'd already done a sweep of the local jails, but it wouldn't hurt to widen the search.

"I'm on it," she said.

A few minutes later, Tori texted him: *Send me a picture of Kaitlyn.*

He found the picture of Kaitlyn on the State Patrol's missing person website. They hadn't taken it down yet. He sent the link to Tori.

Brandon met with Cory in the jail interview room.

"You letting me out now?" Cory asked.

"Not anytime soon."

Cory twisted on the bench. He was in an orange jail jumpsuit and had been handcuffed to the table.

"So what if I beat the hell out of that bastard? He was a rapist, right?"

And what did that make Cory, selling girls for profit?

Brandon wasn't going to go there, though. He'd sent the charging papers up to the prosecuting attorney—assault and promoting prostitution. His only interest in Cory King at this point was his assistance in finding Kaitlyn and solving Arianne's murder.

Brandon got to the point.

"Arianne was murdered last night."

Cory stared at Brandon for a long time, as if determining whether to believe him.

He balled his hand into a fist and pounded it on the table. "Shit!"

Brandon leaned back in his chair. Was this grief, or anger at losing one of his moneymakers?

"I need you to tell me who might have done this," Brandon said.

Cory massaged the side of his head. "I don't know."

"All the time you spent with the girls and neither one mentioned being threatened?"

"Just the usual creeper every once in a while who wanted to do something freaky."

"Did they mention any names?"

"No."

Brandon drummed his fingers on the table. Cory either wasn't capable of being helpful or was choosing not to be.

"You knew Arianne killed Drool," he said.

Cory's eyes widened. "What?"

"She never told you?" Brandon asked.

He waved a hand at Brandon. "Hell no. I don't know about no murder bullshit. I'm a pimp, not a killer."

He studied Cory's eyes. He was telling the truth.

"Okay," Brandon said. "Where would Kaitlyn go if she were to run?"

"You mean you haven't let her get killed yet?"

Brandon leaned forward. "What's that supposed to mean?"

"If I wasn't in here, I could have protected Arianne."

"You call sex trafficking protection?"

"It's all they have. I'm all they have. And I wouldn't have let this happen."

"So you would have stood in front of a bullet for her?"

Cory lowered his head. "Maybe."

"If you care at all about these girls, even one ounce, tell me where Kaitlyn might be."

"I don't know..."

Brandon remembered Arianne's missing cellphone. "What cellphone company did Arianne use?"

"I don't know."

"Okay," Brandon said. He motioned for the guard.

"Wait.."

"What?"

"Can I get my sentence reduced?"

"I'm not making any deals with you."

His shoulders sank.

"Anything else?" Brandon asked.

Cory didn't respond. Brandon turned to leave, then paused. "You have no idea where I might find Kaitlyn?"

Cory shrugged. "All I can say about her is she was the soft one."

"Soft?"

"She wanted a normal life. Believed some guy was going to fall for her, despite her...profession."

"And?"

"So she hung around some kids her age at the fair. Pissed me off. She actually thought she could make friends here."

"Who? When?"

"That's all I know, man. Okay?"

The guard opened the door.

Cory stood. "Now do I get a reduced sentence?"

Brandon stared at him for a long time.

"Maybe when you grow up and start treating women like people instead of a piece of meat. I don't think that's going to happen. So, my recommendation is they throw the book at you."

Cory's mouth slackened. "That's not right man."

Brandon motioned to the guard. "Get him out of here."

The information about Kaitlyn's attempt to make friends around the fair wasn't much, but it gave them something to focus on. It meant they should be talking not just to their main suspects and those employed by the fair, but fairgoers too—especially those in their teens or early twenties.

Knowing Kaitlyn had tried to befriend kids her own age gave Brandon hope—she hadn't given up on a life outside of prostitution yet.

His work cell rang. It was Jackson.

"We've got Phoenix Weaver down here at the fair. She won't talk to anyone but you."

"That's an improvement," he said. "Bring her in."

The fact that she was willing to talk to Brandon meant she had something substantive—he hoped.

He sure as hell hoped she wasn't wasting his time.

Chapter 35

Brandon and Josiah joined Phoenix in the interview room. Brandon went through the usual formalities, recording the conversation.

"What is it you want to say?" Brandon asked.

"Does he have to be here?" she asked, pointing at Josiah.

"Yes, he does."

She huffed. "Maybe I don't want to talk now."

Brandon swallowed his frustration. He didn't have time for nonsense. Kaitlyn was out there, not to mention Arianne's killer. Unless Phoenix was about to confess to murder, she was wasting his time.

"Let's review where we are," he said, opening the folder he'd kept on Phoenix.

She crossed her arms.

"Your panties were in Darren Rule's trailer. I expect the DNA back by tomorrow at the latest." It wasn't an exaggeration. The results were due from the crime lab in the next day or two. "Your fingerprints were in his trailer. And while the tarot card at the murder scene didn't match yours, we found two more that did—one taped to the front door of my house and another used during an attempt on my life."

"I didn't have anything to do with that," she said.

"Which part?"

"The whole card at your house and crossbow thing. You think I'm that stupid?"

When Brandon didn't answer, she continued. "Well, I'm not. And I'm not a killer."

"Where were you last night around 7:30?"

"At home."

"Alone?"

"Yes."

"So you don't have an alibi for Darren Rule's murder and you don't have one for the murder of Arianne Young."

Phoenix jerked her head back. "I had no idea she'd died." She pressed her lips together. "The little slut probably got herself killed. What did she expect?"

Brandon narrowed her eyes at her. "Despite what you think of her, she didn't deserve to die."

"Fine. I shouldn't have said that. But what's my motive? Huh? Don't you have to prove my motive to arrest me?"

"No, I don't. Which is why you need to tell me the truth. The whole truth."

Phoenix eyed Brandon, then Josiah. "Is this going to be public?"

"That depends on what you're about to tell me."

She sucked in a deep breath, apparently gathering her courage, then said, "It's true. I was in his trailer." She cringed. "I mean...I'd had too much to drink."

Phoenix watched Brandon as if to check if he'd accepted her excuse for what she was about to share. He motioned for her to continue.

"And...we did it." She exhaled, and it was as if the anger and vitriol had all drained from her.

"You had sex?" Brandon asked.

"Yes."

"Then what?"

"What do you mean, then what? I went home."

"When was this?"

"A couple of days before he was killed. I...I...thinking about it now, I couldn't find my panties. That explains how they ended up in his collection." She lowered her head. "It makes me sick to my stomach."

"No one is judging you here," Brandon said.

She eyed Josiah. "He is. I can tell."

"Josiah is here in his role as a police officer. You're not judging her, are you?"

Josiah looked to Brandon. "Me? No."

"Okay, Phoenix. Did you interact with Drool again after that evening?"

She nodded. "The next night I spotted him at the fair's pub. We talked a bit, he was mostly bragging, like he did the night before."

"About?"

"How he was expecting to come into some cash. He was going to leave the fair for good."

"How was he going to get the money?" Josiah asked.

"The first night...the time we...anyway, he was intoxicated. We both were. I remembered him telling me about blackmailing some people."

"Did he give you any names?" Brandon asked.

"Just one."

"Who?"

She twisted the loose folds of her dress between her hands.

"Phoenix—"

"He said he'd kill me if I told anyone."

"Darren Rule is dead," Brandon said. "He can't hurt you."

"Yes, his corporeal body is gone."

"You mean his ghost is going to haunt you?" Josiah asked.

"I can feel your doubt, young man. It will be your downfall..."

Josiah sat up straight. "Is that some sort of threat?"

Brandon held his arm out to silence him.

"Phoenix, would you rather deal with Darren Rule's ghost—or prison? Because if you're withholding evidence in a murder investigation—"

"Fine. It was Mr. Sterling. The owner of the fair. Something about shady business deals and Darren found out. I don't know how. He'd already gotten one or two payments from him."

Sterling had claimed he didn't know how Darren Rule could afford the larger, newer motorhome. It might be the RV was one way of keeping him silent.

"Is there anything else?" Brandon asked.

She bunched the fabric of her dress between her fingers. "No."

Brandon stood. "Josiah will write up your statement and we'll need you to sign it."

"You're not going to tell anyone, are you?" she asked.

"About you sleeping with Darren Rule?"

She cringed at the statement. He considered her. "Everyone makes mistakes, Phoenix. I'll do my best to keep it private. Like I said, I'm not judging you. But next time you're confronted with a person who's not living up to your standards, think about this moment."

Her jaw loosened, her eyes a tad softer than they were before.

"Thank you."

Phoenix coming clean most likely cleared her as a suspect in Darren Rule's murder. Her explanation fit the evidence they'd found in the motorhome. But the information she'd provided also opened the door on another suspect. Arianne was still the strongest link to Darren Rule's death, but Sterling's dealings with Rule gave him a motive. Whether he had any connection to the main pieces of evidence—the knives and the tarot cards—that was yet to be discovered. And as far as a nexus between Sterling and Arianne's murder—Brandon couldn't see anything there. Yet.

* * *

Brandon asked Jackson to meet him at the fair entrance. There he briefed her on the interview with Phoenix.

"Wow," Jackson said, speaking of Phoenix's rendezvous with Darren Rule. "I didn't think she had it in her."

"It wasn't her best moment."

They made their way to Sterling's office.

The door was locked.

"Maybe he's skipped town," Jackson said.

"It's possible. I don't see him leaving behind all this," Brandon said. "The fair is probably a cash cow."

"Unless those shady business deals you mentioned are the real source of his income."

"Good point. Let's pay Alex a visit."

Alex was in the security tent at a makeshift desk, speaking to one of his employees.

"What's up?" he asked.

"You got a minute?"

Alex dismissed the security guard.

"We're trying to locate Sterling," Brandon said.

Alex unlatched his radio. "I can call him over."

"Wait," Brandon said. "We don't want him to know it's us."

Alex squinted at them. "What's going on?"

Brandon took the chair next to Alex's desk. "I need to know we can trust you on this."

"I want to be a cop, not a security guard," Alex said. "So if there's been something illegal going on, I'm on your side, okay?"

"Are you aware of anything illegal?" Jackson asked.

His head swiveled. "No way. I wouldn't risk my career for a schmuck like Sterling."

"Good," Brandon said. "Anything you can think of that seemed out of sorts with him?"

Alex thought about it for a minute, then said, "He was upset yesterday. It was after one of those young girls was in his office."

"Who?"

"The prostitutes. The one that likes to talk. She's Asian and Black, I believe."

"Arianne."

They'd found a connection between Sterling and Arianne—meaning he was associated with both murder victims.

"I wasn't going to say anything to him," Alex said, "but then I felt like I had to confront him."

"About?" Jackson asked.

"Soliciting a prostitute. I don't want none of that nonsense on my watch," Alex said proudly.

"You think that's what he was doing?"

"He denied it, but I don't know what else she would be doing in there."

"Arianne was murdered last night," Jackson said.

Alex jerked his head back. "What? How?"

"It's an ongoing investigation," Brandon said.

"You believe Mr. Sterling..."

"We don't know," Brandon said. "That's why we need to talk to him."

"Tell me what you want to do."

"Call him to the tent. Make something up."

"Got it." He grabbed his cell and called Sterling on speakerphone.

"Mr. Sterling, this is Alex in security. We've got a situation here at the tent."

Sterling responded, "I'm busy."

"I think you ought to get here right away."

"Can't you deal with it yourself?"

Sweat beading on his forehead, Alex muted the phone and looked to Brandon. "Should I ask him where he is?"

"No," Brandon said. "That will make him suspicious."

Alex unmuted the call again.

"Sir, this is an emergency. There's a big-shot attorney here threatening to shut us down if you're not here in the next ten minutes."

Alex grinned.

"I'll be there in fifteen," Sterling said.

Alex ended the call.

"He must be in town somewhere," Jackson said.

"He did say something about going to the bank this morning. It couldn't be for a deposit, though."

"Why?"

"I offered to ride along. We usually have security accompany him for the daily cash deposits."

Five minutes later, Brandon and Jackson hid in the recesses of the tent, awaiting Duke Sterling's arrival.

Jackson bent down in the back corner. "Is this really necessary? I mean, he's not going to run."

"We don't know that," Brandon said. More so than most suspects, a man with resources like Duke Sterling was capable of fleeing on a moment's notice.

"He's coming," Alex whispered before stepping out of the tent.

"Where's this attorney?" Sterling demanded.

Brandon and Jackson emerged from the tent.

Sterling turned to Alex. "What the hell is going on here?"

"Sorry, Mr. Sterling..."

"We'll need to speak with you down at the station," Brandon said.

"Some other time," Sterling said. "I was just on my way to the airport."

"You have a private plane?"

"Yes."

"Where were you headed?" Brandon asked.

"That is none of your business."

"It is now," Brandon said, leading Sterling away from the tent.

Sterling turned to Alex. "You deceitful little..."

"I'm just doing my job," Alex insisted.

"You don't have a job," Sterling said. "I want you out. Now."

Dejection crossed Alex's face.

"Sorry," Jackson said.

"Yeah. Me too."

"Don't go anywhere yet," Brandon said.

"He's my employee," Sterling demanded.

"Not anymore," Brandon said. He eyed Alex. "We'll talk later. Give Jackson your contact info."

Chapter 36

Sterling hunched down in his chair at the station's interview room. Brandon knew he had little time before Sterling requested an attorney.

"Tell us about Darren Rule blackmailing you," Brandon said.

Sterling eyed Brandon and Jackson defiantly.

"How much did you pay him?" Jackson asked.

When he didn't respond, Jackson said, "We have his bank account info. Every deposit."

The last bank deposit had been made the day before the murder.

A flicker of fear crossed his eyes, but he recovered quickly. "The only check I've ever written to Mr. Rule was his pay as an entertainer in my employ."

"And when we obtain a warrant for your bank records, we won't find cash withdrawals to match his deposits?"

Sterling sat up in his chair, hands flat on the table. "I paid him bonuses. For his outstanding contribution to the fair."

"You mean how he made everyone hate him?"

"What do you know about entertainment?" Sterling asked, his eyes scrutinizing Brandon's uniform. "Oh, wait. You were that hack actor in the awful production on the Royal Theatre Stage. I could have gotten a better crowd with trained—or *untrained*—mice."

Brandon recalled the audience had been standing room-only, but he kept that to himself.

"Where were you last night?"

"I was out."

"A little more specific, if you don't mind," Jackson said.

"Well, what time?"

"Between 7:30 and 8:30."

"I had dinner in town at the Mexican restaurant. Then I went for a drive."

"Around town? Up to Port Angeles? Where?" Brandon asked.

"I don't know my way around this godawful place. We're in the middle of nowhere in case you haven't noticed."

Brandon stared back at him, waiting for a better response.

"Fine," Sterling said, "I drove toward the beaches. Third beach, second, I don't know. It ended in some sort of reservation so I turned around and came back."

"And that was?"

"I was back by nine."

Sterling was out right around the time of the shooting.

"Do you own a firearm, Mr. Sterling?"

"Yes."

"Caliber?"

"It's .45—I bring my Ruger SR1911 on out-of-town trips."

"Nice gun," Brandon said.

"Thank you."

"What else?"

Sterling sighed. "Back home? A .357, a 9mm, a Remington Rolling Block number one rifle. Buffalo Bill owned one just like it..."

"You don't own a twenty-two?" Jackson asked.

He chuckled. "For what? Hunting squirrels?" He peered at Brandon. "What's this about?"

"Arianne Young was found murdered last night."

He blinked at them.

"Wait a minute," he said, waving his hands at them. "You don't believe...I never met her."

"According to your *former* head of security, you did meet with her."

"In my office. But..." He glanced at the door.

Brandon sensed he was on the verge of requesting an attorney.

"If you have any information that might lead us to the killer, and exonerate you, we need to know. Now."

Sterling's shoulders slumped. "I want you to remember this," he said. "That I'm helping you. I know what you're thinking, too. That I'm going to call my attorney. I just might, but I don't want to drag her into this. Not yet. She's my niece."

"That's nice," Jackson said. "Tell us what you know."

"Do we have a deal?" Sterling asked.

"You haven't given me anything," Brandon said. "Until that happens..."

"Yes. Darren Rule was blackmailing me. I paid him here and there. He promised to stop after one last payment."

"And you believed him?" Brandon asked.

"I threatened him. I knew about his drug use, his selling drugs, and it wouldn't have been difficult for me to dredge up some other crime that would have gotten him locked away, trust me."

"Okay, so you figured it was over," Brandon said.

"What was he blackmailing you for?" Jackson asked.

"He *alleged* I was involved in less than scrupulous real estate investments."

"Were you?" Jackson asked.

"Of course not," he said. "The fool was a performer. He didn't know the first thing about creative accounting."

"Then why pay him if there wasn't anything there?" Brandon asked.

"Let's just say that even the suggestion that I wasn't above board would ruin my reputation."

"So you had nothing to do with Darren Rule's murder?"

"Not at all."

"And the night he was killed?"

"I was in Seattle. I flew in early the next morning. I have witnesses."

Brandon looked to Jackson. She'd followed up on all of the suspects' alibis. She nodded in agreement.

"What's your connection to Arianne?" Brandon asked.

"With Drool gone, I figured everything would return to normal. Then, a few days after his death, I was approached by this young woman."

"Arianne?" Jackson asked.

"Right. She mentioned things that only Rule knew. Somehow she'd gotten ahold of the business correspondence he was holding over my head."

"And Arianne wanted what?"

"Ten thousand dollars, the little shit. I told her to get lost. But then she came to my office again and said she'd settle for a thousand. She brought the documents with her."

"What did you tell her?"

"She asked to meet me outside that crappy diner in town."

"And did you?"

"That's the point," he said. "I was supposed to meet her at 7:30 last night. I waited until eight. When she didn't show, I went for a drive."

They could check the video footage outside the Forks Diner. Cameras had been installed after graffiti appeared on the diner during one of Brandon's earlier investigations. If Sterling was telling the truth, he'd provided himself an alibi. He turned to Jackson. "Go check it out."

When Jackson had gone, Brandon asked. "You were at the bank this morning when Alex called?"

Alex had mentioned the trip to the bank.

Sterling's lips pursed into a frown. "Is there no privacy around here?"

"Not usually," Brandon said.

"I was re-depositing the thousand dollars I'd planned on paying the girl."

Sterling stared down at his hands. "I'm sorry to hear about the young lady. As much as she pissed me off—it was Darren Rule's fault for leaving my documents lying around. This girl Arianne—she was simply taking advantage of a business opportunity. I can appreciate that."

"Did any of your contacts with Arianne involve her friend? Her name is Kaitlyn."

After a moment, Sterling said, "When I asked her how she'd come across the documents, she said *we* found them. She refused to say who the other person was. At that point, I just wanted to get her off my back and get back to Las Vegas."

"That's where you live?"

"One of my homes, yes."

He left Sterling in the interview room. Fifteen minutes later, Jackson was back. Sterling's story checked out. He

325

was in front of the diner from about 7:25 to 8. Arianne's death occurred on the Guthrie property between 7:30 and 8 in the evening.

They collected his contact information, home address, and fingerprints. The latter had taken persuasion, but in the end, Sterling wanted to prove his innocence and avoid any more attention to himself than he'd already risked.

"One more thing," Brandon said, leading Sterling out of the interview room.

"What?"

"Firing Alex Winfield as your head of security makes it look like you have something to hide."

"We already talked about this. I wasn't involved."

"I'm not convinced you're as innocent as you claim to be, especially when it comes to your business."

"So now the police are blackmailing me too?" Sterling asked.

"All I'm saying is you should reconsider your decision to fire Alex. He's good at his job. And it would be a shame if word got out you let him go because he knew something about your business practices."

Sterling glowered at Brandon. "I'll take the matter under advisement."

Josiah had returned from the fair and met Brandon and Jackson in the bullpen.

"Back to square one," Jackson said.

"We're eliminating suspects," Brandon said.

"Hamish and Daisy claimed they were watching television during the time Arianne was murdered," Josiah said.

"How did Hamish take the news about Arianne?" Brandon asked.

"He shed a few tears," Josiah said.

"And Daisy?" Jackson asked.

"She was not happy."

"About Arianne's death?"

"No, about Hamish's reaction. She stormed out of the tent."

"I get it," Jackson said. "Your husband grieving over the prostitute he's been spending all of his time with."

"Daisy's still a suspect," Brandon said. "Her jealousy is motive enough."

"You still believe Arianne killed Darren Rule?" Josiah asked.

"Yes," Brandon said. "My working theory is she used the knife Hamish gave her, also using the serrated knife we found in her purse. She placed the tarot card in his mouth, too. From what deck, I don't know. She also placed Phoenix's cards on my house to frame her."

"It makes sense," Jackson said. "Remember when we were first asking Phoenix about the card we found in the motorhome? Arianne was waiting in line to get a reading from Phoenix."

"She overheard us," Brandon said. "After killing Rule she must have taken the documents from his room. Realizing what she'd found, that led her to blackmail Sterling."

"Except Sterling said more than one person had found the documents, meaning at least two people were involved in Rule's murder."

He knew what she was getting at—Kaitlyn was likely involved.

"Maybe," he said, "or stealing the documents wasn't related to the murder, but came after the fact."

"So who would want to kill Arianne if it wasn't Sterling?"

"The answer is in the documents Arianne found in the motorhome. Someone else she'd attempted to blackmail. Someone with a secret so bad they were willing to kill to keep her quiet."

"And we didn't find any documents in her possession?" Josiah asked.

"Most likely the killer nabbed them," Brandon said.

"I know you don't like this," Jackson said, "but the key to this is finding Kaitlyn."

"Agreed," Brandon said.

Like it or not, he had to accept the fact that Kaitlyn could have been involved in Rule's murder, or at least the blackmail.

His phone buzzed.

It was Tori.

"What's up?"

"I tried the hospitals, morgues, everything," she said. "No one had any news of Kaitlyn."

"It was worth a try," he said. "Thanks for trying. Hey, I'll see you tonight—"

"I wasn't done," she said. "I took the photo you sent and visited the bus station. One driver recognized Kaitlyn from the route back from Port Angeles last night. She was with a group of kids, but seemed closer to one young man in particular."

Kaitlyn was still in town.

"What time?"

"Hold on, let me check my notes."

Jackson and Josiah turned their attention to Brandon. He held his hand over the receiver. "It's about Kaitlyn."

After a moment, Tori said, "The bus arrived in Forks at 6:48 last night."

"Any description of the boy?" he asked.

"Shaggy hair, sweatshirts."

She'd asked for a description. That was impressive.

"Were any of them wearing a white hoodie?" Brandon asked, recalling the shooter at the hotel.

"Sorry, I didn't ask."

"No, you did great. Anything else?"

"They all had skateboards," she said.

Skateboards? David Velazquez was known to hang out at the local skateboard park.

"You are awesome, honey. Thank you."

He ended the call.

Jackson said, "Don't tell me the ex is part of the investigation again."

He cast her a cold stare. She held up her hands. "Sorry. But if my husband was moonlighting a case, you wouldn't be so happy about it."

Jackson's husband was a computer programmer. Tori was an experienced prosecuting attorney. She knew good evidence and how not to corrupt a case.

"What did she learn?" Josiah asked.

"Kaitlyn was seen on one of the busses returning from Port Angeles last night, with a group of skater kids."

"David Velasquez?" Jackson asked. She'd been the first to spot him at the local skate park.

"There's a chance he was part of the group on the bus. Jackson—you search every park or hangout in town—ask if anyone has seen Kaitlyn or David. I'm heading out to the church."

"You want company?" Josiah asked. "Considering what's happened so far."

He had a point. Whoever had shot at Brandon was still out there—and the shooter just might be David Velasquez.

Chapter 37

Brandon flipped his light bar on until they reached the backroads leading up to the church. Eddie had claimed he wouldn't be back from his conference until later that evening. He also said he wasn't sure where David was, but if Tori was right, Brandon might find Kaitlyn and David together. Kaitlyn had to be staying somewhere—why not in one of the empty seminary apartments?

He was half a mile from the church when Jackson called him. He pulled over to take the call, first placing her on speakerphone.

"You found them?" Brandon asked.

"No. But before I left, I got a call from the lab. They found a match on the prints from Darren Rule's phone."

"Who?"

"David Velasquez."

The phone had been missing since Rule's death. Assuming the phone was in Rule's possession when he died, David's prints on the phone very likely placed him at the scene of the murder.

"That changes things," he said.

"Damn right it does."

"But it doesn't integrate with all the evidence against Arianne. The knife, the tarot cards..."

"Unless David was there, too."

"And now he's with Kaitlyn," Brandon said.

"Are you considering they both might have been there when Darren Rule was murdered?"

"I am," he said. "We're almost to the church."

"I don't like this, Chief. Be careful."

"We'll call if we need backup. Just keep checking for those two."

He ended the call.

Brandon parked at a turnoff a quarter mile from the church.

"Why here?" Josiah asked.

"Last time I was here, I heard music coming from the dorms. It went silent when whoever was inside spotted me."

"Dorms?"

Josiah hadn't been to the church property yet.

"The church used to have a seminary. Now it's mostly vacant apartments. David and Eddie Velasquez live in one of the units."

They trekked up the first entrance and sprinted toward the main church. Circling the building to the right, they had a view of the parking lot and the dorms off to the left, nestled against the forest.

Brandon listened for any hint of human presence. The only sound was the chatter of chickadees and other birds occasionally interrupted by the boisterous calls of two crows atop a power line leading away from the church. A car sped by on the road below.

They sprinted to the nearest edge of the apartments, then headed for the back of the building.

Concrete porches stretched from the lower units, balconies from the ones above. The porches were covered in moss and nettles, except the one at the opposite end of the complex—about where he'd heard the music last time. Privacy screens—each one no longer than a single section of a cedar slat fence—separated the units.

"Look," Josiah whispered, pointing to two lawn chairs and a charcoal grill situated on the edge of a short lawn behind the furthest porch.

They crept across the petite yards until they neared the last unit.

The grass was covered in pine cones and branches from some distant winter storm. The cedar privacy screen blocked their view of the porch and the apartment.

Someone laughed. A man.

Another person coughed.

A puff of smoke escaped from behind the partition.

Brandon motioned for Josiah to stay put.

Brandon stepped forward. His boot snapped a thin branch.

The apartment went quiet.

Brandon and Josiah slipped behind the wooden partition.

"What was that?" a woman asked. It was Kaitlyn.

"I don't know," David Velasquez answered.

Feet shuffled out onto the porch. Brandon crouched, holding his breath.

"Probably a raccoon or coyote," David said.

"Freaking scary stuff out here," Kaitlyn said.

"Whatever. No one even knows this place exists."

They went back to talking and closed the sliding glass door. The musky stench of marijuana smoke lingered.

Brandon and Josiah stood.

"We need them outside," Brandon said.

Josiah nodded. "In case one of them is armed."

"Any ideas?" Brandon asked.

Josiah thought about it, his eyes scanning the terrain. He bent down and scrounged through the mossy dirt. He found a hand-sized rock and stood.

"This will do," he said. With a baseball windup, Josiah pitched the rock at the charcoal grill.

The stone bounced off the black metal with a clang, knocking the lid askew.

Brandon chuckled. "Nice."

The glass door slid open.

Unholstering his pistol, Brandon waved Josiah back. "Cover the door," he whispered.

"What the hell?" David said, still unaware of Brandon and Josiah.

"Don't go out there!" Kaitlyn said.

"Who's messing with my shit?"

David balanced his feet on the edge of the concrete porch, hands at his sides.

Unarmed.

Brandon stepped closer. David was scanning the forest, his back to Brandon. His long black hair straggled over the back of his t-shirt. Socks hung lazily off the ends of his feet.

Brandon turned his attention to the sliding glass door. Kaitlyn gripped the handle.

"Out here, now, Kaitlyn."

David spun around.

"Hands where I can see them," Brandon said.

David complied. It took a moment for the surprise to fade from his face.

Kaitlyn moved to close the door.

"You don't want to do that," Brandon said. "I'm only here to help."

"Yeah, right," David said.

Kaitlyn slammed the door shut, locking it.

"Cuff him, Josiah," Brandon said.

Brandon rushed around the near end of the building. He reached the front in time to watch Kaitlyn speed out the door and across the parking lot.

"Stop!" Brandon shouted.

She halted in the middle of the parking lot and wheeled on him.

"Why did you have to come here?"

"We need to talk," he said.

"About what? My dad? My loving family? How I'm missing out on such an awesome life?"

"Kaitlyn...Arianne is dead."

Her demeanor remained stony. Did she know?

"I don't care," she said.

"You're saying you didn't care about her?"

"That's not what I said." She shifted her weight. "You want me to be normal. I'm not. David is the closest thing to normal I'll ever get, and you're ruining that too."

"Did David kill Arianne?"

She scoffed. "No."

"What about Darren Rule?"

Her eyes flitted to him. "What?"

"Was David involved in the murder?"

"Why?"

"We found his phone. David's prints were on it."

Her brow furrowed in genuine confusion. "That makes no sense."

"This isn't a safe place for you," Brandon said.

"You mean David isn't safe. Maybe no one is, maybe I'll never be safe."

She turned and marched away.

"Kaitlyn. You need to stop."

Instinctively, he grasped for his cuffs. He didn't want to do this. She was a suspect in a murder case. He could not let her go, no matter how badly he wanted to believe she was innocent.

"I won't warn you again…"

Kaitlyn slowed, then suddenly burst across the parking lot, lunged into the brush at the edge, and shot down the short embankment to the pavement below.

Brandon paused at the end of the lot. She'd already reached the road. In the distance, the rumble of a semi shook the still air.

Kaitlyn glanced back at Brandon, her expression drowned in sadness and, worst of all, hopelessness.

The truck sped around the turn.

Kaitlyn stepped onto the pavement.

Brandon shouted, "No!"

Chapter 38

Brandon leaped down the embankment. He landed hard on one leg, twisting his ankle. To the left, a logging truck barreled around the corner. Kaitlyn jerked out of his grasp.

Brandon charged ahead.

The truck's shadow swept over Kaitlyn just as Brandon snatched her back. The force of the pull and the swoosh of air sent them tumbling into the brush.

The semi's brakes engaged and the air was rent with the stuttering halt of 40 tons of wood and steel.

Brandon scrambled to his feet and wrapped his cuffs around Kaitlyn's wrists.

The truck settled, straddling both lanes.

Brandon helped Kaitlyn to her feet.

A moment later, the driver jogged up the road. Brandon recognized the familiar panic of a driver who'd nearly killed someone. "Is she okay?"

"She will be."

"I didn't see her," he said.

"I know."

The driver pulled his hat off, rubbed his chest with the other hand. "You scared the hell out of me, young lady."

"I'm sorry."

He asked Brandon, "Do I need to make a statement."

"No. You'd better get out of the road." Brandon offered him a business card. "Call me if there's any trouble with your boss. I'll explain everything."

"Thanks," he said, flipping his hat back on. He shook his head again. "Damn."

Brandon led Kaitlyn back to the church parking lot. "Are you injured?" he asked.

"No."

"What were you trying to do back there?"

She shrugged. "I don't know."

Josiah was waiting out in front of the apartment with David. "I called for a second transport," he said. His eyes scanned Brandon's dust and nettle-covered uniform. "Are you okay?"

"I'm fine. Let's take these two inside while we wait."

They sat David at the kitchen table. Kaitlyn was on the couch. The apartment was messy but nothing out of the norm. It was what you'd expect leaving a teenager home alone for a couple of days—stacks of dirty plates on the stove, empty soda cans, and more dishes on the coffee table.

"You live here with your dad?" Brandon asked David.

"You already knew that," he said.

"Where's the gun?" Brandon asked.

"I don't know what you're talking about."

"You don't own a pistol?"

"No."

"How about your dad?"

David scoffed. "Yeah, right. You do know he's a pastor?"

"So if I searched in here, I wouldn't find a firearm?"

"Nope."

Brandon phrased his next words carefully, considering he didn't have a warrant. Based on case law, however, most judges would consider David, at age 18, able to give consent to a search. "Your dad leaves you in charge of the house when he's not around?"

"Yeah."

Brandon peered down a short hallway that led to two rooms and a bathroom. "You don't mind if I look around, then?"

"Go ahead, but you're not going to find anything."

Brandon headed down the hallway. To the right was a bedroom with mostly bare walls, a double bed, and a simple dresser. The blankets were on the floor, as was a pile of dirty clothes. Brandon did a quick search of the closet, under the mattress, and in the dresser.

He turned to the laundry. There, on top, was a white hoodie.

Brandon stuck his head out of the room and asked Josiah, "Who's headed here?"

"Jackson."

"Tell her to bring in the evidence kit." They would have the hoodie tested for gunshot residue.

"Will do."

He moved to the other bedroom. Family photos covered the walls, a framed copy of the hymn *It Is Well With My Soul.* In the closet were two suits, half a dozen dress shirts, and an assortment of ties.

"Told you," David said as Brandon returned to the front room. "Can we go now?"

"Not happening," Brandon said.

"What are we being charged with?"

"Tell me about your involvement in the murder of Darren Rule."

His eyes widened? "What? I had nothing to do with that?"

"Is that white hoodie yours?"

"Yeah, so?"

"Then I'm most likely going to be charging you with the attempted murder of a police officer and, if that's true, I'm pretty sure you had something to do with the death of Arianne Young."

David's mouth dropped. Then, his hazel eyes suddenly wet, he said, "No. I don't know what you're talking about."

The hoodie connected him to the shootings. And the prints on the cellphone linked him to Rule's murder. Brandon informed David of his rights.

Josiah glanced out the front door. "She's here."

Brandon looked to David. "We'll talk down at the station."

Josiah led David to Jackson's vehicle.

"What are you going to do with me?" Kaitlyn asked.

"I'm taking you into custody until I figure out how you're involved in this."

"But.."

He held up a hand. "We're going to do this on the record."

Jackson appeared in the doorway holding the evidence kit.

"Keep an eye on her."

"Will do."

Brandon hiked down to where they'd parked and retrieved the Interceptor. Once Kaitlyn was safely in the back seat of Jackson's SUV, he instructed Josiah to take David to the station and get him booked.

Jackson helped him do a more thorough search of the apartment and, besides the hoodie, all they came up with was a few ounces of marijuana. It was enough to get David in hot water with his probation officer. But drug charges were the least of his worries.

Jackson and Brandon stood on the apartment's front porch.

"You're convinced he's the one that shot at you?" Jackson asked.

"We'll test for residue on the hoodie. Regardless, we've got him on the cellphone prints."

She looked to the SUV. Kaitlyn sat in the backseat, her head titled back. "You still think she's innocent?"

"Innocent? No. Guilty of murder? I can't tell you."

"I'm sorry, Chief."

"It's part of the job. You know that and I know that."

"Doesn't make it any easier."

He locked and closed the apartment door.

"That's for damn sure."

Brandon and Jackson interviewed David at the Forks Jail.

"Tell us about your relationship with Drool," Brandon said.

David combed a hand through his hair, dragging the bangs from his eyes.

"I didn't have a relationship with him."

"You felt comfortable enough to take your shirt off in front of him," Jackson said.

He sat up in his chair, sneering. "I already told you guys. It was hot."

"Okay," Brandon said. "That was the photo of you in the motorhome. What were you wearing in the photos on Darren Rule's phone?"

"Screw you."

The response confirmed Brandon's suspicions about why he'd tossed the phone. Brandon spread his hands out on the table. "We're going to get the photos. The quicker you confess to what happened, the fewer people that will see them."

David's eyes drifted to the corner of the room. From his years of experience, Brandon recognized this was the moment before a suspect opened up.

Brandon leaned back, letting the uneasy quiet swallow the room. For many, silence itself was enough to compel a confession.

David met Brandon's eyes. "I did some ecstasy, a bunch of other shit too. I don't know what happened. He claimed he had pictures of me wearing nothing."

"Did he?"

"I don't know."

"Did Drool sexually assault you in any way?" Jackson asked.

David lowered his head. Thick strands of his charcoal bangs shielded his eyes. "No."

"You're sure?" Brandon asked.

"Why does it matter?"

"Because, if you need help..."

"You're trying to fricking lock me up in prison. Why the hell does it matter what some perv did or didn't do to me?"

Brandon leaned away from him. "Alright. Then explain to us how you came to possess Darren Rule's phone."

David wiped the sweat off his forehead with the back of his hand.

"You're not going to believe me."

"Maybe we will, maybe we won't. You won't know unless you tell us."

He leaned forward, hands flat on the table. "He texted me that he had some pictures. He threatened to show everyone unless I paid him a grand. I told him to go screw himself."

"When was this?"

"A few days before he died."

"You still have the text?"

"I deleted it."

"We can get the records," Jackson said.

David shrugged dismissively. "Then the next day he tells me he's got something that's going to really piss my dad off. I asked him what but he wouldn't tell me. Right after that, he went to the church and started giving my dad shit."

"And you decided to shut him up for good?" Brandon asked.

"No. I went to his motorhome to steal the phone from him when he wasn't looking or if he was asleep. When I got there, the door was unlocked. I went inside and found him on the bed." He swallowed hard. "He was, you know..."

"What?"

"Dead. The knife sticking out his throat."

"Then what?"

"I grabbed his phone from the dresser and booked it out of there."

"What else did you steal?" Brandon asked.

David eyed Brandon for a few seconds, then said, "The laptop and that's it."

"You're sure?" Jackson asked.

"I thought he might have pictures on there too."

"What did you do with the laptop?" Brandon asked.

"I threw it in the river."

The fisherman hadn't said anything about a laptop.

"In the same location you tossed the phone?"

David hesitated, then said, "Yeah."

Brandon clicked his tongue. "No. That's not right. We have a witness."

David's eyes grew hard. "Your witness is wrong."

"Why didn't you contact police when you found Darren Rule?" Jackson asked.

"The same reason I'm sitting here right now. I knew you would blame me."

"You didn't notice anyone else in the motorhome?" Brandon asked.

"No."

"If it wasn't you," Jackson asked, "then who killed him?"

David stared down at his hands. "I don't know. Maybe a stranger?"

"It wasn't a stranger, David. And if you want to see the light of day anytime in the next couple of decades, I suggest you come up with a better explanation."

"I *don't* know."

"Maybe," Brandon said, "you and Arianne killed him."

They were the two individuals directly tied to the crime scene.

"And then you offed Arianne to shut her up."

"I don't know shit about Arianne. The only girl I met at the fair was Kaitlyn."

"You think she killed him?" Jackson asked. Brandon bristled at the question.

"I don't know," David said. "I hope not."

"Why?"

"She's pretty cool. That would suck if she went to jail."

David was already headed there himself. Unless he was in for a long-distance relationship, he was out of luck.

"You said Rule went to your father," Brandon said. "You have any idea what he and your dad discussed?"

His head swiveled. "I don't want to know."

"Why not?"

David shifted in his seat. "He said it had something to do with my dad."

"It wasn't just the fact that you had burglary charges?"

"Everyone in this piss-ant town knows that."

"What sort of secret might your father have that was so bad that Darren Rule might want to blackmail him?"

"I don't think my dad has secrets," David said. "Everything he does the whole stupid church knows and gossips about. Do you know what it's like having your whole life on display?"

"Yes," Jackson said.

David stared back at her with disbelief.

"I'm a pastor's brat, too," she added.

"Then you know. Everyone wants to know your business. No secrets."

Or, if you had a secret, you had all the more reason to make sure no one found out about it.

"You said earlier the white hoodie belongs to you."

"Yeah."

"When's the last time you wore it?" Brandon asked.

"I don't know, last week."

"And how recently were you at the Forks Inn?"

"Is that where Kaitlyn was staying?"

"Yes."

"Never been there," he said. "I met her when she was hanging down at the park. I saw her at the fair too."

"What's the extent of your relationship with Kaitlyn?"

"You mean like are we having sex?" David asked.

"Okay. Were you?"

He hesitated. "No."

In other words, yes, Brandon thought.

"Does your dad know she's at your house?"

"Not yet. I mean, what's he going to say? Kaitlyn is the one that told me Arianne was trying to blackmail my dad."

Brandon glanced at Jackson. Sterling claimed Arianne had gotten ahold of the incriminating documents Rule had used to blackmail him. It was possible she'd found the secret Rule planned to use against Eddie and David, too.

"You're sure Arianne was blackmailing your father?" Brandon asked.

"Kaitlyn said Arianne wanted to, but we warned him."

"And what did your dad say about that?" Brandon asked.

David shrugged. "He said not to worry about it. That he had nothing to hide."

"Kaitlyn didn't say what the blackmail was about?"

"No."

"Where's your dad now?"

"I don't know. Out of town or something. He's supposed to be back tonight."

That jived with what Eddie had told Brandon.

"And neither you nor your father own a firearm?"

He shook his head no.

"For the recording," Jackson reminded him.

"I said no."

Brandon patted the table. "We're going to get your hoodie tested for gunpowder residue. We'll request copies of your phone records and any communication with Darren Rule. That's just the start."

"I didn't kill him."

"We'll contact an attorney for you," Jackson said. "You want us to notify your father?"

"No."

After the guards returned David to his cell, he had them retrieve Kaitlyn.

"Time for the moment of truth," Jackson said.

Chapter 39

Kaitlyn had been placed on suicide watch upon her arrival at the jail. Her attempt to step in front of a semi-truck was as real as could be. She'd only been there an hour and they were still waiting for the mental health professional to come down. In Brandon's experience, the MHPs meant well, but due to a lack of psych beds across the state, were unlikely to send any but the most dangerous individuals to the hospital. That meant they wilted in jail, waiting for court dates or, worse, were released to the streets.

He wasn't sure if Kaitlyn's dash for the road was due to a mental health issue or came out of a sudden—or chronic—sense of hopelessness about her situation. Either way, she needed help, and as usual, there was little they could do.

In the meantime, they would keep her safe until they understood her involvement in both murders.

The guard handcuffed Kaitlyn to the interview room table and waited outside. Just as David had, she consented to the interview without an attorney. This would be the last shot they had at either of the two without a lawyer present.

"How are you feeling?" Brandon asked.

"Claustrophobic," she said, her eyes scanning the tight-spaced room.

"Kaitlyn," Brandon asked. "Do you know who killed Arianne?"

"No."

"David didn't mention shooting anyone? Maybe even if he didn't kill them?"

Most killers had a hard time keeping a secret. Some force compelled them to confess—or brag about—what they'd done. He imagined David relating the shooting at the hotel to Kaitlyn, especially because he liked her.

"He wouldn't do that."

"What about his dad, Pastor Eddie?"

"I've never met him."

"Did David show you a gun?" Jackson asked.

She bit her bottom lip. "No."

"How did you find out Arianne died?" Jackson asked.

"David's dad told him. He's a pastor."

"Right."

"I mean, the home where they found her, they go to the church and they called him to talk about it."

"Then what?" Brandon asked.

"His dad said he was going out of town. I told David I was afraid, so he let me stay there."

"Why were you afraid?" Jackson asked.

Kaitlyn buried her head in her hands. "I knew this would happen."

"You knew Arianne would be murdered?" Brandon asked.

She nodded.

"How?"

"Because she was always talking shit, bragging about how she was going to use the stuff we found and try to get easy money."

"Wait," Brandon said. He'd nearly missed what she'd said. "You just said the stuff you found. What stuff?"

Kaitlyn's eyes glazed over. She shivered. Jackson scooted her chair closer to the young woman. "It's okay," Jackson said.

She lowered her head. "No. It's not. It's never going to be okay."

"Just tell us what happened, sweetie," Jackson said.

Kaitlyn studied Brandon's face. Her eyes were murky behind a glaze of tears. She swallowed. Her gaze dropped. "You're going to hate me."

He rested his hands on the table, leaning his head to get a glimpse of her eyes. "No, Kaitlyn. I won't. Nothing you can say can make that happen."

She exhaled, releasing her reservations.

"Arianne asked me to go to Darren's that night. She knew he had some documents because sometimes he bragged when he'd been drinking. When we got to his motorhome, he was just getting there. He recognized us and asked us to come inside. I told Arianne it wasn't a good idea."

"Because of what he'd done to you already?" Jackson asked.

"He threatened to kill me if I told anyone."

"And he already knew you'd told Cory."

"Yes."

"What happened next?" Brandon asked.

"He started coming on to us. I told him, no, then he said he could do what he wanted."

"Where did this take place?"

"By the table at the front of the trailer."

The blood splatter indicated the attack had occurred in the bedroom.

"Then what?"

"I was going to leave, but Arianne started doing this thing..."

"What?"

"Acting like she wanted to go back to the bedroom with him. He was headed back there and she told me to search the front for anything we might steal."

"And did you?"

"Just for a minute. Right away I found a bunch of court stuff and bills and tax forms. But then I heard Arianne scream, like freaking out. I ran back and she had a dagger in her hand. She smiled at me and stabbed him again. He was making this horrible noise."

Kaitlyn wrapped her arms around herself. "It was like...gurgling."

"Then what?"

"I asked her what happened and she said, 'the bitch deserves to die'. At first, I thought she was in some sort of trance or something and she was talking about me. But then, she was all calm and wiped her hands on the sheets. She took her tarot cards out. She was laughing, like crazy laughing. She spent like a minute deciding which card, then stabbed it through with the dagger and said she was going to shove it down his throat. He was still gurgling and I started gagging and she told me that if I puked my DNA would be in the trailer and I'd go to jail for the rest of my life."

"What did you do then?"

"I said I was leaving and I swear to God I thought she would come after me next."

"Did you leave?"

"I left the motorhome and called Cory and told him to pick me up."

"What happened after that?"

"I was on the corner outside the fair and Cory pulled up. A second later, Arianne showed up with the documents I'd found. I was about to get in the van and she told me I'd better not tell anyone, not even Cory, or she'd do the same thing to me."

"So you weren't there when she shoved the dagger down Darren Rule's throat?" Jackson asked.

She shuddered. "No."

"So it's your statement that you didn't come to the police because she threatened you," Brandon said.

Tears filled the corners of her eyes. "I told you you'd hate me. I know I should have."

"Why not come to us after Arianne died? She wasn't a threat to you then," Jackson said.

"Because whoever she was blackmailing would assume I was part of it."

"David says you told him that Arianne was going to blackmail his father. Is that right?" Brandon asked.

"Yes."

"So you weren't afraid of him, at least," Jackson said.

"No, but the others...I don't know."

"What others?" Brandon asked.

"The only other one she mentioned was Mr. Sterling."

"Okay," Brandon said. "Did you know Arianne had stolen the tarot cards from Phoenix?"

She frowned. "Yes."

"And that she'd taped one to my door. And tried to shoot another through my head?"

"Arianne told me she put one on your door to scare you."

"What about the crossbow?"

"I didn't know anything about that," she said. "I told her you were trying to be nice to us..."

"Why do you think Arianne killed Darren Rule?" Brandon asked.

"I don't know. I think she just finally lost it. She'd been abused most of her life, and laughed about it like, you know, no one could hurt her. After Drool raped me, she was pissed, talked about getting back at him. I didn't think she'd really do it."

Arianne had briefly mentioned her past to Brandon—including being sexually abused by her mother's boyfriends.

"And who do you believe killed Arianne?" Jackson asked.

"The only people she told me she was blackmailing were Mr. Sterling and Pastor Eddie."

Sterling had an alibi for the time of Arianne's murder and Eddie was out of town.

"Try your best to remember. Did Arianne tell you what the blackmailing was about?"

"For Mr. Sterling, money or cheating on his business."

"And for Pastor Eddie?"

"It was something about their family. Something the pastor wouldn't want anyone to know. I asked her and she wouldn't tell me because she thought I would tell David."

"And you did," Brandon said.

"I only told them what I knew—that Arianne was going to blackmail them."

Assuming she was telling the truth—and he realized that wasn't an assumption everyone would hold—she was guilty of not telling police about the murder. That made her an accessory after the fact, with the extenuating circumstance that she'd been threatened. Sure, she and Arianne had entered the motorhome intending to steal his documents, but she hadn't taken part in the blackmailing.

It was a mess, and he had enough to keep her for now, at the very least for her own safety. Not only had she tried

353

to run into traffic, but she was probably right about being a target as much as Arianne.

"We're going to hold you here," Brandon said.

"What did I do?"

"I could go with criminal trespass. Failure to report the commission of a crime, accessory to murder, albeit after the fact. I need to know more before you can leave, but that means we'll have to proceed with the charges for trespassing and failure to report for now."

The guard returned Kaitlyn to her cell. Brandon and Jackson met up back at the bullpen.

"You really going to go with accessory to murder?" Jackson asked.

"You heard what she said. She witnessed the murder. With the extenuating circumstances, we can talk to the prosecuting attorney about reducing the charge. In the meantime, we get her help. She's been through hell." He crossed his arms, leaning against one of the desks. "Besides, I thought you were the one pressing me to consider her as a suspect in Darren Rule's murder."

"I was right, she was there."

"True," he said.

"I was just trying to make sure you weren't blinded—"

"By my bias?"

Jackson leaned back in her chair. "It seemed you were trying hard to believe she wasn't guilty. I know you put a lot of effort into her."

"I might be biased, but I'm still going to get to the truth," he reminded her.

"Speaking of the truth, where are we at?"

They both turned to the whiteboard where he'd outlined the suspects earlier.

"Considering what Kaitlyn and David told us, we know Arianne killed Rule—nothing to do with blackmail, but instead her history of abuse. That being the case, we can assume David was being truthful when he said he stole Rule's phone and then later tossed it, believing Rule had kept embarrassing photos on the phone. As for the laptop—it doesn't add up that he dropped it in the river. Either he still has it or someone else disposed of it."

"His father?" Jackson asked.

"Likely," Brandon said. "Another question to ask Eddie." He turned back to the board. "After Rule's death, Arianne took over, blackmailing both Sterling and Pastor Eddie."

"As far as the investigation into Arianne's murder," Jackson said, "We've talked to Hamish, Daisy, Phoenix, Kaitlyn, and even David. As far as we know, of all those people, only Sterling and Eddie Velasquez had a strong enough motive to kill Arianne."

"Maybe David, too," Brandon said.

"Right, because Arianne found out something about David's family."

"And there's the hoodie the assailant wore when shooting at me, possibly using the same gun used to kill Arianne. We'll be waiting days for the gunshot residue results."

"My money is on Pastor Eddie," Jackson said. "Whatever this family secret is, it might be motive enough for murder."

"We won't know until we find out what the hell he's hiding. And remember, no firearm, at least according to David."

"Eddie is coming home tonight?"

"That's another thing," Brandon said. "He was out of town during Arianne's murder."

"At least that's what he said."

"Right." Brandon turned to her. "See what you can figure out about Eddie's schedule. The church secretary isn't around most of the time. Get creative. I have a couple of hunches I want to follow up on. Let's meet up later this afternoon."

"Got it."

The only other family that David had, as far as Brandon knew, was his mother. Eddie claimed David's mother disappeared, leaving him to raise David alone. The church secretary, Beatrice, had at least confirmed the part about Eddie being a single father most of David's life. But the events behind the split with David's mom were never divulged. It was just a hunch, but those circumstances might have something to do with the family secret Darren Rule and Arianne were trying to capitalize on.

Brandon searched the state webpage listing all current and previous court cases for the past 18 years. All court filings, from speeding tickets to divorce and custody disputes to major crimes, were listed, along with the case number and jurisdiction. The only exceptions were sealed cases—like adoptions.

He entered Eddie Velasquez's name and selected Clallam County as the jurisdiction. The search came back empty. He expanded his search to the next closest county—Grays Harbor, to the south of Forks.

He found a hit. Susan Velasquez versus Eddie Velasquez. He clicked on the link and it led to the Grays Harbor Superior Court website. Like most jurisdictions, the online system contained scant information on the case—only revealing hearing dates and names of the documents and orders filed.

He scrolled through the list, gleaning what he could from the document titles. To view the content of the filings he'd have to make a trip down to Grays Harbor.

The divorce had been initiated by Susan Velasquez. The initial petition for divorce was there. He scanned for any protection orders—an accusation of domestic violence might be the family secret Eddie was trying to protect. He found motions for continuance, notices of appearance, but nothing about a restraining order. About six months into the proceedings, Mrs. Velasquez had changed attorneys. Mutually agreed upon divorces in Washington State required only a ninety-day waiting period. Something had caused this case to drag on.

Brandon's cursor hovered over the next filing.

A petition to determine parentage.

Either Eddie or Susan Velasquez wanted to prove Eddie was—or wasn't—David's father.

Brandon continued down the list. There had been a ruling on paternity and, soon after that, a final divorce decree. He checked the time. Montesano, the county seat of Grays Harbor, was over two hours away. He wouldn't make it there before the clerk's office closed.

Brandon dialed the number for detective Andy Firth, a Grays Harbor sheriff's detective he'd helped with a case earlier that year. Andy was just about to head out for the day but agreed to download the documents and send them to Brandon via email.

The Velasquez family's court papers could be a goldmine of evidence—and the sort of thing someone like Darren Rule could use to blackmail Eddie. They might be public documents, but most people wouldn't know or care enough to look. Darren Rule, it seemed, was particularly skilled at finding dirt on just about anyone he'd met.

While he waited for the information from Grays Harbor, Brandon would tackle the other missing link between Eddie and Arianne—the lack of a firearm.

Chapter 40

Brandon printed out a photo of Eddie from the church website and headed over to Pistol Annie's—the only gun shop in town. He asked Annie—the blonde, spunky forty-something owner—if anyone resembling Eddie had purchased or inquired about a firearm in the last several weeks.

He placed the picture of Eddie on the glass display case. Inside the display were the typical gun store fare—pistols, revolvers, and even a fully automatic rifle. A sticky note on the rifle read *for display only*.

"He's not been in here," Annie said.

"Not even a visit?" Brandon asked. Even if he'd purchased the gun elsewhere, he might have come to Annie's for ammo.

Annie squinted at the photo. "Sorry, boss. I mean, he looks familiar, like I've seen him around town."

"Thanks, Annie."

"Sorry I couldn't help."

"Give me a head's up if he stops by, will you?"

She considered him for a moment. "I'm not keen on telling the authorities everything that goes on in my shop. It's bad for business."

"This is serious," he said.

"I get that. You know I support the police," she reminded him, pointing to a blue beacon light in the store's window.

"I appreciate that," Brandon said. He handed her his card.

"I'll let you know if I hear anything," she said.

Brandon passed the Forks Diner on his way back to the station. He was reminded of the conversation he'd had with Arianne in front of the diner and her self-assured approach to everyone around her. He thought back to what Sterling had said about Arianne and her business acumen.

What a waste of a life.

Brandon had left Seattle and the homicide unit so he wouldn't have to hear those kinds of stories anymore. But stories like Arianne's were everywhere. Maybe in different tones and in different sorts of neighborhoods, but they were tragedies, nonetheless.

In a few hours, Eddie would return home, and still the only connection between Arianne and Pastor Eddie was the blackmail attempt Kaitlyn had relayed to Eddie and David.

He'd never seen Eddie and Arianne together and had no proof Arianne had even contacted Eddie.

Brandon made a mental note to check both of their phone records.

He recalled something about that conversation with Arianne outside the diner. They'd both noticed Eddie entering the pawnshop across the street. Brandon had noticed the recognition on her face and asked about it. Arianne had denied any personal knowledge of the pastor. Now he knew she wasn't being honest.

Just as important was Eddie's visit to the pawnshop. Pistol Annie's wasn't the only place in town that sold firearms.

The bell above the pawn shop's door jingled as Brandon entered. Ethan Crouce, the shop's owner, peeked out from behind a glass display of watches and pawned wedding rings. A menagerie of guitars, banjos, ladders, power tools, and more crowded the shop's shelves.

"Chief Mattson," Ethan said. "You're just the man I was hoping to see."

"Is that so?"

"I've got a sale on wedding rings."

"Why would I need a wedding ring?"

"Rumor is, you've been seen around with a certain lady—"

"Who told you that?"

"This is Forks," Ethan reminded him.

"Good point."

"Not that it's any of my business. But, you know, good for you. Just because you've been divorced doesn't mean you can't rekindle romance. And how many times have I mentioned you can't stay single forever."

It was the same comment Ethan made any time Brandon dropped in. Checks at the pawnshop for stolen goods weren't a typical police chief duty, but Brandon enjoyed making the rounds, getting to know the town again after his return from Seattle.

If there was one person who had their pulse on the overall state of a community, it was the pawnshop owner. When crime increased, especially drug use, people pawned everything they owned. When they'd emptied their own houses, they stole from their neighbors and pawned the stolen goods, too.

"Thanks for the dating advice," Brandon said. "But I'm here about a gun."

He glanced at Brandon's Glock.

"What're you looking for? Handgun? Rifle? You hunting? I just got a barely used Ruger off a hunter..."

"I'm here on work," Brandon said. "I need to know if you've sold anything to a man named Eddie Velasquez."

"Nope."

"You're sure?"

"I'm sure."

"Alright, well—"

"Hold your horses, Chief. You asked if I sold him a firearm. I didn't."

"Okay."

"I did do a firearm transfer for him."

"From where?"

"Some online gun shop from back east. I don't know why people don't just buy local. We've got us and Annie right here in town. Doesn't make any sense."

"So he bought it online and did the transfer here?"

"Right."

It was illegal for internet retailers to sell and send firearms directly to customers. Any firearm purchased online had to be sent to a federally licensed transfer site, usually local gun stores or pawn shops. There, the buyer would complete the background check and, if they passed, could take possession of the gun. The local transfer site charged a nominal fee for holding the weapon and completing the background check.

"What sort of firearm?"

"I recall it was something I hadn't seen before. Hold on."

He came back a minute later with a receipt. He plunked it on the counter. Brandon read it. "A Glock 44?"

"It's a .22 LR...I read something about it being the first Glock made in that caliber. Sort of a starter pistol."

"It says here you did the background a month ago. When did he pick it up?"

"About five days ago."

Brandon nodded. "Can I get a copy of this?"

"Sure thing, boss."

Ethan returned with a copy. "Did you know he's a pastor?"

"Yep."

"Is he in trouble?"

Brandon stared down his nose at Ethan.

Ethan lifted his hands. "Alright, fine. Don't tell me."

Brandon held up the paper. "Thanks, Ethan. I appreciate it."

As Brandon opened the door, Ethan called out, "Just remember where to come when you decide to settle down again. I've got a whopper of an engagement ring over here. Something to make her proud..."

Chapter 41

Jackson was in the bullpen when Brandon arrived back at the station.

She swiveled away from her computer screen. "You'll never guess what I found out," she said.

Brandon beamed at her.

"What?" she asked. "You got something bigger, don't you?"

He motioned to her. "You go first."

Jackson's lips twisted into a wry smile. "Fine. I checked Pastor Eddie's social media accounts. He hasn't been active the last couple of days, but Beatrice posts regularly on their official page. I logged into my account and sent the church a message."

"Did you get a response?"

She nodded. "I said I was trying to contact Pastor Eddie but heard he was at a conference."

Jackson turned her chair back to the computer screen and brought up the response.

Hello, Pastor Eddie is probably out in the community visiting folks. I'm not in the office today but try again tomorrow. His conference isn't until this weekend, so you still have time to get ahold of him. He has a guest pastor covering for him this Sunday.

"So there was no conference," Brandon said. "At least not yet."

"He was lying."

Jackson leaned back, arms behind her head. "Alright. Shoot. What did you learn?"

"Two things, but first let me check my email." He was waiting to hear back from the detective down in Grays Harbor. Before he headed to his office, he set the copy of the firearm transfer paperwork on the table. "In the meantime, take a look at that."

He logged into his work email, scrolling through the thirty-plus messages he'd received in the last hour.

He found the message from Grays Harbor he'd been expecting. He shot off a thank you email to Andy and opened each of the attachments the detective had sent him.

He returned to the bullpen where the printer was already working on the files.

Jackson nudged the firearm paperwork back to him. "So our pastor got himself a Glock?"

"It's a Glock 44."

She nodded. "I bought one for my husband last year. A good starter pistol because it's got almost no kickback."

Unlike Jackson, her husband had little experience with firearms. He was a work-from-home programmer.

"More important, it's a .22," he said.

Jackson held up her hand, raising a finger with each point. "He owns the same caliber gun used on Arianne, lied about being at a conference during the time she was killed, was being blackmailed by Arianne for God knows what—"

"I think we can answer that last one now."

Brandon retrieved the Grays Harbor family court files from the printer. He split them into stacks and tossed half to Jackson.

"What's this?"

"Divorce and custody proceedings for Eddie and Susan Velasquez."

"Nice catch."

Brandon flipped through the initial petition filed by Susan. There weren't any accusations or dramatic statements. She claimed there were irreconcilable differences and requested equal parenting rights. The attachments included financial statements that normally would have been private, but the detective had been able to access that information, too. Nothing worth noting. An annual income, almost two decades ago, of $35,000 for Eddie, no income for Susan. The child support worksheet included payments to Eddie's wife, but nothing out of the ordinary.

"Check this out," Jackson said, pointing to the papers he'd handed her. "It's Eddie's declaration in response to the initial petition. He says he doesn't want the divorce but asks to be the primary custodial parent. And get this—he mentions something about his wife's *lifestyle and moral choices.*"

"What's the date on that?" Brandon asked.

"February 4th."

"Okay," Brandon said. "I've got a statement in response to Eddie's declaration." He scanned the document. "By February 18th, Susan Velasquez had changed her tune. She's demanding full custody, no visits or residential time for Eddie, and...damn."

"What?"

"I think we've found Eddie's secret."

"What secret?" Jackson demanded.

"Susan Velasquez claimed Eddie isn't David's biological father."

Jackson leaned back in her chair. "I'm pretty sure this is a big enough secret to draw the attention of someone like Darren Rule."

"And Arianne."

Brandon flipped through the papers, finding the final divorce decree.

"I've got the statements of fact from the decree. The DNA results of a court-ordered paternity test are here."

"And?"

"Eddie wasn't the biological father," Brandon said.

He finished reading the documents.

"Mrs. Velasquez continued to claim she didn't know who the father was."

"Meaning," Jackson said, "she was lying, or had intercourse with multiple men during her marriage to Eddie."

"Despite the paternity test, Eddie was awarded parental rights. He'd raised David from birth. And it looks like no one else stepped forward to accept responsibility as David's father."

"What a mess," Jackson said.

"The fact is," Brandon said. "Eddie is David's father. Just not his biological parent."

"What happened to the wife?"

Brandon flipped through the rest of the records.

"Looks like there was some back and forth after the final decree. At some point, she filed paperwork pro se asking to be relieved of any parenting responsibilities."

"Did the court respond?"

"It doesn't work like that," Brandon said. "You can't just give up responsibility, at least not legally."

"Yeah, because we never run into parents who decide not to be parents in this line of work," she said.

Jackson stacked the papers into a neat pile. "So who's he keeping the secret from? His congregation?"

"No," Brandon said. "His son."

367

"So Eddie was willing to kill Arianne to prevent her from telling David the truth about the paternity test?"

"I don't think so."

"Wait, you're confusing me. You don't believe Eddie murdered Arianne Young?"

"I believe he wanted to scare her—but ended up killing her. Think about the rock through the window at the Guthrie place. How he hauled her body to the front porch. He was trying to get her help."

"It's still murder. She might have lived if he'd called 911."

"Agreed. I'm speaking to his motives, not the outcome of his actions."

"So now what?" Jackson asked.

"Eddie claimed he would be home tonight."

"He doesn't know David's in jail yet," Jackson said.

"We can use that," Brandon said.

"That might get him down to the jail, assuming he doesn't know we're onto him. But then what?"

"Eddie would do anything to protect David. That's obvious by what happened with Arianne. If he believes we've charged David with Arianne's murder—"

"Right, and we've got a ton of evidence on our side. The white hoodie, the connection to the crime scene in Rule's murder."

"You ready?"

She checked her watch. "Let me go home and say goodnight to the kids?"

He shook his head. "I'm too nice to you."

"And you're lucky I stick around this one-horse town," she said.

It was 4:30 by the time he left the office. He'd agreed to meet Jackson back at the station at six and head out to Eddie's. They had no idea when the pastor would return. For all they knew, he could have been close by all along. One thing was for sure—he wasn't where he'd claimed to be.

Brandon stopped by the house and found Tori asleep on the couch. She arose as he opened the front door.

Tori yawned. "What time is it?"

"Almost five."

"Sorry," she said. "I was reading and must have dozed off."

"Good for you," he said. "You haven't had much of a vacation."

She stood and wrapped her arms around him. "It's been fun. But I do need to head home tomorrow."

He held onto her. "I know."

They'd never gotten around to what was supposed to happen next.

"You want to go out or stay in?" she asked.

"I can't tonight," he said.

She smiled weakly, letting go of him. "Leaving me alone again?"

"We're close to solving the case."

Brandon explained what they'd learned in the last 24 hours.

"So Kaitlyn's in jail?"

"For now."

She put on her prosecutor's hat. "You could press for reduced charges. It really depends on how good her defense is. What about David?"

"He's already on probation. After this, he'll have a laundry list of violations."

"Too bad."

"It's all too bad," Brandon said.

Tori crossed her arms. "I don't get it. Why didn't Eddie just tell David the truth? He's still David's father, regardless of his DNA."

"The longer you wait to tell the truth, the harder it is."

She searched his eyes. "That's what I love about you."

"What?"

"You come across as Mr. Tough Guy at work but underneath all that you're just a cuddly little philosophical teddy bear."

She kissed him, then motioned to the kitchen. "You'd better get some food in you. It sounds like another long night."

Brandon had planned on microwaving leftovers, but Tori insisted on whipping up "a proper meal." She made enough spaghetti for both of them and he cut up lettuce, carrots, and tomatoes for a salad. By the time he left, his belly was full and he wished he wasn't on his way back to work.

Chapter 42

Brandon and Jackson headed out to Eddie's place just after six that evening.

He slowed the Interceptor as they passed by the church property. "Take a look and see if his car is up there. It's a blue sedan. Ford Taurus."

Jackson craned her neck to scope out the second driveway.

"You're not going to like this," she said.

"What?"

"There's got to be at least a dozen cars."

"On a Thursday night?"

Brandon continued to the next crossroad, did a U-turn, and headed back to the church. They drove through the parking lot. Eddie's car was gone.

They tried the apartment. No one answered so they headed around back to the sliding glass door. The blinds were open but the apartment was dark. Brandon pointed his flashlight over the kitchen table. Things seemed to be the same as they'd left them that afternoon.

"Now what?" Jackson asked. "You think he's not coming back?"

"He won't stay away forever. He has David. Let's try the church."

It was a warm summer evening, still a couple hours from sundown. The church doors were open and they were greeted with the distant, tinny echo of an acoustic guitar and people gathered to sing worship music.

Just inside the foyer, they spotted Beatrice speaking to another woman. She noticed their approach, said something to the woman, then greeted Brandon.

"Hello, Chief. What brings you here?"

The other woman entered the church sanctuary.

"What's going on tonight?" Brandon asked.

"We have recovery groups every Thursday night," she said. "A service, dinner, and then we break out into small groups based on the need. Addictions, co-dependency, that sort of thing."

"That's great," Brandon said. He was genuinely interested in the program. There were a handful of repeat offenders in the area that might benefit from what the church offered. But, at the moment, he had a more pressing issue to address. "Beatrice, we were hoping to speak with Eddie. Is he normally here on Thursdays?"

She frowned. "He's not feeling well tonight."

"You've spoken with him?" Jackson asked.

"I noticed his car in the parking lot this afternoon. I had a question about tonight's service. That's when he said he was ill."

"So he's at home?" Brandon asked, glancing across the parking lot to the apartments.

Beatrice bit her bottom lip. "That's the strange thing. I noticed him drive away about an hour ago. Maybe he went to see a doctor? I hope he's okay."

"Do you mind if we take a peek at Eddie's office?" Brandon asked.

She hesitated, obviously reluctant to let someone into her boss's office alone.

"Beatrice, this is very important," Brandon said. "I wouldn't ask you otherwise."

"Okay," she said.

372

They followed her back to the office, where she flipped the light switch on. She stood to one side as they entered.

"Is there anything I can help you with?"

Brandon ignored the question, scanning the office for any changes since his visit earlier that morning. His eyes landed on the bookshelf where there had been a photograph of Eddie, David, and Susan Velasquez.

The photo was gone. The "World's Best Dad" mug was still there.

"Did Eddie come into the church today?" Brandon asked.

"He could have. I've been in the kitchen preparing for tonight's meal most of the afternoon."

Brandon pointed at the bookshelf. "There's normally a photo there."

"The one of Eddie and his wife with David," she said. "Where is it?"

"I couldn't tell you. I'm surprised he kept it, to be honest with you. Considering what she did to Eddie and David."

"What happened to her?" Brandon asked. "After the divorce."

Beatrice had mentioned she'd known the Velasquez family since David was a baby.

"At the time there was a big court fight. When she lost, she disappeared."

"Do you know the specifics of the custody battle?" He wanted to measure how much Beatrice knew, if anything, about the parentage issue.

"Just that she'd decided not to be a mother." Beatrice's usually kind face pinched into a scowl.

"Anything else we should know about that situation?" Brandon asked, on a hunch.

She tilted her head as if considering the question. "No...just...rumors. Nothing relevant." She squinted at him. "Why are you asking these questions? Is David in trouble again?"

It wasn't David she needed to worry about.

"What were the rumors about?" Jackson asked.

Beatrice heaved in a deep breath, then exhaled. By the guilt on her face, you'd think she was about to reveal a national security secret.

She closed the office door and turned to them. "There was a rumor Susan committed suicide. Out of, you know, guilt."

"Did anyone ever confirm those rumors?" Brandon asked.

"It wasn't my business," she said.

"Who else knows about this?"

"That was a long time ago," she said. "The person I heard it from doesn't even live in Forks any longer."

"Do you believe the rumor?" Jackson asked.

"Not at all. I figure she's still out there living it up with her latest boyfriend."

"Did anyone check to see if she'd actually died?" Brandon asked.

"If she did, it's better David and Eddie don't know. The less they know, the better, in my mind. When a family goes through what they did, being left alone like that, the only way they'll heal is to move on."

Brandon glanced at Jackson. She read his mind. "I'll get ahold of Lisa and see what I can find out."

"Thanks, Beatrice," Brandon said. "I'll let you know if we need anything else."

She looked back at him with worried eyes. "Eddie's in trouble, isn't he?"

"What makes you think that?"

"Just...something in the way he spoke to me on the phone. He sounded irritable. Almost...depressed."

"Any idea where he went?"

"No. I'm sorry."

"You've been a real help," Brandon said, opening the door. "You can get back to the service now."

He closed the door behind her. Jackson was on her cell speaking with Lisa.

"Susan Velasquez," Jackson said. "Hold on."

She turned to Brandon. "She needs a date of birth. Any other info we might have."

"Wait a sec," he said.

Brandon returned a minute later with his notebook and the court paperwork printouts from the divorce and custody case.

He found her date of birth and passed it to Jackson.

Jackson relayed the information. While they waited, she covered the phone. "She's at home but was able to log in remotely."

A few minutes later, they had what they needed.

"I'm putting you on speakerphone," Jackson said. She set the phone on the desk.

"Susan Velasquez," Lisa said. "Died ten years ago. Divorced. Her only next of kin was David Velasquez. The coroner at the time notified Eddie Velasquez of the death."

"You're sure?" Brandon asked.

"That's what it says."

So Eddie had known all along. There was still the issue of the suicide, and whether it really was suicide. It was a question that had to be asked: had Eddie been involved in his ex-wife's death?

"What was the cause of death?" Brandon asked.

"Hold on." A few seconds passed. "It indicates a malignant carcinoma of the breast."

"So she died of breast cancer," Brandon said. "Not suicide?"

"Nothing in here about suicide. Why?"

"Just a rumor."

"Any other questions?" Lisa asked.

Jackson looked to Brandon.

"No."

"That's it," Jackson said. "Thanks, Lisa."

"Hold on," Brandon said.

"Yeah?"

"Where was she buried?"

"I can tell you where she was transferred to," Lisa said. "Looks like Fir Lane. They have a funeral home on-site at the cemetery there."

"I know where that is," Brandon said. "Thanks, Lisa. I really appreciate it."

"No problem, Chief."

Jackson barely suppressed a smile. "See you, Lisa."

"Bye."

"We need to get there," Brandon said. "Now."

"Where?"

"To Fir Lane."

"Why?"

"It's a hunch."

"You think that's where Eddie is?" Jackson asked.

"He took the picture of his ex, the only woman he ever loved by the look of it. Now, he's losing everything else. He has to know we're closing in on him."

"And he has a firearm," she said.

He nodded. "Let's go."

Chapter 43

Fir Lane was a newer cemetery 15 minutes north of town. Brandon had visited there several times. Both his brother Eli and their mother were buried there.

The cemetery gates were still open. The sun was low on the horizon. In less than an hour, it would sink below the tips of the forest to the west.

"Best if we don't announce ourselves," Brandon said, parking in front of the Fir Lane sign.

"We don't even know if he's here," Jackson said.

"He's armed. I'm not taking any risks."

"Good point."

They approached the entrance. The sign indicated the cemetery closed at dusk.

A slight incline led to the main loop through the property. Brandon scanned the landscape. It stretched back several hundred yards, probably ending at the forest. Eli and his mother had been buried near the gates, to their right. There was no sign of Eddie's car.

"We'll have to split up," he said.

"I thought we weren't taking risks."

"There's too much ground to cover. And it's getting dark."

"Alright," she said.

"Call me if you spot him."

Brandon took the road to the left, Jackson moving off to the right. The place was called Fir Lane for a reason. Not only was the cemetery surrounded by a forest, but most of the gravesites were under the shade of one or more of the Douglas Firs and other evergreens spread throughout the property.

It made for a peaceful setting—and lots of hiding places for a shooter intending to target Brandon or Jackson.

He hiked across the lush lawn, trying not to be distracted by the names on the gravestones or the trinkets and flowers left by loved ones. The pungent aroma of lawn fertilizer tinged the pleasant earthiness of the freshly-cut grass.

Brandon had always been drawn to cemeteries. There was something about reading the dates—a person's beginning and end. Sometimes woefully short. Or the men and women—mostly women—that outlived their spouses by 10 or 20 years.

To be alone for that long...

Sort of like what happened to Eddie.

But Eddie could have moved on after his divorce—especially after his ex died.

Brandon didn't want to wait that long—God forbid Tori passed away before he did.

He halted. There, around the curve in the road to the left was Eddie's blue Taurus.

He scanned the field. No sign of Eddie. Brandon shifted a few paces to the right, past the fir blocking his view. Eddie sat cross-legged, 20 feet from the road, with his back to Brandon.

Brandon unholstered his pistol. He crept forward, positioning himself so he would be shielded by the fir.

When he reached the tree, he peeked around the corner. He was about 25 feet from Eddie.

He should call Jackson. But talking would get Eddie's attention. He pulled out his cell and texted her: *To the south, follow the route I took. Be careful.*

His phone buzzed a few seconds later: *Ok.*

Brandon crept around the tree and approached Eddie. He was less than ten feet from the pastor when Eddie grasped for something on the ground in front of him. He lifted a pistol to his temple.

"Eddie, don't."

Eddie turned his head. Unable to see who'd called out, he rose.

"This is Brandon Mattson from the Forks Police Department. Put the gun down."

Eddie pivoted to face him, still gripping the pistol. Eddie's eyes were red, swollen with tears. But the pink blotches spreading over his cheeks and forehead weren't just from his grief—they were evidence of the pepper spray Arianne had used to defend herself.

Brandon pointed his Glock at Eddie's chest.

"Drop it, Eddie."

"Do you think I'm afraid to die, Chief Mattson?"

"No, I don't."

Brandon stepped closer. At Eddie's feet was the framed photo of Eddie, Susan, and David.

"I don't want you to kill me," Eddie said. "I don't want that on your conscience."

"That's great," Brandon said. "I don't want that either. Just set the gun down in front of you."

"I can't do that," Eddie said.

"Why not?"

"I killed that girl."

"Arianne," Brandon said. "I know."

Eddie glanced up at him. "How?"

"We can talk about that later. At the station."

"I'm not going."

"Because you're afraid of jail?"

Eddie scoffed. "No."

"Then what?"

"I deserve to die, Chief. Look at me. My wife left me. My son hates me."

"He doesn't hate you," Brandon said.

"He will once he finds out the truth."

"That you killed Arianne?"

"That I'm not his father," Eddie said. "That I lied to him."

"You did what you thought was best for him. And you are his father. No matter what the DNA test says."

"You know about that too?"

"Yes. David doesn't though."

"That's what they wanted money for," Eddie said. "The girl and that clown from the fair. I wish they'd never come here."

"But they did, and it did happen. Now it's time to make things right."

"She's dead," Eddie said.

"You can still take responsibility for what you did."

"What do you think I'm doing?" Eddie said, his voice suddenly angry. "An eye for an eye."

"Accepting responsibility doesn't mean taking vengeance on yourself," Brandon said. "What was it Jesus said? Forgive others so your father in heaven will forgive you. You don't get to be judge and jury, Pastor Eddie."

Eddie shook his head. "If there was ever a life that seemed ruled by an Old Testament God..."

He raised the gun to his head again. His finger trembled over the trigger. Eddie squeezed his eyes shut.

It was too late.

Brandon hadn't had time to formulate what to say next—the last words Eddie would hear.

"Then David will be charged with first-degree murder."

Eddie opened his eyes.

"What?"

"If you don't come down to the station and make a formal statement confessing what you did to Arianne, I have no evidence he isn't the killer."

It was a stretch, and only partially true. What mattered was getting Eddie out of there. Alive.

Eddie shook his head. "You know David had nothing to do with it."

"We already have proof he was in Darren Rule's trailer the night of his death. David's confessed to stealing the phone and laptop. Arianne was blackmailing your family just like Darren Rule was. He's got motive, he was at the scene, he was hiding evidence—"

"Stop!"

"Not to mention the white hoodie we found in his bedroom. Likely covered in gunshot residue—from the time he shot at me."

"I wore the hoodie. I shot at you."

"The hoodie was in his room."

"It was me. There, you have your confession. Now let me go."

"It doesn't work like that," Brandon said. "But yes, you can off yourself right here, right now. And leave a legacy of what to David? Leaving him to pick up the pieces of what Susan...and now you...have left him?"

Brandon's arms steadied his pistol on Eddie. It was ironic—trying to save a man's life while knowing you might have to take it from him.

Eddie stared at Brandon's feet for several seconds before lowering his pistol.

"That's good," Brandon said. "Now. Put it down in front of you."

This time Eddie obeyed.

"Turn around and hands on your head."

Brandon cuffed him and secured Eddie's pistol.

Eddie slumped to his knees, hands behind his back. He leaned over Susan Velasquez's grave. Tears dropped like watery stars over the family photo.

"I'm sorry, Susan."

Brandon waited for a moment before helping Eddie to his feet.

"I didn't mean to kill the girl. I just wanted to scare her."

"With a gun."

"She wouldn't give me the papers. I tried grabbing them and she pepper-sprayed me. It was self-defense."

"The problem is," Brandon said. "You didn't get her help."

"The rock..."

"You wanted someone else to help her so no one would find out your secret."

"If David found out—"

"In other words, keeping the lie alive was worth more than Arianne's life."

Eddie opened his mouth, then said nothing.

"The thing is, her life was worth something too. She was someone's daughter, Eddie, just as much as David is your son. A life is a life. Period."

Brandon caught his breath, blinking away the white sparkles forming in his vision.

He held his tongue, glad to spot Jackson approach from the north.

He'd have to go over all of this with Eddie on the record. He needed to preserve what little rapport he had with the soon-to-be-former pastor if he wanted to get a clean confession.

Jackson spotted the pistol on the ground.

She read Brandon's face. "You go get the Interceptor and the evidence kit," she said. "I'll stay with Pastor Eddie."

They transported Eddie back to the station, where they were able to obtain a full confession—in writing. According to his version of events, Darren Rule had blackmailed Eddie—not only with the pictures of David on the laptop and cellphone, but with the court paperwork proving Eddie wasn't David's biological father.

Apparently, searching local court files was one way Rule discovered new targets. A quick trip down to Grays Harbor would have let him know he'd struck the jackpot with Eddie and David.

Eddie claimed David came to him about finding Rule's corpse and confessed to taking the laptop and phone. It was Eddie—not David—who'd disposed of the phone and laptop. When they asked him where he'd dumped the computer, Eddie claimed he couldn't recall. Brandon was sure Eddie wanted to protect David from whatever pictures might be on there—and he was willing to go to the grave with that secret. It was still yet to be seen what they would find on Rule's cellphone once the forensic tech team finished their analysis.

Like the crossbow and tarot cards Arianne had used, they would probably never find the laptop.

Eddie had confessed to taking Arianne's phone hoping, he said, to conceal any evidence of her calls to him. What he didn't seem to understand was that call information would be available from the carrier without the actual device.

The shot into Arianne's chest had been an accident, according to Eddie. Brandon believed him, considering his half-assed attempt at getting her help.

Eddie stated he had fired the shots at Brandon outside the Forks Inn. He'd donned David's hoodie hoping to disguise himself, not realizing he'd implicate his son. Eddie repeated more than once that he'd only been trying to scare Brandon off after his failed attempt to search Arianne's room for her copies of the parentage paperwork.

It was a pretty stupid idea, using a firearm to "scare" a cop and then a 22-year-old woman. It had gotten her killed and meant Eddie would be out of his son's life for at least the next two or three decades.

After shooting Arianne, he'd taken the documents. A high price to pay to keep his son in the dark about his biological relationship to Eddie.

He'd burned the papers including, he said, financial documents referencing a man named Duke Sterling. With that, any tangible evidence of Sterling's allegedly shady business dealings went up in smoke.

They met back in the bullpen after the interview. Josiah was covering a late shift and joined them before heading out. They gathered around the table after Brandon made a second pot of coffee.

"It's amazing what some people will kill for," Jackson said.

"At least it was an accident," Josiah said, stirring two packets of cream into his coffee.

"He could have called for help. She might have lived," Brandon said.

"He tried...sort of."

"Sort of doesn't cut it."

"I know," Josiah said. "I'm just saying. It wasn't first-degree murder."

Brandon wanted to say murder was murder, period. But that wasn't true. And irritated as he was at Josiah's statement, he knew the young officer wasn't defending Eddie's actions, he was trying to make a distinction.

Jackson leaned back, hands behind her head. "This was one hell of a case. The tarot cards, the dagger, the crossbow."

"And in the end, it was all about blackmail and revenge."

"Except Arianne," Jackson said.

"That's sort of revenge," Josiah said.

"How so?"

"Revenge against whoever abused her." He looked to Brandon. "I'm not excusing it. But, you know, her motive came from somewhere deeper within her. She was just taking it out on someone else."

"Look at you," Jackson said. "Dr. Phil."

"Whatever," Josiah said.

"It's a good point," Brandon said. "But remember, Darren Rule had raped Kaitlyn. There was a revenge factor there, too. She was protecting Kaitlyn—misguided as she was."

Brandon poured himself a cup of coffee. "Alright. Jackson—that's enough for today. Josiah, have a good shift and be safe."

"You headed home to the wife?" Jackson asked.

386

He stared back at her. Before she could apologize, he said, "Yep, and I'm going to make passionate love to her."

Jackson turned her wrist and checked her watch. She clicked her tongue. "It's 1:45 in the morning. Let me know how that goes."

Chapter 44

Tori was still awake, resting on the love seat. He glanced at the true-crime show on the television.

"Don't you ever get tired of those?"

She yawned. "All done now?"

"We made the arrest. Eddie confessed to killing Arianne."

She stood, stretching her arms.

"Joe Kemba doesn't have a thing on you."

"Who is Joe Kemba?"

Tori rolled her eyes. "A famous detective on television. Hey, did you eat dinner?"

"Before I left, remember?"

"That seems like ages ago. Get changed and let's have a drink. If you're not too tired."

It was already Friday morning. The day Tori was to return home.

"But we do have a couple of hours if you're up to it." She wrapped her arms around him and kissed him deeply.

"I'm up for it," he said.

They talked late into the morning. With each moment, it seemed, time pressed ever more closely in on them. Once she returned home, once things got back to normal and Tori sank back into her work—would they still talk? Would they see each other? They'd meet halfway between Seattle and Forks for the exchanges with Emma. But those five-minute conversations—in front of their daughter—were hardly the foundation for a secure relationship.

The next few weeks stretched out before him. They'd say goodbye, maybe even with the idea that they were together again. They'd talk on the phone once a day, then once every few days. One of them would become irritated at the lack of response...

"What are you thinking about?" Tori asked. She was next to him on the love seat, her legs crossed over his.

"Us."

"You're wondering if we make this real, this thing that's been going on..."

"Will it last?"

"You keep thinking that," she said.

"Thinking?"

She smiled. "Saying, thinking...I know you."

"Well? Will it?"

She slipped her hand over his. "What I know is that I still love you, that I *want* it to work. I know you want more than that, but..."

He was suddenly exhausted. The time he'd put into the case, a double homicide, the situation with Kaitlyn and her family...it all hit him now.

"Let's go to bed," he said.

She considered him for a long time. He waited for her to say something. What was she searching for? Some sign of commitment, a signal that he was done with the lack of knowing what was next?

"Okay," she said.

Brandon changed and Tori was already in her pajamas. They slipped under the covers together and Tori rested her head on his chest. A minute later, they were both asleep.

* * *

389

Brandon didn't hear them arrive until it was too late.

The sun had been up for at least an hour but Brandon still had his arm wrapped around Tori. He sat up, jolted alert by the familiar swoosh of the front door opening.

His first thought was to leap out of bed and grab his pistol from the closet.

Then, he heard their voices.

"Why is your mom's car outside?"

"I have no idea," Emma answered.

Caesar had been sleeping on an unused blanket at the foot of the bed. He sprang up now and scrambled out the bedroom door.

"Hi, Caesar!" Emma exclaimed.

Brandon sat up on his elbow. Emma wasn't supposed to be back for two more days. Had he lost track?

No. He'd marked it on the calendar.

The bedroom door swept open.

"Dad..."

Tori pushed herself up, using the blanket to cover herself.

Emma's jaw dropped. "What...what?"

She set the cat on the floor. Down the hallway, out in the living room, Zach tried his best to pretend he wasn't there. "I'll see you later, Emma."

She didn't respond, her angry eyes set on Brandon and Tori.

Zach disappeared out the front door, closing it quietly behind him.

"Honey—don't..." Tori started. "It's not..."

Emma dropped her sleeping bag and backpack and stomped off to her room.

"Emma," Tori pleaded.

Brandon fell back onto his pillow. "Dammit."

"Well," Tori said. "She was going to find out, eventually."

"Not like this."

Tori leaned over and kissed Brandon. "She'll be fine. Let's just give her space."

Half an hour later, they'd both showered and dressed. Tori began packing her things. Brandon headed to the kitchen to make a peace offering for Emma.

Fifteen minutes later, he knocked on her bedroom door. "I made pancakes...with chocolate chips."

When she didn't respond, he motioned to Tori.

Tori approached the door. "Emma. We want to talk to you about...just come out." Tori opened the door. Emma was on her bed, reading.

Emma turned to them. "I'm busy."

"Come out and eat breakfast," Brandon said.

"Fine."

She swept past them toward the kitchen.

Tori raised an eyebrow at him. "Here we go."

Emma was at the kitchen table, slathering an obscene amount of peanut butter and honey on her pancakes.

She grabbed her fork and stuffed a bite in her mouth.

"Emma," Brandon said. "We didn't know you were going to be home yet."

"I said two weeks."

"That means fourteen days," Brandon said.

"Whatever. I told you I was coming home on a Friday."

"The point is," Brandon said, "mom was going to leave today."

"So," she said, swallowing a bite of the pancakes, "You wanted to get all of the..." she pointed her fork at them, "whatever you were doing in there out of the way before I came home."

"Emma," Tori said, "what your father and I do in private isn't your business."

Emma glared at Tori. "That's right. You can have sex with whoever you want."

"You will not speak to me like that," Tori said.

Brandon wondered what Emma had meant by her statement. He shook the thought away. "She's right, Emma."

"Mom had a boyfriend last week."

"Dating doesn't mean sex," Tori said. "*And* I broke up with him."

"Why, because you're going to get back together with dad?"

"What if we do?" Brandon asked. "Would that be such a bad thing?"

Emma set her fork down. "I don't care."

"You do care," Brandon said, "or you wouldn't be so upset."

Emma rose from the table and put her plate in the sink. She'd only eaten one pancake. Facing her parents, she said, "Let's say you get back together. Great, we're one big happy family again, right?"

She eyed her parents but they both remained quiet at the obviously rhetorical question.

"And then you guys get in a fight and decide to break up again. Then what?"

"Right now, we're just taking this one day at a time, okay?" Tori said.

"So you might break up tomorrow?"

"That's possible," Tori said.

Brandon didn't like that answer.

Would they break it off at some point? He didn't want to think about that. But Tori obviously had.

"Mom and I need to talk about it more. We were going to tell you, but first..."

"I'm going back to bed," Emma said.

Brandon waited for her to slam her bedroom door. She closed it quietly.

"She can be so infuriating," Tori said.

He leaned against the counter, crossing his arms. "Emma has a point."

"About us breaking it off?"

"Well, the way you tell it, there's at least a fifty-fifty chance of that happening in the next week."

"I didn't mean it like that," she said. "But she needs to know the truth. There's no point pretending."

"Still," he said, "You could have said it differently."

She stared back at him. "Let's not go there."

"What?"

"Criticizing how I say things, my relationship with our daughter."

"That's not what I meant," he said, drawing her to him.

They hugged, but he sensed something different between them. A distance that hadn't been there the day before.

She turned away. "I'd better get going."

"Already?"

"It's a long drive. I have laundry to do, work to catch up on."

Chapter 45

It was a long and busy week and he'd only had time to talk to Tori one or two times. By the evening Tori had left, Emma was back to her normal self, content to relate to her dad the most interesting stories from her time as a camp counselor.

Brandon took Emma to the fair one last time before she left for Seattle for the summer. As they strolled by the arena where Brandon had fought Hamish, she insisted on a blow-by-blow account of the melee. When they passed Hamish's shop and Emma realized the size of the blacksmith, she suddenly doubted whether her dad had actually beaten him.

"Are you sure he wasn't injured before the fight?" she'd asked.

"Give me some credit," he'd replied. "Fighting involved brains as much as brawn."

On Emma's last day at home for the summer, they met Tori east of Aberdeen, about halfway between Forks and Seattle. Emma tossed her two suitcases into Tori's car and then hugged Brandon. He wouldn't see her for another couple of weeks. He loved the idea of having her during the long school year, but that made the summers all the more difficult to deal with. She'd still stay over every other weekend, and Brandon would try to make the trip to Seattle as often as he could.

He hugged her goodbye, trying his best to blink away the wetness welling in his eyes. Once Emma hopped in the car, Tori came over.

"Don't be a stranger," she said.

"You, too."

They both sensed the weight of Emma's eyes on them.

"Alright, well, drive safe," he said.

"I still love you, Brandon."

The words were true, he knew that. But what they meant, that was a mystery to him, and her too, he suspected.

"I love you too."

They held each other for a moment. Out of the corner of his eye, he noticed Emma twist away in the passenger seat.

"Call me," he said.

"I promise," she said, then drew him closer, embracing him in a passionate kiss.

They both glanced at the car, where Emma sat shaking her head at them. Their involuntary laughter at her reaction seemed to peeve her all the more.

It had been a whirlwind week, with preparing charges against Eddie and figuring out what to do with David and Kaitlyn. Now that they had the full story on what had happened in Darren Rule's motorhome, David's charges would be breaking and entering and failure to report a crime. There was the issue of him stealing Darren Rule's phone and laptop, too. But David had been blackmailed and likely abused by Rule—whether he wanted to admit it or not. They would never know what sorts of pictures Rule had taken while David was intoxicated. Regardless, there were extenuating circumstances. Hopefully, the judge would consider that.

After a discussion with the prosecuting attorney, they'd charged Kaitlyn with failure to report a crime instead of accessory to murder. She'd witnessed Darren Rule's murder and kept quiet about it, but Arianne had threatened to kill Kaitlyn if she talked to the police. In the end, the prosecutor might drop even those charges.

To Brandon, that was enough to let her go. She'd be released before trial—if there was one.

In the meantime, Brandon had contacted Scarlet Road, an organization dedicated to helping women escape sex trafficking. He was hoping to get Kaitlyn connected with a counselor before her arraignment date. He'd worked with the defense and prosecutor to delay the hearing so he could secure an appointment before she was released.

Eddie's charges were another story altogether. The pastor had fired the weapon that killed Arianne. Even if it was an accident, he'd done little more to get her help than toss a rock through a window. What it showed was that he cared more about concealing his role in her death than saving the young woman's life.

Eddie was charged with first-degree murder. No doubt he'd plea his way down to second degree. But to Brandon, the facts fit murder in the first degree. In Washington State, first-degree murder encompassed situations where the homicide occurred during the commission of the crime of kidnapping.

Eddie had not intended on letting Arianne go until she agreed to drop her attempt to blackmail him. He'd brought the gun to intimidate and hold her. Instead, he'd ended up murdering her.

Then there was the attempt on Brandon's life at the Forks Inn—and the assault on Benjamin in Arianne's room. Eddie had stolen the master key from the front desk—Brandon would have to talk to Benjamin about keeping his keys secure.

Eddie had claimed he was just trying to scare Brandon during the pursuit. No doubt that was the tactic his defense attorney would use—a poor, lost soul shielding his son from the truth.

The problem was, he'd killed one person and almost killed another.

Still, with a decent defense attorney, he'd be out of prison in 20 years or less.

Eddie had been trying to protect his son from the truth that Eddie wasn't his biological father. To Eddie, the concealment and, even the confrontation with Arianne, were acts of love.

Brandon knew it was far too easy to use love as an excuse for hiding the truth. It almost always ended up hurting everyone involved. He hadn't planned his tryst with Tori to be a secret from Emma. He hadn't planned on it happening at all.

Maybe it was a good thing she'd found out earlier rather than later. He'd seen it time and again in suspects he'd interviewed—there was nothing as damaging to the human soul as keeping a secret from someone you loved.

A week after solving Arianne's murder, Brandon finally had time to turn to an issue he'd been delaying for months—hiring retired officer Will Spoelman's replacement.

He'd worked with HR to set up at least three interviews. He knew from experience HR would be on his back if he didn't at least make a show of giving a handful of applications a fair shot.

Brandon had made it clear who he wanted to hire.

Alex Winfield was the last of the three to interview.

Meeting in the station's conference room, Brandon and Jackson led Alex through twelve of the HR-approved questions. Number 13 was last on the list.

"Explain why we should hire you for this position?" Brandon asked.

Alex smiled confidently. He was the best-dressed interviewee of the day, having donned a dark gray suit and vivid blue tie.

"Easy," Alex said. "I've got experience. I've been a cop before. I believe I've demonstrated that I've got street smarts. I can read people."

Alex had shown as much while helping Brandon and his team gather information from the Renaissance fair's cast members. He'd also shown insight and hard work in his research into the tarot cards.

"Most of all, I'm committed. I'm loyal. I'll do what you ask, as long as it's ethical."

"What about Forks?" Brandon asked. "Are you really up to living out here in the middle of nowhere?"

"You mean would I feel comfortable here as one of the few Black men in town?"

"Not what I meant," Brandon said.

"Because that's not a problem for me," Alex said. "If I have your support, I can succeed at my job. No question."

"Good to know," Brandon said. "But what I meant was we get a lot of folks that think they want to live in a small town out near the coast. A few months in, they run back to the big city—what they're used to."

Alex chuckled. "I grew up in Cortena, CA."

"Never heard of it," Jackson said.

"Exactly. I'm a small-town boy at heart. I'm not going anywhere. I've got my daughter up in Port Angeles.

Besides," he said, eyeing Brandon, "I want your job someday."

"Well, you and Jackson can fight for it," Brandon said, chuckling.

"You think I want your job? Following green cops around all day making sure they do their reports on time, dealing with numbskulls like Nolan?"

"Who's Nolan?" Alex asked.

"Let's just say he doesn't work here any longer," Brandon said.

Alex nodded.

"Alright," Brandon said. "Any questions for us?"

"Not at this time."

Brandon stood, followed by Jackson and Alex.

"We'll check your references," Brandon said. "And, I'm not supposed to say this, but as far as I'm concerned, if you want the job, it's yours."

Alex beamed. "Thank you, sir."

"You'll need to complete the background check process, physical fitness, and our state's academy," Brandon said. "Other than that, welcome aboard."

Alex was all smiles as they escorted him to the station entrance. Jackson and Brandon watched him drive away.

"Nice catch," Jackson said. "And to think, you didn't like him at first."

"He was trying too hard," Brandon said, recalling how Alex had inserted himself in the investigation.

Jackson raised an eyebrow. "Usually that's a good thing."

"So I'm not perfect," Brandon said.

"True," she grunted. "If you were, you'd be able to keep a girlfriend."

"Who said I lost a girlfriend?"

Brandon sighed. She'd assumed, correctly, things weren't perfect between him and Tori.

"I mean, if you're going to be with your ex, that's your business," Jackson said.

"You're right. It is my business."

"But either do it all the way or not at all."

"I thought you didn't like Tori," Brandon said.

"I don't like seeing my boss being jerked around."

"That's not—"

"Hold on," she said. "Maybe I thought that at first. But from what I can see, you both have a lot to figure out."

She was right about that.

"So, maybe man up and figure out what you want...Chief."

"*Jackson...*"

She raised her hands, "Just saying..."

He shook his head. "Get back to work, *Officer* Jackson."

"*Detective* Jackson."

"Only as long as I say so."

She rolled her eyes. "Spoilsport."

Chapter 46

Brandon sat in the back row of the courtroom, awaiting Kaitlyn's arraignment. They'd made a deal with the prosecutor and defense to allow her release without bail. Kaitlyn had already met with her counselor from Scarlet Road. They'd already found her a safe home where she could continue to get the help she needed.

After a quick hearing, the judge agreed to the terms and Brandon met Kaitlyn and her counselor just as she was being released.

He met them in the courthouse parking lot.

"Thanks for helping me get out," Kaitlyn said.

"I want what's best for you," Brandon said.

"Did you ever hear back from my dad?"

Brandon hesitated. "No. But don't let that change things. You do what you have to do to take care of yourself."

"I want to say I don't care, but..."

"I get it," he said. Then, he remembered something. "Hold on."

He went to the SUV and hauled out her box of belongings. Brandon asked the counselor, "Can she take it with her?"

"That shouldn't be a problem," she answered.

Kaitlyn lifted the guitar off the top and held it to herself. She strummed a chord.

"It's still in tune."

Brandon grinned. "I might have tuned it this morning..."

"Thank you."

"I'd love to hear you play it someday."

The counselor opened the back of her van and Brandon settled the box in the back and closed the door.

"Kaitlyn, never forget—you are worth more than you can ever imagine. And if you ever need anything, you let me know."

She smiled a genuine smile, still holding her guitar. "I will."

Epilogue

Brandon tightened the cord, securing the hammock between the two gnarled pear trees that occupied a good part of his backyard. It was mid-August and the temperature was just above 80. It was a Sunday afternoon and the sky was a glimmering sapphire.

A perfect day for a nap.

He pressed on the hammock with both hands, then leaned into it, not trusting his own handiwork. Once he was sure he wouldn't tumble to the grass, he leaned back. A warm breeze swept by. Far away someone was mowing their lawn. A bird landed on the tall wooden fence surrounding his yard, considered Brandon for a moment, then fluttered away.

Hands clasped behind his head, he closed his eyes and drifted off.

His phone buzzed in his pocket.

Unable to help himself, he checked the caller ID.

It was Tori.

They'd talked almost daily over the past few weeks, and Brandon had begun to wonder if their long-distance relationship might work, after all. But Tori and Emma were supposed to be on a road trip down to the Redwoods.

Maybe something had gone wrong.

"Hello?"

"Are you busy?" Tori asked.

"Just relaxing."

"Oh."

He didn't like the worry in her voice.

"What happened?" he asked. "Did you break down? Is Emma okay?"

"She's fine," Tori said.

"I thought you were in California."

"We got back today."

"Oh," he said. "Not that you have to have a reason to call but..."

"Brandon."

"What?"

"I'm pregnant."

He sat up. The hammock tilted, spilling him onto the grass. He remained there, unable to stand.

"Are you sure?"

"I took two tests."

"I'll be right there," he said.

"It's not an emergency," she said, chuckling. "We've been through this before, you know."

"Yeah. Eighteen years ago."

They were both quiet.

Tori said, "I'm sorry."

"We did this together. I mean, if it is mine..."

"*Brandon.*"

"Okay, sorry. Have you told Emma yet?"

"Lord, no."

An image of his future flashed before his eyes. Diapers, the toddler years, a pre-teen, God...the teenage years...again. The first time around they'd had no idea what they were getting into. Knowing how hard it was made it so much...harder.

He swallowed. "I'm on my way."

"You don't have work?"

"It's my day off."

She paused. "Brandon. I love you."

404

"I love you too," he said. "And, Tori?"

"Yes?"

"We're going to make this work."

"I know," she said. "See you soon."

The End

Thank You

Thank you for reading *Silent Fool*. If you have a second, please leave a review on Amazon. I read each one and appreciate your time. Please know it makes a difference!

Click here to receive updates on new releases, offers for free books, and more. I promise not to bother you with a ton of emails! Join now and you'll receive a free copy of a Brandon Mattson short story featuring Brandon and Tori working together to thwart a vengeful kidnapper.

I always enjoy researching and writing and *Silent Fool* was no exception. Our family has attended several Renaissance or medieval fairs over the years and many of the sights and sounds in *Silent Fool* come from those experiences. When starting a new story, I outline where I want the plot to go. But sometimes the characters take me in an entirely different direction. That happened a couple of times in this novel—one being Brandon's relationship with Tori. But reading through the first two books again, I can see their reconnection was already brewing—almost inevitable.

While the characters and many locations in my novels are fictional, Scarlet Road is a real organization dedicated to helping young women like Kaitlyn and Arianne flee sexual exploitation. As someone who has worked in social services for over 20 years, I strongly believe that no matter what your current situation is—or how you got there—God loves and cares for you and has a plan for your life. If this is how God views us, shouldn't we see each other in the same light?

Writing is a passion I hope to continue to pursue for many years. I'm currently working full time, so I find time to write before work in the morning and on my lunch break (at times, in the front seat of my car!). I hope to share my characters and their stories with as many people as possible. The best way for me to do that is to get more reviews on Amazon. (Okay—I'll stop pestering you now...)

If you were dissatisfied or found errors, please send me an email. I'm always interested in feedback:
richard@richardryker.com

Made in the USA
Middletown, DE
02 May 2022

65135872R00243